"Like its predecessor, I had a

MW00659047

*Survival Sacrifices*. It's an enjoyable read that begs you to keep turning the page. The tenacity and independence of Christy during her struggles and joys are well balanced by her remembering the key to true peace in all circumstances—something we can all apply in our own lives."

Michele Brock, MBA, CFRE

Marketing & Fundraising Consultant

"An awe-inspiring book that captivates the reader with adventure, love, survival and sacrifice from start to finish. You will lose yourself among the pages until you become a part of the book."

Doriann Whitlock

College Student

"Christy's adventures in *Survival Sacrifices* are even more exciting and unexpected than in the first book, *Survival Skills*. And when she realizes that she can make better decisions when she keeps her faith first and foremost she can accomplish more. Theresa's newest book is a page turner that I thoroughly enjoyed from beginning to end!"

Jennifer Wiederholt

Mother of Three & Pharmacy Technician

Also by Theresa Alt

Survival Skills

# Survival Sacrifices

Theresa Alt

Little Pencil
Publishers

Special thanks to:

**Janell Robisch** at Speculations Editing (speculationsediting.com)
for her insightful developmental editing services

**Jess Denton** at monroe+co (www.monroe-co.com)
for her stunning photography skills in composing the author photo

Everyone who gave me feedback on my early drafts,
helping me to make this book the best it could be:

**Sandy Alt**
**Nicole Trapani**
**Christine Wissink**
**Michelle Langston**
**Susan Repko**
**Tom Ryan**
**Mike Alt**
**Michele Brock**
**Michaela Eipperle**
**Jenny Wiederholt**
**Doriann Whitlock**



Books written by Theresa Alt may be ordered through booksellers or by contacting:
Little Pencil Publishers
http://mkt.com/theresa-alt-books
theresamalt@gmail.com
319-447-1132



ISBN-13: 978-0-6929-7080-5
ISBN-10: 0692970800

Dedicated to the Holy Spirit
in gratitude for
the gift of writing,
the perseverance to finish,
and the opportunity to share my writing with others.

# 1

I swerved around the cars stalled and abandoned on the road. Focusing on the bumpers and headlights of the vehicles that comprised my obstacle course, I strove to avoid the gruesome view that would be seared in my mind if my eyes drifted up to the windows. The inhabitants of those cars that were occupied had been dead for six months. The briefest glimpse inside was enough to turn my stomach.

A grove of trees came into view on the right—a perfect place to relieve myself and catch a quick nap. I eased the car down the embankment and into the field behind the trees. The remnants of the previous year's cornstalks cracked and popped under my tires. The only crop growing in the field this year was an assortment of struggling weeds. Scanning my surroundings, I got out of the car and locked the doors. The fall air made me shiver. I pulled my threadbare sweater tight around me. I circled the vehicle, watching and listening for any signs of danger, and checking to make sure the car couldn't be seen from the road.

The tension in my shoulders eased. I walked into the cluster of trees, confident I was alone but still keeping my right hand on the grip of my pistol. I hadn't gone more than twenty feet when I heard the pound and crunch of hurried footsteps in the field behind me.

I whirled around and ran toward the car, my gun at the ready. Pausing behind a tree at the edge of the grove, I sized up my uninvited guests. Both men were over six feet tall, surpassing me by at least eight inches. They looked to be in their early twenties. Their only weapon was a baseball bat. Nothing I couldn't handle.

I strode forward, my gun aimed at the man wielding the bat near my passenger's side window. "Get away from the car."

He glanced at his partner, who smirked and shrugged his shoulders. They apparently did not feel a nineteen-year-old girl with a nine-millimeter was any threat to them.

He cocked the baseball bat, the muscles in his upper arms bulging as he started to swing. I fired just above his head. He hit the dirt, a string of profanities rising with the dust. He scrambled around the car and bolted after his partner, who had already disappeared into the trees.

These encounters were becoming more frequent, but they still made my palms sweat and my heart pound. At least I'd stopped this one before the men damaged the car or got their hands on the merchandise. I picked up the baseball bat and tossed it in the back seat. That might come in handy.

Six months before, a rash of earthquakes and volcanic eruptions had released huge amounts of methane and carbon monoxide, changing the composition of Earth's atmosphere. A small fraction of the population had been able to adapt to the altered atmosphere. The few people who had survived were now running out of food and clean water. More and more of them were resorting to theft and violence just to meet their basic needs.

In the weeks following the catastrophe, people began calling it the Change. That became our reference point for time. I'd started school at Gerald Ford College eight months before the Change. Scott and I went on our first date six months before the Change. Scott drove away one day before the Change.

It was October, but I knew when I told this story later, I would describe how two men tried to smash my window with a baseball bat six months after the Change.

Inside the car with the doors locked, I took a few deep breaths and my racing heart slowed. Though I felt safer, I was still eager to put some distance between me and the men who might be lurking in the trees. The car rocked and bounced as it accelerated up the embankment and back onto the road. In front of me, the sun slid down the cloudless sky toward the horizon. The bright light in my eyes cast everything else in shadow, including the contents of the vehicles littering the road. Relieved that I no longer had to worry about what I might see, I shifted my attention down the road, planning my route to bypass the obstacles ahead.

After driving another fifty miles or so, I pulled off at another spot where I hoped to safely wait for nightfall, when I could complete my journey with minimal risk of being seen. I surveyed my surroundings from the safety of the car, using the mirrors to help me see what was behind me.

I caught a glimpse of my reflection in the rearview mirror. My face was thinner than it had been a year earlier when I drove from Sioux Falls to Lincoln to start college. I pulled a couple of twigs out of my dark brown hair and combed my fingers through it to try to calm it down. I had always liked wearing my hair long, like my mother's, but it wasn't very practical in my line of work.

Thin lines had popped up around my eyes, carved by persistent fear that demanded constant vigilance. The smile that used to come so easily was a little harder to muster. I forced the corners of my lips up, pointed to the image in the mirror, and said, "You got this."

I looked around furtively, making sure no one had heard. I chuckled. If there was someone within earshot, the possibility that they had overheard me talking to myself was the least of my worries.

Hoping to catch a nap in the two hours of daylight remaining, I reclined the seat. Because I made most of my deliveries at night, I would take sleep whenever I could get it. I closed my eyes, and my memory immediately conjured the image of the man holding the baseball bat.

*I'll just relax with my eyes open. I don't really need to sleep.*

I tried taking deep breaths. I double checked that all the windows were up and the doors were locked. I tried tightening and relaxing each of my muscle groups in turn. Nothing worked to ease the tension that held my body as taut as the head of a snare drum.

*If only Scott were here. I could relax and rest if I knew he was watching out for me.* Scott was my boyfriend. Well, he had been before the Change, anyway. Now I didn't know where he was or even if he'd survived.

A shadow slid across the windshield. I bolted up, aiming my gun toward the unknown intruder. A dry maple leaf floated gently to the ground beside the car. I sighed and put the seat back up. It was obvious there would be no sleeping or relaxing until I reached my destination.

When the sun finally dropped out of sight, I resumed my journey, driving an hour toward the fading oranges and pinks it had left behind. The last glow in the western sky was all but gone when I cut the lights and turned south. I smiled, remembering how difficult it had been to find my way through the winding back roads of Colorado in the dark during my first few trips. Now, after driving the route more than twenty times, it was as easy as finding my way home from elementary school. Still, I couldn't relax and enjoy the hour drive through the scenic foothills. I had to remain vigilant, listening and watching for any sign that I was being followed. If anyone discovered my destination, thousands of lives would be at risk.

I slowed to a crawl when I turned down the gravel road that snaked through the forest to the biosphere. Even though most of the trees had lost their leaves, they still blocked enough moonlight to make it difficult to see the road.

I stopped the car beside the checkpoint. The officer put on his oxygen backpack, covered his mouth and large nose with a mask, and came out of the booth.

"Evening, Christy." The mask amplified the nasal quality of the officer's voice.

"Good to see you, Officer Clement." I gave him the password.

He swept his flashlight around the inside of the car and waved me through.

I followed the road around the corner to the right. Through a clearing in the trees, I saw the moonlight reflecting off the canvas covering the wall of the biosphere. Painted with trees and dense underbrush, the canvas was designed to camouflage the biosphere. This time of year, especially, the disguise was not very effective. The trees painted on the biosphere wall were lush and green, in stark contrast to the real trees, which were all either dead or dropping their leaves in preparation for winter.

After curving to the left and descending into a shallow valley, the road ended at a large pile of rocks. I got out of the car and said the password into a boulder. The rocks in front of the car slid to the side. Behind them, a garage door opened. I drove into the airlock, and the door closed behind me. While fans assisted in the conversion of the atmosphere inside, I unloaded the merchandise from the car. It was a small delivery— five bolts of fabric and a box of winter wheat seed adapted to grow in the altered atmosphere.

Adapted seed was one of the biosphere's greatest needs. Pregnancy rates were high in the biosphere. Early on, the government realized the food that could be raised inside the biosphere would not be enough to meet the needs of the growing population. With the help of my deliveries, the government had started a farming program outside the biosphere, with those assigned to farm work using supplemental oxygen while working on the outside.

The light above the walk-in door turned green, indicating the airlock's atmosphere was now identical to the biosphere's, matching the composition of Earth's atmosphere before the Change. I carried my delivery up the steps to the loading dock, through the now-unlocked door, and into the biosphere. I blinked several times, trying to adjust to the brightness inside. The street lights, though dim and widely-spaced, still far outshone the moon and stars that provided the only illumination at night outside the biosphere.

I turned left, nodding to the airlock operator as I went by her booth. The street was lined with simple two-story wooden structures, punctuated occasionally by narrow alleys. Here, the buildings were designated for manufacturing. In the next block, they housed offices.

The biosphere's official name was the United States Citizens' Survival Bio-Sphere, or USCSBS. My brother and his friends, especially when frustrated by its rules and constraints, shortened the abbreviation to "the B.S." I called it the Bubble, a name inspired by its domed, translucent roof. It had been built by the government in response to scientists' predictions of the atmospheric change. In it, the government had saved a couple thousand people, including my parents and my younger brother, Josh. Prior to the Change, the government had stockpiled non-perishable food, supplies, and fuel to run the massive generators that powered the biosphere and maintained its atmosphere.

Since discovering the location of the biosphere six weeks after the Change, I served as a liaison between the biosphere community and the cabin community, where I had lived after the Change with others who were able to adapt to the altered atmosphere. I negotiated the exchange of knowledge and goods between the two communities, facilitating the survival of both. The leadership in the biosphere and the cabin feared for the safety of the residents if any outsiders found out where they were. I was the only person who knew the location of both communities.

I continued straight ahead two more blocks. The streets were designed to accommodate the maintenance vehicles used in the biosphere, but most days they only saw pedestrian traffic. It was already after nine in the evening, so I was the only person out on the streets of the business district.

The administration building, which housed the biosphere's government offices, had the same simple design as all the other buildings in the district. It was set apart by two rows of meticulously maintained bushes leading to glass double doors. I rang the buzzer to the right of the doors. The security guard looked up from his paper. I flashed him a smile. He waved and hurried to open the door.

"Good to see you, Christy. I trust you had a smooth trip."

I chuckled. "Not exactly." I dropped the merchandise on his desk. "But I made it."

The security guard flipped a few pages on a clipboard. "The Council can see you day-after-tomorrow right after their lunch recess."

"I'll be here." I slipped off my backpack, pulled out a piece of paper, and handed it to the guard. "Here's the list of things they need at the cabin."

"I'll be sure the council members get this first thing in the morning."

"Thanks." I shouldered my backpack and turned to go. "Have a good night."

I hurried to my family's house, offering brief greetings to the neighbors I saw on the way. At first, I had felt claustrophobic when I visited the biosphere. Now the tiny cookie-cutter houses crammed together along the narrow street seemed normal, even comfortable.

Security in the biosphere was tight, keeping crime to a minimum. This was the one place where I didn't have to be constantly on guard. I knew no one would attack me or try to rob me here. A year earlier, when I left home to go to college, I was excited to be out of the house, to finally be my own boss. Now, I was eager to be back under my parents' roof, where I could relax and let someone else take charge for a while.

Before I reached the door, I could smell herbs and tomatoes cooking inside. I knocked, and almost immediately Mom threw open the door and smothered me with a hug.

"I knew you'd be home tonight. Your dad told me to put the soup away, but I said 'No, Matt. Christy is on her way.' "

Though I usually made it back to the Bubble at least once a week, Mom always acted like I'd been gone for months.

She ushered me to the table, just to the right of the front door. The kitchenette was on the other side of the table, along the wall opposite the door. Mom ladled a big bowl of minestrone from the pot on the stove and sat down across from me. The ridges between her eyebrows had almost become a permanent part of her facial expression. But the smile that blossomed when she knew the whole family was safe flattened those peaks into a smooth Nebraska plain.

"How was your trip?" Dad asked, looking up from his paper.

Dad's hair had been thinning on top for as long as I could remember. But it was only in the past few months that I'd noticed how rapidly the black hairs were being replaced by white ones. He and my younger brother, Josh, were sitting just to the left of the door on the couch, which doubled as my bed when I was there.

"It was good." I hesitated. I figured Josh would want to hear all about my encounter with the thieves, but I didn't want to worry Mom. "There were a couple guys who tried to break into the car, but as soon as they saw my gun they took off."

I looked at Josh, expecting him to ask questions, digging for exciting details. His knee bounced, and his glance darted back and forth between Mom and Dad. I don't think he had even heard what I said.

"I would feel a lot better if you weren't carrying a gun." Mom leaned toward me, resting her elbows on the table.

She wasn't alone in the belief that I shouldn't have a gun. I had petitioned the Council several times requesting permission to carry a firearm. All of my requests had been flatly denied. The Council claimed that arming citizens would undermine the authority of the police officers. Then one of my deliveries from the cabin was stolen en route to the Bubble. The council members realized that if I didn't have the tools to defend myself, I couldn't protect their merchandise. They reluctantly allowed the police department to sell me a pistol.

"I was glad I had it today," I said. "If I hadn't, who knows what they would have done with that baseball bat."

Mom didn't know I had ever fired my gun outside of practice. I imagined she would sleep better at night if I didn't mention it.

"So, what's new in the Bubble?" I asked.

Josh stood and walked to the door.

"The Petersons had their baby," Mom said, "cutest little girl you've ever seen."

"I'm going for a walk." Josh left, slamming the door behind him.

"What's up with him?" I asked.

Mom shook her head. "He's been acting really restless this week. And the littlest things will set him off. I've tried to talk to him, but he won't tell me anything."

"I went through my share of moody periods when I was seventeen."

Mom nodded with a wry smile.

"It'll probably blow over if you give him some space," I said.

Mom looked around the small room that functioned as living room, dining room, and kitchen. "I'm afraid space is a little hard to come by here."

# 2

As soon as everyone left for work the next morning, I started on my mail route. Unbeknownst to the leadership of both communities, I was operating a side business, delivering letters between the biosphere and the cabin. Those who gave me letters to deliver paid me with food or homemade items. I traded those items at the market in Lincoln, where survivors met to exchange goods and services. Without this extra source of income, survival on the outside would have been difficult.

I stopped at a couple of houses first, catching a woman just getting home from her third-shift job, and a man who was allowed to stay home and care for his young children.

At nine I headed to the industrial district. This was the busiest area inside the Bubble during the day, which multiplied my chances of getting caught. Because I didn't submit the letters going in and out of the Bubble to the Council for inspection, my actions would be classified as smuggling, a threat to biosphere security. If anyone saw what I was doing and turned me in, it could mean life-long expulsion or worse.

I turned down the alley between the second and third buildings on the right and crouched behind the dumpster.

At 9:20 the side door of the building across from the dumpster opened, and a man stepped out. He took a deep breath and stretched. I couldn't see his face from my hiding spot, but I knew he was surveying the area to make sure we didn't have any uninvited guests. He strolled down the alley, crossing to my dumpster and leaning against the wall of the building right next to me, without ever making eye contact.

"Good to see you, Alex," I said, quietly.

He nodded slightly, pulled an envelope out of his back pocket, and held it out to me. "There's money inside."

"Nobody at the market is using money," I said. "You've got to give me something else, something I can use or trade."

"Fine," Alex said. "Wait here."

He strolled back down the alley and went inside.

I checked my watch. It was already 9:25. I was going to have to leave soon, or I would miss my next rendezvous.

Alex emerged again, carrying a paper lunch bag. He walked a little faster this time, continuing to scan his surroundings. He leaned against the wall, his arm down at his side. I reached up and took the letter and the paper bag from his hand. I quickly glanced in the bag. I recognized the rations containers. Food, I could use.

"Perfect," I said, "I'll make this delivery as soon as I can."

He nodded and walked back to his building.

As soon as the door closed behind him, I hurried to the back of the building and turned left. I stopped two buildings down and crawled under a wooden loading dock. I had just sat down when I heard voices above me. Four feet appeared, dangling over the front edge of the loading dock.

I eased myself closer to the dirty white Reeboks. A small bag appeared, hanging down next to the Reeboks. I grasped the bag and tugged slightly. The hand holding it let go. I opened the bag slowly, trying to avoid making any noise. Inside, I saw a letter and a pair of shoes that looked brand new. I could probably find someone at the market who would trade for new shoes. I emptied the contents of the bag into my backpack. I placed a letter addressed to the woman wearing Reeboks in the bag and eased the bag up in front of the loading dock again. After several seconds, I slowly lowered my hands. The bag stayed in place—she had ahold of it. I breathed a sigh of relief. The transaction was complete. I waited under the dock until both voices and pairs of feet disappeared.

The rest of the morning consisted of a series of meetings in alleys and behind bushes, carefully timed to correspond to the breaks my customers were given during their workday. My busiest time was from noon to one. I sat on a park bench in a small green space that was left in the middle of the industrial district. The newspaper I pretended to read concealed the transactions I made with those who sat beside me on the bench.

I had to cut my lunchtime transactions short, so I could get to the hospital by one. I spotted Jessica as soon as I walked in the door to the outpatient waiting room. In contrast to the anxious expressions on most of the faces in the room, Jessica sported a tentative grin. She stood when she saw me.

I gave her a hug. "Are you excited?"

She nodded and giggled.

Jessica and I had struck up a friendship after I started delivering letters from her brother at the cabin. She was a few years older than me and had grown up in western Minnesota, not far from my hometown of Sioux Falls, South Dakota.

Her husband of just over a year had died a month before, after a fire at the machine shop, where he worked. He had sustained severe burns and developed one infection after another, until his body couldn't fight them anymore and shut down.

Jessica's grief was intense. After excitedly beginning her new life in the Bubble with her new husband, she now found herself totally alone. She hadn't figured out how she could move on. I didn't have any answers for her, but I was glad to provide a listening ear and a few empathetic tears.

Since her husband's death, Jessica had been having a lot of nausea, even throwing up occasionally. She figured it was anxiety-induced. But a couple weeks before, she started putting the pieces together and realized that she was showing all the signs of pregnancy. Though she was still devastated by the loss of her husband, the possibility that she might be carrying his child inspired hope and excitement that she didn't think she would ever feel again.

She was going to find out today if it was really true. She'd asked me to come with her for support.

"Jessica Stewart," the nurse announced.

I squeezed her hand and followed Jessica and the nurse into an exam room. Jessica climbed onto the exam table and the nurse sat on a stool in front of her. I took a chair against the wall.

"So, Jessica," the nurse said, "what brings you in today?"

Jessica shot me a nervous smile. "I think I might be

pregnant."

"What symptoms have you been having?"

"I've been sick to my stomach, especially in the morning before I've had something to eat. And my last period was three months ago."

"Have you had any injuries, illnesses, or surgeries in the past?"

"Just my tonsils out, when I was four, I think."

"Do you have any other children?"

"No, this is the first for Ben and me."

"And Ben is . . ."

"My husband." Jessica's voice softened. "Was my husband. He died last month."

"So you're not currently married?"

Tears streamed down Jessica's face. She shook her head.

I stood and put my arm around her shoulders, giving the nurse a look. I couldn't believe she would ask such an inappropriate question. The nurse was suddenly engrossed in the clipboard on her lap.

"Let's get started on your exam." The nurse didn't look up.

I gave Jessica's shoulders one more squeeze and stepped back.

The nurse checked her blood pressure, heart rate, height, and weight. Someone from the lab came in and took a blood sample. As soon as the lab tech left, a man in a white coat swept in.

"Jessica." He extended his hand toward her. "I'm Dr.

Baldwin."

She shook his hand.

He turned to me. "And you are?"

"Christy," I said, "a friend."

"I'm going to have to ask you to step out so we can complete the physical exam," Dr. Baldwin said.

I looked at Jessica. She gave me a little smile and nodded.

"I'll be right out in the waiting room," I said.

I stepped into the hallway and closed the door behind me. I leaned against the wall beside the door. I didn't want to leave her alone.

"Miss, can I help you?" a nurse asked.

"No, thanks," I said, "I'm just headed to the waiting room."

I walked slowly down the hall. *Lord, be with Jessica, so she doesn't feel alone.*

I sat in the waiting room, absently flipping through magazines while the minutes dragged. Every time the door to the exam area opened, I was ready to jump out of my seat.

Finally, after forty-five minutes, Jessica appeared in the door. I hurried to her, eager to find out what the doctor had said. Her lower lip quivered, and her smile was gone.

I held my question. "Let's get you home." I put my arm around her and guided her to the door.

We walked to Jessica's house, our silence punctuated only by her sniffles. It wasn't until she was sitting on her couch, a glass of water in hand, that I dared ask.

"What did the doctor say?"

Her lower lip started to quiver again. "He said I probably was pregnant, but I'm not anymore." She started to sob.

I put my arms around her. "Oh, Jessica, I'm so sorry."

"I thought this was going to be my chance to move forward," she said through her tears, "a little piece of Ben that would be with me forever. But now that's gone, too."

My heart broke for Jessica. Life seemed so unfair sometimes. I held her and cried with her. There was nothing more I could do.

# 3

After dinner that evening, I suggested that Josh and I take a walk. He had sulked through the meal, hardly saying two words. I thought maybe if I got him alone, he would be willing to open up about what was going on.

"How was work today?" I asked.

Josh shrugged. "Same old, same old."

"Do you think you'll stick with the rations warehouse, or are you planning on looking for something else?"

"I am not working there the rest of my life. But I don't think there's much out there that would be any better. Wherever I go, I'll have to start at the bottom, which usually means backbreaking, mind-numbing work."

I nodded. Work opportunities were pretty limited in the Bubble. School was only offered through age fifteen, so advancement through higher education wasn't an option. A limited number of apprenticeships were available, offering the chance to learn a particular work skill. But there was a lot of competition for a few spots. Josh had been turned down so many times, he'd given up trying.

"How was your day?" Josh asked.

It didn't sound like he really wanted to know. I wasn't sure if he was trying to be polite, or if he just wanted to turn the conversation away from him. Either way, if I was willing to share my struggles, it might help get him to open up.

"It was rough," I said. "I went to the doctor with Jessica. I mentioned she thought she was pregnant, right?"

Josh nodded.

"Well, the doctor said she had been pregnant, but she lost the baby. She was pretty broken up about it."

Josh stopped walking and turned away from me.

"Josh?" I put my hand on his arm. "What's wrong?"

He didn't move.

I walked around him and looked up at his face. His cheeks glistened with tears. He didn't even know Jessica. I couldn't imagine why the news would make him so upset.

"What's going on?" I asked.

Josh sniffed and started walking again.

I matched his speed but left a gap between us. I sensed he needed a little space.

We walked a block in silence.

"It's been happening a lot," Josh said, his voice cracking. "A bunch of my friends have girlfriends who've lost their babies."

Josh hadn't mentioned that before.

"I wonder if there's something about the artificial environment that makes miscarriages more likely," I said.

Josh shook his head. "It has nothing to do with the environment."

"How do you know?"

"All of the girls lost their babies right around the time of one of their prenatal appointments. Every one of them came home bawling their eyes out after their appointment, and none of them will talk about what happened. My friends are convinced that the doctors took their girlfriends' babies. We figure it's part of the Council's population control efforts."

When the government had announced that the Change was coming, pregnancy rates around the country skyrocketed. Hundreds of women were pregnant when they moved into the biosphere, and more were becoming pregnant every day. When the biosphere opened, the government had filled it to capacity to save as many lives as possible. The population had already grown from 2,500 to more than 2,650. The equipment used to maintain the atmosphere had never been tested with that level of demand. If the equipment failed, thousands could die.

I knew the Council, the legislative branch of the Bubble's government, had discarded a lot of individual rights for the purported good of the community. But would they actually go so far as to force people to have abortions?

"There are a lot of pregnant women in the Bubble," I said. "The Petersons just had their baby. Why wasn't their baby taken?"

"I don't know for sure." Josh's voice cracked again. "But it looks like they're targeting unmarried women."

Why unmarried women? I had trouble believing the Council was making some sort of a moral statement. And Jessica didn't quite fit the pattern. She had been happily married, and she was carrying her husband's child. But now her husband was out of the picture. She was too distraught to speak up for herself and had no immediate family members in the Bubble to advocate for her. That must be part of the Council's plan. It would be easier to keep the women quiet if there wasn't a husband involved.

My anger flared. Jessica was already lost in grief for her husband. If they killed her baby, too . . .

"I have to go see Jessica." I turned and hurried down a side street toward Jessica's house.

Josh caught up to me. "You can't tell her I said anything. If word gets back to the Council, they'll think one of the girls talked, and the girls will get in trouble."

I stopped at the corner. "Wait here. She won't see you, and I won't mention your name. I won't even say that it happened to other girls too."

I walked another half block and knocked on Jessica's door. She peeked through the curtain in the window before opening the door. Her eyes were red, but her tears had dried.

I stepped inside and clasped her hands. "I just wanted to see how you were doing."

She shrugged. "I've been better. But it's been so long ago, sometimes it's hard to remember what better feels like."

I hugged her. "I wish there was something I could do to take away even a little bit of your hurt."

She squeezed me tighter.

We sat down on the couch. I tucked my leg under me so I could face her.

"There's something I want to ask you." I hesitated.

Would asking the question just add to her pain? But if

she knew that I knew the truth, that she didn't have to try to keep secrets around me, I was sure that would help.

"I want you to know that you can be honest with me," I said, "and that nothing you say will ever leave this room."

She bit her lower lip and nodded.

"Jessica, did the doctor take your baby?"

Her eyes filled with tears, but she held my gaze. The sorrow in her eyes was even greater than the sorrow for a baby lost. She didn't say a word, but I knew the answer. Hers was a sorrow for a baby taken, a baby killed at the hands of the person who was supposed to be caring for her.

I hugged her again. "Oh, Jess, I am so sorry. I can't even imagine."

I held her until our tears ran dry.

"I better go." I stood and gestured over my shoulder with my thumb. "My brother is waiting for me outside."

Jessica walked me to the door.

I gave her one more hug. "I'll be back. I promise."

The sun was gone by the time I left Jessica's house. I was a little surprised to see Josh's silhouette, highlighted by the street light. I figured he would have given up on me and gone back home.

I walked slowly to him. "You were right. She wouldn't say it out loud, but I could tell. They forced her to have an abortion."

Josh blew out a big gust of air as if someone had just punched him in the gut. He stood still for several seconds. I watched him, trying to make out his expression through the shadows.

Finally, he said softly, "Lauren's pregnant."

"Lauren?"

"My girlfriend. She's—We're going to have a baby."

"What were you—How could—How did this happen?"

Josh and I had been raised with strong Christian values. Both of us had taken purity pledges when we were thirteen, and we understood why God called us to chastity. It hadn't always been easy, but even when it seemed like we were the only ones, we had stuck with our commitment—at least until now.

Josh started down the street. I matched his speed.

"When we moved into the biosphere, it seemed like everything changed," Josh said. "The rules that seemed important before just didn't make sense anymore. The only thing I knew was that life could turn upside down with no warning. I couldn't wait until tomorrow to show Lauren how much I loved her because there might not be a tomorrow."

I shook my head and bit my lower lip. I couldn't pretend that what he had done was okay, but I could understand why he had done it.

"Does anyone else know?" I asked.

"No." Josh shook his head. "She's afraid if she tells her parents, they'll make her go to the doctor."

And if she went to the doctor, they would kill her baby—my brother's baby.

"You two are going to have to get married," I said.

"We're both underage. I don't know about Lauren's

parents, but there's no way Mom and Dad would sign for us."

"If we tell them the whole story, they will."

Josh stopped and turned toward me. "We can't tell Dad about the forced abortions. He won't believe it. He'll say something to one of his friends on the Council to try to clear things up. That's what he did when they had you tied up outside. He went straight to Councilman Jacobs and told him everything. He could have gotten all of us thrown in jail. If he tells someone on the Council that we know about the forced abortions, the girls who lost their babies will get in big trouble for talking. And you know they won't get a fair trial."

We started walking again. My mind raced in search of a solution.

"How far along is she?"

"I don't know. She said she's two months late."

"She could start showing within a month or two. You've got to get married before she starts to show."

"Yes, we do." Josh spoke slowly like he was developing a plan. "Will you back me up when I talk to Mom and Dad?"

"I've got your six."

# 4

I went to the firing range first thing the next morning. My marksmanship had improved significantly in the three months since I got my Smith & Wesson. I didn't need the practice, but I found the firing range relaxing. When I concentrated my full attention on the gun in my hand and the bull's-eye in front of me, it helped me focus my thoughts on the things that were most important. Everything in my life seemed to become clearer.

*Heavenly Father, please let Josh know your forgiveness.* I put on my ear protection and loaded my gun. *Give me the wisdom to help Josh find a solution to this impossible problem. Guide the decisions of the Council. Help the members of the Council to remember, now more than ever, how valuable life is.*

I released the safety and wrapped my fingers around the smooth handle of the pistol. I raised my right arm, stabilizing with the left. Everything disappeared except the red circle marking the center of the target. The muscles of both arms tensed. I squeezed the trigger. The "pop" was accompanied by a slight jerk of the gun. A neat hole appeared at the center of the bull's-eye. *Perfect.*

I tried to think of some way I could save Josh's baby. I wanted to tell Mom and Dad, but I knew Josh was right. If we told them about the girls who had lost their babies, Dad would bring it up at one of his poker games to give his friends on the Council a chance to explain. The Council would assume one of the girls had talked, and the girls would be questioned, or, more likely, punished with no chance to defend themselves. They had already lost their babies. I couldn't put them through any more suffering.

I put the safety on and lowered the gun. I turned my head side to side and circled my shoulders back to ease the tension in my neck and arms. The tight cluster of bullet holes at the center of the target made me smile. Though I hoped never to have to use my gun to do anything more than scare thieves away, I was pleased to know I had the skills to defend myself should the need arise. I crouched down, imagining I was hiding behind something, and took aim again.

Maybe we could somehow hide Lauren's pregnancy. I might be able to get her some larger clothes from the Lincoln market. We could hide her at our house when her pregnancy was too far along to conceal it with clothes. But she wouldn't be allowed to skip more than two days of school without a doctor's note. One trip to the doctor's office, and it would all be over.

I paused to reload.

If I could get my hands on some oxygen tanks and masks, maybe I could sneak Lauren out of the biosphere. Then, after the baby was born, they could move back in. But I had no idea how long an oxygen tank would last. I might need hundreds to get her through her pregnancy. And if I couldn't get all of the oxygen I needed, Josh would lose his girlfriend and his baby.

*God, I am Josh's sister. I should be able to help. What do I need to do to fix this?*

I lowered my gun and stood very still. I didn't hear God's voice or experience any brilliant insights.

"Thanks for the help," I muttered, casting a sideways glance toward heaven.

I holstered my pistol and exited the booth.

I stopped at the rations station to pick up our family's weekly supplies on my way home. I was the first one home, so I started cooking lunch. I didn't mind cooking on Tuesdays, when we had plenty of foods to choose from. On Mondays, when we were using up whatever was left from our last batch of rations, we often ended up with interesting combinations. Just a couple weeks before, we had enjoyed a tantalizing pairing of sardines and sauerkraut.

I was almost done cooking when Mom arrived. She started putting the rations in the cupboard. Josh came in a few minutes later. He looked back and forth at the empty table and the couch a few times before deciding on the couch. He perched on the front edge, his right knee bouncing as if trying to keep time with "The Flight of the Bumblebee."

I handed him a stack of plates and attempted an understanding smile. He nodded but didn't make eye contact. He distributed the four plates around the table and added glasses and utensils.

I was just putting the food on the table when Dad

walked in.

"Mmmm. Smells delicious." Dad went straight to his chair, at the end of the table closest to the kitchen.

Mom took her spot at the opposite end of the table, and Josh and I sat across from each other in the middle.

Dad led us in the prayer before meals. Josh bowed his head with us, but his voice was barely audible.

"Could you pass the bread, please?" I asked.

Josh handed me the cutting board that held a fresh loaf of bread. I winked as I took it from him, hoping to elicit at least a little smile. My efforts went unrewarded.

"I was excited to see fresh bread in our rations." I sliced a piece and spread butter on it. "They must have harvested another wheat crop?"

Josh shrugged. "I don't know where the food comes from. I just put it in boxes."

I knew he was nervous, but he needed to show a little enthusiasm if he was going to convince my parents that he should get married.

"How was work this morning?" Mom asked Dad.

"Good," Dad said, "got a lot done. I'm afraid this afternoon won't be quite so productive. I'm scheduled solid with meetings the rest of the day. How about you?"

"We had one person out sick today," Mom said, "so it was a little hard to keep up on the line. It seems like the foreman would be able to step in every now and then when we're short."

"That's something you have to look forward to," Dad

said. "When they promote you to foreman, then you too can ignore the plight of the common laborer."

Mom laughed. "I could, but I won't. You know that."

Dad smiled. "Yes, yes I do."

"I would like to say something." Josh's voice sounded confident, but his eyes still looked scared.

"Of course," Mom said. "What is it?"

*Lord, give Josh the words to show Mom and Dad how important this is.*

Josh's gaze dropped to his lap. "I proposed to Lauren this morning." He looked up, a little smile playing on his lips. "She said yes."

Mom's mouth fell open. Dad leaned back in his chair and crossed his arms.

"You're engaged?" I tried to make my surprise sound authentic. "Congratulations!"

Josh held his open palm over the table and pressed it toward the tabletop, indicating that I needed to tone it down.

"How did you propose?" I asked.

"I was walking her to school this morning," Josh said.

Maybe he should have left out the part about school. That just reminded my parents that Lauren was even younger than Josh.

"We had a little extra time, and Lauren wanted to take a detour to go by this big old tree they saved when they built the biosphere. It's one of our favorite places to sit and talk. Lauren's face just lit up when she saw the yellow leaves reflecting the morning sun, and I knew it was the right time."

Josh's cheeks flushed.

"And she really said yes?" Since my fake surprise had apparently been a little over the top, I switched to some good-natured teasing. "Did you bribe her?"

Josh smiled. "I was a little surprised, too. But I'm so happy. And no, there was no coercion required."

"Sarah, it's like that time in kindergarten," Dad said to Mom, "when he picked a bunch of dandelions and gave them to Ginger Johnson. He called them her 'bride bouquet.' "

Mom smiled at the memory. I had thought him hopelessly immature at the time. As a wise seven-year-old, I knew that boys and girls should have nothing to do with each other. At age five, Josh had not yet learned of the dangers of cooties.

Dad looked at Josh. "I'm sure this crush will blow over, just like that one did."

Dad knew how to push Josh's buttons.

Josh stood. "Dad, that's not what this is."

If Josh lost his temper, I knew the discussion would be over. I tried to return his "tone it down" gesture, but he wasn't looking at me.

Josh clenched his fists. "I love Lauren. And I'm going to marry her."

"She's a nice girl," Mom said, "but you're only seventeen, and you've only known each other a few months. You need to give it more time before you make that kind of commitment."

"The one thing I learned from the Change is that everything we know and love can be gone in an instant." Josh slammed his fist on the table. "I don't want to be cautious anymore."

Dad stood. I held my breath. He took a step toward Josh.

His voice was low and even. "As long as you are living under this roof, you will not behave like that at the dinner table."

Josh stormed out of the house.

Growing up, Josh had always been pretty laid back. If things didn't go his way, he just dropped a smart remark and moved on. He had handled the move to the Bubble in the same way, settling into his new life with a few sarcastic complaints about having to get a job and losing his collection of signed baseballs. His outburst gave me a glimpse of the loss, uncertainty, and fear Josh experienced as a result of the Change. I didn't realize until now how hard the Change had been for him.

# 5

After helping Mom with the dishes, I walked to the administration building. The security guard at the front door paged the council clerk, who escorted me down the hallway, through the anteroom, and into the council chamber.

I waited just inside the door while the twenty-five men and women of the Council, all dressed in dark suits, finished settling in after the lunch recess. Their desks were arranged in a large semicircle. The chairman's ornate wooden desk, at the top of the semicircle, stood in contrast to the simple metal desks of the other council members.

Chairman Lambrecht called the Council to order, immediately silencing the last of the lunchtime conversations. When he spoke, the other members listened. While Dad had told me of instances when other council members had opposed the chairman, his position always seemed to prevail. It was possible this was due to his persuasive arguments, but I had a feeling it had more to do with his exercise of power.

"Christy Phillips, you may approach," the chairman said.

At first, I had been scared of Chairman Lambrecht, with his stern face and formal speech. Over time, however, I had gotten used to the formality of the council chamber, and my fear receded. The Council needed resources from the cabin community, especially seed adapted to grow in the altered atmosphere. Dr. Franklin, who was in charge at the cabin, had begun developing adapted seed long before the government would even admit the disaster was coming. The leadership in the Bubble had realized early on that the food they could grow inside the biosphere was not enough to support the expanding population. I was the only person who could get the seed and other resources to the biosphere. That knowledge gave me greater confidence that I would not become a victim of any power games the chairman chose to play.

Even though I wasn't scared anymore, I still didn't trust him. When I first showed up at the Bubble, uninvited, I was tied up outside until my fate could be decided, with no trial. It was only after Dad talked to his neighbor, Councilman Jacobs, and told him I might be able to help, that I was given the opportunity to speak up for myself.

I sat in the center of the room, facing Chairman Lambrecht. He had short dark hair that blended to gray at his temples. His salt-and-pepper mustache was always neatly combed. And his tailored suit fit perfectly on his tall, thin frame.

Could he have ordered the forced abortions? Was he so heartless that he would make the decision that a grieving widow should also be stripped of her baby? I had never seen a hint of compassion in my interactions with him. If it served his purposes, I could see him making such a decision. A shiver ran down my spine.

"Your delivery has been inspected and found to be adequate." The chairman directed his gaze above me. "We are able to provide the items requested by the cabin. They will be delivered to the airlock tomorrow.

"In exchange, we need two chemical engineers and two mechanical engineers to review the detailed schematic of our atmospheric conversion system contained in this envelope."

The people living at the cabin were mostly former students and professors from Ford College, which didn't have an engineering program. This demand was going to be hard for Dr. Franklin to meet.

The chairman handed a manila envelope to the clerk, who brought it to me. "Each engineer must write out specific recommendations to improve the efficiency or capacity of the system."

"I don't think there are any engineers at the cabin."

"Then they'll have to find some." He looked me in the eye. "This is a critical need for the survival of our community. In order to impress upon Dr. Franklin the urgency of this request, please inform him there will be no further deliveries from the USCSBS to the cabin until this request is met. It will be a long, cold winter for them if they run out of fuel."

Dr. Franklin frequently traded with the biosphere for propane to fuel the generator used to heat the cabin and power the appliances.

Chairman Lambrecht turned his attention to the papers on his desk. "You will be welcome back to the USCSBS only when you have completed this assignment."

He dismissed me with a wave of his hand. I left the council chamber, my mind spinning. I didn't know anyone with an engineering background who was still alive. Max Reynolds, a friend of mine in Lincoln, Nebraska, was a biochemist. Since the Change, there hadn't been any demand for his expertise in the development of genetic tests. I could ask him, but I doubted if he knew much about atmospheric conversion.

I wouldn't be able to return to the biosphere until I found four engineers and somehow convinced them to help me. I couldn't help Josh if I wasn't even there. By the time I was able to return, it might be too late. On the other hand, if I found some engineers who could help, maybe the government wouldn't have to worry about the growing population anymore, and Josh's problem would be solved. Perhaps this was the answer I was looking for—my opportunity to fix Josh's predicament.

# 6

I stopped at Jessica's house on my way home from the administration building. I knocked several times before she finally opened the door. Her eyes were bloodshot. She was wearing sweats and her red hair was tousled.

I gave her a hug. "How are you doing?"

She shrugged and stepped to the side so I could come in.

"Do you want a glass of water?" I walked to the kitchenette and poured a glass for myself.

"Sure, thanks," Jessica said.

I filled a second glass and brought it to the table. We sat down. I took a sip of water. She stared at her glass.

What was I doing here? There was nothing I could say that would make things better. I couldn't tell her I understood. I had no idea how I would react if I lost my husband and my baby less than two months apart. I wanted to tell her things would get better, but that might not be true. When she lost her husband, we both thought things couldn't get any worse, and then they did.

I put my hand over hers.

"I don't understand." Jessica's voice was flat. "What did I do to deserve this? I just wanted to build a life with Ben, to have a family. Now it's gone. All of it. Gone."

I squeezed her hand. "I don't understand, either. It's not

fair."

"I need to get out of here." Jessica looked me in the eye. "Everything here reminds me of Ben and our baby. I can't handle it."

"Do you want to try going back to work?" I asked. "That might help take your mind off things."

"Maybe," Jessica said. "But even when I'm there, I think of him. How we walked to work together, and he made me lunch every day, and he was always waiting for me when I got off work. I don't know if I can go back."

I nodded. *Lord, I don't know what to say. Give Jessica the comfort and peace that I don't know how to give.*

Jessica stood. "I've got to put myself together and get out of the house for a bit. Thanks for coming."

"Is there anything you need?" I asked. "Anything I can help you with?"

She shook her head.

"Let me know if you think of anything." I gave her another hug and slipped out the door.

*Lord, why would you let all these things happen to Jessica? She's been through so much. I don't understand why one person should have to suffer like that.*

I headed back home, my view of the road blurred by tears. I really wanted to know, to understand why. But my question went unanswered.

*If you won't take away her suffering, Lord, give me the wisdom to help her get through it.*

Mom usually got off work at four thirty. She wasn't home yet at five, so I started making supper. I was just dumping the pasta into a pot of boiling water when she walked in.

"Add an extra serving," Mom said. "Lauren's coming over for supper."

"She is?" I asked.

"I stopped by her house after work. Met her parents. I figure if she means that much to Josh, we need to get to know her a little better."

"Is Dad okay with this?"

"He will be."

I glanced out the window. Josh and Lauren were just passing the house next to ours. Lauren squeezed Josh's hand so hard, her knuckles were white.

They stopped in front of our house. Josh whispered something in Lauren's ear. She smiled, though it wasn't enough to smooth the worry lines on her forehead. She wrapped her arms around his neck. When Josh slid his hands around her waist, there was tenderness in his expression I never thought I'd see from my little brother.

Josh kept his arm around her, and they moved toward the house.

I opened the door. "Come in. It's so good to have you here." I gave Lauren a hug and Josh a punch in the arm.

Josh glanced toward the kitchen. Mom was working at the stove, her back toward us. Josh helped take off Lauren's coat, resting his hand briefly on her abdomen. She smiled at him and put her hand over his. For a moment the anxiety in both of their faces was obliterated by excitement. I could see one thing for sure—they both loved that baby.

I went back to the stove to stir the marinara sauce. Josh started setting the table. Lauren stood just inside the door. She crossed and uncrossed her arms. She looked out the window, looked at us in the kitchen, and then returned her attention back to the window. She shifted her weight from one foot to the other.

I pulled some silverware out of the drawer and handed it to her. "Do you mind helping set the table?"

Lauren smiled. "I'd love to."

I leaned in and whispered, "Congratulations."

Her smile broadened.

Mom was just sitting down after putting the last dish of food on the table when Dad walked in. He stiffened when he saw Lauren and Josh together. I took my seat, and Lauren and Josh joined me at the table. Dad hesitated, as if sitting with us might imply approval of Josh and Lauren's engagement.

After Dad led us in prayer, Mom assumed her role as a gracious hostess, though Lauren could easily have interpreted it as a ruthless interrogator.

"So, Lauren, where are you from?"

"I grew up in New York City."

"That must have been quite a long bus ride to get here."

"Yeah. I'd never gone further than Chicago before we came here."

"Did you like the city?"

"I did. There was always something interesting to see and do, or someone exciting to meet or get to know." Lauren's voice quieted. "I miss my friends a lot."

Josh slid closer to her. I was beginning to see how they had gotten to where they were. She was lonely. He was trying to comfort her. Their lives were turned upside down with the Change. They thought they had nothing more to lose.

"Tell us about your family," Mom said.

"I have—" Lauren looked at Josh, then down at her lap "—well, had two older brothers. They didn't get picked in the lottery. We had to leave them behind when Mom, Dad and I came. We don't know . . ."

Josh reached over and held her hand under the table.

I gave Mom a sideways glance. I thought she knew better than to ask about family. Those kinds of questions always brought up painful memories of leaving loved ones.

I tried to steer the conversation in a different direction. "I got a new assignment from the Council today. It's a tough one. It's going to take me some time to finish, if I'm even able to. It'll probably be a while before I can come home again."

Josh turned to me with eyes wide and a silent question on his lips. He was counting on me to help solve his problem, and now I was taking off for who knows how long. I was letting him down when he needed me the most.

Dad pointed his fork at me. "You're supposed to be negotiating trades between the biosphere and the cabin. Any assignment they give you needs to be carried out by the people at the cabin."

As if I didn't know my own job. "But this time the Council is looking for expertise that no one at the cabin has. And Dr. Franklin keeps everyone on such a short leash; I don't think anyone there would be able to help me."

Dr. Franklin had realized the Change was coming long before the government admitted any such knowledge. He had guided me and many other students and faculty members at Ford College through an acclimatization process, enabling us to survive by adapting to the new atmosphere. But his tyrannical leadership after the Change was one of the main reasons I'd left his community.

"If you're doing all the work, Dr. Franklin needs to pay you for it," Dad said. "Maybe then you could quit your side job."

I shot an accusing glance at Josh. He was the only one in the family I'd told about my illegal mail delivery business. Josh shook his head and shrugged.

"Word gets around, Christy," Dad said. "Is it really worth the risk?"

"When I was stuck at the cabin, wouldn't you have given anything to get a letter from me?" I asked. "All of you risked your lives to talk to me when they had me tied up outside." When I first found the biosphere, the officers guarding the perimeter did not greet me with open arms. "I'm just giving other people the same opportunity—to communicate with those they love."

"Just be careful, sweetie," Mom said. "We don't want to lose you again."

I had successfully diverted my parents' disapproving attention away from Lauren and Josh. But I hadn't come close to convincing them Josh was old enough to make important decisions for himself. They weren't even convinced I was, and I'd been on my own for more than a year.

"Do you think we'll have snow in the biosphere this winter?" Josh asked.

"Oh, I hope so," Lauren said. "I love snow."

"Me too," I said.

"I doubt the upper atmosphere will ever get cool enough for snow to form," Dad said. "The dome creates a pretty strong greenhouse effect."

"I'm sure we'll have frost," Mom offered.

"Tell you what, Lauren," I said. "If you don't get any snow, I'll bring in some snowballs and leave them in your front yard, as long as you promise to throw them only at Josh."

"You better look out." Lauren elbowed Josh. "I have an awesome snowball pitching arm."

"Don't I at least get my own supply of snowballs"—Josh flashed me his puppy-dog eyes—"for self-defense?"

I laughed. "Only if you can steal them from Lauren."

Now that the tension was broken, I tried to poke the elephant in the room. "Have you two thought about wedding plans yet?"

"Only since I was five," Lauren said. "But I'm pretty sure a black-tie event at Old Saint Patrick's followed by a horse-drawn carriage ride to a reception in Central Park is out of the question."

"That sounds beautiful," I said. "If only you guys had met a couple years earlier."

Mom pressed her lips together in a thin line. Dad shook his head. Perhaps bringing up the idea of Josh and Lauren getting together when they were even younger was not a wise move.

"We were thinking a simple service at the church with family, friends, and coworkers," Josh said. "I thought maybe I would ask at work to see if we could have the reception there after hours."

Lauren slouched back in her chair. I couldn't imagine a drabber place for a celebration than the rations warehouse. But there weren't many rooms in the Bubble that would hold enough people for a wedding reception. As soon as Josh turned toward her, she flashed him a smile. But I could tell that the wedding plan was his idea, not hers.

"Have you set a date?" I asked.

Josh put a protective arm around Lauren's shoulders. "Not yet. We're thinking maybe around Thanksgiving."

"It's such a beautiful time of year," Lauren said, "and one of my favorite holidays."

"You'll still be underage next year at Thanksgiving," Mom said to Lauren. "Do you think your parents will give you permission?"

Lauren looked at Josh.

"We're not talking about next year," Josh said.

I held my breath.

He continued, quietly but resolutely, "We're talking

about next month."

Dad slammed his fork on the table. "Out of the question." He crossed his arms.

"Why?" Josh made eye contact with Dad for the first time. "I love Lauren, and she loves me. We want to start building our lives together." Josh turned to Mom. "Why should we have to wait?"

"Marriage is a big commitment," Mom said. "You need to know yourselves and each other better before you jump in."

"I know we love each other," Josh said. "Anything else that comes up we can work through, as long as we have each other."

Josh was beginning to sound like a sappy chick flick. But he did have a point. No matter how old he was, he couldn't predict what challenges marriage would bring. It was the love and commitment they shared that would help them to persevere.

"That may sound good, Josh, but marriage is a lot of work." Mom looked across the table at Dad. "Even the strongest couples sometimes want to throw in the towel."

Had Mom and Dad ever thought about splitting up? I looked at Dad and then back to Mom. I knew their marriage hadn't been perfect. I was just beginning to understand there was no such thing. But I couldn't imagine either of them reaching the point that they were ready to give up.

Mom turned back to Josh. "In a few years, you'll understand better what a lifetime commitment means. Just be patient."

"And what if the dome collapses under the weight of the snow this winter?" Josh jumped to his feet. "What if outsiders attack and breach the biosphere? Then it'll be too late. This is our chance to be a family. If we don't do it now, we may lose that chance."

Even if they weren't working on our parents, Josh's arguments were working on me. If I could somehow have married Scott before he drove away in search of his parents—if we could have been a family, even for a day or two—.

"I said no." Dad put his hands on the table and stood, leaning forward so his face was inches from Josh's. "You can't get married unless we sign for you, and we won't. This conversation is done."

Lauren sniffled.

I bit my lip. Once made up, Dad's mind did not change easily. I flashed Lauren what I hoped looked like an understanding smile.

Josh moved behind Lauren's chair and rested his hands on her shoulders. She reached across her chest, placing her right hand over his left.

Dad sat and put his napkin back in his lap. "Now I, for one, am ready for some dessert. Christy, would you mind?"

Really? Dad expected us to continue the meal like nothing had happened?

I looked at Mom. She nodded slightly.

I stood and walked through the silent room to the refrigerator. I opened the door and pulled out the bowl of fruit cocktail.

"Mr. Phillips."

The strength of Lauren's voice surprised me. I turned back toward the table.

The hand in her lap trembled, but her voice was clear and steady. "I love your son, and I want to spend the rest of my life with him. Josh makes me feel like I'm the most important person in the world, and I want to make him feel the same way. We know this is real, even if no one else can see it. We are going to get married, one way or another." Lauren looked from my dad to my mom. "We would very much like your blessing."

Dad pushed his chair back. "I told you, this discussion is over." He strode to the bedroom shared by Josh and my parents and closed the door.

Josh's voice was barely audible. "I'm going to walk Lauren home." He blinked rapidly, his eyes brimming with tears.

Mom started to object, but I interrupted. "Don't worry about it. I'll clean up."

I returned the fruit cocktail to the refrigerator and picked up the plates. I watched through the front window as Josh and Lauren walked away from the house holding hands, their shoulders shaking.

My heart ached for my little brother. He'd had to grow up so fast. One minute, he'd been a junior in high school in Sioux Falls. The next, he was working full time in the biosphere. Now, just six months later, he was facing fatherhood. He should be enjoying the start of his senior year and trying to find a creative way to ask someone to homecoming, not proposing marriage while trying to find a way to save his child.

Mom and I did the dishes in silence. I tried to think of some way to convince her she could trust Josh to make this decision.

I had just resolved to broach the subject again when Dad came out of the bedroom. "The guys are coming over for poker tonight."

"Do you want me to put out some snacks?" Mom asked.

"That would be great." Dad sat on the couch and started reading the paper.

Mom pulled a couple different kinds of crackers out of the cupboard and arranged them on a plate.

I put away the last of the dishes and hung up the dishtowel. "Why don't we take a walk?" I suggested to Mom.

"Good idea." Mom set the plate on the table and put on her sweater.

As soon as the door closed behind us, I started, choosing my words carefully. "Did you see Josh's face when he left tonight? He was heartbroken."

We turned down the street to the right. The long, flat street was accented by circles of soft light from the streetlamps at each intersection. In the distance, the circles flattened into ovals.

"I know," Mom said. I couldn't make out her expression in the dim light.

"I think Josh might be right about this one."

"I don't think so."

We stepped off the road to allow a utility vehicle to pass.

"No matter how long they wait, they're never going to be prepared for everything that might happen to them when they're married."

Mom waved to a neighbor sitting outside her house. "You're right, but rushing into marriage is not going to make their lives any easier."

"I really do think they love each other. I've never heard him talk about anyone the way he talks about Lauren. He wants to take care of her, to make her life better."

"Josh is hardly old enough to take care of himself. I can't imagine him being responsible for another person, too."

Or two. It was hard for me to imagine as well. But I knew he would figure out a way.

"He's grown up a lot in the past few months. Maybe it's time for you to let him make his own mistakes."

"This isn't like driving too fast or spending too much money on video games. Marriage binds two people so close together. If it's a bad marriage or it ends in divorce—you can't rip those two people apart without causing damage. Sometimes the scars last a lifetime. As a mother, it's my job to protect my children from that possibility until I'm confident they're mature enough to make the decision themselves."

Mom's reasoning made a lot of sense. Short of telling her the whole truth, which Josh had forbidden me to do, I couldn't come up with any more arguments.

We took another right turn, entering one of our favorite neighborhoods. The government had managed to save more of the native trees in this area when they built the biosphere. Especially at night, when you couldn't clearly see the dome of the Bubble, surrounded by thirty-year-old trees, you could imagine you were outside. In the shade of the large trees, the compact buildings felt like quaint cottages rather than mass-produced containers to store people. Even the air seemed to smell fresher in this neighborhood.

I stopped under a massive oak and turned to Mom. "If I could go back in time, I would marry Scott. I wanted to share my life that deeply with him—to love and be loved so much that nothing could come between us. Yes, it would have hurt more when he left. But it would have been worth it."

"I'm so sorry, Christy." Mom put her arm around my shoulders. "I would have given anything to protect you and Josh from all the pain and loss caused by the Change. I couldn't do anything then, but I can now. I can shield the two of you from the pain caused by life-altering decisions made on the spur of the moment. I can, and I will."

I tried to imagine the feeling of helplessness Mom must have experienced while she watched the atmospheric change tear our family apart and turn our lives upside down. A little overprotectiveness following such an event seemed only natural.

When we lived in Sioux Falls, Mom had been pretty laid back, giving us a lot of freedom, at least until we showed we couldn't handle it. Josh never had a curfew. I didn't have one either until Mom found out I had snuck out to go to a party. Now, since the Change, Mom spent a lot more time worrying about us and trying to keep tabs on us.

As his big sister, I felt protective of Josh too. Only I thought the best way to protect him was to let him marry Lauren right away, and Mom thought the best way was to prevent him from marrying as long as possible.

The poker game was still going when we got back to the house. Mom and I sat on the patio, waiting for the party to break up. Councilman Jacobs was the first to leave.

When the door opened, I stood. "Hello, Councilman."

"A beautiful evening, isn't it?" He walked down the street, whistling. He must have been holding good cards that night.

Councilman Jacobs lived a few houses down and had been friends with my father since they moved to the biosphere. He was the first stranger in the biosphere to show me some kindness, ordering that I be untied, and giving me food and water. He still didn't trust me as much as he trusted my father. I was an outsider, after all. But if I was looking for a sympathetic ear on the Council, he was the first person I turned to.

Two other men walked out. They didn't look nearly as happy as Councilman Jacobs.

Mom and I went in and helped Dad and the last remaining guest, Councilman Simpson, clean up. Councilman Simpson lived in a different neighborhood but had recently been invited to join the group by Councilman Jacobs.

"Good to see you again, Councilman," Mom said. "How was the game?"

"I think Jacobs only invited me here to show me up." Councilman Simpson chuckled. "That's okay, though. I picked up on a couple of his signs tonight. Give me another month and I'll give him a run for his money."

"Another month?" Dad said. "If you keep losing, your wife's not going to let you play with us for more than another week or two."

"She's glad to get me out of the house for the evening, no matter the cost." He clapped Dad on the shoulder. "Thanks for a good game."

Councilman Simpson nodded toward Mom and me. "Have a lovely evening." He put on his hat and walked out the door.

Mom returned the remaining crackers to the cupboard. "How did it go tonight?"

"The game was good—friendly." Dad sat at the table. "The Council is really worried about the atmosphere, though. They're already seeing climbing carbon dioxide levels. And the population is still expanding."

"Do you know what they're doing about it?" I wanted to find out if the councilmen had given any hint of their population control actions—anything that would make Dad inclined to believe what Josh's friends were saying.

"Just monitoring right now."

*That's what they want us to think.*

Dad continued, "If things keep moving in this direction, though, they're going to have to take some action."

We finished cleaning up, and I packed my backpack for the trip to Lincoln. It was harder than usual to leave because I knew it might be weeks or even months before I could return. I felt bad that I wasn't able to say goodbye to Josh. He hadn't come back after walking Lauren home. I prayed for his safety, worried he might do something rash in the face of the staunch denial issued by our parents.

The autumn leaves crunched under my feet as I walked toward the airlock. I used to love that sound. But with so many trees outside the Bubble dead, it had become all too common. My thoughts drifted back to the night of the Change. I was supposed to go to the cabin with everyone else who had completed Dr. Franklin's acclimatization program. Ashley came to get me, but I wouldn't go. I couldn't leave my roommate, Kayla. I had stayed with her all night, until . . .

The fear, helplessness, desperation, and grief from that night welled up inside me. I swallowed hard, trying to stuff the memory back into the corner where I usually kept it safely hidden. I was afraid, if I gave those emotions free rein, they would overwhelm me, and I might not be able to regain control. And I had to be in control. If I ever lost it, any number of thieves and government officials would be eagerly waiting to take everything from me.

I needed to think about something safer—something that didn't feel quite so raw. The sound of my shoes shuffling through the dry leaves reminded me of a walk Scott and I took the previous fall. I remembered the feel of his hand in mine and how we giggled as we ran and stomped and threw leaves at each other. I thought then that we would always be together—that nothing could ever come between us.

"Christy."

I thought I heard someone whisper my name. I looked around. I didn't see anyone. *I must be imagining things.* I continued down the street.

A hand grabbed my arm.

I screamed.

A second hand clamped over my mouth.

I drew my free arm back, fist clenched.

"Quiet! Do you want everyone in the B.S. to hear you?"

I recognized Josh's voice and stopped mid-swing, before my fist made contact.

I pushed his hand away from my mouth. "Don't ever do that again."

"Shhh. Come with me." Josh pulled me into an alley.

Lauren stood in the middle of the alley, where the light from the fixtures above the side doors of the two buildings intersected. Her eyes were red, her cheeks streaked with tears. A small suitcase rested on the ground beside her.

Josh stood next to Lauren, facing me. "Christy, we want you to take us with you."

"What?" I asked, confused by his request.

"If we stay here, they're going to kill our baby," Josh said. "Out there our baby will at least have a chance."

"But we don't know if either of you can survive in the

new atmosphere or how adapting to the atmosphere might affect your pregnancy. And I don't know anyone who's acclimatized by sudden exposure."

"We have to take that chance." Lauren grabbed my arm. "Our parents won't let us get married. I'm going to start showing soon. I can't get any new clothes, so I won't be able to hide it for long. Please, you've got to help us."

*Lord, is this your answer? Is this what you want me to do?*

It couldn't be. It was too risky.

"Look, if I take you out of here, chances are all three of you are going to die. I'm not willing to do that." I took a deep breath and tried to think.

"There may be another way." I looked around to make sure there was no one else within earshot. All of my assignments from the Council were strictly confidential. "The Council asked me to find some people who could help boost the atmospheric conversion system. If the system can be made faster or more efficient, the government won't have to worry about the growing population."

"But you said you don't know how long this assignment is going to take," Josh said. "We don't have much time. Where are you going to find people familiar with the workings of an atmospheric conversion system?"

"I don't know," I admitted, "but I will work non-stop until I figure it out. And if I can't, I'll come back and get you."

"Promise?" Lauren asked.

"I promise. But I need you to do two things while I'm

gone. First, see if you can get your hands on oxygen backpacks and masks. If we have to get you out of the biosphere, using the oxygen tanks will be the only way to make your transition gradual.

"Second, I want you to be model citizens—the perfect son and daughter. Convince your parents you're mature enough to make serious decisions and stand behind adult commitments. You need to keep all of your options open."

Josh looked at Lauren. She nodded.

"We can do that," Josh said.

I hugged them both and continued on to the airlock. I loaded my next delivery into the car, mentally reviewing my travel plans. I would hit Pueblo first, then Lincoln, then the cabin. I needed to talk to all of my friends on the outside, to find out if any of them could connect me with engineers who might be able to help.

# 7

I crept out of the airlock, driving slowly to minimize the noise of tires on gravel, my lights off. When I reached the main roads, I turned the headlights on and drove south toward Pueblo, where my best friend Ashley Goodell lived.

Ashley and I had left the cabin together five months earlier in search of our families. Her parents had not been selected for the biosphere. When we'd stopped at her home, we found a fresh grave in the backyard, marked with her mother's favorite type of stone. Ashley had concluded that her dad must have survived and buried her mother after the Change. A car was missing from the garage, but we couldn't find any clues indicating where her dad had gone. Ashley had remained at her home since then, awaiting his return.

It was still dark when I turned onto Riverview Place. I parked on the street in front of Ashley's house and reclined the seat to catch a nap. The government's requirement that all of my biosphere arrivals and departures occur in the dark wreaked havoc on my sleeping schedule.

Someone pounded on the driver's side window. My hand was on the grip of my gun before I even opened my eyes. I was relieved to see Ashley, waving to me through the window. Her blonde pixie cut was tousled from a recent wrestling match with her pillow. The rising sun glinted off her sparkly top which was, of course, perfectly coordinated with her jeans.

I opened the door and slid out. She hugged me so tightly I could hardly breathe.

"It's good to see you, too," I said when she finally let go.

With my delivery schedule, I only made it to Pueblo once or twice a month. I knew she was lonely there by herself. She rarely saw any other people on her cul-de-sac, and when she did, her fear prompted her to hide. My infrequent visits provided her only social interaction.

I grabbed my backpack out of the back seat and walked toward the house.

Ashley practically bounced down the sidewalk. I could see in her grin she had stories to tell.

"So, what's new?" I asked.

"I got all the weeds out of Mom's garden. We'll have to go out and see it. The flowers that survived are really thriving now, and the vegetable seeds you gave me are growing great."

"That's awesome. Your mom would be so proud."

"The neighborhood has been pretty quiet—a few people wandering through but no large groups. I felt safe enough to leave the house a couple times. I went down to the river and tried out Dad's fishing pole. I was only out there for about an hour, and I caught several fish."

"Did you see a lot of dead fish?"

Ashley shook her head. "I wonder if the Change didn't

affect the fish as much as it did the land animals."

"The Change was probably more gradual in the water. Maybe they had more time to adapt. What kind of fish did you catch?"

"I think they were trout. They were small. It was hardly worth the work of cleaning them for the tiny bit of meat I got from each one. Still, it was a nice change from all the canned food."

When we were at college together, I never would have imagined Ashley catching and growing her own food. Her French provincial bedroom spoke of a charmed childhood. The Change had forced all of us far beyond our comfort zones.

"Listen," I said. "I'm not going to be able to stay long today."

Ashley's face fell.

"The Council gave me a big assignment, and I'm under a bit of a time crunch to get it done."

We went through the house and out the back door. While we walked through the garden, I told Ashley about Josh and Lauren's engagement and their worries about the safety of their new baby.

I told her about the Council's request. "Any chance you know where I could find some chemical or mechanical engineers?"

"Mr. Hammond on the corner was an engineer," Ashley said. "Not sure what kind, though."

"Is he still alive?"

"I don't know. I haven't been down to that end of the

street much."

"Let's go pay Mr. Hammond a visit." I turned back toward the street.

We walked to the T-intersection where Riverview Place met Peakview Drive. Ashley knocked on the front door of the two-story home on the corner. No one answered. I tried the door. It was locked. We walked around to the back door. The doorframe next to the deadbolt had been gouged out, and the door stood partway open.

"It looks like we're not the first visitors to the Hammond house." I swung the door open the rest of the way.

Ashley poked her head inside and looked around. "If he is still in here, he's probably not in any shape to help you out."

We entered cautiously, finding ourselves in the Hammond kitchen. The small table was set for two. There were food remnants on the dishes but no mold or ants.

"Someone must be living here," I said. "Maybe he's just out this morning."

Ashley glanced back at the gouged doorframe and shrugged her shoulders.

We walked down the hallway toward the front of the house. I glanced in the room on our left. The doors of the curio at the end of the dining room were standing open, and the contents were strewn all over the floor and large table.

A little farther down and across the hall was the entryway to the living room. A body lay face down on the area rug, limbs askew as if it had been dropped from a passing helicopter. I held my breath and hurried past.

I motioned backward with my thumb. "Mr. Hammond?"

Ashley nodded.

I considered our next move. "Let's look for his office. Maybe he'll have some information about the people he worked with."

We turned and climbed the stairs. At the top of the stairs, I checked the room on the right, and Ashley opened the door to the left.

The bedroom I was looking at had been ransacked, just like the dining room. "If there is anything of value in here, it would take forever to find it."

"Same here." Ashley closed the door.

We walked down the hall, past the bathroom. The doors to the remaining two rooms were standing open. The room on the left was tidy, except for the disheveled covers on the bottom bunk.

"Did Mr. Hammond have a family?" I asked.

"His kids are grown. His wife passed away when I was in middle school."

"I have a feeling Mr. Hammond has some tenants he doesn't know about."

We crossed the hall and looked in the largest room on the second floor. Every throw pillow on the queen-size bed was carefully positioned. The slippers beside the bed were perfectly aligned. The large mahogany desk was free of dust and clutter, supporting only an antique brass lamp.

Ashley stepped back and looked over her shoulder toward the stairs. "You're right, Christy. Someone else is living here. We need to get out of here before they come home."

"There might be something in the desk." I crossed the room. "We have to at least check."

Ashley reappeared in the doorway. "Let's make it quick."

I felt like I needed to put on white gloves before touching the desk, to make sure the new residents of the Hammond house wouldn't find my fingerprints.

I pulled the center drawer open. When I released the handle, it clinked against the plate on which it was mounted. Ashley jumped and emitted a squeak so cute I almost laughed out loud.

"It's not funny," Ashley whispered, her hands in tight fists at her sides.

The top drawers contained a well-organized collection of office supplies. Hanging files filled the bottom drawers on either side of the desk. Grateful for Mr. Hammond's attention to detail, Ashley and I flipped rapidly through the clearly-labeled tabs.

"This is it." Ashley pulled out a file labeled "UTC" and laid it on the desk.

We set aside pay stubs, letters, job descriptions, and outdated project calendars. I was flipping through a packet of letters on UTC Aerospace Systems letterhead when Ashley put her hand on mine. "Stop a sec. What was that?"

I turned back a few pages. "This one?"

"No." Ashley flipped forward one page.

The UTC logo at the top of the page looked the same as all the others. But instead of a letter, this page bore a collection of names and phone numbers, arranged in a pyramid, connected with angled and vertical lines.

"Looks like a phone tree." I pointed to Mr. Hammond's name along the left side of the pyramid. "These must be UTC employees."

"Probably, but what are we going to do with a list of phone numbers?"

Prior to the Change, the government had ordered the shutdown of all communication systems, along with all utilities, for fear of catastrophic results if some of these systems suddenly became unmanned.

"The numbers won't do any good," I said, "but we can use the names to look up some addresses."

I pocketed the phone tree. We flipped through the rest of the file, finding nothing more that might be helpful.

Ashley shoved the papers back in the file folder and stuffed it in the drawer. "Now, let's get out of here."

We had just reached the stairs when we heard voices below us.

"I'm not going to touch the body," a man said.

We froze.

A woman answered, "Well, we can't just leave it in the living room."

I tried to figure out where the voices were coming from. Standing at the top of the stairs, we could see the front door. I hadn't seen any movement there. They must have come in the back door. That meant they were probably in the kitchen.

"If you want to get rid of it, you're going to have to do it yourself." The man's voice sounded closer.

Since it didn't appear they used the dining room or living room much, he was probably headed upstairs. I motioned for Ashley to follow me down the hall. I carefully opened the door to one of the ransacked bedrooms and followed Ashley inside. I closed the door slowly, turning the knob to silence the click of the door latch.

"What are we going to do now?" Ashley whispered desperately.

"We need to get out of here as soon as we can."

"They'll see us or hear us. Who knows what they'll do when they find intruders in their house."

"Maybe we could climb down." I picked my way cautiously through the mess on the floor to the window and looked out. There was nothing attached to the house that we might be able to climb down and no tree branches we could reach from the window. I turned back to Ashley and shook my head.

"We're going to have to hide until they leave or fall asleep," Ashley said.

"I can't wait that long. I have to finish my assignment and get back to the Bubble."

"And you're willing to risk getting shot?"

"We don't even know if they have any weapons. Listen, if we let them know we're not here to take anything from them and we can defend ourselves, I bet we can walk right out the door. Follow my lead." I walked to the door, stomping my feet.

"What are you doing?" Ashley whispered frantically.

*Lord, I hope this works.*

Reaching the hallway, I said loudly, "That's too bad about Mr. Hammond."

Ashley caught up with me. She looked confused but matched my volume. "Yeah, I'm really going to miss him."

"Hey, listen; I really have a craving for fresh meat. Do you want to go squirrel hunting this afternoon? I have my gun with me."

"Sounds delicious." The disgusted look on Ashley's face belied the enthusiasm in her voice. I stifled a chuckle.

I pulled out my pistol. We were halfway down the steps. The path to the front door was clear, but we couldn't see if there was anyone in the hallway behind us.

"I'm getting to be quite a good shot." I reached the bottom of the steps and whipped around, my gun at the ready. "Last time we went I used five bullets and got three squirrels."

I could hear Ashley fumbling with the locks on the front door. I scanned the hallway and the part of the living room I could see.

"Boy, did we feast that night." Ashley swung the door open and touched my arm.

We sprinted through the door. We didn't stop running until we were inside Ashley's house with the doors locked behind us.

Ashley collapsed on the couch, giggling. "I can't believe you pulled that off."

"It's like meeting a wild animal," I said, confidently. "Remember, they're more scared of you than you are of them."

"And squirrels? Seriously?"

"I'm sure they're a delicacy in some countries."

After we caught our breath, Ashley found her phone book, and we looked up the names on the list. We found addresses for about half of them. Ashley planned our route through Pueblo to hit all of the addresses we found. She was reluctant to leave her house unattended, but neither of us wanted to go knocking on doors alone. So, after a quick bite to eat, we set out in my car.

We were grateful to complete our scavenger hunt without any serious threat to our health or safety. However, I was frustrated with our lack of success. Six people were willing to open their doors for us: an administrative assistant, two facilities maintenance workers, two line workers, and a vice president. None of them knew anything about the workings of an atmospheric conversion system.

Back at Ashley's house, I unloaded the backpack of food I had brought for her, and she gave me some more of her parents' clothes to exchange at the market in Lincoln. I had done all I could in Pueblo, so I loaded the clothes in the car and got ready to leave for the cabin.

"Can't you stay tonight?" Ashley asked. "You can start out fresh first thing tomorrow."

I shook my head. "I have to keep working at this. Any delay could mean the difference between life and death for my brother's baby."

Tears welled up in Ashley's eyes. "I think"—she took a deep breath—"I want to go with you."

I was shocked. I had asked her many times before, and she had always adamantly refused to come.

"Of course," I said, after recovering from my initial surprise. "Let's go upstairs and pack your stuff."

We left a note for Ashley's dad, giving him the address of the farmhouse where I stayed when I was making deliveries to the cabin. Then we loaded up the car and headed for the highway. I was thrilled to hit the road with Ashley riding shotgun. We had started our journey side-by-side five months before. It felt right to be traveling together again.

# 8

After driving through the night, we stopped at my house for a quick nap. The farmhouse, located between the cabin and Lincoln, Nebraska, had been our first stop when Ashley and I ran away from the cabin. We had cut pieces of the garden hose on the back of the house to use for siphoning gas.

After finding the Bubble, I'd returned to the cabin with the first trade request. I had stopped at the farmhouse again, emptying the pantry to pay back the cabin community for the supplies Ashley and I had taken when we left. They'd accepted my payment but had yet to accept me back into the community. When Dr. Franklin told me in no uncertain terms that I would not be allowed to stay at the cabin, I set about making the farmhouse my second home. I'd done my best to give its former occupants a proper burial in the cornfield behind the house. I'd restocked the shelves of the pantry with the payments I received for delivering mail. A small bedroom on the second floor with a great view of the sunrise had become my new haven.

The sun was up by the time we awoke.

"Are you sure you want to come along?" I asked Ashley. This was the worst part of my job, facing Dr. Franklin's condemnation every time I brought a delivery to the cabin. Ashley had heard me say many times how difficult and painful it was.

"Of course," Ashley said. "I wish I could have come with you every time."

The term "cabin" did not do justice to the formidable log structure hidden in the woods less than a mile east of the farmhouse. When we were still students at Ford College in Lincoln, we had gone to the cabin for retreats to help prepare us for the atmospheric change through gradual exposure.

Scott had signed up for the acclimatization program, but the Change happened before his turn came up. If only I had talked him into signing up a couple weeks earlier . . .

When the Change started on the West Coast, all of the Survival Skills Club members—students and teachers who had successfully completed the atmospheric acclimatization process—moved to the cabin for safety.

The cabin had provided protection and the support of a community in an uncertain world. Despite its massive size and Dr. Franklin's unforgiving attitude, the cabin still incited in me feelings of comfort and security—feelings of home. Since the Change, other survivors from nearby towns had joined the community, bringing the population up to about 250.

We parked in front and carried the garden tools and containers of propane provided by the Bubble to the tool shed behind the cabin.

Returning to the front of the cabin, I knocked on the door.

*Jesus, please give me strength.*

I didn't recognize the man who opened the door. His

forehead creased when he saw Ashley beside me. He followed protocol, closing the door without a word and retreating to notify Dr. Franklin. Ashley and I returned to the car to retrieve the rest of our delivery and the manila envelope. We left one copy of the atmospheric conversion system schematics in the car. If I found any engineers who could help, I wanted to have the information at hand.

Dr. Franklin opened the door, his broad, six-foot-five frame nearly filling the doorway. He turned his back to us. The horseshoe of graying hair framing his large bald spot had grown bushier since the Change. Perhaps I should request a hair clipper from the Bubble.

We followed him silently down the hall. I smiled at Ashley when we passed the library, the first room on the right. That had been our favorite room in the cabin. During the precious few moments of free time we had when we lived there, retreating to the library afforded us the opportunity to get lost in another world and forget, if only briefly, what was going on around us.

I glanced into the common room, on our left. There were a few groups of people inside, clustered at tables working on projects. I remembered fondly the evening meals we shared there. It was the one time everyone in the cabin got together. I loved listening to other people's stories of the adventures they'd had and the challenges they'd overcome during the day. I longed for those moments of shared experience and celebrated success. If only there were some way to become a part of the community again, without subjecting myself to Dr. Franklin's unreasonable rules and excessive punishments.

We walked through the open door at the end of the hall and into the kitchen. Dr. Franklin closed the door behind us and stood with his arms crossed while we placed bags of batteries and light bulbs on the island.

"The Council delivered everything you requested," I said.

What I had to say next would not make Dr. Franklin happy. I took a deep breath.

"This contains the Council's next request from the cabin." I held the manila envelope out to Dr. Franklin. He made no move to take it, so I put it on the island. "They need two chemical engineers and two mechanical engineers to review the design of the biosphere's atmospheric conversion system and make recommendations for its improvement."

"We don't have any engineers here," Dr. Franklin said. The tone of his voice matched that of a parent scolding a misbehaving toddler.

"I told the chairman that," I said. "He was confident you would be able to find some. He also said there would be no further deliveries from the biosphere until this request was fulfilled."

Dr. Franklin put his hands on his hips. "That is not acceptable."

"Those are the Council's terms," I said.

Dr. Franklin mumbled under his breath, "They won't be so demanding next spring when they're ready to plant and don't have any adapted seed."

"When would you like me to return to pick up the

engineers' recommendations?" I asked.

Dr. Franklin's lips pressed together in a pale thin line that stood in contrast to his reddening ears. "Give me two weeks."

"Yes, sir." I started toward the hallway, with Ashley close behind.

"Ashley." Dr. Franklin's voice brought us to a halt.

We turned to face him. Glancing at Ashley, I saw fear in her eyes. I had seen that same look every time Dr. Franklin confronted us when we lived at the cabin.

"I don't know what Christy has told you." Dr. Franklin's eyes looked as if they would bore a hole through Ashley. "But people who lie and steal from us are not welcome here. You had a chance to be a part of this community, and you chose to leave. You don't get a second chance."

Ashley winced. I took her by the elbow and guided her through the door. We needed to get out of there before Ashley started to cry or said something she would later regret.

I knew how she felt. I was devastated when I heard a similar speech the first time I returned to the cabin. It took me months to realize Dr. Franklin did not speak for the whole community. Many people at the cabin had forgiven and accepted me. I still wanted Dr. Franklin's forgiveness, but I didn't have to have it in order to build friendships with other people at the cabin.

Of course, since Dr. Franklin was the man in charge, I had to build those friendships in secret. Ashley and I drove up the winding driveway until we were out of sight of the cabin.

Ashley shot me a confused look when I pulled off the driveway onto the grass. I grabbed my backpack from the back seat, and Ashley and I walked several yards into the woods. I motioned for Ashley to stop. I stood still, listening for any sound from the direction of the driveway.

For several seconds I heard nothing but the wind rustling the dry leaves.

Then Angela Blanchett stepped out from behind a tree a few feet from us. Ashley jumped.

Dozens of other people from the cabin followed Angela's lead, emerging from their hiding places. Ashley nearly fell over backward.

Angela laughed and ran to give Ashley a hug. Ryan Wright followed close behind. Angela and Ryan had been in Dr. Franklin's class with Ashley and me. We had all gone through the acclimatization process together. Persevering through an experience that was intense beyond what we ever imagined we could endure created a bond no time or distance could weaken.

I stood on the trunk of a fallen tree and addressed the gathered crowd. "It's good to see everyone again. Many of you know Ashley." I gestured toward her. "She's been at her parents' house for the past few months. We're thrilled to have her back with us."

Those who knew her applauded softly.

"News from the Bubble: Doris Feldkamp passed away, six babies were born, and my little brother got engaged."

Soft murmurs arose from the crowd.

"There is still great concern about the ability to maintain the atmosphere in the biosphere given the growing population. If any of you have an engineering background or know of someone who does, please talk to me.

"I haven't yet been to town this trip, so I don't know what's trading well at the market. If you have anything to trade, I'll see what I can do. It may be a while before my next trip to the biosphere, as their demands of Dr. Franklin are going to be difficult to meet. I will be back here in two weeks, to check whether Dr. Franklin has been able to accomplish what they asked. Any questions?"

I looked at the expectant faces gathered around me. Seeing no raised hands, I announced, "Mail time!"

That's what most of those gathered were waiting for. I read off the names on the envelopes and handed them to Ashley or Angela, who distributed them when the people came forward. Some people dropped off outgoing mail or items for trade. A few gave me the names and addresses of engineers who might be able to help with the atmospheric conversion system. After we handed out the last letter, those remaining drifted away.

I cherished the opportunity to bring my friends at the cabin a little joy and news from their loved ones. But it made me sad that I had to do it in secret. I longed to be a full member of the community again.

Ryan and Angela stayed behind to catch up with Ashley. They couldn't quite make it through five months of life stories in the short time they had, but they certainly tried.

After a few minutes, Angela said, "We've got to get going before they miss us at our work assignments. There've been a few incidents when people were away from the cabin, and Dr. Franklin has really tightened the reins."

"And everyone is still just going along with his rules?" I asked.

Ryan nodded. "A lot of people are getting tired of them, but no one is willing to step up and do something about it. We're all afraid he'll kick us out if we complain. No one wants to lose the security of the community."

Angela nodded and turned to me. "Before we go, though, I wanted to let you know your brother wasn't the only one who got engaged this week."

Ryan put his arm around her shoulders, and Angela held up her left hand, revealing a ring woven out of grass supporting a dried baby's breath blossom.

My chin dropped. I knew Ryan and Angela were friends, but I had no idea it was anything more than that. I was speechless.

"Christy, why didn't you tell me?" Ashley hugged Angela.

I understood now why Angela wouldn't leave the cabin when we invited her to come along on our quest to find our families. It turned out there was one particular person she didn't want to leave behind.

"It's beautiful," I said when my chin finally returned to its proper position. "Congratulations!" I pulled Ryan in for a group hug.

"We've got to go." Angela turned back toward the cabin. "We can talk more when you come back in two weeks."

"I'm so happy for you guys," Ashley said. "'Bye."

"I never would have pictured those two together," I said to Ashley, walking back to the car.

Ashley shook her head. "The chemistry nerd and the soprano diva? Not in a million years."

"They're a cute couple."

"Yeah." Ashley opened the car door. "I bet they'll make it work."

I was happy for them. But seeing them together reminded me of how much I missed my own boyfriend, Scott Markham. When the Change began, Scott had driven west to try to find his parents, who were stuck in the traffic jam created by people fleeing the West Coast. Cell service went down shortly after he left, and I had no idea whether he had found his parents or even if he was still alive.

I was so blessed. I still had my family and my best friend. Very few people could say that. But Scott's absence left a big hole in my heart. I hadn't found anything that could fill it.

# 9

After our stop at the cabin, we drove to Lincoln to visit Max. Angela, Ryan, Ashley, and I had struck up a friendship with Max Reynolds when we first went into town after the Change to invite other people to join us at the cabin. He had generously let Ashley and I borrow his SUV when we left the cabin to find our families. Now I helped him with his stand at the Lincoln market, and he gave me tips on the most sought-after items that I could pass on to the people I traded for. I hoped that Max's work as a biochemist before the Change had brought him into contact with some chemical engineers who could help us.

We drove north and caught Interstate 80 West, which took us to the north edge of town. It was a longer route, but it kept us well away from the congestion of the Lincoln market in the center of the city.

Though you could see evidence that many of the houses on Max's street had been broken into, his street was pretty quiet now. Most of the violence in town seemed to happen in areas where more people were vying for resources. There weren't many other occupied homes on his block.

We pulled into Max's driveway and climbed the stairs to the front door of his raised-ranch home. I knocked on the door and stepped to the side. The curtains covering the sidelight moved slightly. Max burst through the door. Ashley stumbled back.

"Ashley! I didn't think I'd ever see you again." Max wrapped his arms around her, almost lifting her off her feet.

"I was going crazy cooped up in that house by myself," Ashley said.

Max held the door open for us. His close-cropped hair came in variety of shades of brown, which helped to disguise the gray. The worry lines that were etched into his forehead and the corners of his mouth since the Change had relaxed some, but his eyes still looked tired.

"How are things in town?" I stepped into the house.

"The market's been a little slow." Max followed us in. "There was some violence at the beginning of the week. People want to make sure things have settled down before they venture out in public. I haven't gone hungry yet, but I am getting a little tired of tuna."

Less activity in the market meant it would be harder to make good trades with the items people at the cabin had given me. At present, though, that was the least of my worries.

We sat in the living room.

"Have you heard any word from your dad yet, Ashley?" Max asked.

Ashley's face fell. "Nothing. Every day it gets a little harder to keep hoping."

"Listen," Max said gently, "whenever you need a dad's shoulder to cry on, just drop by."

Ashley knew one of her parents was dead and didn't

know if she would ever see the other one again. I got to see both of my parents every week or two. I felt horrible for being jealous of Angela and Ryan's relationship. If anyone had a right to be jealous, it was Ashley, not me.

"I imagine Dr. Franklin was happy to see you both," Max said.

"Hardly," Ashley said. "I'd forgotten how much fun his tongue-lashings were. I'm glad we don't have to go back again for two weeks."

"Two weeks?" Max asked.

"Yeah," I said. "The Council asked the cabin for expert advice on upgrading the biosphere's atmospheric conversion system. Dr. Franklin figures it will take at least a couple weeks for him to find someone with that kind of knowledge. You wouldn't by chance know any engineers who could help with that?"

Max shook his head. "We had a few chemical engineers where I worked, but I don't think any of them survived."

Max must have seen the disappointment on my face. "Isn't it Dr. Franklin's job to meet the Council's request? Why are you worried about it?"

"Well, I can't go back to the biosphere until I have recommendations from at least four engineers. That means it might be a while before I see my family again. And—" I took a deep breath "—the biosphere government is forcing single pregnant women to have abortions, to limit the population growth. Josh just told me his girlfriend—I mean, fiancé—Lauren, is pregnant. If we don't find a solution in the next month or two, I might lose my first niece or nephew. Josh is so scared they're going to kill his baby, he wanted me to take Lauren and him with me when I left the biosphere yesterday. They were willing to risk their own lives for the smallest of chances they might be able to save their baby."

Saying these words aloud made me feel even more helpless. I was out of ideas. And now I was hundreds of miles away from Josh. I couldn't even give him a listening ear or an encouraging word.

Max stared at the wall behind me. I looked over my shoulder to find out what had captured his attention. Seeing nothing out of the ordinary, I turned back toward him.

He nodded slowly and met my questioning look. "I think I might be able to help you."

"Really?" I asked, skeptical but interested.

"There's some reason why I survived, and my wife and kids did not," Max said, "why you survived and your roommate didn't. That reason is probably genetic. If we can find the gene that predisposes people for adaptation to the current atmosphere, then we can determine which people living in the biosphere are most likely to be able to survive outside. That could allow Josh and Lauren to leave so they can save their baby. Or it could allow other people to move out of the biosphere, eliminating the population problem inside."

My excitement grew. This idea might actually work.

"All of the equipment we would need to run the testing is available at my lab," Max said. "The machines haven't been used in months. They'll all need to be recalibrated. And the power's off so the incubators haven't been running. We'll need to replace our bacteria supplies."

"What do you need bacteria for?" Ashley asked.

"To produce the enzymes we use to pull apart the DNA so we can copy it," Max said.

"Where can we find the bacteria?" I asked.

"The nearest source is Yellowstone," Max said.

"Yellowstone National Park?" Ashley asked.

Max nodded. "*Thermus aquaticus.* It can only live at the high temperatures created by the thermal features in the park."

A trip to Yellowstone could further delay my return to the Bubble. I wanted to get back as soon as I could, to make sure Lauren and her baby were okay. I felt a pull to stay, to work on finding engineers who could help the Council, so I could return to my family sooner. But what if the engineers' recommendations weren't enough? If I didn't go find that bacteria, I might miss my best chance to save Josh's baby.

I smiled at Ashley. "Sounds like it's time for a road trip."

"No way." Ashley shook her head. "I just left Dad a note saying I would be at the farmhouse. I'm not going to take off cross country with you and risk missing him."

"I'll go with you," Max offered, to my surprise. "I know what to look for to locate *Thermus aquaticus'* habitat, and I can monitor conditions during the drive back to make sure we keep the bacteria alive."

"I just got here, and you're both going to leave me?" Ashley looked like a dejected puppy.

"It'll just be for a few days," I assured her.

"Maybe more like a week or so," Max said. "If you're planning to stay, you can calibrate the equipment and collect some genetic samples. If you can get a good sampling of survivor and non-survivor DNA, we'll be able to start testing as soon as we get back."

Ashley's eyes brightened. "I could do that."

"I would also appreciate it if you could keep an eye on the house while I'm gone," Max said.

"Consider it done." Ashley smiled.

"Great," Max said. "Ashley, you and I will go to the lab, so I can show you what needs to be done. Christy, I need you to go to the market and trade for some food for our trip. Try to get at least two weeks' worth. Don't forget your gun."

"Got it," I said. "I'll also run out to the farmhouse and leave a note for your dad, Ashley, and I'll bring the food from the farmhouse here."

I gathered several items of clothing that belonged to the deceased members of Max's family and drove south to Lincoln's business district. I parked a few blocks away and carried the clothing and some items I had recently received from my mail customers to the market.

Immediately after the Change, most of the people in Lincoln who survived had stayed holed up in their houses, fearful of the violence and theft that were suddenly rampant in the city. When the violence quieted, people started venturing out to find other survivors. They traded goods and services with one another, first to meet their needs and later to make life more comfortable. This eventually developed into the market. People came to the market area every morning, bringing items or offering services. There, they negotiated trades with people from all over the city.

That day, the market was smaller than usual. Several tables of merchandise were set up, but very few people were walking through the market to make trades. Because business was slow, and it was late in the day, I was able to negotiate some pretty good deals. After a couple hours, I made my way back to the car, laden with food and bottled water, almost more than I could carry.

I drove from the market to the farmhouse. I wrote a note for Ashley's dad, giving him the addresses for Max's house and the lab. I also apologized for sending him on a scavenger hunt. Once he knew his daughter was safe, I thought he might appreciate a little levity. I loaded all of the food from the farmhouse pantry into the car.

I stopped at an abandoned car lot on the east edge of Lincoln to trade the car for something more rugged. Our cross-country trip would definitely require some off-roading. When the atmospheric change began in India and Japan, people in the United States fled the West Coast in great numbers, trying to get away from fault lines. Many people were stuck in traffic jams when the Change reached America. Stopped cars littered the roads, especially the major east-west highways, often necessitating detours into the ditch or the median.

I transferred the food and water from the car to the covered bed of a red Silverado. All of the sources of gasoline I knew of between the farmhouse and Lincoln had been depleted. I drove thirty miles north to a dealership in Wahoo and topped off the tank of the Silverado by siphoning gas from cars on the lot.

A few blocks from the car dealership, I found a convenience store. Entering through the broken window, I picked my way through the debris and shards of glass littering the floor and retrieved an atlas from the overturned display. Returning to the truck, I used the atlas to plan a few different routes to reach Yellowstone, using roads that paralleled major highways whenever possible. Tracing the roads that would take us west from Lincoln, memories of Scott's departure flooded over me, creating a familiar ache deep in my chest. Which route had he taken when he left Lincoln in search of his parents? How far had he gotten? Where was he now? Would I ever see him again?

I shook my head, trying to dislodge the memory. I needed to focus on saving Josh's baby. There wasn't time to dwell on the past—especially knowing I would never get it back.

One of the possible routes passed through Colorado, not too far from the Bubble. Was I making the right choice, traveling all the way to Yellowstone to look for some obscure bacteria that may or may not be Josh and Lauren's ticket out of the biosphere? I heard that voice inside me again, urging me to stay and finish the Council's assignment.

I clenched my teeth. *I need to do this. This could be my best chance to save Josh's baby.* I headed back to Max's house.

Max met me at the door. "Nice wheels."

I was glad he approved of the truck. I still felt guilty for not returning the SUV we'd borrowed from him. After someone busted out the window of his SUV while trying to rob Ashley and me, we'd switched it out for another vehicle, abandoning it at a car lot in Kansas.

Max directed me to the living room, where he had collected the things we needed for the trip. We carried the equipment and supplies down the stairs and loaded them into the bed of the Silverado.

I surveyed the contents of the truck bed. "Looks like we're ready to go."

Max rolled the cover over the top and showed me how to latch it in place. "Do you want to leave tonight, or wait 'til morning?"

"I'd like to get started as soon as possible." Even as I said it, I felt an ache in my chest. Ashley and I had just been reunited. I didn't want to leave her already.

"Let's go say goodbye," Max said.

I followed Max up the stairs, into the house, and through the living room to the kitchen. Ashley was sitting at the table, supporting her head with her left hand. She was examining the papers in front of her with such intensity, I thought her eyes might bore a hole through them. Her mouth moved rapidly, then slowly with precision, silently forming the words on her handwritten notes.

"Ashley?" I said.

She jumped, her furrowed eyebrows shooting up. "Don't sneak up on a person like that."

"Sorry." I chuckled. "Did Max teach you everything he knows?" I gestured toward the papers spread across the table.

Ashley nodded with one corner of her mouth turning up in a wry smile. "And I still don't know anything."

"Not true," Max said. "She picked up on things so fast, she'll be ready to take over my job by the time we get back."

Ashley smiled, her cheeks flushing slightly. "I'm just glad to have something to do. Sitting around waiting was driving me crazy." She pointed at Max. "You better hurry back, or I'll be good enough to be your boss before we see each other again."

Max sported a smug grin. "Lucky for me, the company put a freeze on promotions"—his eyes dropped to the floor, his smile gone—"the day they sent us all home and told us not to expect any more paychecks."

I tried to imagine what that was like for Max, walking away from the career he had spent his life building, knowing he might never be able to return. Maybe that's why he was so eager to help me with this project. It gave him a chance to use his skills and knowledge one more time.

"Do you have any questions, now that you've had a chance to look things over?" Max's tone was all business, but it couldn't suppress the sadness in his eyes.

Ashley shook her head. "I don't think so. If I do, I'm sure the answers are in here somewhere." Ashley picked up a handful of papers and let them fall onto the table.

"We're going to head out tonight," I said.

Ashley sighed.

I continued quickly, "So we can get back as soon as possible."

Max put a hand on her shoulder. "Thank you for taking care of things at the house and lab while we're gone."

Ashley stood and gave Max a hug. "I hope you find what you're looking for."

She turned to me.

"I'm going to miss you." I wrapped my arms around her.

"Me, too." Ashley's voice cracked, but she held her tears at bay. "Hurry back."

"I promise." Reluctantly, I pulled away. I squeezed Ashley's hands and turned to go.

By the time Max and I reached the edge of town, the sun had dropped below the horizon, leaving a breathtaking tapestry of pinks and oranges in its wake. I looked at Max and back at the western sky. For the first time, I felt confident. This trip held the key that I needed to save my brother's baby. We were going to find what we were looking for—we just had to.

# 10

The morning light nudged me awake. I shifted in the passenger's seat and tried to stretch.

"Morning, sunshine," Max said.

I yawned. "This is not the most comfortable place I've slept."

*It's not the most uncomfortable either.* My thoughts went back to the two nights I'd spent outside the biosphere with my wrists and ankles duct taped together after I arrived there uninvited.

I looked at my watch. It had been more than three hours since I'd handed over the wheel. I had been sound asleep for most of that time. "Do you want me to drive for a while?"

"No, I'm doing fine."

He eased the Silverado in and out of the ditch to get around the cars blocking the road. I tried to imagine what it was like when all of these cars were moving—or trying to move. With traffic jams clogging all of the major eastbound highways, people were driving on the shoulder, in the median, or even going the wrong way in the westbound lanes, in an effort to escape the cataclysmic seismic activity wracking the West Coast. And in the midst of all that, Scott was driving upstream, headed west in an attempt to find the particular traffic jam in which his parents were stuck. As challenging as it was to drive on these roads now, I couldn't imagine adding honking horns and countless desperate drivers fleeing for their lives.

"So, how did you convince Ashley to leave Pueblo?" Max pulled me back to the present.

"I didn't. I didn't even ask her this time. She just said she wanted to come. I think she's really been lonely."

"I can understand that," Max said, quietly.

"You've never told me much about your family."

There was a long pause. Maybe it was too soon to ask him about those he'd lost.

"Kathleen was beautiful," he said with a sad smile. "The first time I saw her, I couldn't take my eyes off her perfect features. Then, after I got to know her, I realized she was even more gorgeous on the inside.

"She was quiet, took care of everyone. She kept the house running and the schedules straight. She was always in the background, letting everyone else shine.

"During the past few years, we were so busy with work and the kids' activities, we didn't have much time for each other. We drifted apart. I figured once the kids left home we would have time to reconnect." Max blinked back tears. "I was wrong."

I nodded. "Even though I knew what was coming, I didn't understand what it would mean for me and the people I loved until it was too late."

Max cleared his throat and sniffed. "Ethan was our oldest. He and I were inseparable when he was growing up. He wanted to be just like me—which, quite honestly, terrified me. Somewhere along the way, though, he figured out I didn't know everything. I think it was around the same time he realized he did." Max chuckled. "He and I had a couple of rough years, but I looked forward to seeing the man he would become. He would have started college last month.

"Taylor caused me the most sleepless nights. She was fun-loving and beautiful, the spitting image of her mother. I was afraid that combination would get her into some serious trouble in high school and college. It's not that I didn't trust her. It was the high school boys I was worried about."

"For good reason," I said.

"Chris was our athlete. He played every sport he could, and he was good. I have no idea where he got his talent—certainly not from my genes. He was super competitive on the field, but once he got off the field, he just wanted everyone to get along. He would have grown up to be either a professional basketball player or a foreign ambassador."

"I wish I could have met them."

"Me, too." Max turned to me and smiled, still blinking tears away.

There were fewer stopped cars on the road now, so we were making better time. It seemed odd, though. Highway 18 had grown more and more crowded the farther west we drove, up until about twenty miles back.

Soon we discovered the reason. Just outside of the South Dakota Black Hills, halfway between Oelrichs and Hot Springs, the road ended abruptly, dropping off into a huge canyon. Max stopped the truck, and we got out to look. Steam escaped in threads and spurts from a crack running down the middle of the canyon. My eyes traced the crevice all the way to the horizon. The canyon was so long, I couldn't even see the wall on the opposite side. I crept to the end of the road and peered over the edge. A few trees clung desperately to the canyon wall. Mangled cars rested on the floor of the canyon, a half mile or so below where the road used to be.

I stumbled back from the edge, imagining the terrifying seconds before impact.

"How did this happen?" I searched Max's face for reassurance.

Max shrugged. "Probably an earthquake."

Scott had been driving west, looking for his parents, when the earthquakes and volcanic eruptions that precipitated the Change were just beginning. What if he was on the road right in the middle of things, and the earth collapsed under him? I shook my head, trying to erase images of Scott's Corolla twisting and flipping as it plummeted toward the canyon floor.

I pointed toward the cars below. "Is that going to happen to us?"

"There's always a lot of seismic activity in Yellowstone. I'm sure there were some big earthquakes around here leading up to the Change. I doubt there'll be any more landscape-altering quakes for a few hundred years."

I felt a little better. But I still thought Max was way too calm considering what we were looking at.

Max walked back to the truck. "I'll check out the maps

and find another route. You want to take the wheel for a while?"

"Sure." I slid in and moved the seat forward.

We backtracked to the next major intersection, then drove south to Highway 20. It had more obstructions than Highway 18, but it did successfully bypass the crater. Seeing no more evidence of collapsed roads, my tension eased.

"What kind of future did you have planned, before the Change?" Max asked. "I don't imagine over-the-road delivery driver was your career goal."

I laughed. "At this point, I'm just glad to have a job. I'm not going to be picky. This was not my plan, though, you're right. I was studying to be a high school chemistry teacher."

"I should have taught you how to calibrate the lab equipment, instead of Ashley."

"No, Ashley catches on to things a lot more quickly than I do. And since we didn't even get to finish our first year at Ford, I haven't had any more chemistry classes than she has."

"Ah. So, you were going to inspire young minds with the fascinating world of chemistry. Anything else?"

"I figured I would marry Scott, teach for a few years, and then stay home and raise our kids." I could feel a blush creeping up my cheeks. "Don't tell Scott, though. I don't want to scare him away."

Max smiled. "You still haven't heard anything from him or his family?"

I shook my head. "I just wish I knew. I want more than anything for him to come walking up to my door some morning. But if he—" I couldn't bring myself to say it. "If he's not coming back, I want to know, so I can let him go."

Max put his hand on my shoulder. "You can hold onto hope, but don't let it stop you from living your life."

I smiled at him through my tears.

By nightfall, we were both exhausted from twenty-four hours of traveling. We decided to stop and rest, rather than risking one of us falling asleep behind the wheel. Max insisted I sleep in the bed of the truck, where the cover provided some protection from the cold night. He stretched out on the ground beside the Silverado. I was grateful he had thought to bring blankets. Exhausted, I fell asleep right away, despite the rough ridges of the truck bed floor.

We awoke early, refreshed but stiff. We were less than a hundred miles from the east entrance to Yellowstone. I looked forward to a much shorter travel day. Mid-morning, we passed through the town of Cody, Wyoming, about fifty miles outside the park. We drove thirty-five more miles before the road became impassable. The road had cracked and buckled, forming potholes that would have swallowed Ashley's Prius whole. Even our four-wheel-drive Silverado couldn't handle it.

"Looks like we're going to have to make the rest of the trip on foot." Max turned off the truck.

I opened my door. The smell of sulfur seared my nostrils.

"Eau de rotten eggs," Max said, "my favorite."

I pulled my backpack out of the bed of the truck and put it on. "Why is the road such a mess? Did earthquakes do that, too?"

"Probably." Max strapped on his backpack and grabbed a stick out of the truck bed. "Yellowstone is an active volcano. Things are always shifting and changing because of the movement of molten rock below the surface. All of the seismic activity leading up to the Change probably accelerated that process."

I surveyed the pock-marked landscape. "I've never been so glad to live in the boring Midwest."

We picked our way around the potholes. Max used his stick periodically to test the stability of the ground. We had to watch our step, but we still maintained a pretty good pace for the first couple of hours. Then I took a step and felt the pavement give way. I screamed and scrambled backward. Max grabbed me around the waist.

"Are you okay?" He set me back on my feet.

I nodded. "It just surprised me."

"The surface is getting more unstable. I want you to follow directly behind me. Try to match your footsteps to mine."

Max walked along the center line, testing the pavement in front of him every few steps with the stick. I stretched to match his stride length.

At random intervals, puffs of steam erupted around us or hissed out of the cracks in the road. A stream of water flowing along the shoulder appeared to change colors from one mile to the next.

Max periodically stopped and moved carefully to the edge of the road to test the temperature of the water. He was looking for the ideal habitat for *Thermus aquaticus*: a wet environment with a temperature around 158 degrees Fahrenheit. We watched for yellow, pink, or red coloration of the bed or banks of the stream, which might also indicate the bacteria's presence.

By mid-afternoon, Max had to test the ground with each step he took. Conversation was sparse as we focused on maintaining firm footing. Every time Max's stick broke through the pavement, my breath caught in my throat.

The constant tension was exhausting. It wasn't even five o'clock, and I was ready to call it a night.

Max tapped the pavement with his stick, easily cracking the surface. I heard a low rumble, like water on the stove right before it starts to boil.

Max wheeled around. "Get back!"

I stumbled back a few steps, then turned and ran. Several times, my foot sank into the pavement, making me lurch to the side and stagger to recover my balance. I could hear Max's feet pounding the road right behind me.

The rumble crescendoed to a roar. The drops of water hitting my face felt like needles piercing my skin. When I was clear of the falling drops, I slowed to a stop and turned around. A great column of water rose from the spot where we had been standing just seconds before. I glanced at Max, who had stopped beside me. I could see red spots where the scalding water had hit his face. He appeared to be transfixed. I turned my attention back to the roaring spout, in awe of the power of the water and thankful for our narrow escape.

After several minutes, the newly-formed geyser shrank, leaving what looked like a boiling pot of water, some fifty feet across.

"Well, that got rid of a lot of pressure that had built up under the surface," Max said. "Unfortunately, I doubt it improved the stability of the ground."

Max began testing the ground in front of us. In most places, a light tap of his stick made the surface crack like the thin sheet of ice covering a pond in early spring. He found solid ground to his left and gingerly stepped onto it.

I didn't follow. "Maybe we should go back."

Max looked over his shoulder at me, one eyebrow raised.

"I mean, do you think it's worth it?" I asked. "We haven't even found where the bacteria might be. And we're one misstep away from turning into human stew."

Max pivoted to face me. "*Is* it worth it?"

I looked at the boiling pool in front of us. I closed my eyes, trying to get rid of the images of what might have happened to Max and me if we hadn't gotten out of the way in time. Immediately, an image appeared. Josh stood with his arm around Lauren. Following Josh's gaze, I saw a bundle in Lauren's arms. I didn't know the baby hidden in that bundle. I didn't even know if it was a boy or a girl. But I knew I would do anything to protect that baby.

"Yes, it is." I turned to Max, blinking back tears. "I can't let them take Josh's baby."

Max nodded. "If it's worth it to you, it's worth it to me."

My determination was renewed, but that didn't make our travels any easier. It took more than an hour to find a safe path around the geyser and back to the road. Max plodded carefully, testing each step, and I tried to place my foot right in the center of the spot vacated by his.

The sun had just dropped below the horizon when Max stopped walking. I looked up to see what had interrupted his forward progress. Fifty yards in front of us, on the right side of the road, I spotted the famous "Yellowstone National Park" sign with the National Park Service arrowhead. The sign tilted forward. One of the posts supporting the sign had disappeared into a pool of boiling mud.

Despite my exhaustion, I smiled. *We made it.*

I looked around. The pavement in front of us had fractured into a million pieces. The landscape was dotted with columns and tendrils of rising steam, bubbling pools of mud, and intermittent eruptions of water creating rivulets that fed the stream along the road. I couldn't see any areas of intact ground greater than a few square feet between us and the park entrance. It looked to me like we had reached a dead-end.

"What is all this?" I asked.

"A living textbook of hydrothermal features." Max pointed out different spots in the hydrothermal field. "That's a mud pot. There's a geyser. Those are steam vents. It looks like there might be some hot springs just beyond the entrance."

He turned to me. "I think it's time to call it a night. We'll work on getting through this in the morning."

Max tested the ground behind us to find a stable area large enough for both of us to lie down. We sat and ate some of the food from our backpacks. I pulled the shoes off my sore feet and stretched my aching legs.

Max spread one of the blankets out on the pavement. "This area is very unstable. Things could change any moment. We're going to have to wrap one blanket around both of us."

I looked at Max, alarmed. "Hold on. I am *not* sleeping with you."

"We need to be connected to each other, so that if the ground under one of us gives way we won't fall in, as long as the other person is still on solid ground."

"I don't think so." I shook my head.

"Think about it, Christy. What happens if the crust where you're sleeping collapses, you land in a mud pot, and I can't reach you to pull you out?" Max's voice softened. "Or what if a geyser pushes me into one of those bottomless potholes, and I can't help you save your brother's baby?"

I reluctantly agreed to Max's plan. He lay down on his back on the blanket. I lay down where instructed, on my right side with my back to Max. He pulled the ends of the blanket over us and secured them together with safety pins. He spread the second blanket on top.

"Good night," Max said.

I didn't answer.

He chuckled. "Asleep already?"

I tried to scoot farther away from him. I could only move a half inch before the blanket stopped me. I lay there, wide awake, for what seemed like hours, unable to relax.

At long last, I drifted off.

The rocky ground dug into my hip, nudging me back to semi-consciousness. I rolled onto my back, relieving the pressure on my hip only to shift it to my tailbone. I tried to look around. The clouds obscured every source of light, making the view with my eyes open identical to that with my eyes closed.

I heard the syncopated glub glu-glub of gas escaping from pots of mud. I imagined a witch, complete with a black hat and long warty nose, standing over the mud pot, stirring. The sulphuric fumes from her brew snaked across my face, burning my nose.

A loud hissing noise startled me fully awake. I stifled a scream. I knew it was only steam escaping from an opening in the road, but in my mind, I saw a snake curled up beside me, head poised and ready to strike. I covered my face with my arms, trying to block the gusty breeze that felt like the flick of a snake's tiny tongue against my cheek.

When my racing heart calmed, I heard another sound—the rhythmic whisper of Max's breathing. My tension slowly melted. I wasn't alone in this strange place. I was going to be okay.

The rising sun found me resting shoulder-to-shoulder with Max. I didn't feel awkward anymore. I felt secure.

I lay still, enjoying the warmth of the sun, until I felt

Max begin to stir. I eased out of our shared blanket, trying not to disturb him. Using the stick to test the ground, I ventured away from our sleeping area in search of some privacy. I had just squatted when I heard Max frantically yelling, "Christy! Christy!"

"I'm right here," I hollered back, laughing. "Just give me a minute."

I walked carefully back to the road. "Can't a girl have a moment to herself around here?"

Max smiled sheepishly. "I panicked. I couldn't imagine where you'd disappeared to."

"Next time, pick a hotel with restrooms, and you won't have to worry about me wandering away."

"I'll see what I can do," Max said. "I'm glad you're okay.

# 11

I packed up our bedding while Max explored the edge of the field of hydrothermal features that surrounded the entrance to the park. At several different spots, he walked a few feet into the field, testing the ground with every step, and then backed out.

I hoisted my backpack and gingerly made my way over to Max. "Any luck?"

He shook his head. "It's too unstable. We're going to have to go around."

He followed the edge of the field toward the left. I fell in step behind him. The repeated tap of his stick followed each time by a gentle footfall created a rhythm that reminded me of a slow-motion gallop. The cadence was interrupted when Max's stick sunk into the soft ground in front of him. He stopped and tested the area around us. The only solid ground led into the trees, and away from the hydrothermal features.

Before heading into the woods, Max squatted and dipped the thermometer in the pot of bubbling mud beside us. After several seconds, he pulled it out and wiped the mud on his handkerchief. He examined the thermometer, rotating it to get a clear view of the mercury. "Too cold." He shook it down and returned it to the side pocket of his backpack.

I followed Max into the trees. "How can it be too cold?

That mud was boiling."

"It wasn't actually boiling. Pockets of gas rise up and then pop through the surface of the mud, making it look like it's boiling. That gas also gives it its lovely smell."

The odor didn't bother me anymore, except when I was trying to eat. The smell of rotten eggs seemed to make everything taste bitter.

The path of solid ground carried us far into the forest. Several times we had to climb over trees that had been recently uprooted. There were only a few places where we got close enough to the hydrothermal field that Max could check the water temperature. Each time the outcome was the same: not warm enough.

It was noon before we made it past the unstable ground surrounding the park's east entrance and got back on the road. Here, several yards past the Yellowstone National Park Sign, the street was mostly intact, with only a few steam vents cracking the pavement. Max's cadence accelerated to a steady trot.

"Yellowstone is such a popular tourist destination," I said. "I'm really surprised they don't maintain the roads better."

"The National Park Service will definitely be getting a strongly worded letter from me when we get back." Max smiled.

"Good thinking, skirting around the entrance so we didn't have to pay to get in."

Max laughed. "I'm pretty sure it would have been easier to pay the admission."

After we rounded a curve, I noticed the road in front of

us seemed to disappear a short distance ahead, as if we were nearing the top of a steep hill. But it didn't feel like we were walking up much of an incline. Near the end of the visible road, I noticed light tan and gray rocks on and around the road. I hadn't seen them in other places we had walked. The rocks were full of holes like a sponge, but they were hard and brittle.

I soon realized the road did, in fact, end—at the edge of a crater so wide I could barely see the other side. On the floor of the crater, a huge pool of molten lava writhed and hissed. My breath caught in my throat.

Max picked up one of the gray rocks. "I was afraid of this."

"Afraid of what?"

"Looks like Yellowstone erupted recently—first time in more than half a million years. This pumice came from that eruption." Max looked around. "It was a small one, though, which means a bigger one could be coming."

Max turned to me. "We may be able to outrun a geyser, but we wouldn't stand a chance with an erupting volcano."

"But what about the bacteria?"

"We can try a different part of the park, but continuing to look around here would be suicide."

I took one more look into the crater before following Max back down the road. Max settled into a brisk power walk. I had to jog a few steps every couple of minutes to catch up.

We got back to the hydrothermal field surrounding the park entrance without incident. I fell in line behind Max as he navigated around it to the right. On the muddy or dusty parts of the route, we could still see our footprints from the first trip, which made our trek a little easier.

We had made it about a quarter of the way around when our footprints disappeared. Things had shifted in the few hours since we traveled this route. Max tested the ground all around us and found nothing stable enough we could walk on, except back the way we came.

We retraced our steps and tried to bypass the field to the left. Our path was blocked by unstable ground even sooner on that side. We were trapped between a volcano that could erupt at any moment and a field of geysers, steam vents, and mud pots. There was no way out. No way back to the truck, back to Lincoln, back to the Bubble.

"We're going to have to go across." Max was undaunted.

"Across?" I looked over a landscape that could have come directly out of a sci-fi movie. "How are we going to do that?"

"We'll walk on logs. That will help distribute our weight and hopefully keep us from sinking in."

Hopefully? Was that the best he could do?

A steam vent hissed to life right in front of me. I jumped back. One thing was certain—we couldn't stay here. I was skeptical of the efficacy of Max's plan, but I didn't have any better ideas. I joined Max in his search for fallen trees that were wide enough to walk on but light enough to carry.

We slid four tree trunks out into the hydrothermal field, keeping one end on solid ground. I stepped onto my logs and eased forward, searching the surface of the log to find sure footing. As we advanced farther into the field, the logs became more unstable, rolling or sinking under our feet. I clutched Max's hand with a death grip each time I took a step. I was pretty sure I knew exactly where, when, and how I was going to die: right there, right then, by drowning in a pool of bubbling mud.

We stopped after traversing about three-fourths the length of the logs. Max checked the temperature of the mud pots and hot springs around him. I looked up. It didn't seem like we were any closer to the stable ground at the far edge of the hydrothermal field than when we started. What if we didn't make it? What if we couldn't get out? I would never see my family again. I would never get to meet Josh's baby. And Ashley—if Max and I didn't make it back to Lincoln, she would be so lonely.

I couldn't think about that. I just needed to take one step at a time. I swallowed and focused on the logs under my feet.

At Max's direction, I knelt down on one of my logs. The bark bit into my knees. Despite the discomfort, I was grateful for the rough surface that helped keep me from sliding off. I grabbed the branches sticking up from the log beside me and lifted. The log I was sitting on did a nosedive, pitching me forward. I dropped the other log and grasped at branches to keep myself from being thrown off.

I closed my eyes and took a deep breath. The hissing and popping around me seemed to grow louder. I opened my eyes again. Reality was frightening enough. I didn't need my imagination to exaggerate the danger.

I scooted back, closer to the middle of the log, and tried again. Instead of lifting, I slid the log forward, inch by inch, stopping after each movement to make sure I still had my balance.

After sliding all four logs forward, Max and I resumed our hand-in-hand walk.

We passed the partially-sunken sign. From this side, it read "Leaving Yellowstone National Park." *That's what we're trying to do.* We'd made it out of the park, but we still had a long way to go to reach stable ground—and even farther to get back to the truck.

I squeezed Max's hand and stepped forward. The log I was standing on rolled to the side. I screamed, scrambling to stay on the logs. I could not go down. Not here. My right foot slipped off the log and hit the ground, breaking through the surface and plunging into scalding water. The searing pain flooded my eyes with tears. Max's arms were immediately around me, lifting me up. I had no idea how he'd managed to get behind me. My pain and fear were overshadowed by relief.

When my gasps calmed, Max said, "See if you can walk."

I realized I was standing on one leg, my right foot tucked up like a flamingo's. I gingerly put my foot down. The moment it touched the log, flames seemed to explode through the sole. I jerked it back up, tears streaming down my face.

After several seconds, still holding me securely, he said, "Try again."

I swallowed hard. I did not want to feel that pain, but I

knew we had to keep moving. Reluctantly, I lowered my foot. The burning sensation made me gasp, but it wasn't as bad as the first time.

"Try to take a step."

I eased my right foot forward and started to shift my weight. Excruciating pain shot up my right leg.

I squeezed my eyes shut against the pain. "I can't," I whispered.

"All right." Max released his grip on my waist. "I'll hold your logs still while you get down on your hands and knees."

I held onto the branches in front of me.

"Right leg first," Max said.

I slid my foot back and carefully lowered myself onto my knee. The pain decreased to a strong ache. I brought my left knee down on the other log. The air rising from the ground hit my face like an Arizona summer wind streaming over a pile of rotten eggs. Through the hole where my foot had broken through, clear water hissed and bubbled over a red floor, several yards down. I shuddered. If Max hadn't caught me . . .

"I'll stabilize your logs while you crawl to the other end," Max said.

I worked my way down the logs. Branches scratched my arms and face. My forward progress was slow, but I felt safer on hands and knees. Now only inches below, spurts of steam, roiling water, and bubbling mud reminded me that disaster was just one misstep away.

I stopped several feet before the end of the logs and did my best to hold them still while Max started his journey.

Halfway down he switched to his logs, afraid the two of us together would be too much weight as we neared the end of the logs. The far left log sank further and further into the ground until he had to abandon it.

"Are you doing okay?" Max asked when he caught up with me. He looked worried. The sun had already dropped behind the evergreens, most of which were no longer green. We weren't even halfway across.

I nodded. "It's feeling a little better."

I started sliding the free log forward.

Max pulled out the thermometer and lowered it into the pool of water on his left side. It periodically bubbled or released a hiss of steam. The yellow color on the sides and bottom of the pool made it look like a bowl of Mountain Dew. He pulled the thermometer out, looked at it, and put it in again.

"Christy." He held the thermometer up. "This is it."

"What?"

"One hundred sixty degrees." Max grinned. "If there are any *Thermus aquaticus* bacteria in this park, this is where they would be."

*Thank you, Jesus. I just know this is going to be the solution to all our problems.*

"The collection supplies are in your backpack," Max said. "Can you hand it to me?"

I eased my backpack off and gave it to Max, keeping a firm hold on the log with one hand throughout the process. While he collected samples from the walls and floor of the pool, I slid the second log forward. He packed the samples in an insulated container and returned the backpack to me. Max joined me on the logs I had already moved forward and pulled up the remaining log.

By the time we repeated the slow process of crawling and walking along the logs twice more, twilight had surrendered to the darkness. The light of the moon made the night seem less menacing. I was grateful, though I knew clear skies meant a colder night.

I'd never been so exhausted or so glad to be on somewhat solid ground as I was when we made it to the other side of the hydrothermal field. We returned to the spot where we had slept the night before. At Max's instruction, I reluctantly removed my right shoe and sock. Even in the dim light, I could tell my foot and ankle were bright red. The lightest touch was excruciating.

"The skin is intact." Max examined my foot on all sides. "It should heal up just fine. It's a good sign that it hurts so much. That means your nerve endings aren't damaged."

"So I should be glad I'm in so much pain?"

Max smiled. "It'll feel better in a couple days. You'll need to elevate it tonight, so it doesn't swell too much."

He spread out the blanket and stacked the backpacks on one end. I lay down and propped my foot on the backpacks. Max wrapped the blanket around us and pinned the ends together. I was so tired, nothing could keep me from falling asleep—not even the rocky ground, the hissing steam, my throbbing foot, or the man lying beside me who was old enough to be my father.

# 12

It seemed like I had only been asleep for a few minutes when I felt a nudge at my side.

"Time to get up, Christy, we've got to keep moving."

I opened my eyes. The sun hadn't even reached the horizon yet. I groaned and tried to roll over. The blanket cocoon prevented me from moving.

"No snooze button this morning." Max unhooked the safety pins. "We're still too close to the volcano."

I slowly pushed myself to a sitting position. He opened one of the backpacks and pulled out some crackers and two bottles of water.

"When we get back to the truck we'll test the samples to see if we found what we were looking for," Max said between bites of breakfast. "If we didn't, we'll try another part of the park."

I felt better after drinking some water. I put the sock and shoe back on my right foot. It wasn't quite as tender as it had been the day before, but it still hurt to force it into a shoe that barely fit. I stood and tried to take a few steps. I could put enough pressure on it to take a short step with my left foot. Still, I couldn't imagine spending the whole day walking on it. I continued testing it out while Max packed up our bedding.

Max wore both backpacks, one on the front and one on

the back. He found a branch he could use to test the ground and gave me the other stick to use as a walking stick. I held onto his right arm, and we set out, side-by-side.

We had a little more difficulty finding a path to walk since we now needed stable ground wide enough for two. With both of us testing the ground in front of us, that didn't slow us down too much. Max was wise to get us going early, though, because I had to stop and rest often.

When we took a break mid-afternoon, my foot continued to throb, even when I sat down and propped it up. Max checked the bacteria samples and activated a chemical heat pack to maintain the desired temperature.

"I don't think I can keep going." I wanted to show Max I was tough and strong, but the thought of standing on my foot again made me want to curl up in a ball and cry.

He studied my face. "The worst part is over. Pretty soon we'll be on stable ground."

I shook my head.

"We'll stay here a while longer, take a little siesta," Max said.

I lay back on the ground. The warm sun felt good on my face, but I wanted to stick my foot in a bucket of ice to numb the constant burning pain. I drifted toward sleep. As the world around me faded, so did my pain. *If only I could stay asleep until my foot was better.*

"We've got to get going if we want to make it to the truck before dark."

Max's voice brought me out of blissful sleep back to

painful consciousness. I didn't want to sleep on the ground again, but I also didn't want to walk any farther.

"I don't know if I can," I said weakly.

"Don't worry, I've got you." Max wrapped his right arm around me and lifted me to my feet.

I winced when my right foot touched the ground.

Max held me tightly to his side. "Lean on me when you're standing on your sore foot."

I pressed against him and took a step with my left foot. My right foot didn't feel quite so bad. After a few steps, I didn't have to lean on Max as much. Still, he continued to support me with his arm around my waist.

The final stretch of our journey seemed to take forever, even though the pain was better with Max's help. When I finally spotted the red Silverado, barely visible in the waning light, I felt a flood of relief. I couldn't believe we had made it.

I looked at Max, grateful for all the sacrifices he had made to help me get through the day. The deep creases on his forehead softened, and his clenched jaw relaxed. He smiled, scooped me up in his arms, and carried me to the truck. He set me down on the tailgate, my left leg dangling over the edge and my right leg supported beside me.

I held a flashlight while Max assembled the equipment to test the samples for *Thermus aquaticus*. The first two samples came up negative. The disappointment in Max's eyes felt like a knife in my gut. What if all of our hard work and pain was just wasted effort?

Several minutes into the test for the third sample, Max's

face transformed. His eyes widened, and the corners of his mouth crept up.

"We got it." He laughed, holding up a test tube of yellow liquid. "Here it is."

He put the tube down and grabbed my shoulders. "Christy, we did it."

His grin was contagious. We'd found what we were looking for. All of the struggle and fear and pain we'd gone through was worth it. We had the bacteria we needed to develop the genetic test that I was sure would help me to save Josh's baby.

I put my hands on Max's arms. His dark chocolate eyes, so often shadowed with grief, now sparkled with joy. He leaned in and pressed his lips tenderly against mine. I closed my eyes. I felt safe and cared-for. I wanted those feelings to crowd out the pain and exhaustion. The musky scent of his cologne mixed with the sharp smell of sweat. He was so close; I could hear every short, trembling breath. I leaned forward and found his lips again. His arms circled around me, pulling me in, carrying me away from the harshness of the world.

I relished his gentle kiss and protective embrace a moment longer before I pulled back. "I'm—I can't, Max. I'm sorry." I turned away.

I was confused. Six months ago, Max was a married man with three kids not much younger than me. Six months ago, I had a boyfriend, who might still be alive somewhere and looking for me. Max was my friend, nothing more. At least, he wasn't supposed to be anything more.

I was embarrassed. I should have answered his kiss with a congratulatory hug or a peck on the cheek. Instead, I leaned in for more. His kiss made me feel things I hadn't felt in a long time. I wanted those feelings to continue. I wanted Max to support me and take care of me, so life wouldn't be such a struggle. I didn't want our embrace to end, even when I pulled away.

Max quietly finished his testing and returned the positive samples to the insulated container, adding a hot pack to bring them up to temperature. I could only imagine how he felt—angry, betrayed, confused. I was too ashamed to look him in the eye. He unstrapped the blankets from the backpacks, handed them to me, and climbed into the cab of the truck without a word.

I spread the blankets out in the bed of the truck and lay down, crying softly. The last thing I'd wanted to do was hurt Max, especially after all he'd done to help me. He'd saved my life more than once just on this trip. He'd traveled all the way to Yellowstone with me, placing his own life at risk to try to save the life of someone he would probably never meet. Now, all of a sudden, things were so awkward between us that I couldn't look at him, and he couldn't—or wouldn't—speak to me.

# 13

When I awoke, Max was already up.

I slid out from under the truck bed cover and sat on the tailgate.

"Let me know when you're ready to go," Max said. "Your clothes are behind the seat if you want to freshen up. I put some food and water in the cab, so we can eat breakfast on the road."

His voice was natural, friendly. Maybe everything would be fine. Maybe we could forget about last night and go back to the way things were.

"I walked down the road a little ways to check it out," he said. "It looks pretty much the same as it did when we arrived. We shouldn't have any trouble driving out of here."

"Great!" I responded, a little too enthusiastically. "I'll take care of a couple things, and we can get going."

In the fog of recent sleep, I slid off the tailgate without thinking about my sore foot. When it hit the ground, the pain made me gasp, and I almost went down on my knees. Max looked up. Concern showed in his eyes, but he made no move to help me. I was grateful. I didn't know how I would react if he tried to touch me.

I limped around the Silverado, holding onto the side, and pulled a clean shirt out of my bag. Max turned his back to me, giving me privacy so I could change and answer Mother Nature's call without having to venture too far away.

"Okay, I'm ready," I said, shuffling back to the truck.

"I'll drive, so you can keep your foot up." Max opened the driver's side door. "That means I'll need you to keep an eye on our bacteria."

"I can do that." I climbed into the passenger's seat.

Max had put a pile of blankets on the floor to support my right foot. *That was so thoughtful.* But was it thoughtful like a father caring for his daughter or like a man I wanted to take care of me for the rest of my life? I felt a stab of pain between my eyes. That was a question I couldn't answer.

"The temperature needs to stay between these two marks." Max showed me the thermometer on the side of the container holding the bacteria. "If it gets too hot, crack the lid open. If it gets too cold, activate one of these hot packs and put it inside."

"Got it." I took the container from him and carefully placed it on the seat between us.

"There's water and food in the glove compartment." Max started the truck and made a multi-point turn, avoiding the largest potholes and roughest patches of pavement.

I ate my breakfast quietly. I didn't want to distract Max while he navigated over the rough road. Every few minutes I checked the bacteria temperature.

When the road smoothed out, my silence continued. I still felt confused and uncomfortable, sitting beside Max. I realized, no matter how much I wanted to, I couldn't just forget about what happened.

I cleared my throat. "Max, I'm sorry about last night. I was tired and scared and hurting."

"Sorry about what?" Max asked, softly.

"Pardon?"

"Are you sorry about the kiss or sorry about pulling away?"

My face flushed. "The kiss." I hesitated. "Well, maybe both. I don't know. I wanted to do it, but then it felt wrong."

"Christy, you are beautiful and kind and good-hearted. You would give your life for Ashley or for your family. You are a wonderful human being, and I care about you deeply."

"But you're married."

"I *was* married. Now I'm trying to figure out how to start over again." Max stopped the truck and turned to me. "The more time I spend with you, the more I realize I don't want to do it alone. I want to build a new life with you. I can't promise you an easy life. Seems like nothing's easy anymore. But I can promise that I will take care of you. I want you to be safe and happy, Christy. I think I can give you that."

I wanted what Max was offering. I wanted someone to protect me, someone to help shoulder my burdens, someone to assure me that everything was going to be okay. So many parts of me wanted to say yes—the hurting parts, the lonely parts, the scared parts. But my heart wasn't in it. Max deserved more than I could give.

"You have been so kind and generous," I said, "coming out here with me, risking your life and saving mine, all to try and help my family. There's no way I could ever express how grateful I am. You've offered me everything. But I can't make the same offer to you, because—" I started to cry "—I still love Scott."

Max put the truck in drive and resumed our winding path down the crowded road. I looked over and saw tears in his eyes.

"I never wanted to hurt you, Max," I whispered. "I am so sorry."

Max wiped a tear away. "I'm sorry, too."

# 14

Conversation the rest of the morning was limited to comments about the traffic jams, navigation instructions, and reminders to check the thermometer on the bacteria container. I directed Max to take a more southerly route, steering well away from the canyon that slowed our progress on the way out. I was glad to be off my foot, though that morning's emotional pain felt rawer than my foot had ever felt.

We stopped around noon to stretch and have a bite to eat. I was pleased I was able to walk with less pain and only a small limp. I offered to drive for a stretch, but Max refused. He insisted my foot was feeling better because I had been elevating it, and I needed to keep it up.

We had only been back on the road a few minutes when one of the stopped cars caught my attention. It was one of the few cars we saw that was facing west. There was something familiar about the car. Riding by, I saw it had California plates, and I knew.

"Stop!" I yelled. "Stop the truck."

Max slammed on the brakes, his eyes wide with alarm.

Tears spilled over before I even got my door open. I ran back to the car we had passed. I was afraid of what I might see, but I had to check. I had to know.

I went straight to the driver's side of the dark red

Corolla and peered in the window. I saw a jacket on the passenger seat, but there was no one inside. I laughed with relief. I tried the driver's side door. It was locked, but I could see the passenger's side door wasn't. I hurried around the car, opened the door, pulled out Scott's jacket and hugged it to my chest. When I stood up, I noticed Max standing near the rear bumper, watching me.

"It's Scott's car," I said, apologetically. "He's not here, so that means he could still be alive."

Max came to me and put his arm around my shoulders. I tensed at his touch.

"I'm glad." His voice sounded tired but sincere. "I hope you find him."

My tension melted, and my tears flowed even faster. Max wanted what was best for me. He wanted me to be happy, even if it wasn't with him. I knew then, that Max truly loved me. But I couldn't return his love, at least not in the way he wanted.

In my rush to get to the car, I had forgotten to favor my right foot. Now it was throbbing. I leaned on Max and limped to the truck.

Max pulled the Silverado back onto the road. I repositioned the blankets supporting my foot. Checking the thermometer on the bacteria container, I added a hot pack. I was thankful for these tasks that briefly kept at bay the hurricane of emotions threatening to overwhelm me. I was elated Scott might still be alive. But the chances of finding him were infinitesimal. I had no idea where he had gone when he left his car. There was no way to contact him. I could search for decades with no guarantee I would find him. Despair engulfed my joy.

*Lord, show me your will. I thought Scott was the one you chose for me. But I don't know if I'll ever see him again. Maybe I heard you wrong, I don't know. Just—tell me what I'm supposed to do.*

I looked at Max. His eyes were fixed on the road ahead, as he navigated around the vehicles littering the highway. Streaks on his cheek marked the paths of his tears. *He loves me.* I don't know why I didn't see it before. He always looked out for me, making sure I had what I needed. He had made a huge sacrifice coming on this trip, leaving his livelihood for several days to help my family. I was so grateful for his care and friendship, yet it seemed I couldn't stop doing and saying things that hurt him.

I focused my attention on the bacteria thermometer, trying to hold back my tears.

Max turned toward me. "How's your foot?"

"Better, thank you"—I looked at Max—"for everything."

He nodded and turned his attention back to the road.

# 15

We arrived in Lincoln the next day, shortly after sunset.

Immediately after the Change, I had feared for my life whenever I had to go to Lincoln. The people there were suspicious and unpredictable. Friendly neighborhoods had given way to locked doors and gangs in the streets.

This time, though, I was relieved to be back in the city. Compared to the instability of Yellowstone, Lincoln seemed like a bastion of safety and security. In Lincoln, I had new tasks to complete and other people to occupy my time and attention. Maybe I could stop thinking about finding Scott and about how much I had hurt Max.

We drove to the industrial area of town, just to the east of Max's neighborhood. Max pulled around to the back side of the lab, parking between the building and the railroad tracks.

"Can you bring the samples in?" Max asked.

"Got it." I shouldered the container of bacteria samples and opened my door.

The rumble of the generators reminded me of the growl of the earth just before a newly-formed geyser nearly blasted us into the sky. I hesitated, glancing at Max. He was walking toward the building, oblivious to the sound.

I took a deep breath and gingerly stepped down. After a few steps, I was able to walk smoothly, almost normally. I followed Max through the back door of the building, down a short hall, and into a long, narrow room labeled "Sample Storage."

"You can put the bacteria there." Max motioned to a table along the right wall, just inside the door.

I put the container down and walked with Max to the large metal box beside the table.

He flipped the switch on the front of the box and then pressed and held the button labeled with an up arrow. "This is how you set the temperature on the incubator. Here's the set temp." He pointed at the display to the right of the buttons, which now read 158° F. "This shows the current temp." The display to the left read 75° F.

Max turned to the opposite wall, which was lined with refrigeration units. Through the glass doors, we could see several racks of test tubes. Each tube was labeled in Ashley's flowery script.

"Looks like Ashley was busy while we were gone," I said.

Max nodded. "Everything's ready to go. We'll be able to get started first thing tomorrow." He smiled for the first time since learning we'd found the bacteria. "I'm going out to top off the generator fuel. When the temperature gets up to one fifty-eight, take the bacteria samples out of the container and put them in the incubator."

We finished our tasks, locked up the lab, and made the short drive to Max's house. Ashley sprinted out to meet us, reaching my door before Max could turn the truck off.

I leapt out of the truck, careful to land on my left foot,

and hugged Ashley. "It's so good to see you."

"I'm glad you're both okay," Ashley said. "You wouldn't believe all of the horrible things I imagined might have happened to you."

I smiled. "Your imagination might not have been too far off." I pointed to my swollen foot.

"Oh, no." Ashley knelt to get a closer look. "Are you all right?"

"It's getting a lot better."

I turned to pull my things out of the front seat. Ashley went to the back to help Max unload the bed of the Silverado.

"Did you find the bacteria?" Ashley scanned the contents of the truck bed.

Max nodded. "We already dropped them off at the lab."

"That's awesome!" Ashley hugged Max.

"Did you manage all right while we were gone?" I asked.

"The lab equipment is all primed and ready to go," Ashley said, "and the market is a lot of fun."

I carried the extra food from our trip into the pantry. Every shelf was full.

I poked my head into the kitchen. "Ashley, where did you get all this food?"

Ashley laughed. "I told you, I love hanging out at the market."

"We are definitely going to make you our designated shopper." I gave up on finding room in the pantry and left our food on the kitchen counter.

We went back to the truck to bring in another load.

"It looked like you had collected quite a few DNA samples," Max said.

Ashley wrinkled her nose and nodded. "Next time, I'm going to take the road trip, and you two can collect hair samples from dead people.

"I didn't get as many samples from survivors as I'd hoped to. I got a few from people I traded with at the market, but Dr. Franklin wouldn't let me take samples from anyone at the cabin."

"I'll go there tomorrow," I said, "see if I can bypass Dr. Franklin. The cabin is our best chance to get a wide variety of survivor samples."

"You're not going anywhere until we get that foot taken care of," Max said.

"It's fine," I protested. "It feels a lot better today. I'm sure it will heal on its own."

Max motioned toward the couch. I could see in his face he would not take no for an answer. I sat and propped my foot on the coffee table.

The initial sting of the burn cream brought tears to my eyes. The cooling sensation that followed washed over me in waves of relief. I didn't realize how much my foot hurt until it finally started to feel better. Max's gentle touch as he smoothed on the cream and wrapped my foot with an elastic bandage stirred up emotions that had been battling inside me for two days. I fought to blink back tears.

"How's that?" Max asked, arranging pillows beside me

on the couch to support my foot.

"Better," I answered, unable to look Max in the eye.

"Now, I want to hear all about your trip," Ashley said.

Max and I took turns recounting the obstacles we had encountered and our excitement at finally achieving our goal. We left out certain personal details. I needed to talk to Ashley about what had actually happened on the trip, but not while Max was in the room.

"On the way home, Christy made a discovery almost as exciting as the bacteria," Max said after we finished the story of our adventures in Yellowstone.

Ashley looked at me expectantly.

"We found Scott's car," I said.

Ashley's eyes widened. "Was . . . he . . ."

I shook my head. "No, which means he could still be alive somewhere."

"Oh, Christy." Ashley wrapped her arms around me. "That's great."

"Only, I have no idea where he is or how to find him." I started to understand how Ashley must have felt, waiting at home alone for months, hoping against hope that her dad would come home.

Ashley squeezed me tighter. "They'll find us," she whispered. "I know they will."

# 16

The next morning, Ashley and Max walked to the lab to begin amplifying and sequencing the DNA samples she had collected. I drove to the cabin to try to collect more survivor samples, taking Ashley's Prius, which we had left at Max's house when we borrowed his SUV.

I parked the car near the beginning of the driveway, out of sight of both the road and the cabin. I went through the woods, skirting wide around the cabin to avoid being spotted by Dr. Franklin on my way to the agricultural fields. Every few minutes I stopped and listened for sounds of someone moving or working. I heard nothing but an occasional surviving insect buzzing by. The fields where I had worked when I lived at the cabin were all empty. I'm sure many more fields had been planted since I left, but my fear of getting lost kept me from venturing into unknown parts of the cabin grounds.

Reluctantly, I turned back toward the cabin. If I couldn't find anyone out in the fields, I was going to have to figure out a way to convince Dr. Franklin to let me take DNA samples.

I emerged from the woods and was surprised to find the yard around the cabin also deserted. The vague anxiety I had been feeling ramped up to all-out fear. Something was wrong. Had violent survivors attacked the cabin, forcing everyone to flee or hide? I ran to the front door, the ache in my foot intensifying each time it hit the ground. I had to make sure my friends were okay.

I pounded on the door and waited. No one answered. I eased the door open, afraid of what I might find. I was relieved to see familiar faces but disturbed by their somber expressions. People rushed in and out of the library. Others huddled in small groups deep in discussion. No one noticed me standing in the doorway. I spotted Ryan and Angela near the kitchen. Weaving around the clusters of people, I made my way to the end of the hall.

"What's going on?" I asked, touching Angela on the shoulder.

She jumped, then grabbed me by the hand and pulled me down the hall.

"Thank goodness you're here, Christy." Her words tumbled out. "We need your help."

She pulled me into the library and forced her way through the crowds of people gathered inside. "Dr. Franklin is very sick. We need you to take him to a doctor right away."

"But I don't know any doctors," I said. "There's nothing I can—"

The words caught in my throat when I saw Dr. Franklin. He was lying on a cot they had brought up from one of the two large sleeping wards that made up the basement of the cabin. Light from the picture window highlighted his colorless, waxy skin. If it weren't for the barely perceptible rise and fall of his chest, I would have thought it was already too late.

"What happened?" I choked out, scanning the anxious

faces keeping watch over Dr. Franklin.

"We don't know." Brad shook his head. "He hasn't been feeling well for several days—weak and coughing. Yesterday morning he walked in here and just collapsed. He's been unconscious ever since and feels like he's burning up. We couldn't get him to swallow Tylenol. We've tried cold washcloths on his head and soaking his socks in vinegar. Nothing we've tried has helped."

"You have to help him." Megan grabbed my hands, her eyes wide. "None of us have any medical training." Her arms dropped to her sides, and her voice was barely audible. "If we don't get him to a doctor, I don't think he's going to make it."

"There are a couple of nurses who offer first aid in town," I said. "I could check and see if one of them would be willing to make a house call."

Brad shook his head. "We can't take that risk. You're going to have to take Dr. Franklin into town."

I nodded. Bringing someone out to the cabin who had not agreed to join the community and follow its rules could place the lives of everyone there at risk. If someone outside of the community saw the flourishing farm fields and the resources available at the cabin, the threat of a robbery or even a hostile takeover would be amplified significantly.

"I'll go get the car."

My throbbing foot made it difficult to hurry up the winding driveway. I drove down and parked in front of the cabin. Under Brad's direction, several people carried Dr. Franklin out on a sheet and laid him across the back seat, bending his knees so they could get the door closed. I secured the center seatbelt around him.

I sped up the driveway under the watchful and worried eyes of the entire cabin community. The supplies for collecting DNA samples were still on the seat beside me. That task would have to wait.

I parked as close to the center of town as I could. I knew of two nurses who usually offered their services at the Lincoln market. I ran three blocks to the corner where one of the nurses usually set up her stand. The corner was empty. I asked nearby vendors, but no one had seen her.

I hurried two more blocks and rounded a corner. I was relieved to see the other nurse, a balding man whose dark blue scrubs stretched tight across his large belly, sitting behind a table.

I ran past the line of people waiting and straight to the table. "There's a man who is very sick." I struggled to catch my breath. "I'll take you to him."

The nurse gestured toward the people in line and continued bandaging a wound on a man's foot.

"But he could die," I pleaded. "He needs your help right away."

"I'll see him when I'm done with these people." He did not look up from his work. "You may take your place in line."

I walked to the back of the line. I checked my watch. I tapped my foot. I leaned to the side to try to see how close he was to finishing the treatment. I'm sure his clients were very appreciative of his meticulous work. I just wished he would hurry up. I counted the people in line in front of me—seven. That could take hours. I checked my watch again, dread swelling inside me. I was certain, by the time we made it back to the car, we would find Dr. Franklin dead in the back seat.

When it was finally my turn, I spoke quickly. "He's a few blocks away, in my car. He's been unconscious for two days."

I walked briskly down the street, motioning the nurse to follow.

"Hold on," he said.

I stopped and turned around. "What?" I asked impatiently.

"What can you offer me as payment?"

In my rush to reach the nurse, I hadn't thought about how I would pay for his services.

"I can deliver letters to people in the biosphere or at the cabin," I said. It was a long shot. Few survivors had any friends or relatives who were still alive.

"Sure you can." He rolled his eyes and continued packing up his supplies.

"No, really," I said. "I run a delivery service between the two communities."

He stopped and looked at me.

"I've heard about you." He approached, pointing at me. "It's really true, then?"

I nodded.

The nurse grabbed my arm. "Take me to the biosphere." His eyes were bright with expectation.

I shook my head. "I can't do that. I'll lose my job if anyone ever finds out where the biosphere is."

His face fell. "My fiancé is there—or at least she's supposed to be. I have no idea if she ever made it. I would give anything to know she's all right."

I knew exactly how he felt. "I will find out if she's there and how she's doing." I put my hand over his. "I promise."

He looked up, the sorrow in his eyes now mixed with hope. "Let's go help your friend."

I led the way, hurrying through the crowded streets. The thought of Dr. Franklin as my "friend" made me smile. He seemed to oppose everything I stood for and constantly criticized my choices. But still, I probably wouldn't have survived the Change without his help. I owed him my life. Now his life hung in the balance.

*Father, keep Dr. Franklin in your care. Guide the nurse to the truth, so he can help Dr. Franklin back to health.*

When we got away from the clamor of the marketplace, we picked up the pace and I filled the nurse in. "The patient is Dr. Richard Franklin."

"Doctor?"

"Ph.D. Biology, I think. He's had a cough for several days. Yesterday morning he collapsed, and they haven't been able to wake him up since."

Reaching the Prius, I opened the back door. The nurse squeezed into the backseat and knelt on the floor beside Dr. Franklin. Despite the cramped conditions, his examination was thorough and efficient. He checked Dr. Franklin's vitals, listened to his lungs, shone a flashlight in his eyes, and examined his skin and fingernails.

"He's septic, probably from bronchitis." The nurse completed his assessment and slid out of the car. "His temp is one-o-five, and his pulse is barely palpable. You need to get him to a hospital right away."

"But there aren't any hospitals open."

"Maybe not in Lincoln."

The only hospital in operation that I knew of was in the biosphere. If I took Dr. Franklin there, it would be in direct violation of my contract with the government of the biosphere. I would most certainly lose my freedom and possibly my life. There must be something else we could do to help him.

"Don't you have some antibiotics you can give him?" I asked. "I'll pay you for them."

He shook his head. "I don't have any IV medicine. If I tried to give him oral antibiotics, in his condition, he'd probably aspirate and end up with pneumonia too." He handed me a small piece of paper. "Give this information to the doctor as soon as you arrive."

My mind raced. There had to be another way. If the government put me in jail or executed me, I couldn't help my brother, and he would probably lose his child. Was it worth saving one man's life, if it might mean the loss of two others?

He wrote a name on another piece of paper and gave it to me. "This is my fiancé. If you find her, tell her Jerrod says hi." His eyes clouded over. "Tell her that I miss her and that . . ."

Jerrod shook his head, blinked several times, and turned

back to the car. "You'll need to hurry. He doesn't have much time left." He closed the door and faced me. "Thank you for looking for Bridget for me. You have no idea how much I need to know she's okay."

Jerrod disappeared down a side street. He had made it clear what I had to do. If I didn't get Dr. Franklin to a hospital, he would die.

I slid into the driver's seat and began driving east. I had to get Dr. Franklin to the biosphere, no matter the consequences.

Memories of my first, uninvited visit to the Bubble flooded my mind—the suffocating fear when the barrel of a gun was pressed to my temple, the isolation that threatened to push me beyond the limits of sanity when I was left outside the biosphere, bound and blindfolded. The recollection made my pulse quicken and my breaths come fast and shallow. If I broke the rules, I could expect the same or worse treatment. I couldn't put myself through that again.

I turned the car around. Surely Dr. Franklin would understand. He was a stickler for following the rules, no matter what. I would just take him back to the cabin. Brad and Megan had always been his loyal helpers. They would take good care of him.

Besides, Jerrod was probably overreacting. Dr. Franklin was healthy, and he wasn't that old—probably in his sixties. With time and rest, maybe he would get better on his own. And if he didn't . . . Well, he would probably want to be with people he knew at the end, not in an unfamiliar hospital, surrounded by strangers.

This had to be the right decision. I would keep my life and my freedom. I would have a chance to help Josh and Lauren. I was doing my job, obeying my contract, following the rules.

But it didn't feel right, no matter how much I tried to justify my decision. There was a critically ill man in the back seat. I had the power to get him the help he needed. I was, quite possibly, the only person who could save his life. Dr. Franklin and I seemed to always be at odds, but without his help, I probably wouldn't be alive. He had been there for me when I needed him. I couldn't abandon him now.

I turned the car around again. My imagination bounced among the possible consequences of my decision to take Dr. Franklin to the Bubble. Dread swelled inside my chest until it constricted my throat. This decision was going to cost me—maybe my job and my right to see my family, perhaps my freedom, or possibly even my life.

Despite the knowledge of what I might be giving up, I felt a sense of calm, a feeling of peace deep inside that had been missing when I was headed toward the cabin. That kind of peace could only come from God. I knew that I had made the right decision.

# 17

By the time I turned back to the west, it was well past sunset. I was going to be hard-pressed to make it to the Bubble while it was still dark, but I had to try. I picked the quickest route I knew, one I could navigate without even a glance at my maps. I sailed around obstacles and maxed out the speedometer on every open stretch of road.

The eastern sky glowed in my rearview mirror when I crossed the Colorado state line. Driving to the biosphere during daylight hours was strictly forbidden because of the risk someone might see me and try to follow. I knew I couldn't wait until sunset to get Dr. Franklin the help he needed. I kept going, watching and listening vigilantly for any sign I was being followed. The sun was well above the horizon when I turned down the dirt road toward the biosphere.

Officer Clement was stationed at the checkpoint that morning. He stood in the middle of the road with his left arm in front of him, signaling me to stop. When I came close enough, he recognized me through the windshield. He stepped to the side of the road and raised his right hand to wave me through. But before I could take my foot off the brake, he spotted my passenger in the back seat. His right hand flew to his holster. He drew his gun and aimed it at my head.

I raised my hands in the air and mouthed, "He needs

help," tilting my head toward the back seat.

Keeping his gun trained on me, the officer opened the driver's side door. "What do you mean, bringing an outsider to the biosphere?"

"It's Dr. Franklin."

Officer Clement looked confused.

"The head of the cabin community. He's the person the Council negotiates trades with. He's very sick and needs a doctor." I tried to keep my voice calm. The fear and desperation I had felt during my first encounter with an armed man outside the biosphere welled up inside me. I couldn't help Dr. Franklin or Josh if the officer shot me before I even made it to the biosphere.

"You know you're not allowed to bring anyone here. You have compromised the safety of everyone in the biosphere, including your family." Officer Clement gasped for breath. Without an oxygen tank, I knew he could only stay outside the controlled environment of the checkpoint booth for a few minutes.

"He was unconscious the whole trip. He has no idea where we are."

"Don't move." Keeping his eyes and gun trained on me, the officer backed into the booth and closed the door.

He spoke into the radio clipped on his shoulder. I couldn't tell what he was saying. The distrustful expression on his face did not change. We watched each other for several minutes, while he maintained an unwavering grip on his gun, and I held my hands in the air.

My attention shifted to a cluster of people walking down the road toward me. Each person wore a mask attached to an oxygen tank, so I knew they had come from the biosphere. The five men at the front of the group had their guns drawn. When they spotted me, they broke into a run. I tensed, more convinced than ever I would not make it into the Bubble alive.

"Get out of the car," one of the armed men yelled. His words were loud and clear, even through his mask. "Keep your hands where I can see them."

I reached down slowly with my right hand.

"Hands up!" he screamed.

"Seatbelt?" I squeaked out.

A barely perceptible movement of the lead officer's head started two other officers in motion. One grabbed both my wrists in an iron grip. The other reached across to release my seatbelt. The officer holding my wrists dragged me out of the car. The other officer got hold of my legs and flipped me on my stomach. Dust filled my nose and mouth, making me cough. A heavy boot pressed down across my shoulder blades. The officers wrenched my arms behind my back, sending pain shooting through both shoulders. I cried out, my mouth filling with dirt again. A rough cord bit into both of my wrists.

I heard footsteps approaching, followed by muffled voices and the sound of car doors opening and closing.

"In the back seat."

"Unconscious."

"Seventy-six over palp."

"Sats sixty-eight."

I felt dizzy. I tried to take a deep breath but couldn't overcome the weight pressing my chest into the ground. The voices sounded far away.

". . . get him inside."

"Use the sheet."

"Lift on three."

"One, two . . ."

Sharp pain in my shoulders brought me back to consciousness. Two men pulled me up by my elbows and dragged me down the road. I struggled to get my feet under me to take the pressure off my shoulders.

I blinked several times, trying to clear my blurry vision. I struggled to stay on my feet as the men pulled me to one side and then the other, navigating around the ever more tightly-packed trees. I looked around. I couldn't see the road, the biosphere wall, or any other familiar landmarks.

We emerged into a clearing. The morning sunlight streaming over the tops of the trees forced me to close my eyes. The men pressed me forward. My toe caught on one of the recently-cut tree stumps that littered the floor of the clearing. I looked up, catching sight of the small log structure just before the men shoved me through its open door. I lost my balance and pitched forward. They caught me, barely preventing my face from slamming into the opposite wall. Using another cord, they secured my bound wrists to an eye bolt seated in the wall and turned to leave.

"Wait!" I wanted to ask what they planned to do with me, but I was afraid to hear the answer. "Where is Dr. Franklin? Is he okay?"

"Our medical team is looking after him," one of the officers replied. He slammed the door and secured the padlock.

I was hoping for a little more information than that, but I was relieved to know he was getting medical care.

My eyes slowly adjusted to the dim light admitted by one small, high window. I could tell by the dirt floor, the lack of furnishings, and the door that locked from the outside, that I was not in someone's vacation cabin. Apparently, after my first uninvited visit to the biosphere, the Council had decided to construct a jail cell, in case such a thing should happen again.

With no guns pointed at me, I could relax a little. I surmised that if they planned to execute me, they would have done it already. As long as I was alive, I held out hope that someone would listen to my story and empathize with the impossible choice I'd had to make.

Fatigue overtook me. It had been well over twenty-four hours since I last slept, and that time had been filled with anxiety and internal conflict. My wrists were secured to the wall at waist level. I couldn't sit or lie down. I leaned against the wall and closed my eyes, trying to relax. Whenever I came close to drifting off, I started to slide down, threatening to dislocate my shoulders.

I tried to dig with my feet in the dirt to build a hill to sit on. I could scoot the dust around, but below the top half inch, the compacted dirt wouldn't budge. The effort made my foot throb. I remembered Max's tender and comforting touch, and I wanted him there with me. Why was he the first person to come to mind when I was lonely and hurting? I tried to convince myself it was only because he'd made my foot feel better. But I couldn't shake the feeling there was more to it than that.

Desperate to get some sleep, I decided to try to cut the cord securing me to the wall. I found a rough spot on the eye bolt and rubbed the cord back and forth across it. After several minutes, the increased pressure on the cord caused both of my hands to tingle and throb, and there was no evidence the cord had weakened at all. But it was the only thing I could think to do, so I kept at it. Soon, both hands went completely numb. Exhaustion and anxiety combined to make me sob uncontrollably. Through my tears, I continued to frantically rub the cord back and forth over the rough spot.

The sound of footsteps in the woods brought my futile efforts to an end. I sniffed and tried to swallow my tears. I heard someone fumbling with the padlock. The door swung open and the lead officer from the party that met me at my car stepped inside. The light streaming through the door glinted off the blade of the knife in his hand. I squeezed my eyes closed and held my breath.

"It's time for your trial," the officer said gruffly.

He sliced easily through the rope securing me to the cage wall and wrapped one of his hands around both my wrists. He used the other hand to sheath his knife and pull out his gun.

Pressing the barrel of the gun to my back, he commanded, "Walk."

I stumbled out of the jail cell and through the crowded stand of trees. Their dry branches scratched my face, bringing tears to my eyes again.

We emerged from the trees right beside the entrance to the Bubble. Without releasing his grip on me, the officer spoke into one of the boulders. The rocks in front of us slid to the side, and the airlock door opened. The officer forced me inside.

Waiting for the atmosphere in the airlock to complete its transition, I remembered the first time I had been invited into the Bubble. I had been met by President Bentley herself, with a hero's welcome, because I was bringing seed that could be cultivated outside of the biosphere, ensuring the people in the biosphere would have enough food. Now I was returning as a criminal.

The officer forced me up the stairs and through the door into the biosphere. Another officer was waiting just inside. The two officers escorted me straight to the administration building and into the council chamber. Everyone in the room turned and looked when we entered. I saw condemnation in the eyes of nearly every member of the Council. I could see "innocent until proven guilty" was not one of their guiding principles. I caught a spark of sympathy in Councilman Jacob's expression, but it didn't come with an encouraging smile. I closed my eyes and took a deep breath. It was not going to be easy to convince them I'd made the right choice.

The officers pressed me forward and forced me into a chair near the center of the room. They stood on either side of me, each keeping a hand on his gun. Officer Clement sat a few feet to my right.

Chairman Lambrecht struck his gavel. "This trial will now commence. Officer Clement, please state your case."

"Honorable chairman, members of the Council," the officer said, "this woman—"

He pointed his finger at my head, just as he had pointed his gun a few hours before. I shuddered.

"—Christy Phillips," Officer Clement continued, "was seen approaching the biosphere during daylight hours, voluntarily bringing an unauthorized individual with her, in direct violation of her contract."

The officer proceeded to read the contract I had eagerly signed months before to gain release from captivity under biosphere law enforcement. When he reached the final section of the contract, listing the possible consequences of violating its provisions, he landed heavily on each word: *fines, incarceration,* and *death.*

"Ms. Phillips' actions have compromised the safety of thousands of people. If we let her go with only a fine, she will have the opportunity to place all of our lives at risk again. If we hold her in the jail cell, she will be a drain on our already limited resources. It is for these reasons I recommend execution."

The word sent a chill through me. Officer Clement had

always been cordial to me, though the requirements of his job demanded a degree of formality that precluded friendliness. Still, his recommendation of the death penalty shocked me. Perhaps he was trying to impress his colleagues. Maybe he had aspirations of joining the Council and wanted to demonstrate for them his ability to exercise authority. Or perhaps he just wanted to make sure I knew the power he had over me.

The council members asked Officer Clement a few questions, looking for specifics about my arrival time, the condition of my passenger, and my behavior when detained.

The chairman then turned to me. "Ms. Phillips, you may now state your case."

My mouth felt like it was full of cotton. Everything Officer Clement had said was true. I had no idea what to say in my defense.

*Lord, give me the words.* I stood to address the Council.

The officers standing guard converged on me and forced me back into the chair. I had appeared before the Council dozens of times. I couldn't believe that now, when it mattered most, I forgot the simple rule that anyone addressing the Council must do so from a seated position.

I swallowed hard and tried to collect myself. The officers hovered inches away, poised to react should I make any other inappropriate moves.

"Chairman, ladies and gentlemen of the Council." My voice was barely audible. I cleared my throat. "Officer Clement has spoken truthfully about my actions."

A murmur rippled through the Council.

"However," I continued, "I disagree with his claim that I put the lives of the residents of the biosphere at risk. While I did approach the biosphere just after sunrise, I made sure no one was following me, stopping several times to listen for the sound of footsteps or other vehicles. Dr. Franklin, the unauthorized individual in the back seat of the car, was unconscious for the entire trip because of severe sepsis. And even if he had momentarily regained consciousness, he was lying across the back seat and could not have seen enough through the window to tell where we were traveling. I assure you, Dr. Franklin has no idea where he is or how he got here."

My words tripped over one another in their eagerness to get out. I paused, trying to organize my thoughts and slow my speech.

"I did violate the terms of my contract, but I did it to save a man's life. There are no hospitals available outside of the biosphere and only a few nurses offering their services." I didn't know Dr. Franklin's condition. If it had deteriorated, the rest of my argument would not hold water. "Without the help of your physicians, Dr. Franklin would be dead by now. Remember the knowledge and resources Dr. Franklin has shared with you, to help make sure you can feed the growing population in the biosphere. The actions I took to save his life are actually helping to ensure the survival of your community, not its destruction."

I sat on the edge of my chair, scanning the faces of the council members, looking for any sign of empathy or understanding. I saw none.

Chairman Lambrecht finished writing on the pad in front of him and looked at me. "Ms. Phillips, you were instructed to return here only after you had obtained information about how we can improve our atmospheric conversion system. Do you have that information for us?"

I slouched back in the chair. "No, sir."

"That means your arrival here is also in violation of our most recent trade agreement. That makes three charges against you, none of which you can refute."

Fully expecting the next words out of his mouth to be a sentence to the death penalty, I made one more desperate attempt.

"Maybe there's another way I can help you preserve your atmosphere. I have a friend on the outside—a biochemist—who's trying to determine the genetic factors that enable some people to adjust to the altered atmosphere. If we can develop a genetic test, the people who are able to acclimatize to the air outside could choose to leave the biosphere. With fewer people in the biosphere, the atmospheric conversion system would be able to keep up, without modification."

"Ms. Phillips." Condescension dripped from Chairman Lambrecht's voice. "We have committed to provide for the basic needs of everyone who was invited to live in the USCSBS. The residents know how lucky they are to have been chosen to live in the protection of this community. No one would choose to leave, even if they knew they could survive on the outside."

I knew that wasn't true, but I didn't think it would be

wise to contradict the chairman, who held my life in his hands.

"The Council will begin deliberations now. You are dismissed." The chairman pounded his gavel.

The officers pulled me to my feet and pushed me through the door into the small anteroom outside of the council chamber. I sat in silence, thinking about what I had said, how I might have said it better, and what I had planned to say but forgot.

I ran my tongue around my teeth and tried to swallow but couldn't overcome the dryness. "Could I have some water, please?" I asked, timidly.

"Anything for the princess," one of the officers mumbled, grudgingly leaving the room.

His comment stung. I didn't think my request was unreasonable.

The officer returned and held a glass of water out to me. I turned to show him my hands were still tied behind my back. He rolled his eyes and put the glass to my mouth. He tilted it up, dumping much of the lukewarm water down my shirt. Still, the little I swallowed helped rinse away the feeling of cotton mouth.

When it became apparent the Council was not going to reach a quick decision, I decided to strike up a conversation with my escorts. "So, I suppose this is a little different from your normal workday, huh?"

The officer standing at the door to the council chamber shot me a derisive look. "Thanks to you, we're pulling doubles."

The officer standing over me snorted. "The chairman's

right, you don't belong here. We shouldn't have to waste our time with you."

His colleague added, "With any luck, you'll be dead by nightfall, and we'll be relieved of babysitting duty so we can go back home to our families."

A chill swept over me again. These same officers had cheerfully waved me through each time I came and went from the biosphere. People I thought were my friends now all seemed to think it would be better if I were dead.

Trying to get my mind off the subject, I introduced another topic. "In your line of work, you must get to know a lot of people."

No one responded.

"I've been trying to get in touch with Bridget Gehling, but I haven't been able to find her. Do any of you know where she lives?"

The officer standing by the door looked up as if startled when he heard her name but then quickly returned to an intent examination of his boot.

The other officer slid over to him and elbowed him in the ribs. "How 'bout it, Charlie? Do you know anyone named Bridget?"

I could see red creeping up Charlie's neck. He didn't say a word. I was glad to know Bridget was alive but concerned about Charlie's apparent interest in her. I didn't want to have to take the news back to Jerrod that his fiancé had moved on. At least I knew that, if I ever was released, tailing Charlie for a couple days would undoubtedly lead me straight to Bridget.

There was a sharp knock on the council chamber door. Charlie opened the door. The other officer yanked me to my feet and pushed me into the council chamber. Charlie forced me into the chair, pushing me so hard the chair almost tipped over.

Officer Clement entered from the opposite side of the room, casting me a smug glance as he crossed in front of me to his chair.

The chairman pounded his gavel, bringing the proceedings to order again. "After careful consideration, the Council has reached its decision. Ms. Phillips, the charges brought against you are grave and irrefutable. However, consideration must be given to the motivation for your violations and the contributions both you and Dr. Franklin have made to the preservation of the people of the USCSBS in the past.

"Let the record show Ms. Christy Phillips is guilty on three counts of breach of contract, including approaching the USCSBS in daylight, bringing an unauthorized individual to the USCSBS, and returning before completing her contracted duties. Know, Ms. Phillips, that this conviction is a permanent part of your record and will be taken into account in sentencing for any future infractions.

"The Council has determined to impose a fine as punishment for these crimes. That fine will be implemented through the withholding of food rations until such a time as you produce a list of three hundred residents who are able to survive outside of the USCSBS without supplemental oxygen. If you are unable to produce such a list within thirty days, you will again appear before the Council for reconsideration of your sentence. I assure you, Ms. Phillips, thirty days from now, our tendency will not be toward leniency."

I was relieved my life and freedom would not be taken from me but concerned about the Council's future plans.

"Thank you, Mr. Chairman, for your understanding of the difficult decision I was forced to make. If I may ask, how does the Council plan to proceed after receiving the list of names?"

"That is not your concern," Chairman Lambrecht answered sharply. He pounded his gavel. "You are dismissed."

# 18

The officers escorted me back to the anteroom where they cut the cord that held my wrists. The sudden rush of blood into my swollen, numb hands sent pain shooting through each of my fingers. I bit my lip to keep from crying out.

The officers left me alone in the anteroom. I let the tears flow—tears of pain and tears of relief. After coming so close to losing my life, I was free again, at least for the next thirty days. The task the Council had given me was nearly impossible. Since I had been unable to collect samples at the cabin, Max and Ashley only had a few DNA samples from survivors to compare to the samples from non-survivors. I had enough supplies in the Prius to collect samples from fifty people in the biosphere. But we couldn't do anything with those samples until we knew what we were looking for.

I wasn't sure what to do with my newly regained freedom. I needed to get the supplies out of the car, still parked at the checkpoint. I wanted to stop at the hospital to see how Dr. Franklin was doing. But before any of that, I needed to see my family. I hurried out of the administration building and through the streets to my biosphere home.

I knocked on the front door. The impact made my swollen knuckles sting. Mom cracked the door tentatively. I never arrived home in the middle of the afternoon. She grinned and threw the door open. A gasp erased her smile.

"Christy, what happened?" She clasped my swollen hand between hers, making me wince. "Your hands! What did they do to you?"

"I got back a little late, and with an uninvited guest," I said. "Earned the right to try out the new jail."

Mom ushered me in, and we sat on the couch. She massaged my hands while I told her the story of my untimely arrival and my subsequent incarceration and trial.

Mom shook her head. "I can't believe no one even told us you were here—and that they would treat you like that when you were just trying to save someone's life."

I didn't mention the part about the Council reconsidering my sentence if I didn't produce the list within thirty days. Mom worried about me enough. I didn't need to add to her anxiety.

"I bet you haven't had anything to eat all day." Mom jumped up and hurried to the kitchenette. "I'll get you some lunch."

"No, I don't need anything. They're only going to give you rations for three, now. I can't eat your food." I knew my growing brother was already giving part of his rations to his fiancé to keep her and her baby healthy. I couldn't take any more food away from them.

Mom turned to face me. "We can spare a little. It's no big deal."

"I'm fine, Mom."

She held my gaze for several seconds, then sighed and

turned to the sink to fill two glasses with water.

I smiled while her back was turned. When I was growing up, Mom had always been tenacious, especially when it came to matters of discipline. I was pleased to see that some of her determination had rubbed off on me.

She handed me a glass of water and sat beside me.

"How have things been going here?" I asked.

"Not much new. Lauren's been over for dinner a few times. She is a nice girl."

I nodded. "I can see why Josh fell for her."

"Josh has really surprised me. I figured after we vetoed his wedding plans, he would sulk around and avoid us whenever possible. But that's not been the case. He's home every day right after work. He's been helping more around the house. His mood has been pleasant, even when dealing with your dad's grouchiness."

I smiled. It sounded like Josh had actually listened to his big sister's advice. "My little brother is growing up."

By the time Dad and Josh returned home from work, I was asleep on the couch. They tried to keep the noise down to avoid waking me, but in such a small house, it was impossible. I pretended I was asleep until they finished supper, so they wouldn't feel bad about eating in front of me.

It felt great to finally get some rest, but I still felt weak in the knees and a little lightheaded when I stood. I needed to find some food. I invited Josh to take a walk with me to the airlock.

"How's Lauren doing?" I asked when I was sure we were out of earshot of the house.

"She's still getting sick a lot. Her parents want her to see the doctor to get treated for the flu. She's afraid if she goes they'll figure out what's going on, and it will all be over."

"Have you talked to her parents about getting married?"

Josh nodded. "It did not go well. They don't want Lauren to marry for at least five years, and I'm positive they don't want her to marry me ever."

"So our only hope is to get you out of here."

"You got it."

"Have you managed to get your hands on some oxygen tanks and masks?"

"I got ahold of two masks and backpacks, but the oxygen tanks come at a pretty high price. I can't cut back on Lauren's food, so it's going to take me a while to save up for them."

"Do you think you can get some before she starts to show?"

Josh shook his head. "She's already two months along. I might be able to get one or two tanks, but not enough to get her through the rest of her pregnancy."

"Keep trying. We've got to keep as many options open as possible."

"What other options are there?"

"There's nothing for sure yet, but Max and Ashley are working on figuring out the genes that make one person more likely to survive than another. I'll take genetic samples from you and Lauren back with me. I don't know how long it's going to take, but I think it's our best shot."

"The sooner, the better."

"Do you think some of your friends would be willing to be tested, too?"

"Definitely."

"I have to give the Council a list of three hundred people who might be able to survive on the outside within thirty days. I don't know what they plan to do with the list."

"We don't care. My friends and I would do anything to get out of this B.S."

Josh was careful not to use his shortened version of the biosphere's abbreviation in front of our parents. Since we were alone, he let it drop with all the aversion he could muster.

"I have enough supplies to collect fifty DNA samples. See how many of your friends you can get to stop by the house tomorrow afternoon."

"You got it."

"When you're done talking to your friends, go to Lauren's house. I'll meet you there to get samples from both of you."

I knocked on the window of the airlock operator's booth to get her attention. I explained to her that I needed to get supplies from my car to start the assignment given to me by the Council. She unlocked the doors in succession to let me out.

The walk from the biosphere to the checkpoint seemed to take forever. My stomach had long since ceased growling.

My feet felt heavy, my head, light. Every time I hit an uneven spot on the road, I thought it was going to throw me to the ground; a couple of times it did. At long last, I spotted the Prius ahead. I went straight to the trunk, where I normally kept enough food for the round trip to the biosphere. I hadn't packed as much this time because I'd planned to go straight back to Lincoln after my stop at the cabin. The granola bar and bottle of water weren't nearly enough to satisfy my hunger, but they gave me sufficient strength to start on my next task.

Back in the Bubble, I packed several DNA sampling kits in my backpack and dropped off the rest at home. Then I started on my delivery route. Normally I would accept almost any type of payment for delivering a piece of mail. That day, though, I was only interested in two things: DNA samples and food. I declined every other payment offered.

By the time I reached Lauren's house, my hunger was satisfied, and my backpack contained seven DNA samples. Josh had talked to Lauren and her parents, and they were all ready to offer a sample, bringing my total up to eleven.

I stopped at Jessica's house on my way home. She was still grieving but had been able to get back into a daily routine. Her angry phases were getting farther apart. Most days were marked by sad resignation. I could see in the downward turn of her eyes and mouth that this was one of those days.

We shared a hug and sat on the couch together.

"How are things going at the new job?" I asked.

She shrugged. "It keeps me busy. It's good to be busy."

It seemed to take a lot of effort for her to raise her eyes

and look at me. "What's new with you?"

"Well, I got to take a little trip to the biosphere's jail," I said. "That was fun."

"You're kidding. What happened?"

"I've talked about Dr. Franklin, the guy in charge at the cabin? Well, he got sick, and I couldn't find anyone on the outside who could help him. So, I brought him here. Bringing an outsider to the Bubble is, like, the ultimate violation of my contract, so they threw me in the slammer."

"How did you get out?"

"There was a trial of sorts," I said. "I was found guilty, of course. But I made them an offer they couldn't refuse, and they let me go with just a fine."

"What kind of offer was that?"

"A friend of mine is working on developing a genetic test to determine who might be able to survive outside the Bubble. The Council wants a list of people who have a predisposition to adapt to the altered atmosphere.

"You said once that you wanted to get out of here—to get away from the memories. Would you like me to test your DNA to see if you might be able to leave?"

Jessica looked around the room, and then her eyes dropped to her lap.

After several seconds, she looked up. "The constant reminders are still tough sometimes, but I can't just walk away. I don't want to forget. Some days the happy memories are the only thing that keeps me going."

I nodded. "That makes sense. If you ever change your

mind, let me know."

"I will."

I found out from my dad where Officer Charlie lived, and I headed there first thing the next morning. I planned to hide near his house and follow him when he went out, hoping he would lead me to Bridget. Unfortunately, he had already left his house by the time I reached his neighborhood, and he spotted me coming down the street before I had a chance to take cover. I formulated a new plan.

"Good morning, sir," I said cheerfully.

He looked down his nose at me and didn't respond.

"I'm sorry I caused so much trouble for you and the other officers."

He stopped and looked me up and down. "You most certainly did."

He started walking again, mumbling, "I don't know why it's so hard for some people to follow the rules."

Quelling the urge to defend my actions, I turned and jogged a few steps to catch up with him.

"You really care for Bridget, don't you?" I asked.

He kept walking, looking straight ahead.

"I ran into a friend of Bridget's in Lincoln. This friend wanted me to let Bridget know her friend is okay." I avoided using male pronouns that might give Charlie a clue to the nature of Bridget's relationship with her friend.

"If you tell me where I can find her, I'll be sure and let her know you helped me get this message to her. I'm sure she would be forever grateful to the person who made it possible for her to get good news from the outside."

Charlie paused. I knew he didn't want to help me. But I could see in the flush of his cheeks that he would do almost anything to impress Bridget.

"Follow me," Charlie said begrudgingly and strode off.

I hurried to keep pace with his long legs throughout the silent quarter-mile walk. Charlie strode up to one of the houses and knocked on the door. The curtain covering the window next to the door moved to the side and then fell back in place. The door opened, and a woman stepped out.

"Hello, dumplin'." The woman wrapped her arms around Charlie and puckered her lips.

Charlie cleared his throat and stepped back. "Bridget, this is Christy."

Bridget turned toward me, her cheeks pink. "It's nice to meet you." She smiled and extended her hand.

"She has a message for you." Charlie leaned against the house, his eyes following my every move.

I shook Bridget's hand, making eye contact and angling my head toward the door, hopeful she would invite me in.

"A message?" Bridget's brow furrowed, though her smile remained. "From whom?"

I took a step closer to the door. Bridget didn't move. It looked like I was going to have to say what I came to say in front of Charlie.

"I ran into a friend of yours the other day." I tried to sound casual but chose my words carefully. "Your friend is working as a nurse at the public market in Lincoln."

Her eyes opened wide. She knew exactly who I was talking about.

She glanced at Charlie. He was still watching me and didn't appear to have noticed her reaction.

"How is my friend doing?"

"Helped me save a man's life the other day—the best nurse at the market."

"I'm sure." She put her hand on my shoulder. Her smile widened. "Thank you for letting me know."

"I couldn't have done it without Charlie. He was more than happy to help me find you, so I could share some good news with you."

I started toward the street. "Your friend will be glad to know you're doing well."

Bridget waved goodbye, and she and Charlie went into the house. I tried to imagine how she was feeling. Learning that her fiancé, whom she hadn't heard from in six months, was alive, had to be exciting, but the chances that Bridget and Jerrod would ever see each other again were slim. Undoubtedly, she had some tough decisions and maybe some challenging conversations ahead of her. But I knew by the look on her face, telling her was the right thing to do. The appreciation I saw in her expression and so many others' was the best part of my delivery job.

# 19

A steady stream of people came and went from our house that afternoon. Between my family, Josh's friends, and several neighbors, I had filled all fifty test tubes by dusk. Though I hated to cut my time with my family short, I was eager to get back to Lincoln, where we could begin testing the samples and where I could more easily find food. My mail route had generated enough food to get me through the day before, but the hunger pangs returned full force by evening.

The outgoing mail was already secured in the hidden compartment in my backpack. I packed up the DNA samples, said goodbye to Mom, Dad, and Josh, and headed out.

I had two stops to make before I could leave the biosphere. The first was risky, but the look in Bridget's eyes when I last saw her and the potential of a snack to sustain me through my trip spurred me on. I needed to let Bridget know I could get a letter to her fiancé.

I approached her house cautiously, watching for any signs that Charlie was visiting. I stopped under a window on the side of her house. I could tell by the variations in the light streaming out the window that someone was moving around inside, but I didn't hear any voices. I stepped up to the front door and knocked lightly. I waited several seconds. Hearing nothing, I knocked a little harder.

"I'll get it," a man's voice said.

I sprinted down the street, seeking shelter in the shadows beyond the next house. Over the pounding of my heart, I heard the door of Bridget's house slam. I hoped the man had returned to the house and wasn't out looking for the troublemaker playing ding dong ditch.

I waited several minutes. Hearing nothing, I crept out from behind the house, looking around cautiously. As soon as I reached the circle illuminated by the streetlight, I heard footsteps running toward me. I sprinted in the opposite direction.

"Stop!" The man yelled.

I didn't look back.

By the time I reached the business district, it felt like my lungs were about to burst. I ducked between a dumpster and an office building. I was certain everyone within a block could hear me gasping for breath. When my breathing finally calmed, I crept out from behind the dumpster. I couldn't hear anything. It struck me that, here in the Bubble, there wasn't even the rustle of the wind to disturb the silence.

Fearing someone might be waiting in the street for me to emerge, I went to the alley behind the buildings. I walked down a couple blocks before returning to the street. I checked my back every few steps.

I stopped before reaching the door of the hospital to try to smooth out my hair and brush the dumpster dirt off my clothes. I certainly didn't look my best, but I hoped I was presentable enough they would let me in.

When brushing off my backside, I felt something poking through the bottom of my backpack. I moved closer to the streetlight and took the backpack off. I opened it and found that the seals on several of the tubes had broken, and the swabs had come out. That meant the samples were contaminated and could no longer be used. I chastised myself for taking unnecessary risks with the precious samples. There was nothing I could do about it now, though. Before I could take any more samples, I had to return to the lab in Lincoln and get more supplies. I cleaned up the mess in my backpack as best I could and entered the hospital.

The waiting area was empty, and the receptionist was happy to show me to Dr. Franklin's room. If it weren't for the buzzing and beeping of the machines monitoring his condition and pumping antibiotics into his veins, I would have thought he was sleeping peacefully. It looked like a little color had returned to his cheeks. I said his name a couple times. He didn't stir. It was hard to believe this man, whom I had seen as a ruthless dictator, had been rendered completely helpless by the tiniest of organisms.

I held his hand and prayed quietly, "Father, please keep Dr. Franklin comfortable. Give him strength and peace as he works through this. Guide the doctors with your wisdom to give him the treatment he needs. Amen."

Dr. Franklin's eyelids fluttered slightly. I smiled and squeezed his hand. I didn't know what his relationship with God was like, or if he even had one, but his reaction convinced me he had heard my prayer.

My departure from the biosphere was routine. I could do it in my sleep, and, since it always happened at night, it often felt like I was asleep. I backed out of the airlock, cut my lights when I reached the checkpoint, and crept along the tree-lined gravel road in the dark. After driving five miles, I turned on the headlights and picked up a little speed.

I stopped at an abandoned car lot just over the state line in Nebraska and selected a chocolate brown Jeep Grand Cherokee. I switched vehicles every few weeks to help avoid arousing suspicion during my frequent trips between the cabin and the biosphere. I found a couple cars on the lot that still had gas in their tanks and siphoned enough to fill the SUV. The biosphere government kept me well-supplied with gas, but sources outside the biosphere were rapidly drying up. It wouldn't be long before the mere fact that I was driving a motor vehicle would stir up suspicion.

Back in Lincoln, I went straight to Max's house. There was no one there. I needed a nap, but the deadline hanging over my head compelled me to keep going. I found Max and Ashley in the lab, hard at work testing samples.

"I was afraid I'd never see you again." Ashley ran to me, almost tackling me with a hug.

"I'm glad you're all right." Max kept his distance, but his expression was sincere.

"It's so good to see you guys." I smiled, relieved to be back with my two best friends.

"When you didn't come back on Wednesday, I went to the cabin looking for you," Ashley said. "After they assured me you were okay, I explained what we were working on. Everyone was eager to help. We just started sequencing the last of the samples from the cabin."

"Did you get the non-survivor samples done?"

Max nodded. "We finished those yesterday. When all of the samples are sequenced, the computer will compare the results from the two groups. We'll use that comparison to develop the genetic test."

"How long will that take?"

"It depends on how complex the genetic fingerprint for survivorship is. Sometimes it takes weeks or even months."

The probability of meeting my thirty-day deadline was rapidly moving from unlikely to impossible.

"Most of the time, though, we're comparing a group of people with a certain condition to the general population—some members of which may develop the condition in the future. In this case, our groups are clear and mutually exclusive. Everyone in the survivor group was able to adapt. Everyone in the other group wasn't. That should make it easier to isolate the differences between the two groups. I can probably have the test up and running within a week or so."

*I hope that's soon enough.* "How can I help?"

Max taught me how to prepare samples for sequencing. While we worked, I shared the story of my less-than-warm welcome back to the biosphere and my assignment to produce a list of three hundred survivors in thirty days.

"Based on the survival rate out here," Max said, "you're probably going to have to test every person in the biosphere to get three hundred positives."

I nodded. "And they won't tell me what they're going to do with the list. A lot of people there don't trust the government. I can't imagine I'll be able to find many people willing to give the government their DNA."

"Can we give them something in return?" Ashley asked.

"We can't afford to bribe thousands of people," I said, "not if we want to be able to eat for the next six months."

"After we run these samples, there won't be much for you girls to do until I finish putting together the test. You should both go to the biosphere tomorrow and work on collecting more samples."

"Are you trying to get me thrown in jail?" I asked. "I will never see freedom again if I show up at the Bubble with another passenger."

"Then let's pick a place to meet near the biosphere," Ashley said. "You can collect the samples and I'll run them back here to the lab. That way we can test the samples as we collect them, and you won't have to waste time driving back and forth."

"That might work," I said. With the three of us working together, maybe we could accomplish this seemingly insurmountable task.

I drew Ashley a map to one of my favorite car lots in northern Colorado. We agreed to meet there in three days, on Tuesday evening after dark.

# 20

When I reached the biosphere checkpoint the next evening, the officer detained me until two others arrived. The three officers, all wearing oxygen masks and backpacks, searched me and my vehicle thoroughly, combing through the contents of every box and even looking under the spare tire. I hadn't been subjected to such an inspection in months. Just two weeks before, the officers had welcomed me as a trusted emissary. Now, they were treating me like a common criminal.

Shame filled my chest, making it hard to breathe. The sting of the officers' actions surprised me. I had tried to convince myself and those around me that I was tough and strong. I needed to be tough enough to stand up to the thieves that threatened to keep me from doing my job. I had to be strong enough to keep going even when memories of Scott, my roommate Kayla, and so many other people I might never see again weighed me down. I had begun to believe that I was as tough as the persona I tried to project. But now I just wanted to run away and never come back.

The officers finally cleared me to continue toward the biosphere. The two officers who had been called out to meet me walked on either side of the Grand Cherokee as I snaked my way down the dirt road. I pretended that I was an important dignitary, and they were my Secret Service detail.

When the officers weren't looking, I even snuck in a wave to the imaginary throngs gathered along the road to watch me drive by.

The officers spoke into the rock to signal the operator to open the airlock. They supervised the unloading of the SUV and accompanied me to my parents' house. After exchanging nods with my mother and handshakes with my father, the officers finally left. Though I saw them walk away, I couldn't shake the feeling that we were being watched.

I was grateful for a restful night with my family. I resisted the urge to sleep in. I had too much to accomplish to waste daylight hours sleeping. As soon as she heard me stir, Mom got up, too. I grabbed a bite of breakfast from my cargo while she bustled around the kitchen trying to turn their meager rations into an appetizing meal for Dad and Josh. I filled my backpack with test tubes and swabs.

"Bye, Mom," I whispered, trying not to wake the guys.

"Wait." Mom turned off the stove and slipped on a sweater. "I want to come with you."

"You don't have to. I'll be fine."

She fumbled with the buttons on her sweater. "I think it would be good for us to spend more time together."

"Okay." I shrugged. "If you want to."

She flashed me a little smile and then looked away.

We stopped at a few houses we had already visited, to replace samples that had been damaged when I was running for my life. Then we made our way through the rest of the neighborhood. We quickly discovered things went better if

Mom rang the doorbell and explained what we needed. She was a familiar face in the neighborhood. Based on the suspicious glances I received, it seemed word of my transgressions had already spread.

I enjoyed spending time with Mom. My visits to the Bubble were usually brief, and the house didn't afford much privacy. I finally told her about finding Scott's car and hoping against hope that he was still alive. I opted not to give many other details about our trip to Yellowstone. Mom hadn't met Max, and I didn't want her imagining him as a dirty old man preying on innocent girls.

We finished the neighborhood a little before noon. It had been a successful morning, with fifty new DNA samples ready for delivery. We stopped at home to drop off the samples, pick up more supplies, and have some lunch.

Our productivity stalled after lunch. We were canvassing neighborhoods farther from home. Fewer people knew Mom, and no one was about to let a perfect stranger stick a swab in his mouth without a good reason. The afternoon wore on, and our frustration grew. We finally gave up around five with only three new DNA samples.

"I need to go to the firing range, blow off some steam," I said. "I'll see you at home."

"Sure, Sweetie." Mom seemed reluctant to let me go. "You'll be home for supper?"

"Probably a little after. I don't want to be tempted by the smell of your wonderful cooking."

I walked down a side street. When I turned toward the

firing range, I glanced back and saw Mom, still standing where I left her. I tossed her a wave and continued down the street.

Despite our disappointing afternoon, I couldn't help but smile when the firing range came into view. It was my second home in the Bubble. It was there I gained the confidence to venture out into the world without paralyzing fear. When my life was spinning like a car that was going too fast on an icy road, I could step into the firing range and be in total control again.

My smile broadened when I saw a familiar face at the desk. "Hey, Sam. Is stand six open?"

Sam glanced up at me and then back down. He cleared his throat. "Um, Christy." He shifted in his chair. "I'm not allowed to let you shoot."

"What? Why?"

"There's a list." He held up a piece of paper, his eyes still firmly fixed on his desk.

I snatched it from his hand. The top of the paper read "No access to facilities and services designed for use by residents of the USCSBS." Christy Phillips was the only name on the list.

"Come on, Sam. I just need to de-stress a little. Give me ten minutes."

He shook his head. "I can't do it."

"Five minutes, then. No one will know."

He looked up, making eye contact for the first time. "You need to leave now."

I opened my mouth to object, thought better of it, and

turned to go.

"I'm sorry, Christy."

I glanced back at Sam and continued out the door.

Instead of relieving my frustration, my trip to the firing range had only amplified it. I wanted to scream or punch something, but there was no place in the Bubble where I could do those things without raising suspicion. Maybe I just needed to get out of there. Life on the outside could be unpredictable and dangerous, but at least there was no one there telling me what to do.

But if I didn't give the Council what it demanded, I wouldn't be able to come back. I wouldn't be able to see my family ever again. I couldn't let that happen.

I walked slowly toward the house, trying to think of a way to get the samples I needed and to convince the people who used to be my friends that I was still a good person.

Rounding the corner onto our street, I saw two people standing in front of the house. Drawing closer, I recognized my mom. She was talking with a uniformed officer. By the time I reached the door, the officer was gone, and Mom was inside.

"Is everything all right?" I asked.

"Fine. Why?" Mom asked.

"I saw an officer here. Did something happen to Dad?"

"No, Sweetie."

"Josh?" My sense of alarm intensified.

"Everyone is fine," Mom insisted.

"Then why was he here?"

Mom was suddenly preoccupied with the can opener.

"Was he checking up on me?" I asked.

Mom sighed. "Yes. He just wanted to make sure everything was okay."

I remembered Mom's odd behavior that morning. "They're having you keep tabs on me, aren't they?"

Mom turned away to stir something on the stove.

"You weren't interested in spending time with me. You were spying on me."

Mom faced me again, with tears in her eyes. "Sweetie, you know I would never do anything to get you in trouble."

She tried to put her arm around me. I pulled away.

"But things are different since the Change," she said. "We have to play along and pretend to support whatever the government does. Otherwise, people get hurt.

"The government wants to make sure you're working on your assignment while you're here, and not participating in any more illegal activities. If we didn't agree to keep an eye on you, they would have had an officer watching your every move. If the officer saw the slightest violation of the rules, it would be game over for all of us. And if he got tired of his post, all he would have to do is make something up. It would be his word against ours."

She was right, of course. But I still couldn't believe my own mother agreed to spy on me.

"I'm sorry," I mumbled.

I went out on the patio. I needed to be alone, and that was as close as I could get.

Even when my friends in the Bubble turned against me,

I'd been confident my parents were on my side. Now I wasn't even sure of that. Was there anyone I could trust absolutely?

Of course there was. "Jesus," I whispered, "I really need a friend right now. Can you help me get the samples I need? And please keep my family safe. I don't want them to get in trouble because of me."

I heard Josh's distinctive whistle as he came down the road.

"Good day at work?" I asked.

Josh shrugged. "Same old, same old.

"Guess what I got for Lauren." He held out a small package wrapped in brown paper.

"Baby clothes?" I guessed, whispering to make sure no one overheard.

"Better." His eyes sparkled. "A pot roast."

"No way. Where did you get it?" There hadn't been any fresh meat in the rations for months.

"Finely tuned business acumen," Josh said in an exaggerated British accent, "and a little blackmail."

"She is going to love it."

# 21

I awoke the next morning still trying to figure out how I could get nine hundred more DNA samples. The approach we had been taking was obviously not working.

"When we take a break for lunch, do you want to come with me to pick up our rations?" Mom asked. "Sometimes it's helpful to have an extra set of hands."

"Sure, that'd be fine." I was still lost in my thoughts.

I turned to her. "Wait, what did you say?"

"Today is ration day. We can get our supplies at noon."

"Ration day." A smile spread across my face. "Gotta go, Mom. See you later."

"You know I have to go with you."

"Then hurry up and get ready," I said, filling my backpack with kits for DNA collection.

Ration distribution had just begun when we arrived, each carrying a backpack and a box full of test tubes and swabs. A long line snaked around the ration building. Mom started near the entrance to the building. I started at the end of the line.

"Excuse me, sir?" I addressed a man tapping his foot impatiently while stretching to see how close he was to the beginning of the line. "The Council is requesting DNA samples from all citizens."

The man's nose wrinkled as if he had caught a whiff of sour milk.

"We need a swab of the inside of your cheek," I said. "Open up for me."

The disgusted look stayed on his face, but he let me take the sample. I stuck the swab in a plastic tube and sealed it.

I handed him a spiral notebook. "Please write down your name and address."

I copied the man's name onto the test tube.

"Thank you, sir."

*That was easy.* Apparently, what happens at the rations station is assumed to be official government business.

At the next group of people, I tried opening with "President Bentley is requesting a DNA sample from each of us." People reacted more favorably to that approach. Abigail Bentley had been responsible for the creation of the biosphere, saving thousands of lives. She served as the kind, encouraging public face of the government, leaving the difficult and often unpopular decisions to the Council.

We worked steadily through the morning. Late in the morning, traffic slowed. I carried the samples we had collected home and brought more collection materials and some snacks.

Noon brought a big rush. Most of the people were in a hurry, so it was hard to get them to stop for us.

Near the end of the noon rush, I ran into Lauren, waiting in line for her family's rations. Her head hung down, and she bit her lower lip.

"Lauren, it's good to see you," I said. "How are you feeling?"

She looked up, her chin quivering.

I put my hand on her arm. "What's wrong?"

"Mom figured out"—she looked around to see who might be eavesdropping—"why I've been so sick."

"Was she really upset?"

"Disappointed, mostly, which is even worse." Tears welled up in her eyes. "She scheduled a doctor's appointment for me in three weeks."

I wrapped my arms around her. "Max and Ashley are working in the lab non-stop."

"I'm so scared, Christy," Lauren whispered. "You have to help me."

"Don't worry. I'm going to get you out of here."

By the end of the day, Mom and I had collected almost five hundred new DNA samples. It took us a couple trips to get all of the samples and my family's rations home. My feelings of betrayal turned to gratitude when I realized that if I'd been alone, I would have collected only a fraction of what Mom and I collected working together. If she hadn't agreed to spy on me, I would still have some seven hundred empty test tubes.

I was exhausted, but I wanted to get the samples to Lincoln right away, and I knew Ashley would be waiting for me. After a quick nap, I enlisted the help of my family to carry the DNA samples to the airlock.

Snacking helped me stay awake for the ninety-minute drive to meet Ashley. As soon as I turned into the parking lot, she jumped out of her car and ran to meet me.

"You made it," she said. "Did everything go okay?"

"More than okay." I opened the back of the Grand Cherokee.

Ashley's jaw dropped when she saw the bags and boxes of DNA samples.

I laughed at her expression. "I'm feeling a little better about that thirty-day deadline."

We transferred the DNA samples to Ashley's car and the testing supplies and food she brought to my SUV.

"Lauren's mom figured out she's pregnant and scheduled a prenatal appointment in three weeks," I said. "If we don't get her results before then, it might be too late."

"With Max and me working together in the lab, once the test is up and running, we should be able to move pretty fast."

"Great. I sure hope this works."

Ashley closed the trunk of her car. "Should we meet here again in three or four days?"

"Let's make it a week. The best time to collect samples seems to be ration day. That doesn't come around again until next Tuesday."

"Tuesday it is."

"Hey, do you know the nurse who works in the market?"

"The perky one with a voice like Snow White?"

"No, the balding one who's a pathological perfectionist."

"Sure, I've seen him around."

"He's the one who took a look at Dr. Franklin and told me to get him to the hospital. In exchange, I promised to check on his fiancé. Could you find him and let him know that Bridget is living in the biosphere and doing well and that she was glad to hear from him?"

"No problem." Ashley got into her car.

"Are you sure you can find your way back okay?"

"I got this. Don't worry." Ashley started the car. "I'll see you in a week."

I couldn't return to the Bubble right away because then they would know I hadn't driven all the way to Lincoln and back. If the Council found out I had directed someone partway to the biosphere, life as I knew it would be over. That meant I had about twenty hours before I could head back to the Bubble—plenty of time to catch up on sleep. With the doors locked and my pistol in my right hand, I fell sound asleep on the back seat of the Grand Cherokee.

# 22

Late in the morning, the warm sun on my face gently pulled me out of my deep sleep. Through my closed eyelids I sensed the sun's light dimming. *A little cloud must be floating across the sun.* I smiled at the thought.

Then I heard a man's voice.

I sprang up to sitting and aimed my gun in the direction I thought the voice had come from, blinking the sleep out of my eyes. The man on the other side of the window took a couple steps back. I looked around, counting at least ten men. I was surrounded. I could try to frighten them off with my gun, but if they decided to fight back, there was no way I could take them all.

I decided to try a little negotiation but kept my finger firmly on the trigger in case I had to resort to my backup plan.

"What do you want?" I yelled through the window.

"We need some food for our families." The man in my sights held his hands in the air. He looked scared.

I looked around at the other men. The week's supply I had wouldn't go far split ten ways.

"I have a little," I yelled. "What do you have to trade for it?"

I heard a loud crash as a projectile shattered the window behind me. I screamed and whirled around. A man's shoulder struck my chest, cutting my scream short and slamming me into the side of the SUV. My head whipped back, smacking the wall. The pistol went off, shattering another window. Splotches of darkness raced to obscure my vision from every direction. I struggled to resist, but the darkness overcame me. I slumped to the floor.

When I came to, I heard only the pounding in my head. I pulled myself up onto the seat. It felt like the world was spinning and tilting around me. I gripped the seat and willed the world to slow down. Even when I closed my eyes, the whirling wouldn't stop. I lay down on the seat.

When the pounding had let up a little, I tried sitting up again. The world tipped to the left, rolled, and righted itself. I turned my head carefully to assess the damage. All of my food was gone. There was no sign of my pistol. The DNA collecting supplies Ashley had left with me were strewn about the SUV and the parking lot. Most of the test tubes I could see had been crushed.

I climbed out of the Grand Cherokee to try to salvage any of the supplies that were still usable. I bent to pick up a tube that appeared to be intact. As soon as I tilted my head forward, I vomited. I pulled myself into the front seat and reclined it. Somehow I needed to get a new vehicle and a week's supply of food. But I had nothing to trade. I couldn't tolerate sitting up for more than a minute or two. And Ashley wasn't coming back for six more days. I drifted off with these thoughts swirling in my head.

The cool breeze coming through the broken windows woke me. The dark was intense, with the sliver of a moon only occasionally peeking through the clouds. I couldn't remember where I was or how I had gotten there. I sat up and promptly threw up in my lap.

*Ah, yes, my concussion.* The confusion started to clear.

Now that it was dark, I needed to get back to the Bubble. I lay back on the reclined seat. *But it wouldn't hurt anything to wait and rest one more day.*

The breeze was getting colder. Whether or not I tried to get back to the Bubble that night, I needed a new vehicle. My busted up SUV did not give me enough protection for a November night in northern Colorado.

I opened the door, slid off the seat, and sat on the running board for a few minutes. The pounding in my head quieted. I stood, keeping a firm hold on the frame of the vehicle. I felt shaky, but the nausea stayed at bay. The clouds parted enough that I could see the outlines of other cars behind the SUV. I inched forward, sliding my feet along the ground, keeping both hands on the side of the Grand Cherokee.

When I reached the back, I had to let go of the SUV. I stood for several seconds with my arms out in front of me, my gaze focused on the nothingness ahead. I took one small step, then another. I celebrated my success—two steps without falling or getting sick. I was careful not to move my head during my internal celebration.

I continued taking tiny steps for what seemed like an hour until finally my shin struck the bumper of a car. Relieved, I reached down for the hood of the car. Instantly, waves of nausea washed over me. I stood up again, trying to still my churning stomach. The quick movement made the earth tilt and begin to slide out from under me. I clutched the car and eased myself onto the ground. I couldn't keep from heaving, but there was nothing more to bring up.

My stomach and my head finally settled down, but I was afraid to stand. I scooted along the ground until I could open the back door. I pulled myself into the car, lying across the back seat with my feet on the floor. The relative warmth of the inside of the car soothed me back to sleep in seconds.

When I awoke in the morning, the sunlight streaming through the window reignited the pounding in my head. The events of the previous day were coming into focus. I cautiously pushed myself up to sitting, pausing after each little movement to make sure I wasn't going to get sick or dizzy. The world was no longer tilting and spinning, but the smell of vomit on my clothes, amplified by the small enclosed space, roused my nausea. I wanted to bolt out of the car to get some fresh air, but I knew that would create more problems than it would solve. I slid over to the door and opened it, careful to avoid any sudden movements.

The crisp morning air made me shiver, but it still felt good on my aching head and tainted nostrils. I inhaled the fresh air deeply, gingerly placed my feet on the ground, and stood up. My legs felt a little wobbly, but my head was clear, my stomach, calm. I took a few steps forward. I felt pretty good. I turned around to walk back to the car, and a surge of nausea threatened to overtake me. I stopped moving, and the queasiness slowly ebbed. I still had to move slowly, but at least I could function.

Walking to the section of the lot I had not yet tapped for gas, I realized how hungry I was. My shaky knees had much more to do with my lack of nourishment than with my concussion. I found a purple Honda Civic that still had half a tank and parked it near the Grand Cherokee. I sorted through the ransacked supplies, leaving the tubes that were crushed or had broken seals, and carefully packing the intact testing supplies in the car.

My final task before returning to the Bubble promised to be the hardest. I hadn't eaten in almost two days, and whatever I ate before then I had since regurgitated. I couldn't last much longer without some sustenance. And once I reached the biosphere, my only source of food would be my family's limited rations. I needed to find several days' supply of food, and I needed it now.

By that time, several months after the Change, all of the businesses and homes that might contain food had been looted. The few wild plants that had survived or germinated since the Change weren't strong enough to produce much fruit yet. Like humans, most of the animals died in the Change. Many of those that survived didn't last long because their food sources were gone. My best hope was to find another city with a market like Lincoln's. There were a number of towns in this part of northern Colorado but nothing even approaching one-tenth the size of Lincoln.

Luckily, the towns were in close proximity. I drove through one after another, looking for any sign of organized trade. Finally, in Sterling, I spotted a table full of trade items in someone's front yard. There wasn't a structured or centralized market, but the people manning the table directed me to others nearby. It was difficult to find people willing to accept my limited trade parameters. I only wanted food, and I could only offer to deliver letters to people in the biosphere in return. I felt a little guilty making that offer. While I was under constant surveillance, delivering letters in the Bubble would be impossible. But as long as the letters eventually reached their destination, I figured it was a fair trade.

After canvassing the entire town of Sterling, I only had enough food for a few days. The sun had just touched the horizon. Even if other towns in the area had a market, it would surely be closed by the time I got there. I didn't want to wait another day before returning to the Bubble. I needed to get back and collect more DNA samples. I was just going to have to make do with what I had.

I was wiped out, even though I had spent more of the past forty-eight hours asleep than awake. The strain of trying to accomplish important tasks while making no sudden moves and keeping my head still at all times was exhausting. But there was no way I was going to risk letting someone steal the food I had just collected. I would just have to wait until I got back to the Bubble to rest.

At the checkpoint, the officers repeated their lengthy ritual, inspecting every inch of me and my vehicle, after extensive questioning about why I had switched vehicles again so soon. I thought I might fall asleep standing up before they finally finished their inspection and cleared me to enter the biosphere, still under escort.

Despite my fatigue, I was not going to bed until I cleaned up, replaced the clothes I had been wearing for three days straight, and brushed the horrible taste out of my mouth. I had to give my worried parents a quick recap of my encounter with the thieves before I could finally rest my aching head.

Even though I was secure in my parents' home, I slept poorly, waking often to the imagined sound of a window shattering or sensation of being struck on the back of the head. When the glow of sunrise finally gave me permission to leave my unsettling dreams behind, I found myself dreading the day when I would have to venture outside the Bubble again.

# 23

Mom and I set out first thing in the morning to collect more DNA samples. We hit the industrial sector, stopping at workplaces to catch employees on their breaks. We picked up a few samples, but more often we were flatly refused or run off by supervisors who feared we were interfering with the efficiency of their workforce.

On Saturday, we stopped at the homes of those who had willingly given samples the week before, to collect from the members of their households who were at work or school the last time we stopped. The approach proved successful. With brief stops at the house to grab a bite to eat, drop off collected samples, and pick up more sampling kits, we continued until well past dark, collecting more than three hundred samples.

Mom and I stopped to see Jessica a few times in the evenings. After hearing Jessica's story, Mom revealed that she had had several miscarriages before she got pregnant with me. She understood Jessica's grief in a way I never could. On our second visit, as we were getting ready to leave, Jessica pulled me to the side.

"I want to do it," she said softly. "I'm ready."

"Ready?" I asked, confused.

"I want to get out of here," she said. "I can take the good memories with me, but I need to get away from the Council and the doctors and the threats they made to keep me quiet. I want you to test my DNA."

"Sure." I always kept a few sampling kits on hand. I swabbed the inside of her cheek. "I can't make any promises, but I'll be happy to do the test."

She wrote her name and address in the notebook. "This could be my get out of jail free card. I hope it is."

While I was in the Bubble, I parceled my meager food supply into equal daily portions. After a few days, the growling in my stomach ceased, leaving behind a constant feeling of emptiness. I ate in private, so my family wouldn't know how little food I had. Whenever I had to sit down quickly because I was feeling lightheaded, Mom noticed and tried to get me to eat some of the family's food. I declined every entreaty, though the aching hunger threatened to break my resolve as the week went on.

Mom and I visited Dr. Franklin at the hospital every day. When we arrived on Friday afternoon, I poked my head in the door to his room. I was surprised to see him sitting up in a recliner, the remnants of his lunch on a table in front of him.

"Are you up for visitors?" I asked.

He looked up and waved us in.

"How are you feeling today?" Mom asked.

"Exhausted," Dr. Franklin said, "but thankful to be above ground."

I sat down on the edge of his neatly made bed. Mom

took a chair beside the recliner.

"It must feel good to be out of bed," I said.

He nodded. "I was getting a little stir-crazy. It sure was a lot of work to get over here, though. They might need to call Barnhart to get me back in bed."

I chuckled. Barnhart was a popular crane service provider in Lincoln, where Dr. Franklin had lived before the Change.

"We take so many things for granted until we lose them." Dr. Franklin rested his head against the recliner. "I've had a lot of time to think, lying on that bed. And I still can't make sense of everything."

This was a side of him I hadn't seen before. As a professor and as leader of the cabin community, Dr. Franklin had always been confident, often to the point of condescension. His illness had changed him. While it was refreshing to hear him admit that he didn't have it all together all the time, it was also a bit disconcerting. I wasn't sure how to relate to Dr. Franklin 2.0.

I took a deep breath. "It's hard when you can't see the big picture."

He tilted his head and looked at me. "Yes, it is. I don't know how I can make decisions when I can't even guess what the consequences will be."

"As much as I would like to be in control, I know that things would not go well if I were in charge of the world." *Lord, give me the courage to speak the truth.* "God sees the big picture. Even the stuff that doesn't make any sense to us, he can turn into something good."

Dr. Franklin nodded slowly. He opened his mouth as if he wanted to say something but then closed it again. Leaning back, he shut his eyes.

"We better go, let Dr. Franklin get some rest." Mom stood and turned toward him. "It's good to see you up and around. We'll be back tomorrow."

I followed Mom out of the room.

Walking down the hall toward Dr. Franklin's room on Monday, I noticed that nearly every bed was full. "Business has really picked up here this week."

Mom nodded. "A lot of the patients are on oxygen. I wonder if there's a respiratory virus going around."

"I hope we don't catch something, hanging out here every day." I knocked on the open door to Dr. Franklin's room and stepped inside. There was no one on his side of the room. "Do you think they sent him back to the cabin?"

"I doubt it," Mom said. "He's still way too weak."

We walked back down the hall to the nurse's station. A woman wearing dark blue scrubs was standing behind the counter, writing on a clipboard.

"Do you know where Richard Franklin is?" Mom asked.

The nurse pointed toward the hallway behind her with her pen, and then returned her attention to her clipboard. Mom and I exchanged a confused glance and turned down the hallway she had indicated. We immediately spotted Dr. Franklin, walking toward us. His steps were cautious, and he leaned heavily on a walker. An aide held onto the back of a wide belt around his waist and pulled a wheelchair behind him.

We had covered about half the distance to Dr. Franklin when he glanced up. His clenched jaw and tight frown relaxed briefly into a little smile.

"It's so good to see you on your feet," I said.

"Piece of cake," Dr. Franklin grunted, sliding his right foot forward.

Mom smiled. "The first steps are the hardest."

Dr. Franklin paused and took a deep breath. "That's what they keep telling me."

We joined him on his arduous journey down the hall. In contrast to Dr. Franklin's wing, most of the patients in this wing were infants or children. A lot of them were on oxygen, too.

"Seems like the hospital is pretty full," Mom said to the aide. "Is there a respiratory flu or something going around?"

The aide shrugged. "A lot of people with elevated heart rate and blood pressure. Doctors aren't sure what's causing it. Some think it's just the stress of living here. Others are afraid the atmosphere of the biosphere is failing."

I had thought, up to this point, that the Council was probably overreacting to a threat that didn't actually exist or one that wouldn't become a problem until the distant future. But the hospital was filling up, and some of the doctors thought it was because of the atmosphere. I looked at Mom. My new little niece or nephew might not be the only member of the family who was at risk.

I felt a renewed sense of urgency for my mission. "We should go. I want to collect some more samples before the workday is over."

I headed toward the main entrance. "Looking good, Dr. Franklin," I said over my shoulder.

There was a pause before I heard Mom's footsteps behind me, hurrying to catch up.

# 24

The next morning, Mom and I got to the ration building before sunrise. As soon as people started lining up at the locked doors, we started collecting samples. In most households, the same person picked up the rations each week. Still, we got quite a few samples from those we had missed the week before due to the sheer volume of people.

Our steps were light on the way home, despite the heavy load of DNA samples and rations we carried. Once we got home, though, my excitement at the success of our collection activities was replaced by anxiety. I had to leave the Bubble that night and meet Ashley in the same parking lot where I had been robbed and knocked unconscious. Everything within me resisted the thought of leaving. Even if it meant not meeting my thirty-day deadline and being subject to a harsher punishment from the Council, I did not want to go.

In desperation, I abandoned my packing and ran out of the house. Mom followed close behind me, continuing her twenty-four-hour surveillance. Though I knew I didn't have friends there anymore, I went to the police station.

The receptionist greeted me with a guarded smile. "What can I do for you, Christy?"

"Listen, Kate, I have to leave tonight, and—" I faltered "—the last time I was on the outside a bunch of guys knocked me out and took my gun and all my food." Saying it out loud brought back a flood of emotions and a sharp pain in the back of my head. "I need another pistol. I can't go back out there without any way to protect myself." Tears welled up. I tried to blink them away.

"What can you offer for payment?"

I had saved the proceeds from my mail delivery business for weeks before I'd had enough to purchase my first gun.

"Nothing," I said quietly, my eyes downcast. "But I'll pay you as soon as I can. You know I'm good for it."

"I'm sorry, Christy." Kate's eyes were compassionate, but her voice was firm. "We can't take IOUs."

"Okay, thanks," I mumbled, turning and quickly exiting the police station.

As soon as the door closed behind me, I burst into hysterical sobs. "I don't want to leave. They're going to hurt me again."

Mom held me in a tight hug. "You don't have to go, Sweetie. You can stay right here. I won't let them hurt you."

"But there's not enough food," I said through my tears. "And—and—they'll put me back in jail. And they'll kill the baby."

"What?" Mom pulled back, still holding me by the shoulders.

I realized my mistake, and my sobs stopped short.

"Nothing." I backpedaled. "Just a . . . a dream I had."

"Whose baby?" Mom asked.

"Nobody's. I don't know."

If Mom figured out Josh's secret, it could put his baby even more at risk.

We walked back to the house in silence. Mom kept her arm around my shoulders. I could tell she knew I was keeping something from her.

I finished packing without a word. Dad and Josh gave me goodbye hugs.

Mom walked me to the airlock. When it was time to say our goodbyes, she faced me and took me by the shoulders again.

"I don't care whose it is," she said, softly but emphatically. "You do what you need to, to save that baby."

I wrapped my arms around her. "I will."

She held me and combed her fingers through my hair. "Your dad and I pray for you every day. God's going to keep you safe. I know he will."

"Thank you," I whispered, giving her one more squeeze before entering the airlock.

# 25

Mom had succeeded in bringing my fear under control. Still, as I neared the spot where I'd been attacked, I felt panic creep in again.

"The Lord is my light and my salvation; whom should I fear?" I repeated the verse from Psalm 27 out loud, over and over again. "The Lord is my life's refuge; of whom should I be afraid?"

The sight of the ransacked Grand Cherokee I'd left in the car lot made my stomach turn and my heart race.

*Lord, you are my refuge. Take away my fear.*

As soon as I stopped the car and opened the door, Ashley nearly tackled me with a hug. "Oh, Christy, I'm so glad to see you. When I saw the SUV, I thought for sure you were killed or kidnapped or—I don't know. I can't believe you're okay."

"Watch the head," I cautioned, chuckling.

Ashley pulled back, gingerly. "Oh, did they hurt you? What did they do?"

"Just a little concussion." I touched the back of my head lightly. "No big deal."

"I shouldn't have left you here alone. I should have stayed with you until it was time for you to go back."

I shook my head. "It wouldn't have done any good. There were ten of them, and they had me surrounded before I even woke up. Besides, I needed you to get those samples back to Max. How are things going at the lab?"

"Great. The test protocol is up and running. We started testing the samples from the biosphere this morning. If you can spare the time, we could use your help in the lab."

"Sounds good. We got more than the thousand samples we were going for. Hopefully that's enough." I couldn't imagine the Council would have a problem if the list I gave them was a few short of three hundred. But then again, the Council did a lot of things I couldn't imagine until they happened.

"They filled me up before I left," I said. "Let's take my car."

Ashley loaded the belongings and supplies she brought into the Civic, and we hit the road. She offered to drive so I could sleep, but I knew the roads better, and I wanted to get there as soon as possible. It felt good to be moving.

I was grateful to have some one-on-one time with Ashley. We hadn't had a chance to talk—I mean really talk—since our drive back from Pueblo.

"I'm so glad you decided to come back to Lincoln," I said.

"Me too, most of the time." Ashley sighed. "But I feel like I'm so much farther away from my dad now. Like if he tried to find me, I might be just out of reach."

"When he sees the note we left at the house, nothing will stop him from finding you."

"Yeah, but what if the note gets lost? And travel is so difficult, what if he can't make it to Lincoln? What if he gets there, and I'm not home, and he gives up?" Ashley was close to tears.

"Your dad would never give up on you. He loves you."

Ashley's tears spilled over. "I love him, too, but I gave up. I left our home and my mother's grave. I got tired of waiting, and I left. What if he gets tired of looking?"

"You didn't give up, Ashley. You're living your life. That's what your mom and dad would want you to do."

"It's not fair. I miss them so much. I want to believe I'll see Dad again, but I don't want to spend the rest of my life waiting for something that might never happen."

"During our road trip, Max said to me 'It's okay to hold onto hope, but don't let it keep you from living your life.' I think he was right."

We rode in silence for a few miles, both of us lost in our thoughts. I believed what Max said was true, but was I acting on it? When I embraced my role as liaison between the cabin and biosphere communities, I felt like I had it all figured out. I was embracing the future. I even felt a little sorry for Ashley, who was stuck in the past, waiting at home for her father to return. But now, as I watched Ashley move on and create a new life for herself, I realized I was the one stuck in the past, desperately clinging to a futile hope. Were my feelings for Scott and my irrational belief that he was still alive keeping me from seeing the opportunities right in front of me?

"What else did Max say on your road trip?" Ashley asked.

I flinched. "What do you mean?"

"Well, it seemed like you guys were different when you got back, like something had changed between you."

I took a deep breath. "He kissed me."

I looked at Ashley. She nodded, her eyes still on the road.

"We were exhausted, and he took such good care of me after I burned my foot, and we were so excited we had found the bacteria." I turned to Ashley again. "I kissed him back."

She met my eyes with an expression of understanding and not a hint of shock or surprise.

"It felt amazing, and I didn't want it to end." The memory of the kiss brought a flush to my cheeks. "But it also felt wrong, so I pulled away."

"He's a good man."

"He is, and I know he loves me." I'd known it for a long time, but this was the first time I'd said it out loud. The ache in my chest intensified. "The last thing I wanted to do was hurt him."

"Do you love him?"

I thought of all the things he'd done for me and for Ashley, all the ways he'd taken care of us. "Yes, but not the way he wants me to. Not the way I love Scott."

We arrived in Lincoln late on Wednesday morning and went straight to the lab. Max showed me how to do the testing. The three of us worked together, with Max supervising and helping us to refine our technique. When he was confident we had it down, he suggested we work in shifts, so there would be someone there to record the results of each test as soon as it was finished.

I volunteered for the overnight shift since I was accustomed to staying awake at night when I was traveling. Max and Ashley agreed and sent me to Max's house to get some rest. I didn't find out until later that Max had been up all night working in the lab and needed the rest as much as I did.

It made me nervous going to the house alone. I wanted to suggest we bring in some blankets and sleep at the lab. But I knew we needed to keep an eye on Max's house. So I swallowed my fear and set out. The bright afternoon sunshine did little to bolster my courage. I had been attacked in broad daylight. No time or place seemed safe anymore.

Despite my fatigue, I slept lightly, jumping at every noise. The sun hadn't yet touched the horizon when I gave up on my efforts to get rest and went back to the lab. I was surprised and encouraged by how much Ashley and Max had gotten done while I was gone. Both working on little to no sleep, they left soon after my arrival.

I was alone again, but in the lab, it didn't seem as scary. No one had ever tried to break in while we were there; there wasn't anything in the lab of value to most people.

While not as cathartic as the firing range, the repetitive work of the lab did give me some time to think.

My mind drifted back to my first date with Scott. I'd thought we were just joining the rest of the choir for supper at Subway after Sunday night Mass. It wasn't until Scott paid for my meal that I realized it was something more. It might not have been what I'd imagined as the ideal first date, but somehow it was still perfect.

The results from the first samples tested would come in the next day. I just knew this test was my brother's ticket to a new life outside of the Bubble. I pictured Josh and Lauren building a house with their own hands, and Lauren rocking a baby while Josh prepared the land for planting with a horse-drawn plow.

I remembered what Mom had said to me before I left the Bubble. Even though she knew I was hiding things from her, she believed in me. She believed I would make the right choices. And she believed I could accomplish my goal, though she didn't even know exactly what it was. It boosted my confidence knowing my mom had that kind of faith in me.

The night flew by, while the results of my work accumulated on the table in front of me. Ashley returned early in the morning, and we worked together for a few hours. Max came around noon. We shared the lunch he had brought, and I went back to the house to sleep.

When I returned to the lab that evening, Ashley met me at the door.

"We got the results for your family." Ashley beamed. "Your mom and your brother are both survivors."

"But not Dad?" I asked.

Ashley shook her head.

"What about Lauren?"

Ashley looked at Max, still hard at work at his bench.

"It doesn't look like it," Max said.

"That can't be right." I hurried to Max's bench. "Lauren has to be a survivor."

"With three people in your family who can adapt to the atmosphere," Ashley said, "chances are pretty good the baby will be able to also."

"But if Lauren can't get out of the biosphere, the baby might never get that chance."

*Lord, do you want Josh's baby to die? Is this your will?*

If it was, I didn't want to have any part of it.

# 26

I continued going through the motions in the lab for a few more days. I appreciated my friends' dedication to helping me meet the Council's deadline, but I didn't see the point. What would it matter whether I was free or in jail if I couldn't save my brother's baby?

We hadn't finished the testing yet, but it was the day before Lauren's doctor's appointment and I felt compelled to go back to the Bubble. Maybe Josh and I could talk to Lauren's parents. Or I could try to get Lauren's appointment postponed. I wasn't sure what I could do to help, but I knew I couldn't do anything as long as I was hundreds of miles away.

I took the list of those who had tested positive, showing a predisposition to survival in the earth's new atmosphere—225 people so far. Perhaps if I gave this partial list to the Council, they would ease up on my restrictions, and I could more easily help Lauren and Josh.

The trip to the Bubble took longer than normal. I made several side-trips in search of untapped sources of gasoline. In addition to fueling my vehicle, I also needed to restock the gas supply we were using to keep the lab generator running.

I stopped at the biosphere checkpoint and popped the trunk for the vehicle inspection.

"What's in here?" The officer pointed at the red plastic

containers filling the trunk.

"Gas."

"We fill up your car every time you leave the biosphere. What do you need more gas for?"

"To fuel the generator I need to run the tests."

"What tests?"

My frustration mounted. "The DNA tests the Council has asked me to do."

The officer stared at me for a few seconds before retreating to the checkpoint booth. There he removed his oxygen mask and spoke with great animation into the radio on his shoulder.

After several minutes, appearing satisfied, he donned the mask and stepped out of the booth. "You will need to remove the containers from the vehicle before you can proceed."

Frustration turned to exasperation. I knew arguing would get me nowhere, so I began unloading the containers of gas, placing them along the side of the road. "You'll make sure nothing happens to them, right?"

The officer continued to watch me, silently.

By the time I finished emptying the vehicle, two more officers had arrived, both wearing oxygen backpacks and masks. I drove into the airlock under their watchful eyes, and they escorted me to the administration building. The security guard at the front desk put me on the Council's agenda for 1:00 p.m.

The officers followed me to my parents' house. Even

though it was three in the morning, they insisted on pounding on the door, waking my parents and Josh, to make sure someone would keep an eye on me. I was exhausted but still had trouble falling asleep. My mind kept bouncing around from one mediocre idea to another, trying to come up with an irrefutable plan to save my brother's baby. Lauren's appointment was in just a few hours. If I didn't figure something out soon, it might be her first and last prenatal check-up.

Despite my late arrival, I was up as soon as I heard movement in the bedroom. Mom was first out of the bedroom. I had hoped she would sleep in, so I could talk to Josh in private before he started work. Now that she was awake, I knew she wouldn't be more than a few steps away from me the rest of the day.

Josh and Dad joined us at the table for breakfast several minutes later.

"I need to stretch my legs this morning," I said to Josh. "Okay if I walk with you to work?"

I often accompanied Josh on the way to or from work when I was in the Bubble. It gave us the chance to catch up without other listening ears around. In fact, the first time I met Lauren was when I joined Josh after work, and we stopped at the school and walked Lauren home.

Josh's eyes shifted toward Mom and back to me. He

frowned and raised one eyebrow.

If I joined Josh on the walk to work, that meant Mom would be tagging along, too. I could tell he didn't want Mom chaperoning while he walked Lauren to school.

"Josh can keep tabs on me," I said to Mom. "I'll be back within an hour."

"You know that's not enough," Mom said. "You'll be walking back alone. There's a pretty high risk that someone will spot you and tell the authorities."

"Okay, fine," I said.

Dad put his dishes in the sink and gave Mom a kiss.

"I love you," Mom said. "Have a good day."

"I love you, too." Dad put on his jacket and went outside.

Dad and Mom had always shared a goodbye kiss in the morning, but I didn't remember them saying "I love you" as often back at home in Sioux Falls. It was good to hear them say it.

Mom stood and picked up her dishes. I followed her to the sink.

"Listen," I said, keeping my voice low, "Josh and I like to talk about . . . stuff when we walk together. If you could just hang back a little, I'd really appreciate it."

She looked hurt, but she nodded.

I turned back toward the table. "Ready to head to work?"

"I guess." Josh sighed.

Mom kept her word and stayed a few steps behind us. But I knew she wasn't fully out of earshot, so I spoke softly and chose my words carefully.

"Did you talk to Lauren's parents about postponing the appointment?" I asked.

"Lauren tried to convince them it was just the flu and it was getting better," Josh said, "but she throws up every morning at six-thirty like clockwork. Her Mom knows, and nothing we could say would convince her otherwise."

"Did you try telling them the whole story?"

Josh shook his head. "We couldn't risk it. If they started talking—whether it was because they believed us or because they thought we were crazy—then everyone would know about Lauren's . . . condition."

I glanced back at Mom. She was waving to a woman who had just come out of her house. It didn't look like she was paying any attention to us.

"Her appointment is this morning," I said.

"I know," Josh said loudly.

I looked back again. Mom walked faster, her attention now firmly fixed on the two of us.

"What are you going to do?" I whispered.

"She's going to try to convince the doctor it's something else," Josh said, "like an allergy or something."

"They do a blood test," I said. "You can't fake a blood test."

Josh's face went white.

But that wasn't the only way to know if someone was pregnant.

I grabbed Josh's arm. "I've got an idea. Just follow along."

I turned around. "Mom, Lauren's got a doctor's appointment this morning, and her Mom can't take her because she has to work. I think we should go with her."

Mom shrugged. "That's fine. As long as we're back in time for your appointment with the Council."

"Great," I said. "We'll swing by and pick her up before we drop Josh off at work."

I faced Josh. There was still worry in his eyes, but one corner of his mouth turned up.

"I got this," I said.

*I sure hope this works.*

Lauren opened the door as soon as we knocked. Her eyes widened when she saw me but a smile appeared as soon as she spotted Josh next to me.

She was ready to step out, but I stayed right in front of the door, leaving her nowhere to go.

"Mom and I wanted to come with you to your doctor's appointment," I said, "you know, for a little moral support."

I put my foot on the threshold. She stepped back, and I stepped in.

"I just remembered, though, that I forgot something at home." I walked to the kitchen. "I just need to borrow a small container with a lid—maybe a jar or a container for leftovers."

I opened a cupboard door. "You don't mind, do you? I'll return it as soon as I'm done."

I closed the door and opened two more. "This'll work." I pulled out an empty glass jar with a pizza sauce label that was half gone and a metal lid.

I turned around. Ignoring the confusion on Josh's face and the appalled expression on Mom's, I asked Lauren, "Do you have some paper and a pen I could borrow as well?"

She pointed to the table next to the couch.

I opened the drawer of the end table. "Perfect." I pulled out two sheets of paper and a pen. "Thanks so much."

I put the items in my backpack and walked to the door. "We're going to drop Josh off at work first, and then we'll take you to the doctor's office."

I held the door and motioned for Mom to go out. I followed her and began walking briskly down the street.

She fell in step beside me. "What was that all about?" Her volume was low, but her tone was sharp.

"Sorry," I said. "I just forgot a couple things I'm going to need today, and I knew we didn't have a lot of time before Josh had to be at work. I'm sure Lauren and her parents don't mind."

"That doesn't mean it's okay for you to barge into their house and help yourself to their things."

"I really do need the things I took, and I promise I'll return them all. I'll explain it all." I glanced back at Lauren and Josh. "I just can't do it right now."

When we reached the rations building, I tried to convince Mom that we should wait around the corner from the employee entrance, but she insisted on staying near the door.

Josh and Lauren shared a hug and a quick peck on the lips, and Josh went inside. Lauren turned toward us, her lower lip trembling. I wanted to tell her my plan, to ease her fears, but I couldn't say anything with Mom standing right there.

I put my arm around her shoulders and gave a squeeze. "Now, let's get you to the doctor and see what he can do about this pesky flu."

I kept chattering all the way to the hospital, trying to keep Lauren's mind off of what was coming. Despite my best efforts, the color drained from her face, leaving it white as a hospital sheet. When the outpatient entrance came into view, she stopped walking.

"It's going to be all right," I whispered. "I'll make sure everything works out."

She swallowed, looked at me, and nodded. We resumed our walk toward the entrance, moving a little slower this time.

I held the door open for her, and Lauren and I walked up to the reception desk together.

"Lauren Cosgrove here for an eight o'clock appointment," I said.

The receptionist's fingers flew rapid-fire over her keyboard. She paused, watching her screen, and then looked up. "You're all checked in." She smiled. "You can have a seat."

I leaned forward and lowered my voice. "Could you direct me to the public restroom?"

She pointed toward her right. "Down to the end of that hallway, then turn left. You'll see it right there."

"Thank you."

I turned to Mom. "We're going to the restroom. We'll be right back."

"I'm good," Lauren said. "I'll just wait out here."

I took her gently by the elbow. "No, I need you to come with me."

Lauren looked at me, her head tilted to the side.

"Please." I started down the hallway. "I'll explain later."

We walked into the bathroom. I scanned the ceiling and walls for any sign of a security camera. I didn't really know what I was looking for, but I didn't see anything that looked suspicious.

The first two stalls were occupied. I couldn't risk saying anything out loud. I motioned Lauren to go in the last stall, and I took the stall next to hers. I took off my backpack, pulled out the pen and paper, and tore off a small strip.

"I have a plan," I scrawled. I slid the paper under the partition between the stalls.

"Before we leave, you need to flush all of these pieces of paper."

Lauren picked up each note as soon as I slid it across.

"When the doctor asks for a blood sample, pretend you are scared of needles—not just scared, terrified. Scream if you have to."

The toilet in the stall on the other side of mine flushed. I waited until I heard water running at the sink before passing the next note.

"They'll ask for a urine sample. When you go in the bathroom to get the sample, you'll pour my urine in the specimen cup instead."

"Understand?" I wrote this on a larger piece of paper and passed both the pen and the paper to Lauren.

I pulled out the jar I had gotten from Lauren's kitchen and sat down on the toilet.

*Lord, I hope this works.*

I was so nervous, I had trouble going.

The paper and pen slid across the floor toward me.

"Do you think it will work?" Lauren had written.

"You have to sell it," I wrote. "If they try to force you to do the blood draw, promise them you'll come back and do it later, when your mom can be here with you."

I put the paper on the floor and then picked it up again.

"You can do it!" I wrote in big letters across the bottom. I slid the paper into Lauren's stall.

I took a deep breath and tried to relax. I was finally able to produce the sample I needed. I secured the lid on the top of the jar and wiped off the outside with toilet paper. I slid the jar under the partition.

I heard the sound of paper tearing and then the flush of the toilet in Lauren's stall. I stepped out and joined her at the sink. I smiled at her in the mirror. She still looked scared but gave me a tentative smile.

We returned to the waiting room and sat next to Mom. I was afraid if I said anything, I would give something away. I flipped through a magazine, occasionally offering Lauren an encouraging smile.

A nurse stepped through the door beside the reception desk. "Lauren Cosgrove," she announced.

I jumped to my feet. Lauren was slower to rise.

"Do you want us to come in with you?"

She shook her head. "I think it'll be easier if I'm by myself."

I squeezed her hand. "We'll be right here waiting."

I watched her walk into the hallway where the exam rooms were. When the door closed behind her, I felt like everything was suddenly out of my control. This could be the moment when they would try to kill my brother's baby. I had done everything I could, but I didn't know if it was enough.

I wanted to follow her. I wanted to be there with her to make sure nothing happened to her or to the baby. I was scared. I couldn't do anything sitting in the waiting room.

I knew, though, that I couldn't do anything more, even if I went in with Lauren. The doctor would send me out like he did when I was there with Jessica. It was all completely out of my hands.

Somebody more powerful was going to have to take over. That's when I remembered. There was something more that I could do.

*Father, I turn this whole situation over to you. Surround Lauren and her baby with your angels. Keep them safe. Protect them from any evil intentions. I know you are Lord over all things. You can act where I am powerless.*

How many times in recent months had I tried to do everything myself, tried to stay in control? When was the last time I truly put my trust in God?

*Jesus, I trust in you. Hold Lauren in your care. Blind the doctors to the truth about her pregnancy. Give Lauren the courage to keep her baby safe.*

"No! No needles!" The hysterical scream passed through several walls and was clearly heard in the waiting room. Everyone in the room looked up. Glances were exchanged—some worried, others amused.

Mom looked at me, her eyes wide. "Is that Lauren?"

I nodded. "She told me in the bathroom that she's deathly afraid of needles. It'll be all right. I'm sure they can find some other way to do the tests they need."

I stifled a smile. I'd had no idea what a good actress Lauren was.

I didn't hear any more screams. I started to get nervous again. What if she had given in? If they got a blood test from her, it would all be over.

*Jesus.* I took a slow breath in.

*I trust in you.* I let all my air out.

I repeated that mantra until my pounding heart calmed.

Mom stood. I looked up and saw Lauren walking toward us, a huge grin on her face.

I hurried to her. "What did the doctor say?"

Lauren assumed a serious expression. "He thinks it's stress-related. He gave me some pills for nausea and anxiety. If it's not better in a couple weeks, he said to come back and he'd give me a recommendation for a good counselor."

"That's wonderful." I gave Lauren a hug.

Over Lauren's shoulder, I noticed Mom's confused expression.

I quickly added ". . . that they finally figured out what was wrong."

We walked to the door.

"Do you want company on your way to school?" I asked.

Lauren shook her head. "No. I'm good."

I had a feeling she might not be headed straight to school. I was glad. I knew Josh was worried sick by now. It would do him good to hear the news from her.

# 27

Mom and I had just started cleaning up the lunch dishes when there was a sharp knock on the door. I dried my hands and opened the door. Two officers stood outside.

"Time for your appearance before the Council," one of the officers said.

"Oh. Okay." I didn't realize I was going to have a police escort.

I pulled on a jacket. One officer tapped his toe. The other checked his watch. I slung my backpack over one shoulder.

"Ready," I said, smiling at the officers.

They exchanged an annoyed look and stepped to the side. I passed between them and started down the street. I had only taken a few steps when one of the officers grabbed my elbow and doubled his speed, forcing me to jog to keep up. We reached the administration building with twenty minutes to spare. I didn't know why the officers were in such a hurry.

After a short night's sleep and an anxiety-filled morning, I was grateful for a few moments to relax in the anteroom. I must have dozed off while we were waiting. When word came that the Council was ready for me, the officers grabbed my arms and pulled me to my feet. I reflexively pulled away. One of the officers twisted my arm behind my back. The pain dropped me to my knees. He hoisted me onto my feet. It felt like my shoulder was going to pop out of its socket.

"Okay, okay," I said. "I'm sorry."

The officer eased his upward pressure but still kept my forearm pinned against my back, using it to propel me into the council chamber. The officers pushed me into the chair in the center of the room and assumed their posts on either side of me, so close I couldn't shift my weight without touching one of them, causing a heavy hand to come down on my shoulder.

"I trust you have some good news for us, Ms. Phillips." Chairman Lambrecht crossed his arms, looking as if good news was the last thing he expected to hear.

"Oh—yes." I fumbled to open my backpack.

I stood to give the list to Chairman Lambrecht. Two hands forced me back into the chair. One of the officers took the list from me and handed it to the chairman.

"Our early tests have produced this list of people who are likely to be able to survive outside the biosphere."

The chairman flipped through the list. "How many names?"

"Two hundred twenty-five, sir." I quickly added, "But there is more testing in progress. We anticipate adding several more names to the list."

"You only have one more week."

"Yes, sir. I believe we can finish the list in one week."

The chairman summoned his secretary and handed her the list. "Draft a letter to each of these individuals, informing them they will be moving out of the USCSBS in two days. They can bring with them any belongings they can carry."

I scooted to the edge of the chair, alarmed. "But you can't do that!"

The officers grabbed my shoulders and pushed me back. My neck struck the top of the chair, and my head whipped back. Darkness crowded my vision. I blinked several times, trying to keep it from overtaking me. I took a deep breath. The secretary had almost reached the door, holding the list I created that had just turned lethal.

In desperation, I yelled, "They'll die if you kick them out."

"Ms. Phillips." Chairman Lambrecht's sharp tone silenced me. "You will continue to be denied access to services, including rations, until you produce the remaining seventy-five names." He pounded his gavel. "You are dismissed."

The officers pulled me to my feet and dragged me toward the door.

I made one last plea over my shoulder. "You can't tear these families—"

One of the officers thumped me on the back of the head. Searing pain shot through my head. My legs crumpled, and the world went dark.

# 28

I somehow ended up on the couch in my parents' house. I drifted in and out of sleep for hours. When I was awake, all I could do was sob and say, "I'm so sorry. It's all my fault."

Going to Yellowstone, developing the genetic test—that had all been a mistake. God had tried to tell me that wasn't what I was supposed to be doing, but I ignored the little voice inside and did what I wanted instead. My throbbing headache intensified. I whimpered and pressed my hands against my temples.

Mom was immediately at my side. She held my head up and coaxed me to drink something. It burned my throat and made me cough, but after a few minutes it dulled the pounding in my head, and I was able to get some restful sleep.

When I awoke early the next morning, the fog clouding my brain had started to clear. I only had one day to figure out how to save the lives of 225 people. I chastised myself for wasting a day. I had made this mess. I needed to fix it.

I moved to Josh's bed and gently shook him awake.

"Josh, I need to talk to you," I whispered.

He sat up, rubbing the sleep from his eyes. I handed him a coat and motioned for him to follow me outside.

"You were a basket case last night." Josh yawned. "What was wrong with you?"

"Yeah, sorry about that. A few too many knocks to the head, I guess."

"So, what's with the early wake-up call?"

I lowered my voice. "You know the DNA samples Mom and I collected?"

Josh nodded.

"Well, the Council is using the test results to force people out of the biosphere."

"What?"

I could hear the accusation in Josh's voice.

"I didn't know that's what they were going to do with the results—I asked them, and they wouldn't tell me."

"That didn't clue you in to the fact that it probably wasn't anything good?"

"I'm sorry. You're right, I should have known. But I wanted to save your baby, and I couldn't do that if I was in prison or dead. I didn't think I had a choice."

"Are you going to save my baby?"

I turned away. That question was the reason I pulled Josh out of bed, but I didn't want to say the words.

I faced him again. "Josh, your test was positive, but Lauren's was not. She's going to have to stay in the biosphere."

"No. No. She can't stay." Josh's voice cracked. "I will not let them take our baby."

I put my hand on his arm. He pulled away and stepped back.

"I know Dad's always backed the Council." I imitated Dad's voice. " 'Without them, we'd all be dead,' 'They're doing what's best for the community,' and all that. But as soon as he hears that they're kicking you and Mom out, he'll turn into the Council's biggest opponent. Wait until they get the letter about the forced evacuations, and then tell Mom and Dad what the government is doing to unwed mothers. They'll believe you. I'm sure they will. And they'll let you get married. You have to do it today. That's the only way you can save your baby. Tomorrow you're going to have to leave the biosphere."

"I will not leave Lauren," Josh said through gritted teeth. "I can't keep her safe if there's a wall between us."

"I'm so sorry, Josh. I never meant for this to happen."

I wanted to stay and comfort him, but as long as he blamed me, my presence would only be an aggravation. Besides, I needed to get away from the house before Mom woke up and resumed her police-mandated surveillance.

I pulled my coat tight around me. Even in the stagnant environment of the Bubble, the morning air still held a touch of the crisp smell of winter. I hurried toward the hospital.

Visiting hours hadn't started yet. I waited in the shadows outside the hospital, watching through the glass doors. When the security guard was deep in conversation with another employee, I slipped inside.

I strode through the halls as if I belonged there, nodding to the nurses I passed. A few responded with confused looks, but no one tried to stop me. I tapped lightly on Dr. Franklin's door, entered the room, and closed the door.

Dr. Franklin was sitting up in bed, reading by the light of his bedside lamp. His roommate was snoring in the darkness on the far side of the room.

"Christy." Dr. Franklin took off his reading glasses. "Isn't this a little early for you? I remember how much you loved our 6:00 a.m. trips to the cabin."

I smiled. It was good to see Dr. Franklin getting his strength and sense of humor back. Though, come to think of it, when I was in his class I didn't believe he had a sense of humor.

"I need your help." I kept my voice low to avoid disturbing his roommate. "We don't have much time."

"What's going on?" Dr. Franklin set his book aside.

"My friend, Max, developed a genetic test to determine who is likely to be able to survive in the new atmosphere. I asked him to do it so I could help my brother. But now the Council is going to use that information to kick a bunch of people out of the biosphere. I tried to tell them that wouldn't work, but they wouldn't listen to me.

"I need you to develop a plan for acclimatization, show it to one of your doctors—someone who would understand why gradual exposure would be more likely to work than sudden exposure—and ask him to present it to the Council.

"It has to be done today. They're planning on making everyone leave tomorrow, including my mom and my brother. Can you help us?"

Dr. Franklin already had his glasses on and a pad of paper in his lap. "Tell me more about the airlock."

"I don't know much about it."

"How big is it? How do they regulate the composition of

the air inside?"

"It's big enough a large pickup truck or cargo van can turn around inside it. The ceiling is maybe fifteen feet tall. After I come into the airlock from the outside, big fans run for four or five minutes before I can open the door to the biosphere."

"Alright, I'm going to need you to get more information about the airlock." Dr. Franklin made a list along the left margin of his pad of paper. "Find out the total volume, how they monitor the composition of the air inside, and whether they can control the amount of air coming in from the outside."

He tore the top sheet off the pad and handed it to me. "Meanwhile, I will write up the parameters for acclimatization. My primary doctor rounds first thing. I'll talk to him right away this morning. Get that information back to me as soon as you can. Once my doctor starts his office hours, he probably won't be able to get away until after the council session has ended."

I was thrilled Dr. Franklin was willing to help but concerned about my ability to obtain the information he needed. I could hardly find anyone who would give me the time of day. I didn't know how I could talk someone into giving me detailed schematics of the inner workings of the airlock.

I decided to take the same technique that had gotten me through the hospital halls before visiting hours: pretending I was there doing my job. I used the walk to the airlock to practice my approach.

After getting the attention of the airlock operator, I launched into my speech. "I'm sure the Council has informed you of the plan to transport a number of residents out of the biosphere tomorrow."

The operator nodded, hesitantly.

"I helped the Council compile the list of residents, so I am responsible for making sure the transition to the outside is successful. In order to do that, I need some information about the airlock." I didn't think it necessary to mention I had assumed that responsibility of my own accord, without the knowledge or approval of the Council.

"What do you need to know?" The operator still looked skeptical. She had seen me entering the biosphere under the custody of two officers and knew from internal communications that my access to biosphere services was still restricted.

"Total volume of the airlock," I said, my pen poised to write.

"Fifteen thousand cubic feet."

"How is the composition of the air inside monitored?"

"A gauge shows us the relative concentration of oxygen."

"What is the process for returning the atmosphere in the airlock to the composition of the air in the biosphere?"

"I can't give you that information."

"That information is critical for a successful transition tomorrow." I leaned over the counter separating us. "The lives of almost three hundred people depend on it."

I could see the struggle in her face. I kept my eyes locked on hers.

She finally gave in to my request. "Fans on either side of the loading dock bring in air from the biosphere, while fans in the ceiling expel the lighter air outside."

"Is there any way to control the volume of air entering the airlock from the outside?"

"No. Air only enters the airlock from the outside through the garage doors. There's no way to control it."

"Thank you for the information." I dropped my commanding tone. "It will help us to make sure those people stay safe."

I hurried back to the hospital. The eastern sky glowed orange. I hoped I wasn't too late to catch Dr. Franklin's doctor. I waited outside until the security guard was distracted. I slipped through the door undetected.

I had just turned the corner toward Dr. Franklin's room when the security guard's voice stopped me. "Where do you think you're going?"

I turned toward the guard and held up the piece of paper. "Delivering some test results."

The guard walked toward me. "Let me see that."

I knew it would be all over if I let the guard get ahold of the paper. I could only see one viable option. I turned and sprinted down the hall.

"Stop her!" the guard yelled. A clatter of footsteps exploded on the tile behind me. It sounded like the entire hospital was chasing me.

I burst into Dr. Franklin's room and threw the paper at him. "Hide it!"

I darted out of the room and continued down the hall. I knew I couldn't avoid capture, but I hoped to minimize the chance of casting suspicion on Dr. Franklin. I turned into another patient room and clasped the hand of the stranger lying unconscious in the first bed.

"I love you, Grandma," I said.

The security guard wrenched my arms behind my back and pushed me into the hallway.

"I'll come back as soon as I can," I yelled over my shoulder.

# 29

The security guard propelled me down the hallway to his desk by the front door. With one hand firmly holding my wrists behind my back, he used the other to radio the police dispatcher.

Within minutes two officers appeared—the same officers who'd handled my arrival and appearance before the Council the day before. They did not look happy to see me. One officer tied a cord tight around my wrists. The other pushed me roughly through the door.

I'd hoped they would return me home, to my mother's supervision. But we were walking in the opposite direction.

"Where are we going?" I asked.

The officers didn't respond.

The administration building loomed ahead. If I had to appear before the Council again, I was sure my sentence would be death or imprisonment.

"Look, I'm really sorry. I just wanted to visit a friend."

The officers were silent.

I breathed a sigh of relief when we passed the administration building.

We turned down the street leading to the airlock.

"Wait, I need to see my family. Take me back home, and I promise I won't sneak out again."

The officers exchanged a glance. I hoped they were considering my request. Instead, they sped up. I scrambled to stay on my feet.

The airlock operator's mouth fell open, and her eyebrows shot up when she saw me with the two officers.

"Ms. Phillips will be leaving now," one of the officers said, curtly.

The officers escorted me into the airlock and forced me into the driver's seat of the Civic. Only then did they cut the cord securing my wrists. They returned to the biosphere. The garage door leading to the outside opened.

I burst into tears. If Dr. Franklin didn't succeed in getting a message to the Council, Mom and Josh would be dead tomorrow, and it would be my fault. And I didn't even get to say goodbye. Josh's baby would be killed soon. I would only get to see Dad again if I provided the Council with another list of survivors, so they could rip them away from their families.

I looked over my shoulder at the open garage door. I had a feeling once I went out that door I would never see my family again. But I didn't have a choice. I backed out of the airlock, my vision blurred by tears. I watched the garage door close and the rock wall slide shut. It felt like my heart was caught between the rocks, squeezed so hard it could barely beat.

When my tears finally dried, I turned the car around and drove to the checkpoint. I put the containers of gas back in the car, though there was no need to keep the lab up and running anymore. I was not going to do any more testing for the Council. I would not be responsible for getting even one more person kicked out of the Bubble.

*Nothing that I've tried has worked, God. Why do I even bother? What's the point?*

I didn't want to go back to Lincoln. I didn't have anything to deliver to the cabin. I could pick up some mail, but I would probably never be able to get it to its destination. More than that, though, I didn't want to tell Ashley and Max the long hours they'd invested day after day to help me had accomplished nothing we'd hoped for.

When I reached Interstate 80, I impulsively turned toward the west. I wanted more than anything to find Scott. If only I could feel his arms around me again, I would be able to make it through whatever the future held. Maybe Scott was at his uncle's house in Reno. His parents had stayed there when they had to evacuate because of the California earthquakes. Or maybe he and his parents had made it back home to Pasadena.

But even if I could make it to Reno or Pasadena, I would have no idea where to begin looking. I didn't know Scott's address or his uncle's. I could ask around, but that would more likely lead to me getting robbed or shot than to me finding Scott.

Continuing to drive west was not going to lead me to the man of my dreams or make my problems disappear. Instead, it would lead to an empty gas tank, leaving me stranded, far from everyone I loved.

I turned around.

*Lord, I want to hold on. I want to see Scott again. But if*

*Scott is gone, please give me the strength to let him go.*

The return trip to Lincoln took longer than usual. Though I wanted to see Ashley and Max again, I dreaded the conversation I would have to have with them. I chose crowded roads where I had to slow down to navigate around obstacles, delaying the inevitable as long as I could. When I got to Max's house, I sat in the car for several minutes, trying to muster the courage to go inside.

When I finally knocked on the door, their warm and excited greeting made the story pour out of me. I told them about my appearance before the Council, my conversations with Josh and Dr. Franklin, and my subsequent expulsion from the Bubble.

"I don't know what's going to happen to the people on that list or to my brother's baby. I can't go back without bringing another list of names to the Council. And I will never ever give them even one more name.

"I'm so sorry I dragged you into this. I thought we were going to help the people in the Bubble to survive. I had no idea the Council would just kick people out."

"You didn't drag us into this," Max said, gently. "We wanted to help."

Ashley nodded. "And we would do it again for the possibility that we might be able to save your little niece or nephew."

We shared a group hug. I couldn't put into words how relieved I felt, knowing Ashley and Max didn't blame me for what had happened or resent their involvement.

"There is one other way you could get back to the biosphere," Max said, "if you're able to bring them the information they requested on how they can improve their atmospheric conversion system."

"That's right." In my zeal for the possibilities of genetic testing, I had forgotten about my original mission. "Ashley, we'll go to the cabin tomorrow and see if they've found anyone who can help. Max, can you ask around the market tomorrow to see if you can find any chemical or mechanical engineers?"

Max and Ashley traded a knowing smile as if I had brought up an inside joke.

"Already done," Ashley said. "While Max was developing the genetic test, I was scouring the city for engineers. I found three people who are willing to help, but they're asking for a lot in return."

"What do they want?" I asked.

"One of them wants adapted seed, horses, and horse-drawn farming equipment," Ashley said. "Another is asking for a six-month supply of food and fresh water. And the other one will only help if he has the chance to talk to his daughter, who is in the biosphere."

"They're asking a lot," I said.

"They're offering us high-level knowledge that could save a lot of lives," Max said. "They probably felt like that gave them some bargaining power."

"There's no way the three of us can meet all of those demands," I said. "Hopefully, the people at the cabin want to resume trade with the biosphere bad enough to help us make those payments.

"I don't know about that last one, though. The Council would never let anyone get close enough to talk to someone inside the Bubble, even by walkie-talkie. Would he settle for exchanging letters?"

Ashley shook her head. "He insisted on talking to his daughter. He would not accept anything else."

"Well," I said, "I hope Dr. Franklin found two other engineers who could help before he got sick."

We spent the rest of the evening painstakingly reproducing the schematics and information about the atmospheric conversion system, so we could give each of the engineers a copy. The tedious work hardly seemed like work at all, because of the great company. Gratitude for good friends and hope that I would see my family again reinflated my crushed heart.

# 30

Ashley and I awoke early, leaving Lincoln before sunrise. We waited outside the cabin until we saw light coming from the windows. The light was dim and flickering.

"Do you think they're out of propane?" I didn't hear the familiar rumble of the generator.

"That or just trying to conserve it," Ashley said.

We knocked on the front door of the cabin.

Megan answered the door. "Ashley, Christy, it's so good to see you." She gave us each a hug. "Come in."

My heart swelled with gratitude. I smiled at Ashley. We were finally welcomed into the cabin without suspicion or reservation.

She held the door open for us. "How's Dr. Franklin doing?"

"He's getting stronger every day," I said.

"I'm glad to hear it." Megan followed us down the hall.

We stopped at the door to the common room, which was buzzing with activity. People were rearranging furniture and assembling cardboard dividers on the tables. Someone squeezed past us carrying a large box and placed it near the door. I sensed anticipation and excitement in the people's actions and faces. Under the light of the candles, even the shadows danced.

"What's going on in there?" Ashley asked.

Megan grinned. "It's election day. We're choosing representatives to serve as our governing body and voting on articles for our constitution."

"You've been busy since I was here last," I said.

Megan laughed. "We had to work fast. We didn't want anyone thinking they could step in and take over Dr. Franklin's role as supreme ruler."

Megan had been one of the leaders of the Survival Skills Club, the group organized by Dr. Franklin to help students prepare for the Change. I was surprised to hear her refer to Dr. Franklin's leadership in a negative light.

"Speaking of Dr. Franklin," I said, "do you know if he found anyone with ideas about how to modify the biosphere's atmospheric conversion system before he got sick?"

"I'm not sure," Megan said. "Brad's been following up on that. Let me go get him."

Megan disappeared into the kitchen at the end of the hall.

I turned back toward the common room, admiring the commotion. "Elections—that's awesome. I hope they're able to come up with something that works."

"It's got to be better than Dr. Franklin's dictatorship," Ashley said.

"I don't know. I felt like Dr. Franklin did have the best interests of the community in mind when he made decisions. Not all elected officials share that same focus."

"You mean the chairman of the Council?"

"Sometimes it seems like he wants what's best for the people, but other times it just seems like he wants the power and prestige that go along with the position."

"Hello, ladies." Brad walked down the hall with Megan close behind. "Welcome to the Democratic Republic of the Cabin."

Ashley laughed. "The first job for the new government should be coming up with a catchier name."

Brad opened the door to the library, across the hall from the common room. "Let's talk in here, where it's a little quieter."

We stepped into the dimly lit room. There were no candles in the library. The large picture window let in a little light from the earliest rays of the morning sun.

Brad closed the door. "Megan tells me you were asking about the last request we got from the biosphere. I'm afraid Dr. Franklin wasn't able to make much progress on the assignment before he got sick. We've continued to work on it since he left, giving it a high priority on the list of tasks for our resource acquisition teams. So far, they've only found one mechanical engineer who could help. Here are her recommendations." Brad handed me several sheets of paper covered in scrawled handwritten notes.

Megan motioned around the room. "We've started conserving fuel to make sure we have enough for winter, just in case we aren't able to resume trade with the biosphere by then."

"We found three engineers in Lincoln who might be able to help," Ashley said, "but they're demanding a pretty steep price. Would you guys be willing to help cover the cost?"

"We want to start trading with the biosphere again," Brad said, "but I can't authorize any distribution of our resources. You'll have to take it up with the new government. Come back tomorrow afternoon. I'll see if I can get you on the agenda."

A few people stopped us on our way out to give me letters to deliver. I told each of them I didn't know how soon I would be able to return to the biosphere, but I would keep their letters safe until they reached their destination.

We stopped at the farmhouse before going back to Lincoln. The sight of the faded note we had left on the front door for Ashley's dad brought a lump to my throat. Even if I never saw my family again, I had already spent several more months with them than Ashley'd had with her parents. I felt horribly selfish for focusing only on my loss. Ashley was working hard to give me the chance to see my family again. But she could only wait and hope she might someday see her dad again.

I put my arm around her shoulders. Tears filled her eyes, but she was still able to flash me a smile.

We collected some things we might be able to trade at the market and drove back to Lincoln. We walked from the car to Antelope Valley Parkway, the street where most of the market vendors set up their booths. Turning onto the street, Ashley stopped short. I looked up. The usually bustling thoroughfare was nearly empty. There were only a handful of tables set up, and their proprietors looked quite bored.

"Was there some violence or something this week?" I asked.

"The market's been busy all week," Ashley said. "I didn't hear about any violence. Maybe something happened yesterday afternoon after we packed up our booth."

We began walking slowly down the street, alert for any other signs that something was amiss.

We hadn't walked a block when it dawned on me. "What's today's date?"

"Um, the twenty-fourth, I think."

"Thursday, November twenty-fourth. Ashley, today is Thanksgiving."

"You're right." Ashley laughed. "I had no idea. Happy Thanksgiving."

We hurried through the market, scanning the booths that were open, and making trades where we could. The vendors were eager for business, so we made a few good deals. But with limited selection, we didn't get the quantity we were looking for.

Within a couple hours, we were back at Max's house. We scanned the contents of the pantry. We couldn't find any turkey or cranberries, but we did manage to locate some canned chicken and instant potatoes, a can of gravy, and a box of Stove Top stuffing. It was by no means the feast we were accustomed to enjoying on Thanksgiving. But, as I shared it with Max and Ashley, I realized I had a lot to be thankful for.

We headed back to the market with more items for trade as soon as the sun was up the next morning. The pushy salespeople and hurrying customers were back. Only it seemed like everyone was more cheerful than normal. Taking a day out to be thankful can do wonders for a person's mood.

We focused on trading for food and water. By noon the trunk of the Civic was one-third full. It wasn't enough to meet the engineer's demands, but it was a start.

Ashley and I returned to the cabin. Though my previous experiences made me nervous about the prospect of standing before another governing body, I was excited to see who had been elected and how the new government functioned.

We were on the agenda for the Board of Representatives at one thirty. While we waited, we had time to catch up with other people at the cabin. I collected a few more letters for delivery to the biosphere. I felt a new sense of freedom, walking through the cabin and grounds without Dr. Franklin's judgmental scrutiny and constraints.

After checking out the greenhouse, we came in the back door and found Angela in the kitchen cleaning up the lunch dishes. We shared a soapy hug, and Ashley and I grabbed a couple of dishtowels to help out.

"How are the wedding plans coming?" Ashley asked.

Angela giggled. "It is so not the wedding I've imagined since I was five, but I'm having so much fun. We got ahold of an old treadle sewing machine, and Sue is making a dress for me out of worn-out clothes and sheets."

"Your very own coat of many colors," I said.

"Ryan and I have been working every night on decorations and centerpieces. And Ryan is writing the service. Though, with his new job on the Board of Representatives, he hasn't had a lot of time to work on it."

"He was elected to the Board?" I asked.

Angela nodded, with a proud smile. "The youngest member."

"That's awesome," Ashley said.

Angela's excitement was contagious. I couldn't wait to see her walk down the aisle in her one-of-a-kind wedding dress. At the same time, I felt a stab of jealousy. Angela seemed to have it all together. She was beautiful and talented. She got to live in the security of the cabin, no longer subject to Dr. Franklin's strict rules and harsh punishments. And on top of that, she was eagerly making plans to marry Mr. Right (actually, Ryan's last name was Wright).

I wanted that—all of it. I wanted to live where I was surrounded by friends who had my back; where I didn't have to be constantly on guard. I wanted a voice like Angela's. I wanted to sit down with Scott and make centerpieces while we talked about spending the rest of our lives together.

Only I doubted I could talk Scott into making centerpieces with me unless they required geometric calculations or used a Fibonacci sequence. But I would love to hear what Scott would come up with if he were writing our wedding service. Knowing his sense of humor, I was sure it would be the most memorable wedding any of my friends had ever seen.

When the dishes were finished, we moved into the hallway to await our turn in front of the Board. At one twenty, the administrative assistant called us into the library. I saw several familiar faces on the Board. I wasn't surprised to see Brad and Megan there. Both had been respected leaders within the group even before the Change. I spotted Ryan and gave him a discreet thumbs-up. I recognized a couple of my professors from Gerald Ford College. I was surprised and happy to see Sue, who had moved to the cabin after the Change with her husband and three kids.

Brad stood to introduce the topic. "Trade between the biosphere and the cabin has been suspended, as we have not yet met the request last made by the biosphere. Christy and Ashley are here to give us more information."

Brad returned to his seat and motioned toward us.

"Thank you, Brad," I said. "The biosphere government has asked us to provide them with input from two mechanical engineers and two chemical engineers on alterations to their atmospheric conversion system to improve its output or efficiency. You have already obtained feedback from one engineer. We have located three others who are willing to provide input, but we are not able to give them the payments they have requested."

Ashley detailed the demands of the engineers she and Max found in the marketplace. "We are requesting your help in providing food, water, seed, horses, and farming implements in payment to the engineers. Know that, even with these payments, there is no guarantee we will meet the biosphere's requirements, since gaining the input of one of the engineers is dependent on the biosphere government's willingness to allow him to speak to his daughter. However, without these payments, we see no possibility of resuming trade with the biosphere."

We answered a few questions from the representatives, after which they dismissed us for deliberations. We waited in the hallway for thirty anxious minutes.

When we returned to the library, one of my professors stood and spoke. "It is our desire to meet the demands you have outlined, in order to show our faith in the biosphere community and resume trade relations. However, we are unable to do so without significantly compromising our ability to provide for our own people. Therefore it is the decision of the Board that we will provide half of the requested food and water and all of the adapted seed. We will also offer to the engineer the use of two horses and appropriate farming implements for a period of one week in the fall and one week in the spring.

"Representatives on the Board will help you to load the food, water, and seed into your car, on the condition that, if this payment is not accepted, you will return it all to the cabin. Is that understood?"

Ashley and I nodded. "Yes, sir."

Ashley and Brad went to the shed to get the seed. Sue and Ryan helped me get the food and containers of filtered stream water from the pantry. I felt a sense of déjà vu. Except the last time I loaded food from the pantry into a car, it was in the middle of the night and certainly not with the permission of the established government. Our theft of food from the cabin was one of the reasons Dr. Franklin was unable to forgive Ashley and me for leaving the cabin community.

When the trunk was full, we drove to Max's house. We took more food from the pantry to supplement the payment offered by the cabin, leaving enough to sustain the three of us for a few days. With copies of the atmospheric conversion system schematics in hand, Ashley and I drove to the market. I stayed with the Civic. We couldn't risk leaving our precious cargo unattended. Ashley walked through the market, looking for the engineers she and Max had spoken with earlier in the week.

It made me nervous sitting unarmed in a car full of valuable commodities. I jumped at every sound or perceived movement. I started the Civic and drove around the block. Somehow a moving vehicle seemed safer than a stationary one. Given our dwindling sources of gas, though, I couldn't keep driving around. I got out of the car to get a better view of my surroundings. I got back in, concerned I would draw more attention standing near the car than sitting inside of it.

At long last, I saw Ashley walking down the street. A short, portly man was half a step behind her, sweating with exertion despite the late November chill.

I got out of the Civic and handed Ashley the keys. She opened the trunk and the back door.

"This is what we can offer you, in exchange for your expertise," Ashley said.

The man's eyes widened. Packed into a small vehicle, it looked like a lot of food.

"We are unable to negotiate further, as we have nothing else to offer," Ashley said.

"I'll take it," the man said eagerly.

"You can have half now," Ashley said. "The rest will be delivered after we receive your written report."

The man nodded.

"Where would you like us to deliver it?" Ashley asked.

"I'll ride with you," the man said, "show you the way."

Ashley and I exchanged a glance.

"I'm afraid we can't do that," Ashley said.

The man grudgingly gave us his address and brief directions to his house.

"We'll meet you there between five and six this evening." Ashley got in the Civic and signaled me to do the same. We closed our doors and drove away.

When we were out of sight of the man, Ashley held up her hand.

I gave her an enthusiastic high-five. "You dominated back there. You had him eating out of your hand."

Ashley laughed. "It wasn't that hard. He would have done anything to get out of working for a few months."

"Do you think he'll be able to help? He didn't really seem like the super-smart engineer type."

"Hopefully. He says he's worked with similar systems in

the past."

Ashley found another spot to park a few blocks away. "I'm going in for engineer number two. Wish me luck."

"May the force be with you."

Ashley's confidence had rubbed off on me a little. I still kept a close eye on my surroundings, but the tension in my neck and shoulders had eased.

Ashley returned a short time later with a tall, slender man sporting a graying beard and mustache. He did not look pleased. I imagined Ashley would have a little harder time convincing him to accept altered terms.

Ashley pulled out one of the boxes of seed and opened it. "This seed came from plants that grew last summer, after the Change. It's guaranteed to be genetically suited to the current atmosphere."

"How did you get enough plants to grow after the Change to produce this much seed?" the man asked.

"One of the professors at Ford College started cultivating plants that could adapt long before the Change," Ashley said.

He ran his fingers through the seed. Ashley and I watched his face.

When it appeared he was satisfied with what he saw, Ashley jumped in. "You can take all the seed you requested right now. When you return your report to us, we will bring you written confirmation of your access to two horses and appropriate farming implements for one week each spring and one week each fall."

"That's not what I asked for," the man said.

Ashley looked at her feet. "Well, no, but . . ."

"It's even better," I said. "You don't have to worry about feeding the horses the rest of the year. And if the equipment breaks or the horses get sick, you don't have to pay to replace them."

He nodded slowly. "How long would this agreement be in effect?"

"As long as the community who offered it still has the equipment and you still need it," Ashley said.

The man thrust his hand forward. Ashley jumped back.

"You have a deal," the man said.

Ashley recovered enough to grasp and shake his hand.

We set up a meeting time and place for the following week, to complete the last part of the exchange. He walked toward the market, carrying the boxes of seed and a copy of the schematics.

Back in the car, we resumed our celebration.

"Success number two," I said, raising the roof.

"Tell you what, I'll pretend to be our last engineer's daughter," Ashley said. "Then we can get them all taken care of today."

I laughed. "I'm sure that would work. I mean, it's been, like, eight months since he last saw her. I'm sure he doesn't remember what she looks like."

It felt good to laugh. And it felt good to see our efforts finally pay off.

Ashley delivered the schematics for the atmospheric conversion system to the third engineer, with the promise that we were working with the biosphere to try to arrange an opportunity for him to speak with his daughter.

That night Max pulled out a bottle of wine to celebrate our success and toast to the future. When I touched my glass to his, I could see in his eyes the future he imagined was still different from the one in my mind. The future I hoped for, with Scott by my side, was unlikely to ever come to fruition. I tried to picture a future with Max. Maybe it was time for me to be more realistic with my dreams.

# 31

Ten days later, I was on the road again, headed toward the Bubble. This time, my fear of being robbed was overshadowed by my fear of what I would find when I arrived.

In my nightmares, I saw Chairman Lambrecht pushing people out of the Bubble and the people dropping dead, right in front of the rock wall. I heard Lauren crying. My brother tried to reach her, to comfort her, but something always got in his way. And she never stopped crying.

I timed my trip so I didn't have to stop and wait for nightfall. I was not going to risk another attack. When I reached the turn-off for the gravel road leading to the Bubble, I almost turned around instead. Maybe it would be better not to know. Then I could always remember my family as they were, together and happy.

I forced myself to go on.

When the checkpoint officer spotted me coming, he ran to the middle of the road, waving his arms wildly while talking into the radio on his shoulder.

I stopped at the booth. The officer walked around to the driver's side window. I knew most of the checkpoint officers, but I didn't recognize this one. His eyes were wide and his jaw quivered.

"Name and password." His voice cracked.

"Christy Phillips. S-P-H-E-R-E-4-6-9."

"Ms. Phillips." He cleared his throat. "I cannot allow you through."

"I have the information the Council requested." I held up a manila envelope.

"Wait here." The officer went into the booth, where he appeared to have an animated conversation with himself.

I was surprised he didn't put on an oxygen backpack and mask before exiting the booth.

He returned to my window. "I'm sorry, Miss, but you can't go any further without the approval of the Council. You'll have to wait here until the Council convenes tomorrow morning."

"Okay. Thank you, officer." I fought to conceal my frustration. I couldn't afford to make anyone else mad at me.

I reclined my seat and tried to get some sleep. It was difficult to relax, knowing the officer was watching my every move. Fear had become my almost constant companion. And I had good reason to be afraid—for my life and the lives of those I loved.

My thoughts drifted back to family weekend, the previous fall, when Scott met my family for the first time. My biggest fear then was that my family would scare Scott away. Thankfully, that didn't happen, but I was mortified when Mom shared embarrassing stories from my childhood. It was all worth it, though, when Scott tried to even the score by sharing some of the trouble he got into during his younger years. The image of Scott at age two, chasing the family cat around trying to cover it with chocolate frosting made me laugh so hard it brought tears to my eyes.

I glanced up. The officer was standing in the checkpoint booth, his eyes fixed on me. I realized, with the armed officer watching, I could at least be confident no one else would attack me. I relaxed and drifted off to sleep, something I thought I'd never do in a vehicle again.

I awoke to the sunlight filtering through the trees. I opened my door. The officer was instantly standing in front of me, gun drawn.

I held my hands up. "It's all right. I just need to squat behind a bush for a minute."

The officer's ears turned red. He lowered his weapon and turned his back to me. I was grateful. The bushes in the area didn't have any leaves and therefore did not provide much privacy.

"Thank you, sir," I said, after I finished. "Any word from the Council yet?"

He turned toward me again, shaking his head. "Their session doesn't start for another hour and a half."

"Are you a new officer? I don't remember seeing you here before."

He nodded, reluctantly. "I finished training last week. They promised me nothing ever happens on checkpoint duty. I thought I was going to have a quiet night until you showed up."

I smiled. "Sorry to spoil your peaceful evening."

He shrugged. "That's okay. At least I didn't have to

worry about falling asleep on the job."

He looked over his shoulder. "Listen, you better get back in the car. I'll get in trouble if someone sees you standing out here."

"You got it." I slid into the front seat and tried to tame my hair. I noticed the officer didn't return to the checkpoint booth right away, and he didn't seem to be struggling to breathe at all.

I was getting restless, sitting in the car, when I noticed the officer speaking into his radio again. A short time later, two more officers arrived. They weren't wearing masks or carrying oxygen tanks. The officers inspected me and my almost-empty car. Finding no reason to detain me, they escorted me and my Civic down the road.

When we rounded the corner, I was shocked to see that the woods to the right of the road had been cleared to make way for a collection of log structures. Each building was about the size of a small backyard storage shed. Most of the structures were topped with a chimney. The people working among the buildings stopped and stared as I drove by. I returned their stares, trying to understand what I was seeing.

The officers remained outside when I drove into the airlock. After the air exchange was completed, two different officers came in from the biosphere and escorted me to the administration building.

They took me straight into the council chamber. I searched for a friendly face among the council members. Every one of them looked extremely irate that I had interfered with their scheduled agenda yet again.

"Ms. Phillips," Chairman Lambrecht bellowed before I even sat down, "you better have a list of names for us."

I swallowed hard. Max had told me I should take the rest of the DNA test results back with me, but I refused.

"I do not, sir."

An aggravated murmur arose among the council members. The chairman raised his hand to dismiss me from the room.

"But," I quickly added, "I do have the requested feedback from mechanical and chemical engineers regarding modifications to improve your atmospheric conversion system."

I handed the envelope to one of the officers. He gave it to the chairman, who removed its contents and flipped through them. He handed the papers to the councilman on his right.

"I see input from three engineers," Chairman Lambrecht said. "Were you not instructed to obtain recommendations from four engineers?"

"Yes, sir," I said. "We found four engineers who were willing to give their recommendations, but one would do so on a condition only you could meet."

The chairman pulled his glasses off. "And what was that condition?"

"He would like to talk to his daughter, Janelle Cole. He believes she is living in the biosphere."

Chairman Lambrecht pounded his gavel. The council members sitting closest to him jumped. I thought I heard one of them swear under his breath.

"The Council will begin deliberations," The chairman said. "You may wait outside."

The officers escorted me into the anteroom. It was several hours before we were allowed to return to the council chamber. I scanned the faces of the council members again. Several of them still looked irritated, but most sported satisfied smiles. Apparently, the vote had not been unanimous.

"The decision of the Council is as follows," Chairman Lambrecht said, "Ms. Cole will accompany you this evening when you transport Dr. Franklin back to his community."

I tried to conceal my surprise.

"She will be issued a twenty-four-hour supply of oxygen," the chairman said. "If you do not return within that time frame with Ms. Cole and the report from her father, you will be placing her life and your freedom at great risk."

"But that's hardly enough—"

The bang of the gavel stopped me short.

"That is the decision of the Council." The chairman's voice was cool and measured.

The officers escorted me to my parents' house, where they turned me over to my father's watchful eye and, once the door closed behind me, his welcoming embrace.

"I didn't think I'd ever see you again," I said into his shoulder.

When he pulled back I saw tears in his eyes.

The house that had been crowded with four residents had become a spacious, albeit cluttered, bachelor pad. Dad moved a ration box out of the way so we could sit on the couch.

"Tell me everything that happened since I left," I said. "Did they really kick everyone out? Are Mom and Josh okay? Do you ever get to talk to them? How is Lauren doing?"

"Hold on." Dad laughed. "One question at a time."

"Okay." I looked at Dad sheepishly. "Do I have a new sister-in-law?"

Dad nodded. I tackled him with another hug.

"Tell me all about the wedding," I said. "No, wait. I want to hear it from Lauren. Tell me what happened after the wedding."

"Well, Lauren and I helped your mom and Josh pack. There were a lot of tears. Then we left Josh and Lauren alone for a while. They didn't have much time to get used to being husband and wife.

"Your mom and I stayed up most of the night, walking, sharing memories, saying goodbye."

Tears welled up at the picture Dad painted of the precious, heartbreaking family moments I'd missed. Our family might never be together again, and I wasn't there for the last night.

Dad caught my eye. "We were worried about you when you disappeared that morning. Mom pushed the wedding back as far as she could, hoping you would come home."

"They wouldn't let me," I said through my tears. "I

wanted to come back, but they made me leave."

Dad held me until my sobs quieted.

"They all had to be at the airlock by 7:00 a.m." Dad's voice was softer. "The officers were dragging people out of their homes, without even giving them a chance to grab their luggage. Some of them were forced out into the cold with nothing but the pajamas they were wearing.

"When everyone was accounted for, they sent half the group into the airlock, including your mom and Josh. A half hour later they came out, looking like they'd run a marathon across the Sahara. There was nearly a riot when they tried to send the other half of the group in. The officers and their billy clubs were pretty persuasive.

"They kept doing it, over and over again. Sometimes, when they came out, people who could barely stand were trying to carry people who had passed out. Lauren and I watched from a block away. They wouldn't let us come any closer. I tried to yell 'I love you' to Mom and Josh. I don't think they could hear me, but I couldn't leave them to suffer that torture alone."

Dad stared at the wall behind me as if riveted by a movie portraying the events he described.

"Just after noon, the officers made an announcement. I couldn't hear what they said, but I could guess by the panic it aroused in the crowd. I just kept yelling 'I love you, I'll miss you' over and over again until the door of the airlock closed behind the first group. When the door opened a half hour later, no one came out."

I knew what it was like to watch someone struggle through the acclimatization process, powerless to help them. But I couldn't imagine watching the love of your life, your spouse of twenty-two years, suffer like that without even being close enough to offer a comforting touch or word.

"I'm sorry, Dad." I put my hand over his.

"I had no idea how far the Council was willing to go," Dad said. "I didn't want to believe it when Josh told me about the forced abortions. But when I saw what they put those people through—" he looked at me, his eyes glistening with tears "—what they did to your mother and your brother, with no compassion or remorse. Our government has lost all sense of decency and humanity."

"Do you ever get to see Mom and Josh?"

"I can talk to them on the walkie-talkie once a week, for five minutes. But the officers listen to every word, so we can't really say anything. They're doing well. They had a few chilly nights before they got the roof on their house, but now they say it's quite cozy.

"After Josh told us about the forced abortions, your Mom realized what really happened to Jessica's baby. She invited Jessica to share their house.

"They still get their rations every week. Josh says Mom is getting pretty good at cooking over an open fire. They're being reassigned to jobs outside the biosphere. Josh just started officer training. Once their house is finished, your mom will be helping with the crop farm.

"I think Josh is enjoying the adventure. Your mom just

wants us to be together as a family again."

"We've been separated before," I said. "Somehow we always manage to find our way back together."

"I don't know." Dad's eyes clouded over. "The wall seems thicker than it ever was before."

"I just came from the cabin. They have a new representative government, and they just voted on articles for a constitution. It seems to be working pretty well for them."

"We need to do something different with our government," Dad said. "But the people I know on the Council would never be willing to risk losing their power and position in an election."

"What about President Bentley? She was elected by the people as President of the United States. Surely she isn't okay with a council that's trampling all over the rights our nation was founded on."

A knock at the door brought us both to our feet. I glanced out the window and then flung the door open, wrapping Lauren in a bear hug.

"Look at you, Mrs. Phillips." I pulled back and looked her up and down. "You are just glowing."

I guided her to the couch. "How have you been feeling?"

"Much better," Lauren said. "I haven't thrown up in, like, two weeks. It's been great."

"And the baby?"

"Doctor says she's a healthy fourteen-week-old."

"She?"

Lauren laughed. "I can't call my baby 'it,' so I alternate

between 'he' and 'she.' "

"Good plan," I said, "as long as you can remember which it is after the baby's born."

"I don't think that'll be a problem."

"Just to be on the safe side, maybe you should avoid those gender-neutral names like Taylor or Drew."

"Good advice." Lauren stood. "I'm going to get lunch started."

"Dad, are you making her cook for you?" I asked, following Lauren to the kitchenette.

"He's not making me." Lauren laughed. "I need the practice." She held her hand up beside her mouth as if to prevent her words from reaching my dad. "And your dad really can't cook."

"I heard that," Dad said.

"Listen, you sit down and put your feet up," I said to Lauren. "I'll do the cooking."

I started the rice and then sat at the table with her to chop some vegetables. "Now, I want to hear all about the wedding. I can't believe I missed it."

Lauren shrugged. "There's not much to tell. We didn't have a lot of time to put everything together. Thankfully, the minister and the church were both available. My mom stood up with me, and your dad stood up with Josh. I think I cried the whole afternoon. I was so happy I was becoming Josh's wife. I had dreamed of that day for months. But I didn't know how I would be able to make it when he was gone. I couldn't bear the thought that I might never see my husband again; that he might never get to meet his child.

"I love Josh so much. I can't think of any better way to have spent our last day together than declaring our love in front of God and our families.

"That night we talked about our plans for the future, what we might name our baby, and how many more we would have." Lauren wiped away her tears. "For a few hours it felt like we were a normal couple and we were going to have a normal life. The next morning, reality hit full force. Nothing has been normal since."

I'd had similar dreams about the future I would share with Scott. Every day it became a little harder to believe those dreams could ever come true. I could offer Lauren comfort, but I didn't have enough hope to spare.

Dad and Lauren insisted I join them for lunch. I left some of the food I had brought to replace the food I ate.

"Dad, do you have to get back to work?" I asked, after putting away the last of the lunch dishes.

"Nope," he said. "You're my job today."

I sighed. "You really don't have to babysit me, Dad. I promise I'll behave."

"I believe you," he said, "but for some reason, the Council is less trusting. Might have something to do with a recent footrace through the hospital halls."

"Sometimes you have to break the rules," I said. "Without that footrace, Mom and Josh probably wouldn't have survived the transition to the outside."

"I know," Dad said. "That's why it's better to have me as

your guardian than one of the officers."

"Yeah." One corner of my mouth raised in a crooked smile. "And you can't run as fast as most of the officers can."

"You wanna test that theory?" He crouched down like a runner at the starting blocks.

I laughed. "Maybe some other day. I need to get to bed. My next assignment has a tight deadline—I have to drop something off at the cabin and pick something up in Lincoln and make it back to the Bubble in twenty-four hours. If I don't sleep now, it'll be a long time before I get another chance.

"Lauren, it was great to see you." I gave her a hug. "You take good care of that baby."

She squeezed me back. "I will."

# 32

Dad woke me around nine o'clock. I freshened up and had some supper before we left for the airlock.

Dad stumbled as he stepped outside, grabbing the doorframe to catch his balance.

"Are you all right?" I asked.

"Sure, I'm fine." Dad brushed off my concern. "Just having a little trouble with my vision."

"Do you need new glasses?"

"The eye doctor said that wouldn't help. She said carbon dioxide levels in the biosphere are rising, causing a lot of people to have vision problems."

If carbon dioxide levels were going up, that meant the atmospheric conversion system wasn't keeping up—even after the population inside the Bubble was reduced by more than two hundred people. How long would it be before the carbon dioxide reached lethal levels? The chances that my dad could survive outside the Bubble were slim. If the Bubble became uninhabitable, he and hundreds of others would be out of options.

"I gave the Council some information to help improve the atmospheric conversion system this morning."

But what if that wasn't enough?

I stopped walking and turned to Dad. "Do you think I

should give the Council the rest of the names?"

"Do you trust them?"

"No. They've shown over and over again that they have no problem trampling on people's rights."

I started walking again, slowly. "But I do think most of them are trying to do what's best for the community."

"Then you have to decide which is more important, the rights of the individual, or the well-being of the community."

"Can't we have both?"

"I don't know." Dad took a deep breath. "I hope so, but I don't know."

I walked up to the airlock operator's booth, more confused than ever. I did not want to let the Council tear apart any more families. But was I jeopardizing Dad's and Lauren's lives—and maybe even the baby's—by withholding the genetic testing results from the Council?

"Everyone else is already inside," the airlock operator said, gesturing toward the door.

*Everyone else? How many people are coming on this little trip?*

I opened the door to the airlock. There were two cars inside. A thin woman, probably in her twenties, with long blonde hair sat in the passenger's seat of the Civic. Dr. Franklin was in the back, along with an officer.

I slid into the driver's seat of my car.

"Janelle?" I extended my hand. "I'm Christy. It's nice to meet you."

She returned my handshake without a word, casting a

nervous glance toward the garage door in front of us.

The officer driving the other car gave us a thumbs-up, and the garage door opened. I glanced in the rearview mirror and saw the officer in the back seat slip a cloth bag over Dr. Franklin's head.

"What are you doing?" I whipped around to face the officer.

"We can't risk him seeing anything that would clue him in to the location of the biosphere," the officer said.

"He is not a criminal," I said. "Take that bag off."

"Christy, it's okay." Dr. Franklin's voice was muffled.

"Why does he have to wear the bag and not Janelle?" I asked.

"Invited residents of the biosphere committed to secrecy about its location before they got on the bus to come here. Janelle knows that revealing the location of the biosphere to anyone would put her life in jeopardy. Richard has no such motivation for keeping our secret."

The officer held my gaze, his lips pressed together in a thin line. Nothing in his expression indicated a propensity toward compromise. If I pushed the issue, they might not allow me to take Dr. Franklin back to the cabin. I couldn't take that risk. I swallowed my objections and started the car.

I glanced at Janelle. She stared out the open door with a look of terror.

"It's going to be all right," I said. "It's not as scary as people think. Besides, there's someone out there who really wants to see you."

I handed her the mask attached to the oxygen tank at her feet. "You better put this on now."

She flashed me a little smile and put on the mask.

We pulled out of the airlock. The other car followed close behind. The drive was quiet and tense. I was afraid to say anything with the officer present. Janelle appeared to be lost in fear. By the time we reached the highway, I could see the bag covering Dr. Franklin's head bobbing in the rearview mirror. I was pretty sure he had fallen asleep.

After we had driven for a couple of hours, the officer instructed me to pull off the road. I turned onto a side street and stopped. The officer took the bag off Dr. Franklin's head and opened the door.

"Remember, that oxygen will only last twenty-four hours." The officer got out of my car and joined the other officer in the car behind us. They turned around and headed back toward the Bubble.

With a sigh of relief, I pulled back onto the highway. "I can't believe they did that to you, Dr. Franklin. I'm really sorry."

He shrugged. "They wouldn't let me go until I agreed to it." His voice quieted. "I've had a lot of practice being at the mercy of other people and feeling helpless over the past few weeks." He stared out the window. "It's a frightening feeling, but I'm getting used to it."

I nodded. I had experienced that same scary feeling over and over again since the Change. But Dr. Franklin had somehow managed to maintain the sense that he was in command, even when everything around us was in chaos. It was only when he got sick that he'd lost his power and control.

We filled the rest of the trip to Lincoln with small talk. When Janelle could focus her attention on us, instead of on the often horrifying views in the cars we passed, her fear eased.

She directed us to her parents' house, but there was no one home. I imagined her dad was probably already at the market, but I had no idea where to find him there.

We drove to Max's house. Max was there, but Ashley was not. Max had met the engineers once, but he didn't know near as much about their routines and favored locations as Ashley. After I explained our time constraints, he got in the car with us, eager to help.

We parked as close as we could to the center of the market. I didn't think we could safely bring Janelle into the market with us. Her mask and oxygen tank would attract too much attention. Plus the brisk walk would deplete her oxygen supply. Dr. Franklin stayed in the car with Janelle. Max and I split up, looking and asking for Ashley and Mr. Cole on opposite ends of the market.

I saw a lot of familiar people, many of whom were quite irritated that I wouldn't stop to trade, but I didn't see the people I was looking for. I had only gotten through about a quarter of the market when I had to head back to the car to make the one-hour meeting time Max and I had agreed on.

Max also showed up empty-handed. We checked on Janelle and Dr. Franklin. Janelle was breathing rapidly. Through the mask, I could see her lower lip quivering.

I opened the car door and grasped her hand. "We're going to find your dad soon, okay?"

Janelle didn't respond.

"And then I'm going to get you back to the biosphere, safe and sound. Do you believe me?"

She took a deep breath and nodded twice. I squeezed her hand and shut the door. My confidence was fading fast. I was glad someone believed me.

Max and I hurried back to the market. Eleven hours had already passed since we left the Bubble. I only had thirteen hours left to find Janelle's dad, get Dr. Franklin to the cabin, and get Janelle back to the biosphere. Panic threatened to overwhelm me.

This time I didn't stop to ask people if they'd seen Ashley or Mr. Cole. I darted through the streets, stopping only briefly to inspect clusters of people before passing by.

After about a half hour, I finally spotted her.

"Ashley," I yelled, running to her.

I grabbed her by the arm, pulling her away from the vendor with whom she was bartering.

"We need you to find Mr. Cole." I spoke in a low voice. "The Council agreed to let him talk to his daughter in exchange for his knowledge. We have her here."

Ashley's eyes and mouth opened wide. "She's here?"

I nodded. "A few blocks from the market. But she can't stay long. She has a limited oxygen supply, and we have to get her back to the Bubble tonight."

Ashley took off down the street. I raced after her. She

checked at three booths with no luck. When she finally spotted Janelle's father, she broke into a sprint. I caught up with her just before she reached him.

"Don't make a scene," I said under my breath.

"Mr. Cole." Ashley tapped him on the shoulder.

He turned around. Seeing Ashley, he looked up and sighed. "What do you want?"

Ashley maintained eye contact. "We have obtained the trade item you requested from us."

Mr. Cole frowned, and his brow wrinkled.

"In exchange for your knowledge about our air conditioning unit," Ashley continued.

Mr. Cole's eyes widened.

"The trade item is available for only a limited time," Ashley said. "Would you like to come with us to inspect it?"

Mr. Cole nodded vigorously.

We walked at a brisk pace but tried not to attract attention. The last thing we needed was someone following us.

As soon as we were out of sight of the market, Mr. Cole asked, "Where is she?" his eyes sparkling with anticipation.

"Corner of E Street and Fourteenth," I said.

Mr. Cole sprinted seven blocks to the car. Though he had at least twenty years on us, there was no way Ashley and I could catch him. We rounded the corner just in time to see Janelle throw herself into his arms.

I didn't want to interrupt the family reunion, but my time crunch was getting tighter by the second. "I'm going to take Dr. Franklin back home. Janelle, you have about twelve hours of oxygen left. I'll pick you up here in two hours. Mr. Cole, we'll need your payment at that time."

Mr. Cole and Janelle waved me away without a word. Ashley stayed to update Max when he returned.

I watched Janelle and her father in the rearview mirror as we pulled away.

"Before the Change," Dr. Franklin said, "I told you I thought it was going to be harder on those who survived than on those who didn't."

I thought of all the challenges I had faced in recent months that I could never have imagined before the Change. "I think you were right."

Dr. Franklin motioned with his thumb toward Mr. Cole and Janelle. "It's those moments that make it all worth it."

I nodded.

I remembered that conversation. It brought to mind a question I'd never had the chance to ask. "Dr. Franklin, who did you lose in the Change?"

Dr. Franklin sighed. "My ex-wife."

His answer surprised me. If they were already divorced, it seemed like he would have had a chance to recover from losing her before the Change.

"I thought maybe if she had more time to heal, eventually she would forgive me," Dr. Franklin said. "I tried to convince her to go through acclimatization, but she didn't want to have anything to do with it, or me."

I could hear the anguish in his voice. I knew the pain of losing someone you loved. I was with my college roommate,

Kayla, when the Change took her. Though it wasn't easy, I was able to let her go with no regrets. I had done everything I could to make her last moments comfortable, and I was confident that she was at peace at the end. I couldn't imagine how difficult it would be to lose someone who used to love you; to lose all hope that they would ever love you again.

"Forgive you for what?" I asked softly.

There was a long pause. Dr. Franklin looked straight ahead.

Finally, he answered, "For the death of our daughter."

He took a deep breath. "I was driving Chloe to school like I always did. She was chatting about the other kids in her class and what they were going to do at school that day. She expressed her frustration with one of the particularly annoying kids in her class. I flashed her an empathetic look, and that's when I saw it.

"A car was speeding down the country road toward the highway we were on. There was no way he was going to be able to stop in time. I slammed on the brakes and tried to swerve away, but it was too late. The car ran right into us, pushing us across the road and into the ditch on the other side. I did CPR on Chloe for ten minutes before the ambulance arrived, but I couldn't save her."

Dr. Franklin's shoulders shook, and tears streamed down his face.

"At first, her mother and I grieved together and tried to help each other through. But when she couldn't make sense of what had happened, Deborah decided she had to blame someone." He choked out the words. "She picked me."

"I'm so sorry."

"I sent her money and took care of things for her. I told her how sorry I was I don't know how many times. I thought after she worked through her grief a little more, she would see how much I loved her and Chloe, and she would forgive me. But we ran out of time."

Dr. Franklin struggled to contain his emotions.

"At first, I blamed myself too. I should have sped up instead of slowing down, so he wouldn't have hit directly on Chloe's door. I should have taken a different route to school or left home a little earlier. If I had done one thing differently, we would have been able to watch Chloe walk across the stage to receive her high school diploma last year.

"But I knew, deep down, it wasn't my fault. It was the driver of the other car who was speeding and didn't notice the stop sign." Dr. Franklin's voice quaked, anger mixing with his grief. "He is the one who stole my daughter from me and ripped my family apart.

"I dedicated my life to stopping people like him. I advocated for harsher punishments for those who broke traffic laws. If he had been going the speed limit and paying attention to the signs, he would have been able to stop in time. So many tragedies would never happen if everyone followed the rules.

"I thought if Deborah saw me doing these things to save other people from the pain we'd experienced, it might soften her heart. I thought she might come back home."

He looked out the window and sighed. "Maybe she

would have, eventually."

I began to understand where Dr. Franklin's stoicism came from and why his punishments for those who broke the rules were so severe. It made sense now.

"Christy." Dr. Franklin pulled me out of my thoughts. "I was wrong."

That was a statement I never thought I would hear him say.

"I thought following the rules was the best way to prevent tragedy and end suffering," he said. "But you put your life on the line for me. You broke the rules to save my life. Thank you."

I nodded, unable to get any words out through my tears.

# 33

We had barely pulled ourselves together by the time we reached the cabin.

"Things have changed a little since you left," I said to Dr. Franklin. "Wait here. I'll let them know you're back."

I knocked on the front door, where I was met with a hug and immediately ushered in. I smiled, contrasting this with the cold greeting I had received when Dr. Franklin was in charge.

The Board of Representatives was in session. I requested a brief audience. After fifteen minutes, the administrative assistant ushered me into the library. The representatives' friendly smiles put me immediately at ease, quite unlike the accusatory looks I had recently received from the biosphere's Council.

"Thank you for seeing me on such short notice," I said. "I have a brief report for you. Both engineers accepted the payments you offered. Thank you for your generosity. We are in the process of obtaining a report from the final engineer. After that, it is anticipated that normal trade relations will resume with the biosphere."

The announcement was met with smiles and nods.

"Dr. Franklin's medical treatment was successfully completed, though he is still working on recovering his strength."

Smiles broadened in response to more good news.

"And he has returned here to the cabin."

The representatives exchanged glances, their smiles disappearing.

Ryan spoke up. "The Board has drafted a new contract for citizens of the cabin. Dr. Franklin will need to sign the contract in order to return to our community.

"The Board also approved a motion to invite you to rejoin the community, Christy. If you sign the new contract and continue to provide delivery services to the cabin, you are welcome to stay here and share meals with us whenever you're in the area."

My heart flooded with gratitude. The cabin had been my home, months ago. When everything around us was falling apart, the cabin was our safe place. But Dr. Franklin's iron fist had made it unbearable for me there. I'd wanted nothing more than to get away from the cabin. In doing so, I had broken the bond of trust with the community. I had tried to right the wrong I had done, and most of the people at the cabin had forgiven me for my actions. But I had never been invited to be part of the community again, until now. And now, more than ever, I wanted to be part of this community.

"Thank you," I said. "I would love to."

The Board's administrative assistant ushered me out and handed me two copies of the contract. I returned to the car and gave Dr. Franklin one of the copies. I skimmed my contract and signed it. Dr. Franklin gave his a little closer scrutiny.

When he finished examining the last page, he looked at me. "This is good. Even if I'd never met these people before, I would want to be a part of this."

He signed the contract and handed it to me.

I motioned toward the door of the cabin. "Come on in, Dr. Franklin."

The administrative assistant delivered our signed contracts to the Board. Moments later, she invited us into the board meeting.

"Do you have any questions about the contract?" Sue asked.

Dr. Franklin and I shook our heads.

"Do you clearly understand what you are agreeing to?"

"Yes," we answered.

"Welcome back," Sue said. "We're glad to have you here."

Out in the hallway, I noticed the grin on my face wasn't reflected on Dr. Franklin's.

"It's going to be different for you here," I said. "Are you going to be okay?"

"I've had a lot of practice not being in charge the past few weeks," Dr. Franklin said, "but it's still hard for me to trust other people. Ever since the accident, I've felt like if I want something done right, I have to do it myself."

I motioned toward the library. "The people in that room care about this community, and they have good ideas about how to make it safe and prosperous. You don't have to do it on your own anymore. Let them take that responsibility off your shoulders."

Dr. Franklin nodded. "I'll try."

Dr. Franklin had opened up to me so much. I wanted to stay, to help him with his transition back to the cabin in his new role. But I was already running late.

"I have to go get Janelle," I said. "I'll come back as soon as I can.

"Dr. Franklin?"

He raised his downcast eyes to meet mine.

"You're welcome," I said. "I would do it again in a heartbeat."

# 34

By the time I got back to our meeting place in Lincoln, it was noon. Janelle only had nine hours of oxygen left.

Driving up, I saw the joy in Janelle's face turn to panic. She wrapped her arms around her dad.

I stepped out of the car.

"Janelle, we have to go," I said, gently.

She held tight and said nothing.

"I'll deliver letters for you," I said. "You can still stay in touch."

She whispered something in her dad's ear and slowly released her grip on him.

"Mr. Cole, I'll need your report on the atmospheric conversion system for the Council."

"It's not done yet," he said.

Now it was my turn to panic. "We cannot return to the biosphere without that report. And if we don't get back to the biosphere, your daughter will die."

"I'll write it along the way," he said, moving toward the car.

"You can't come with us," I said. "Janelle and I will both be thrown in jail if we let anyone else get near the biosphere."

"Then take me part way." Mr. Cole seemed awfully nonchalant considering his daughter's freedom and life were at stake.

"Okay, that might work." My mind was spinning. "I could pick you up on my way back and bring you back to Lincoln."

"Or I could find my own way back." Mr. Cole winked at his daughter.

"Now, hold on," I said. "You cannot follow us to the biosphere."

"Of course not." Mr. Cole smiled.

"If anyone is following me, I can't go to the biosphere. If you follow us, I will not be able to take your daughter to safety."

Janelle and her dad got in the back seat of the Civic. Mr. Cole directed me to his house.

While he was inside retrieving some supplies and the start of his report, I instructed Janelle, "You're going to have to turn your oxygen off for one minute every fifteen minutes, to make sure we have enough to get back to the biosphere." I showed her how to open and close the valve. "If that seems too long, you can turn it off for thirty seconds, but then you have to remember to do it every seven minutes. If you don't do that, you could end up with no oxygen for the last half hour of the trip or more. You probably wouldn't make it."

For Janelle's sake, I wanted to take the quickest route to the Bubble. However, since we had an unauthorized passenger, I needed to deviate from my normal path to throw him off track if he ever tried to find the biosphere. I wound through the country roads, heading north and west.

I heard a lot of casual chatter from the back seat, but every time I looked, Mr. Cole was writing and flipping through the information I had given him about the atmospheric conversion system.

As time wore on, I grew more and more nervous.

"Let me know when you're done with your report, Mr. Cole. You know I can't take you farther than four hours from Lincoln," I said. "Janelle, are you remembering to turn your oxygen off?"

They both gave me a little wave and continued their conversation.

At 4:30 p.m. I pulled off to the side of the road. "This is where you get out, Mr. Cole."

He looked at his daughter, then back at me. "I need one more hour to wrap things up."

"You can't have another hour." My frustration threatened to boil over. "I cannot drive you any further, and I have to get Janelle back to the biosphere before she runs out of oxygen."

"Alright. Give me a minute to say goodbye," Mr. Cole said.

I stepped out of the car. Mr. Cole and his daughter shared a hug and a few words. He gave her several handwritten pages.

He got out of the car, shouldered his backpack, and handed me a packet of paper, stapled together, each page covered in his precise, tiny handwriting. "I hope they find this helpful. I would do anything to ensure my daughter's well-being."

Flipping through the pages, I could tell this report had not been written in a moving vehicle. "You had this done all along?"

"I wanted a few more hours with my daughter. I'll probably never get to see her again."

My anger receded. I would have done the same thing if I got to see Kayla or Scott again for one last time.

"I'm sorry," I mumbled.

"Don't be," Mr. Cole said. "Without you, I wouldn't have had the chance to see her at all. Thank you."

"We've got to get going," I said, "but I'll deliver letters to Janelle anytime you want."

"I would like that."

I opened the driver's side door. "I'll be coming through here, probably in two or three days. Do you want me to stop back and pick you up?"

"That would be great."

I slid into my seat.

"I love you, Daddy," Janelle yelled before I closed the door.

Mr. Cole crossed his arms over his chest as if he were still holding his daughter close. "I love you, too," he mouthed through the window, tears streaming down his face.

I drove north until I was certain Mr. Cole could no longer see us and no one was following us. I took two left turns and drove south back to one of my usual routes. I made up a little time going south because the roads weren't as crowded as those going east and west. Still, our detour had cost us a lot of time.

Every five minutes I asked Janelle to turn her oxygen off for half a minute. I tried to engage her in small talk, but she wasn't in the mood, and I needed to focus on the task of driving if I was going to get her to the Bubble in time. Within an hour after we left Mr. Cole, it was completely dark. While I frequently drove these roads in the dark and knew every curve and obstacle, I didn't feel like I could max out my speed with a passenger and a highly flammable oxygen tank on board.

Several miles from the Bubble, I cut the lights and stopped to look and listen for any sign someone might be following us. I turned and looked in the back seat. Janelle appeared to be sleeping. I checked the oxygen tank. It was empty. We had at least fifteen minutes to go and no more oxygen.

I took one more look at the deserted road behind me, and then I floored it. I didn't stop again to make sure I wasn't being followed. The sound of my tires on the rough country road seemed deafening in the stillness of the night. I didn't care if someone heard me. I only cared about getting Janelle back to where she could breathe again.

"Lord, send your angels to fly us to the Bubble and to keep Janelle breathing," I whispered. I recited a prayer I had learned as a child. "Angel of God, my guardian dear, to whom God's love commits me here, ever this day be at my side, to light and guard, to rule and guide."

The full moon peeked out from behind the clouds,

illuminating the turn-off for the gravel road leading to the Bubble.

"Thank you, Lord," I whispered.

I sped around the corner. The back tires slid on the gravel, nearly spinning the car around.

The crunch of tires on gravel woke Janelle. She gasped for air and yanked the oxygen mask off her face.

I gripped the steering wheel, attempting to regain control.

"We're almost home, Janelle." I tried to sound soothing, but I couldn't keep the panic out of my voice. "Hang in there a little longer."

I skidded to a stop in front of the checkpoint and jumped out of the car. "Janelle is out of oxygen. We have to get her inside right now."

The officer held up his hand. "Not until the inspection is complete."

He punched a button on his radio, to inform the other officers of my arrival. He made no move to leave his position in the center of the road.

I opened the back door and lifted Janelle out of the car. I staggered a few steps down the road, but I couldn't handle her weight.

"Do you think you can walk a little?" I asked.

She nodded, still struggling to breathe.

I put her feet on the ground and wrapped my arm around her waist to guide her down the road.

"Stop right there," the officer commanded.

"Either help us or get out of the way," I yelled.

The officer looked bewildered. While he talked excitedly into his radio, we skirted around him and continued down the road.

As soon as we could see the village outside of the Bubble, I yelled for help. Within seconds, several people emerged from the village. Two men picked Janelle up and carried her toward the biosphere. I ran ahead to try to get the operator to open the airlock. Along the way, I met the two officers who were coming to assist with the inspection.

"Janelle's out of air," I yelled, without breaking stride. "We've got to get her inside, quick."

After a moment's hesitation, the officers ran after me. I wasn't sure if they were trying to catch me or help me, but as long as they were headed in the right direction, I didn't care. They were on my heels when I reached the rock that serves as an intercom with the airlock operator.

"Janelle needs to get inside, right now," I yelled into the rock.

I turned to one of the officers. "Give her your authorization."

"I'm afraid I can't do that," the officer said, "not until our inspection is complete."

"Then inspect already," I said, "while Janelle suffocates."

One officer examined me, while the other checked Janelle over. They gave us a thorough pat-down, combing through the contents of every pocket.

Janelle's eyes were closed, and she took quick, shallow

breaths. She couldn't stand without help. When the officer found the pages Janelle's father had written for her, he began to read through them.

"Look, you can read our mail later, just let us in," I said.

The officer looking at the papers ignored me.

I appealed to the officer who had searched me. "You know what it's like to be in air you can't breathe. Don't you remember when they were getting you ready to come out here?"

The officer looked at me. He stepped up to the rock, then stopped and looked over his shoulder at the other officer.

"Please," I said. "She's not going to last much longer out here."

The officer turned back toward the rock, gave his credentials, and requested the airlock be opened.

It seemed to take forever for the rocks to slide to the side and the garage door to begin to rise. I ran toward the barely-open door and rolled under it. I sprinted across the airlock and up the steps and pounded on the door to the biosphere. "Open up! Janelle needs to get in there. Now!"

I glanced back. The men supporting Janelle ducked to get her inside the airlock.

"Everyone's in," I yelled. "Close the garage door, and let us in."

The garage door reversed direction and began to close. As soon as it reached the floor, I resumed pounding on the door to the biosphere. I heard the fans hum to life. Apparently, protocol was always to be followed, even when someone's life was at risk.

"Take her over there." I pointed to the fan embedded in the wall beside the loading dock. "That's where the good air comes in."

Every minute seemed to last an hour. Finally, Janelle's breathing slowed, and her pained expression relaxed. Several long minutes later, the door opened.

A medical team hurried in. They lifted Janelle onto a gurney. After a rapid and coordinated examination, they carried the gurney up the steps to the loading dock.

I followed them through the door into the Bubble.

The team rolled the gurney down the street toward the hospital.

I collapsed on the ground in tears. I had done everything I could to get Janelle back in time, but I didn't know if it was enough. Was it worth it to give Janelle a few hours with her father, if it might cost her her life?

When my tears dried and I mustered the strength, I pulled myself to my feet. It was then that I noticed the officer waiting to escort me to my dad's custody. I was embarrassed he had seen me break down but also irritated that I was still being held under house arrest.

Dad was waiting for me on the patio. When the light from the street lamp hit my face, he ran out to meet me. "Christy, are you all right?"

I nodded.

"Thank you, officer." Dad was more brusque than usual and seemed eager for the officer to go.

"What happened?" Dad put his arm around my shoulders.

We walked toward the house.

"Janelle got to see her dad, and Dr. Franklin made it to the cabin, and I hurried back as fast as I could, but I don't know if we made it in time. They took Janelle to—"

I stopped short when Dad opened the door, revealing a house full of people.

"Dad, what's going on?"

"Christy, I know you've had a hard day, and I'm sure you're exhausted. But these people want to talk to you, and this was the only time I knew for sure you'd be home."

"Okay," I said tentatively.

I scanned the room, recognizing many of the people as my mail delivery customers. I hoped my illegal activities hadn't gotten them in trouble.

A woman sitting at the dining room table stood and offered me her chair. "You probably know, people have been protesting in the streets all week, demanding the government reunite families now divided by the wall."

I shook my head. That hadn't come up in my conversations with Dad and Lauren the day before.

"Well, the Council won't listen to what they have to say. And the officers are getting more violent toward the protestors every day. Since the Council doesn't seem to be interested in looking for a solution, we want to offer them one. All of us here would be willing to live outside the biosphere if that would enable people who are now outside to rejoin their families."

"Did you see what the people who moved outside went through to get there?" I asked.

Everyone nodded, some reluctantly.

"If they can do it, so can we," said a voice from the back of the room.

"And what about you guys?" I asked. "You would have to leave your families and neighbors, too."

"I don't have any family in the biosphere."

"My fiancé is out there."

"I've always wanted to live like a pioneer."

"I didn't sign up to live in an oligarchy."

People from all corners of the room gave the reasons they were ready to leave the Bubble. I think if I had offered to lead them out right then, every one of them would have followed me, no questions asked.

"All right," I said. "What can I do to help?"

A man stepped forward. "We need you to test all of us, to see which of us could live on the outside."

"That should be no problem," I said. "We still have some DNA sampling kits here."

"And," the man said, "we need you to present our case to the Council, without revealing our identities until they have agreed to let the same number of people back in as they let out."

I frowned. "That's going to be more difficult. The Council does not take too kindly to people bringing up topics that aren't on their agenda."

The people looked at me hopefully.

I forced a smile. "I'm sure I can figure something out."

I wasn't sure. But I would try anything to get my family back together. Christmas was less than a month away, and I knew it would break Mom's heart if we weren't all together for the holiday.

Dad pulled out the unused DNA testing kits I had left at the house. Those whose samples we collected first went out and spread the word, creating a steady stream of people going in and out our front door. By the time Dad and I finished collecting and labeling samples from everyone, I could hardly stay on my feet. Twenty-seven hours without sleep was catching up with me.

After I stowed the last sample, I collapsed on the couch.

# 35

I awoke the next morning—actually, it was afternoon—with a feeling of excitement. I had accomplished what I'd set out to do the day before, though not on the time schedule I had planned. And I now had a new mission—one that would be a challenge to complete but one that might give me the opportunity to reunite families and save lives.

First, though, I needed to check on the results of my mission from the day before. I got cleaned up and, at Dad's insistence, had a bite to eat. They still weren't providing any rations for me, and I hated to take Dad's food.

Then I went straight to the hospital. Of course, Dad had to tag along with me, continuing his babysitting duties. Under Dad's supervision, the security guard at the front door allowed me into the hospital. I felt like everyone was watching me as we walked down the hall. Apparently, I had made quite an impression during my last visit.

"Can you tell me where Janelle Cole's room is?" I asked the man seated at the nurse's station.

He nodded, his eyes directed over my shoulder.

"I'll show you." The deep voice came from behind me.

I turned around. A security guard towered over me, his broad chest straining the buttons of his dark blue uniform shirt. He strode down the hallway, taking frequent glances back to make sure Dad and I were still with him.

When we reached Janelle's room, the security guard stood beside the door, arms crossed. I walked past him and into the room, trying to avoid eye contact. Dad waited in the hallway.

I was relieved to see Janelle sitting up in bed, awake and smiling. I hardly recognized her without the oxygen mask. I ran over to the bed but stopped before reaching out to hug her. She might not be quite ready for that, considering she had nearly died in my care less than twenty-four hours before.

She reached out and clasped my hand. Her eyes glistened with tears.

"Thank you for taking me to see my dad," she whispered. "I never imagined I could be that happy again."

She pulled me in and wrapped her arms around me.

"I was so worried about you," I said. "How are you feeling?"

"Just a little weak. They said I should be able to go home tonight. It might be a few days before I can go back to work. That's okay, though. It'll give me more time to write letters to Dad."

I glanced over my shoulder at the door before whispering, "I will deliver every one of them."

After she assured me a few more times that she was going to be okay, I left so she could get some rest before her return home. The security guard followed Dad and me to the front door of the hospital.

Our next stop was at the airlock. I knocked on the

window to get the operator's attention.

"I left all of my things in my car." I raised my voice so I could be heard through the window. "May I go out and pull my car into the airlock?"

"The officers already brought it in for you." The operator motioned toward the door. "Go on in."

"Want to come in with me?" I asked Dad.

He looked around nervously.

"Don't worry," I said, "they're not going to open the outside doors while we're in there."

"I'll hold the door for you." Dad's offer allowed him to keep one foot in the biosphere.

I grabbed my backpack and the report from Mr. Cole out of the front seat. I was relieved to find the papers the officer had taken from Janelle in the back seat. I knew she would want them, and I was glad to have an excuse to pay her another visit.

I had hoped, though, that retrieving my things from the car would give me the opportunity to visit Mom and Josh. I hadn't seen them since they moved out of the Bubble. It looked like that visit would have to wait until it was time to leave.

We walked from the airlock to the administration building. I had been surprised there wasn't an officer at our door at eight that morning to escort me to appear before the Council.

I gave the attendant Mr. Cole's report and requested a slot on the Council's schedule. He went into the council chamber to deliver the report and returned a few minutes later.

"The Council put you on their agenda tomorrow at ten."

"Thank you, sir," I said. "I'll see you tomorrow."

I still had some mail in my backpack, but I didn't dare deliver it while Dad was hovering. He knew of my extralegal activities, but if he were ever questioned, I wanted him to be able to truthfully say he had seen nothing.

"Let's have Lauren over for supper," I suggested.

"Good idea."

"I'll head home and start cooking. You can go to Lauren's house and invite her."

Dad shook his head. "You know I can't do that."

"I promise I'll go straight home."

"I'm sure you will. And if the wrong person sees you walking home alone, we'll both be in hot water."

I sighed. "Okay, fine." I felt like I was being treated like a six-year-old. I couldn't even walk down the block without holding my daddy's hand. But I knew Dad was right. It was better to be under his protective care than to have officers breathing down our necks twenty-four seven.

We walked together to Lauren's, and she accompanied us back to our house. The three of us enjoyed a relaxing meal together. It felt like a normal family dinner, though the empty chairs at the table reminded us that the family was incomplete.

After sleeping all morning, I had trouble falling asleep when evening came. Lying awake, I tried to think of a way to bring up the people's proposal to the Council. It would work best if I could somehow make it seem like it was the Council's idea. It would help if I could do something to get me back on their good side. Maybe delivering the final engineer's report would be enough to restore my reputation with the Council. I drifted off with these thoughts bouncing around in my head.

Despite my difficulty falling asleep, Dad still had to wake me so we could make it to the council meeting on time. The clerk ushered me in almost immediately after our arrival. I sat facing the chairman. It felt strange to be in the council chamber without officers hovering over me.

"Mr. Chairman, sir," I said, "I trust you received the final engineer's report I delivered yesterday."

"Yes, we did. We found the input from your engineers to be exceedingly helpful. Some of their recommendations are being implemented as we speak. Well done, Ms. Phillips." He sounded astonished that I had accomplished the task.

"Thank you, sir."

"We would be happy to resume trade with the cabin at such time as further needs arise."

"That is very good news, sir."

"Thank you for your service to our community. You are dismissed."

Chairman Lambrecht raised his gavel. Before he could bring it down, definitively concluding our interaction, I spoke up.

"Sir."

He paused, gavel in the air.

"Would you consider terminating my probation?"

He placed the gavel on the desk and folded his hands. "Ms. Phillips, the termination of your probation is contingent upon you producing a list of three hundred people genetically predisposed to survival outside of the USCSBS. So far, we have only seen two hundred twenty-five names."

"You'll be happy to know, sir, that I collected more genetic samples yesterday. I should be able to add to your list within the next two weeks."

"I'm glad to hear it." The chairman pounded his gavel. "You are dismissed."

It took great restraint to walk calmly out of the room. When the door of the anteroom closed behind me, I allowed myself one silent leap for joy. Chairman Lambrecht had given me an opening to talk about the people's proposal the next time I appeared before the Council.

The only problem was, I might have to relinquish seventy-five more names—people who would be forced out of the biosphere against their will—before the Council would consider my request. I wasn't sure if I could bring myself to do that, without knowing for sure whether the Council would agree to the people's proposal.

Dad spotted my grin and smiled tentatively. "Well?"

"The good news is they loved the engineers' reports. The bad news is"—I patted Dad on the back—"you have to babysit me a little while longer."

"Happy to do it." Dad tipped his invisible hat toward me. "As long as you don't start running off like you did when Mom was your guardian."

"I can't make any guarantees. Urgent early morning errands sometimes come up."

We walked from the administration building to Janelle's house. We returned the papers her father had given to her. She looked stronger than she had the day before. When my dad went to the kitchen to get glasses of water for us, she slipped me a letter to give to her dad. I left her house confident that she was going to be okay and that we had done the right thing, taking her to see her father.

Unable to complete any more errands under Dad's watchful eye, I decided to leave the Bubble. That would give me time to visit with Mom and Josh before nightfall, when I could start my drive to Lincoln. Dad helped me carry the DNA samples to the airlock and hugged me goodbye.

"It'll take at least a week to run all of these samples," I said. "I'll be back as soon as I can."

I could see the loneliness clouding his eyes.

"I'm going to do everything I can to get Mom and Josh back in here before Christmas," I said. "Can you hang on until then?"

Dad nodded. I gave him one more hug and stepped into the airlock. He closed the door.

I pulled out of the airlock and parked the Civic a few yards from the entrance. I approached several people before I found someone who knew my mom and brother. She directed me to their house. I knocked on the door. I didn't even see the door move before I found myself smothered in a hug from Mom.

She eagerly invited me in. Smoke hung heavy in the room. I tried to suppress my cough. A stovepipe extended from the ceiling halfway down to the beginnings of a brick and stone fireplace, sending only a fraction of the smoke out of the house.

"It'll be better when we finish the fireplace," Mom said. "Josh is busy with officer training. I work on it as much as I can, but once my fingers go numb I have to stop working and build a fire so I don't get frostbite."

We sat on the single bunk built into the right side wall. I thought about how this home compared to our two-story in Sioux Falls. "I'm so sorry I let them send you out here."

Mom's chipper demeanor turned serious. "This is not your fault. You can't control what the Council does. None of us can. Until we can get a new kind of government in place, we have to live with their decisions and make the best of them."

"But Dad says none of the council members will give up their power. If anyone tries to push for a new form of government, the Council will throw them out."

"I don't know how it's going to happen, but I know it will. Everyone knows, now, what the Council is capable of. Somehow, we will find a way to get back to a government that supports the values this country was founded on."

"Are you talking about a revolution or something? People could get hurt."

Mom nodded. "Some things are worth sacrificing for. I don't want my grandchild to grow up in a world of fear."

I thought about what Mom said. I had repeatedly subjected myself to Dr. Franklin's condescension in order to reconcile with the cabin community. I had risked my life and freedom to see my family and to save Dr. Franklin's life. But would I be willing to place my life on the line for a chance of changing an unjust system—for the chance of giving the people who came after me a better life?

"Do you have everything you need?" I asked.

"Sure," Mom said. "We get extra rations because of the cold temperatures. We have to collect our own water and firewood, but there's plenty of both in the area. We have more freedom out here—we can go anywhere we want inside the perimeter of the checkpoints. I had forgotten how much I missed the fresh air."

I smiled. The air inside the Bubble did have a certain stagnant, manufactured smell to it.

"Josh and I really are having fun and learning a lot. The government provided us with the stovepipe and all the tools we needed. After we helped a couple of our neighbors build their homes, we put this together all by ourselves. Next spring we're hoping to add on another room there." Mom pointed to the wall across from the door.

I smiled. Despite the rough conditions, Mom did look like she was enjoying the adventure.

"I'm sorry I couldn't stop by earlier," I said. "My recent trips have been on a bit of a time crunch."

"Don't worry about it. That gave me time to get the place spiffed up for your grand tour. Last week, before we got the roof on, it was still pretty drafty."

The door swung open, and Josh walked in. The fatigue in his face vanished when he spotted me. I ran across the room, reaching him in two steps.

"It's so good to see you." I wrapped my arms around him, and he gave me a squeeze. "I hear you joined the dark side."

Josh laughed. "Well, you get in trouble so much, I figured entering law enforcement would be the easiest way to stay in touch. Besides, there are a few more opportunities for advancement as an officer than as a packer of ration boxes. I'll be able to provide a better life for my family." His face was a mixture of awe and joy and anxiety. I could tell that he was both thrilled and overwhelmed to say the words *my family.*

"How was training?"

Josh dropped a bucket of rocks he had collected next to the fireplace. "Fun and exhausting." He flopped down on the lower of two bunks built into the wall across from us. "We were working on pursuing and apprehending suspects. That's one part of the job that would be a lot easier in the B.—" he glanced at Mom and corrected himself "—in the biosphere, where they can only run so far."

"Still better than your last job?" I asked.

"Way better."

I contributed some of the food I had brought and helped Mom prepare supper. As soon as everyone's plate was dished up, we lit a few candles and put out the fire.

The door opened and Jessica walked in. I almost overturned my plate when I jumped up to give her a hug.

"Careful," Jessica said, "you're going to get dirty."

I pulled back and looked her up and down. Soil crusted

her shoes and gloves and was ground into the knees of her jeans.

"Are you on the mud wrestling team now?" I asked.

Jessica smiled. It was the first smile I'd seen in months that made it all the way to her eyes.

"More like the turnip wrestling team," she said. "We've been planting and weeding winter vegetables." She pulled off her gloves. "It's a dirty job, but somebody's got to do it."

I handed her a plate of food. "You can take my spot." I motioned to the place I had been sitting on the right bunk.

"No way." Jessica sat on the floor, her legs crossed. "I'm not going to get my bed all dirty."

I sat beside Mom and picked up my plate. "Dad told me your acclimatization was pretty intense."

Mom winced at the memory. "There were people who couldn't even walk, and the officers kept making them go back in."

I shook my head. I had endured the acclimatization process a year before. I remembered the feelings of panic and desperation like it was yesterday.

"Did you know the Council was planning on kicking everyone out without giving them time to acclimatize?" I asked. "It was Dr. Franklin who convinced them people needed time to adjust. If he hadn't . . ."

I didn't want to think about the alternative. I was so lucky that my whole family had survived the Change. I couldn't imagine losing them now.

Eager to change the subject, I said, "Lauren looked

good."

Josh's face lit up at the sound of her name.

"We had her over for supper last night," I said. "She got to hear the baby's heartbeat this week."

"Thank you for looking out for her," Josh said. "I would give anything to be in there taking care of her myself."

Jessica looked down at her plate, blinking rapidly.

I'd done it again, speaking before thinking. "I'm so sorry, Jess."

"It's okay." She sniffled. "I don't want you to feel like you have to walk on eggshells around me. I just have to figure out how I'm going to deal with all these things that can set me off."

"You know this is a safe place to express what you're feeling," Mom said. "If you need to cry or scream or just talk about stuff, you can always do it here."

Jessica nodded.

After supper, we worked in the dark to build up the wall around the fireplace, embedding bricks and rocks into the fresh mortar Mom mixed. With four of us working, we made a lot of progress before the chill demanded we build another fire.

I warmed my hands over the stove. "I've got some good news from the Bubble. There's a group of people who want out, but they're only willing to go if the Council will let people who have been separated from their families come back in."

"And the Council agreed to that?" Mom asked.

"Well, we haven't exactly asked yet," I said, "so don't start spreading any rumors I can't deliver on. I'm still on probation as far as the Council is concerned, so they're not going to give me any special consideration."

The feeling had returned to my fingers. "I've got to get back to Lincoln to start testing my newest batch of DNA samples."

"I'll walk you to your car," Josh said.

"I think I can make it okay," I said.

Josh held the door open for me. "It's really dark out there, and the village isn't exactly arranged in a logical pattern. I'm coming with you."

I exchanged smiles with Mom. It was sweet to see Josh looking out for someone besides himself. I was becoming more and more convinced that he was going to be a great husband and father.

Josh guided me through the village and back to the road. He was right. It would have been easy to get disoriented if I'd been weaving through the maze of houses alone.

I opened the car door. "I'll be back in a week or two."

"Christy." I couldn't see Josh's face, but I could hear the intensity in his voice. "I need to be with my wife and baby."

"I will do everything I can. I promise."

Josh gave me a hug and watched me drive away.

# 36

I was impatient to start testing the new samples. After causing my family to be split apart, I was eager to do something that might bring them back together. But before I could head for Lincoln, I had to take a northern detour. I retraced the route I had taken to the Bubble so I would be heading south when I reached the spot where I had left Mr. Cole. I still couldn't risk giving him any hint as to the location of the biosphere.

I stopped at the spot where I had dropped Mr. Cole off. I didn't see anyone in the area. I imagined he had sought shelter somewhere nearby. I was nervous about attracting the wrong kind of attention, but I wanted to get on my way as soon as possible. I turned on my emergency flashers so Mr. Cole would notice I was there. I scanned my surroundings and then began examining each business lining the street, looking for signs of life inside.

I was intent on the dry cleaners on the left side of the street when someone knocked on my passenger's side window. I jumped and stifled a scream.

I turned and saw Mr. Cole, smiling at me through the window.

I took a deep breath and reached across the car to open the door.

"Thanks for picking me up." Mr. Cole slid into the

passenger's seat and closed the door.

I wanted to chastise him for delaying his daughter's return to the biosphere, and for slowing me down when I was trying to do my job. But then I remembered that he had just said goodbye to his daughter for the last time. He would never get to see her again in this life, even though they only lived a few hundred miles away.

"I'm glad you're okay." I handed him an envelope. "This is from Janelle."

"Thank you," he said, "so much."

It took a week to test all of the new DNA samples. As the results came in, I committed the names of those who tested positive to memory. I couldn't risk bringing a written list to the Bubble. If the Council got ahold of it before they had agreed to the people's terms, all we were working toward would be lost.

When I wasn't running tests or checking results, Ashley and I spent our time in the market. Not knowing how active the market would be during the winter, we wanted to stockpile essentials.

I also made a couple visits to the cabin to pick up outgoing mail and a list of items the Board needed from the biosphere. Joy had obliterated the dread that used to accompany my visits to the cabin. It was wonderful to be forgiven and fully accepted back into the community. The months I had spent serving the community, trying to demonstrate my remorse and my desire for reconciliation, now all seemed worthwhile.

It warmed my heart to see Dr. Franklin pitching in to help around the cabin as his strength allowed. The smile on his face seemed all the more remarkable considering the personal tragedies he had experienced. I hoped he would one day be able to forgive the man responsible for the accident. I was grateful for my glimpse into Dr. Franklin's past. It helped me to understand his attitudes and actions and to appreciate even more the difficult adjustments he had to make now that he was back in his community but no longer in charge.

Angela and Ryan had set their wedding date for New Year's Day. Despite the limited resources available for decorations, clothing, and food, Angela was thrilled to share with me her wedding plans and preparations. If all went as planned, I would get to enjoy Christmas in the Bubble with my newly reunited family and spend New Year's with my friends at the cabin, celebrating the Wright wedding.

Halfway through the drive back to the Bubble, big wet snowflakes started to fall, sticking to everything they touched. The sight of snow-covered trees, cars, and signs, sparkling in the light of the setting sun, reminded me that Christmas was almost here. If I didn't convince the Council to agree to our plan within the next few days, my family wouldn't be able to celebrate the holiday together.

Approaching the checkpoint, I could see the silhouette of the officer standing in the middle of the road holding his hand out, signaling me to stop. I didn't realize until I had almost reached him that the officer was Josh.

I hopped out of the car, ran over, and gave him a hug. "Look at you, all handsome in your uniform."

Josh cleared his throat. "A little respect for my position, please."

I pulled away. "Yes, sir."

I expected to see a glint of humor in his eyes, but he was dead serious.

"Officer Phillips, I come bearing information requested by the Council," I said. "I would like to request admittance to the biosphere and an audience with the Council."

Josh rolled his eyes. "You don't have to be like that," he whispered. "Just make it look good for them." He motioned over his shoulder with his thumb toward the two approaching officers.

"Got it, Officer Doofus," I whispered back.

"Ms. Phillips' personal inspection is clear." Josh turned to face the other officers. "Ready to begin the vehicle inspection."

The three officers examined every nook and cranny of the Civic.

"All clear," one officer said, closing both doors on the passenger's side.

"We'll escort you in now," the other officer said.

I moved toward the driver's side door. He closed it just

before I got there.

"This way, Ms. Phillips." He motioned toward the front of the car.

Confused, I walked around the car. Perhaps they were going to drive me to the airlock.

The other officer cut me off before I reached the passenger's side door. "We'll be going on foot, Ms. Phillips." He motioned down the road.

I shot Josh a questioning look, but I didn't argue. When we could see the entrance to the airlock, the officers guided me off the road to the right. We wound through the village, stopping at Mom and Josh's cabin.

"This is great," I said, "but I need to speak to the Council."

"They'll send for you when they are ready to see you," one of the officers said.

The officers turned and left.

I was concerned. What if the Council didn't get the message that I was there? I was surrounded by people who wanted to get back into the Bubble to be with their families. And dozens of people inside the Bubble were willing to trade places with them. But that couldn't happen unless I was able to speak to the Council.

I knocked on the door. After peeking to see who it was, Mom flung the door open, put her arm around my shoulders, and hustled me into the warm cabin.

Mom, Josh, and Jessica had completed the fireplace. The house felt homier already, without smoke clouding the room.

They even had a little Charlie Brown-style Christmas tree in the corner, with a few ornaments made out of the containers the rations came in.

"I love it, Mom," I said, admiring all of the little improvements she had made. "I'm afraid it might get a little crowded, though. It looks like I'll be staying here until the Council invites me in."

"That's wonderful," Mom said, bustling around the cabin tidying up. "It's been so long since we've been able to spend time together. I'll sleep on the floor, and you can have my bed."

"No, Mom. I'm not going to kick you out of your bed. I'll take the floor."

"You can help me finish the Christmas presents, and when you do go in, you can take your father's present to him."

"I'm still hoping to get you and Josh in, so you can deliver it yourself."

Mom stopped and looked at me. "Do you really think that might happen?"

"I don't know, but I'm going to try."

Tears welled up in her eyes. "That would be wonderful."

Mom and I were cleaning up after breakfast the next morning when someone knocked on the door. It was the first time I eagerly greeted an officer at our door.

"The Council is ready for you," the officer said.

I grabbed my backpack, gave Mom a quick hug, and followed the officer out the door. He escorted me to the airlock and gave the code to open the door. I waited alone in the airlock until the atmosphere had been converted. Another officer opened the door into the biosphere and escorted me to the administration building.

*Only one officer? Either they're short-staffed, or I've lost my status as public enemy number one.*

We stopped briefly in the anteroom while the clerk announced my arrival to the Council.

*Lord, please give me the right words to say.* I knew I only had one chance to get this right. If I couldn't convince the Council, my parents may never be together again.

The officer escorted me into the council chamber. He stood by the door while I took my seat in front of the chairman. I felt lonely in the center of the large room.

"Do you have the final list of names?" Chairman Lambrecht asked.

I swallowed. "Yes, sir, I do. In fact, instead of seventy-five names, I have a hundred and fifty."

A murmur rippled through the Council. I had succeeded in getting their attention.

"However."

The room fell silent again.

"The individuals who submitted to the DNA testing will allow their names to be released under one condition."

"Ms. Phillips." The chairman addressed me as if I were a two-year-old who wouldn't quit playing in the toilet. "You are still on probation. You most certainly are not in a position to negotiate."

I feared at any moment his gavel would fall, and the conversation would be over.

"You are absolutely right, Mr. Chairman. But I must honor the agreement I made with the people who gave me their DNA samples."

Chairman Lambrecht crossed his arms and leaned back in his chair. "And what is that condition?"

"The people whose DNA tests were positive will leave only if, for each person who voluntarily moves out of the biosphere, you allow one person who was forced to leave to come back in and reunite with their family."

"And how, exactly, will that help to decrease the demand on the atmospheric conversion system?"

"It won't, sir," I said, my voice barely audible.

"Give us the list of names, Ms. Phillips, and then step outside while the Council considers your proposal." The chairman held out his hand, palm up.

"I don't have it," I said.

"Excuse me?"

"I don't have a list, sir."

"So you were lying when you said you had one hundred fifty names."

"I was not lying, sir. I do not have a *list* of names. The names are in my head. I can't share them with you until you agree to the terms set forth by the people."

Chairman Lambrecht's ears turned red. "Ms. Phillips,

you are dismissed."

The officer opened the door, and I stepped into the anteroom.

I'd had my chance, and I'd blown it. I thought about all the things I could have said. Maybe it would have helped to share a story about families torn apart. Though empathy didn't seem to be the Council's strong suit. Practical arguments might have been more convincing if I could have come up with any.

The door to the council chamber opened, and the officer escorted me back in.

"It is the decision of this Council that, after one hundred fifty people voluntarily leave the USCSBS, seventy-five people, selected at random, will be allowed to return." Chairman Lambrecht pounded his gavel. The officer strode toward me.

"Mr. Chairman, sir," I said, louder than I intended.

The chairman glanced at me, waved his hand toward the door, and returned his attention to the papers on his desk. The officer pulled on my arm, trying to coax me to my feet.

"The people who are now living outside the biosphere have been trained to work on the outside," I said. "If those who return to the biosphere to live continue to spend their workday on the outside, that will decrease the demand on the atmospheric conversion system, so more people can move back into the biosphere."

"The decision of the Council is final," Chairman Lambrecht said. "You will leave the list of names with the secretary on your way out."

"I can't do that, sir."

The chairman stood and leaned forward, his hands resting on the desk. "What did you say?"

"I can't release the names to you unless you agree to the conditions the people put forth. I can inform them of your offer, but I can't give you their names until they give consent."

"Ms. Phillips." Chairman Lambrecht's face flushed bright red. I wouldn't have been surprised if I'd seen steam coming out of his ears. "At eight o'clock tomorrow morning, I expect to see one hundred fifty people at the airlock entrance, ready to move out. If I do not see that, you will answer to me."

A slight jerk of the chairman's head prompted the officer to force me to my feet. Eager to escape the chairman's threatening glare, I hurried to the door.

Outside of the administration building, I took in a big gulp of fresh air and blinked back tears. My heart was racing, and my legs felt like they would hardly hold me, but I did not want to break down in front of the officer. I hurried down the street, trying to stay one step ahead so he couldn't see my face.

"That's really nice, what you're doing to help get families back together," the officer said.

"Thanks." I slowed my pace a little.

"You know, the Council is just trying to keep everyone safe. It's not an easy job."

I sped up again. "It wouldn't hurt them to listen every now and then."

We walked half a block in silence.

"My wife and son are on the outside," the officer said. "I didn't even know they got tested until the council representative showed up at our door telling them to pack and get ready to leave."

"I'm really sorry. I had no idea the Council was going to force people out."

The officer hesitated. "Do you think you could do the DNA test on me?"

"Absolutely. We have some testing kits at the house."

I unlocked the door and motioned the officer in. "Sorry about the mess. Dad isn't used to picking up after himself."

I pulled a notebook and a box of testing supplies out of the cupboard.

I handed the notebook to the officer. "Your name and address, please."

I swabbed the inside of the officer's cheek and put the swab in a tube.

"Officer Parizek." I copied his name onto the tube. "It's nice to meet you. I'll let you know as soon as I get the results." I put my hand on his arm. "I hope you get to be with your family again soon."

I put the sample and testing supplies away.

"I'm sure you've got to get back to your patrol." I opened the door. "Thanks for walking me home."

The officer stood but made no move toward the door. "I can't leave you alone, not as long as you're on probation."

I sighed. "You don't have to babysit me. I promise I'll be good."

"Maybe I could help you contact the people on your list."

I hesitated to involve another person, but I didn't know where Dad was. It was going to be difficult for me to get to everyone by the end of the day, working alone. And Officer Parizek seemed sincere.

"Do you have a directory?" I hadn't committed the addresses to memory. It had been hard enough just remembering the names.

"I can get one." Officer Parizek walked briskly toward the door. "I'll be right back."

While he was gone, I wrote down the list of names. It made me nervous to have the names in writing, but the officer wouldn't be able to help me unless he knew who we were looking for.

When he returned, he circled the names in the biosphere directory, while I finished writing the list.

We started in the neighborhood right around my house. Officer Parizek flipped through the directory to identify all of the people on the list who lived in the area. I knocked on doors and explained the Council's partial approval of their terms. Many people expressed their anger and frustration with the Council, but only a few absolutely refused to leave. Most were undecided. I tried to encourage them, pointing out that reuniting families was a worthwhile goal, even if we weren't able to reunite as many as we first hoped to.

The officer and I worked through one neighborhood after another. It was well past dark when I finished talking with the 173$^{rd}$ person. I had fudged my numbers a little when talking to the Council, in case some of the people changed their minds. I hoped the Council's altered terms wouldn't deter too many people. I did not want to imagine what my punishment would be if 150 people didn't show up at the airlock the next morning.

My feet were aching by the time Officer Parizek and I made it back to the house. Though only a fraction of the population of the United States had fit in the Bubble, it was still a large area to traverse on foot.

The officer turned me over to the watchful eye of my father. Dad insisted on giving him a bite to eat before he left. I put the directory and list of names in the cabinet with the DNA testing supplies and joined Officer Parizek at the table. I didn't realize how hungry I was until I sat and took the pressure off my weary feet.

# 37

I left the house at seven fifteen the next morning, fearing I would be the only one who showed up at the airlock. When I came within sight of the airlock entrance, I was relieved to see a large cluster of people.

Drawing closer, I heard a lot of yelling and noticed the officers around the perimeter of the group had their guns drawn. I ran toward the crowd.

"There she is." A voice projected above the din.

The crowd surged toward me, but the officers kept them from reaching me. I stopped and looked around, trying to make sense of the scene in front of me.

A man broke free from the group and ran toward me. His face looked like that of a linebacker headed for a member of the opposing team. I wanted to run, but my feet were frozen to the ground. He stopped before making the tackle I expected, his face only inches from mine.

"You gave us your word." His voice dripped with accusation. "We trusted you."

I took a step back. "I kept my word. I let all of you know what the Council had agreed to."

"Was that before or after you gave them our names?"

"What? I never—what do you mean?"

"There were officers at our doors this morning,

rounding us up to come here, whether we wanted to or not."

"But I didn't tell the Council . . ."

No, I didn't tell the Council. But I did tell Officer Parizek.

I stepped to the side and spoke to the nearest officer. "Where is Officer Parizek?"

The officer shrugged his shoulders. "I haven't seen him this morning."

I circled the group, looking for Officer Parizek and asking people on the perimeter if they'd seen him. I came up empty.

I sprinted to the administration building.

"Miss? Can I help you, Miss?" the receptionist asked as I flew past her desk.

An alarm blared. The halls filled with the noise of pounding footsteps. I picked up speed. I had to make it to the council chamber before they caught up with me.

"There she is," someone behind me yelled.

I threw open the door to the anteroom and slammed it behind me. I pushed a chair against the door, jamming the back under the door handle. I hoped to slow down my pursuers so I would have time to say my piece to the Council.

I took a deep breath, carefully opened the door to the council chamber, and slipped inside.

". . . reminded the people today who's in charge," Chairman Lambrecht addressed Officer Parizek, "and what happens when the people try to manipulate the Council. You, young man, are on the short list for the next open council seat."

Though I disagreed with his methods, I'd thought Chairman Lambrecht based his decisions on what he thought was best for thc pcople of the biosphere. Now I saw that he wasn't looking for the common good at all. He was just trying to preserve his power.

The chairman left his desk and walked to the center of the room, where Officer Parizek was seated. "Congratulations, Officer." They shook hands. "Well done."

Officer Parizek smiled and nodded. I couldn't believe I had trusted him. I had believed his story about wanting to see his wife and son. But he was just using me to advance his own political career.

Turning back toward his desk, the chairman spotted me.

I strode toward him, keeping my eyes locked on his. "You cannot force people to leave. They were all promised safety and protection in the biosphere. You can't go back on that promise."

"We are doing what we have to, to keep the people in the USCSBS safe."

"I'm sure I can find other people who want to leave. Give me another week. The people you rounded up this morning—they didn't even have time to pack their things or say goodbye to their loved ones."

"Well, now, that's your fault, isn't it?" Chairman Lambrecht crossed his arms. "If you had given us the names yesterday, we could have given them plenty of time to prepare."

The door behind the chairman's desk flew open, and officers flooded the room.

"But I promised—"

An officer tackled me. I landed hard. By the time I caught my breath, I was stumbling down the long hall behind the council chamber, my hands tied behind my back, trying not to fall as four officers pressed me forward.

We exited the administration building by a back door and went straight to the airlock. I was grateful the back alleys we took didn't go by the crowd of people about to be forced out of the biosphere. The officers shoved me into the airlock and locked the door behind me.

*Why did I trust Officer Parizek?* By accepting his offer of help and letting him see the list, I had effectively gone back on my word to almost two hundred people. The officer had reinforced my growing belief that I couldn't trust anyone. If something important needed to be done, I resolved to just do it myself.

# 38

The door opened again, and the crowd filed in. I knew some of them had come voluntarily, but still, every one of them looked angry. I crouched in the corner, willing myself to become invisible. But the elevated loading dock gave every person who entered a clear view of the entire room. Those who spotted me weren't afraid to say exactly what they thought of me.

"Traitor!"

"We trusted you."

"Liar!"

"How could you do this to us?"

"You're a fraud."

"Evil. Just evil."

The words washed over me like acid, making me want to crawl out of my seared skin. Maybe I was a bad person. I had tried so hard to do the right thing and just ended up hurting the people who trusted me. My job as liaison between the Bubble and the cabin, which used to give me such a sense of purpose, now only seemed to cause pain.

The walk-in door closed, and the garage door opener rumbled to life, opening the door leading to the outside about a foot. The people near the door immediately began gasping for breath. They hurried toward the opposite wall in search of breathable air. Several crowded up the stairs, shaking the doorknob and pounding on the door to the biosphere.

I moved toward the cluster of people nearest to me. I hesitated while I was still a few feet away. They probably didn't want to hear anything I had to say. I took another step toward them. "It will be a little easier if you spread out and give each other some space."

They looked at me with disdain and crowded closer to each other and farther from me.

I moved to a group of people who were struggling more than most to catch their breath. "Let me help you with your breathing. If you can slow it down, it won't be so hard to adjust."

A man turned away from the group and stepped toward me. "You have . . . a lot of nerve," he said between gasps, "forcing us in here . . . and then trying . . . to tell us . . . what to do."

I turned away, blinking back tears. Their suffering was my fault, and there was nothing I could do about it.

After several minutes, the garage door closed. Though breathing was still difficult, the fear that marked everyone's eyes when the door was open faded. People spread out through the room, and some sat down to get comfortable. I stayed in a corner near the garage door, trying to avoid making eye contact.

I listened for the whir of the fans to bring in the biosphere air and give the people a reprieve. Instead, I heard the garage door opener grind to life again. The rush of fresh air from the outside felt good to me but prompted the others to hurry away, pressing against the far wall.

Fear welled up inside me. Dr. Franklin had recommended a return to the biosphere's atmosphere after each stage of the acclimatization process. Whoever was in charge had ignored that part of Dr. Franklin's protocol. I didn't know how the body would react when forced through the process without a break.

The pounding on the biosphere door intensified. A few people frantically groped the walls of the airlock, looking for some other way out. I approached one of them.

"Look, they aren't going to let us back into the biosphere. It'll be easier if you—"

The woman shoved me to the side. With my hands still tied behind my back, I couldn't reach out to break my fall. I tucked my chin so I wouldn't hit my head. The hard landing knocked the wind out of me. While I lay there trying to catch my breath, someone stepped on my leg and stumbled, nearly falling on top of me. Though I still felt lightheaded, I struggled to my feet. The floor was not a safe place to be.

I heard the thud of someone else hitting the floor. I hurried over to see if I could help. The people gathered around her saw me coming and closed the circle, preventing me from reaching her. I returned to my corner. It tore me apart to watch people desperately trying to catch their breath or find a way out, while I was powerless to help.

*Jesus, are you even there? I've tried everything I could think of, and I've only made things worse. I don't know what to do. How can I make things better?* I cried softly, feeling more alone than I ever had before, even though I was in a room full of people.

*My grace is sufficient for you, for power is made perfect in weakness.* The verse crept into the back of my mind. I realized I had been trying to fix everything using my own plans. Every strategy I tried seemed to backfire. I knew, now, that I couldn't do it without help, that any plan I came up with on my own would probably fail.

*Jesus, I'm sorry for trying to take control. I want your will in this situation, not mine. If there is anything I can do to help carry out your will, I'll do it. I don't need to see the big picture, Lord, just the next step you want me to take.*

*Jesus, please give these people the peace and comfort only you can give. I know how much they're struggling, and I can't help them. Fill this room with your presence to bring calm and to help them persevere.*

*I don't know how it can happen, now, but Lord I pray that you would give the people living outside the Bubble the chance to be with their families again. I thought I found a way to make that happen, but it was my way, not yours. But I know your power can shine through my weakness.*

The garage door closed. I continued to pray. The door opened three more times, a foot off the ground each time. The people gave up their desperate attempts to escape. It was all they could do to breathe. People were passed out all over the floor of the airlock. Even those who were still awake looked like they'd given up and were waiting to die.

I felt a stirring inside of me to say something

encouraging.

*But Lord, they all hate me. They don't want to hear anything from me.*

The impulse grew stronger.

I stood and cleared my throat. A few faces turned toward me. Their pained expressions almost made me turn away.

"I'm so sorry I put you all through this." I resisted the urge to justify my actions or throw the blame back on the Council. "I know you've been scared and desperate, and many of you are ready to give up. I felt that way, too." More faces turned toward me, bolstering my courage. "You just need to hang in there a little longer. Pretty soon it's going to get easier. You're almost there."

My speech was interrupted by the grind of the garage door opener. I turned toward the door and was surprised to see it opening the rest of the way.

*Thank you, Lord, for helping everyone make it to the end.*

# 39

I walked toward the garage door. I could already see the navy blue uniforms of the officers waiting on the other side to escort me to jail. But I wasn't upset or scared. I knew that I could do just as much good behind bars as I could in the thick of things—maybe even more. Prayer was my most valuable tool. As long as I was locked up, I didn't have to worry about my goals getting in the way of God's will.

As the door rose further, though, I saw that the officers had their backs to us. Beyond the officers was a crowd of people. Had someone on the outside figured out where the biosphere was? Were we under attack?

The noise of the crowd outside swelled, and the people surged forward. All six officers drew their weapons, halting the crowd's momentum.

I scanned the crowd, spotting several familiar faces. This wasn't an invading army. It was a group of people from the village.

One man stepped forward, hands in the air. All six officers trained their guns on him.

"Stop right there," an officer yelled.

The man's face was blocked from my view by one of the officers. I stepped to the side so I could see. It was Josh.

I wanted to yell at him to get back before someone got

hurt. But I didn't want to risk escalating the situation.

*Lord, please keep him safe. I don't know what's going on here, but give him your wisdom.*

"This is a peaceful exercise of our right to free speech."

The people quieted as soon as Josh began to speak.

"The people inside the airlock agreed to leave the biosphere only if an equal number of people were allowed back in."

One of the officers said, "The government's directive is to resettle these people in the village. No one is moving back in."

"We can't allow that to happen," Josh said.

An officer gestured toward the airlock with her head. "Get 'em outta there," she said to the officer beside her.

The officer turned around and stepped inside.

The crowd surged again, but not toward the officers this time. They fanned out, forming a semicircle several people deep, completely surrounding the airlock entrance.

The officer inside the airlock said, "All right, everybody out."

No one moved.

He grabbed the arm of a woman standing near him. "Come on, let's go."

She sat down on the floor, letting her arm go limp.

The officer took a deep breath. "Look, we can do this the easy way or the hard way. Either way, you're all going to end up out there." He gestured toward the door with his thumb. "And those of you who cooperate will be the first to get a house.

I'm telling you, you're not going to want to spend too many nights outside in this kind of weather."

Glances were exchanged around the room.

A man sat down on the floor beside the woman and linked his arm with hers. One by one, people linked elbows, forming human chains. I was thrilled to see such a demonstration of solidarity. The woman at the end of the chain nearest me coaxed the others in her group closer to me. She slid her arm through the narrow space between my left arm and my body. I didn't think anyone would want me as a part of their chain. I flashed her a grateful smile. Soon every person in the room was connected to at least half a dozen others.

The officer backed toward the door. "I'm going to need some help in here," he said over his shoulder, keeping his eyes on us.

". . . the only way to get rations to you." An officer on the outside was trying her hand at a persuasive speech. "If you don't let these people out, you're cutting off your only source of supplies."

"The Council claims it's doing all this to preserve the lives of the people of the biosphere," Josh said. "If they really have our best interests in mind, would they let us starve out here?"

"If you persist in violating the law, they will have no other choice."

"There's always a choice," Josh said.

The officers huddled together, exchanging whispers while still scanning the crowd. After several minutes, the officers made a triangular formation and slowly moved forward, guns still drawn. The villagers parted, allowing the officers through.

The officer at the center of the base of the triangle said, "When you get hungry enough, you'll decide to end this game."

The semicircle closed behind them, and the officers picked up speed.

As soon as they were out of sight, applause erupted, both inside the airlock and out. I ran outside and searched the milling crowd for Josh. I spotted him standing on the rocks next to the airlock entrance, trying to get the people's attention.

I ran to him. "Josh, you were amazing. I can't believe you just did that—and got all these people to go along with you."

"Yeah, but if we don't keep it together, the officers will have control again before we know it."

I turned around, pursed my lips, and gave a shrill whistle.

The crowd quieted.

"Thanks, I owe you one." Josh reached down to give me a fist bump. I shrugged my shoulders, my hands still tied behind my back.

He stood and addressed the people. "I had hoped that the Council would at least listen to what we had to say today. But it looks like they decided to try to wait us out, instead of hearing us out. Are they going to outlast us?"

"No!" the crowd yelled.

"Then we're going to have to stay organized and alert.

We'll take twelve-hour shifts in the airlock. When you're on the outside, you'll need to be working in the fields or hunting for food. We've saved up some rations, but they're not going to last very long.

"If you have the opportunity to talk with officers or Council members, our demands are simple. We will discontinue our protest when one hundred seventy-three people are allowed back into the biosphere to reunite with their families.

"I need a dozen volunteers to collect materials we can use to make sure they don't close the door on us, and to protect the people inside from the weather."

Several hands went up.

"Great, thank you. The people inside the airlock need some more time to adjust and rest. Who can provide them with some bedding?"

More hands were raised.

"Excellent. Finally, I need thirty people to take shifts guarding the entrance to the airlock. If you can help with guard duty, meet here at the entrance and we'll assign shifts.

"If we all work together, we can make this happen. We have to stay strong, so the Council will know that they can't push us around. Are you with me?"

Cheers erupted all around. The people from the village scattered to complete their assignments.

Josh organized those who volunteered to guard the entrance into groups of ten and scheduled them for eight-hour shifts. I admired his confidence and command of the situation.

My little brother really had grown up a lot in a few months. I knew he was willing to do anything to reunite with his wife. As I watched him interact with the other people from the village, I was convinced that he had their best interests in mind as well.

At Josh's prompting, one of the volunteers slipped over to me and cut my hands free. I flexed and extended my fingers and rubbed my wrists.

After dismissing the volunteers, Josh gave me a quick hug. "I've got to say a few words to the people inside."

I followed Josh, stopping at the entrance to the airlock.

"Thank you all for your willingness to make sacrifices so that other people could be reunited with their families. We're doing everything we can to make sure the Council honors your sacrifice. I know the last few hours have been more difficult than you could've ever imagined—I've been there. I wish I could offer each of you a luxury hotel room with a pillow-top mattress and free Wi-Fi, but I can't. What I can offer you is a day to rest and adjust, knowing that there are people guarding the door, keeping you safe."

He slipped his backpack off. "I'll be coming around with packets of food and water. We can't offer you much. Try to make it last through the night. If you have any questions, I'd be glad to answer them when I get to you."

I walked around the room with Josh, helping him pass out the small bags while he fielded questions. The most common was "How long?"—how long could we hold on without rations; how long were we willing to wait for the Council to come around? Josh said hopeful, encouraging things, but he couldn't give any specific answers.

After we finished handing out supplies, Josh and I parted the heavy blankets that had been hung over the entrance to the airlock and stepped outside. People were still working to block the garage door and sliding rock wall so they couldn't be closed using the controls inside the biosphere.

"Josh, I'm so proud of you." I gave him another hug. "Did you organize this whole thing?"

One corner of his mouth raised in a crooked smile. "I just suggested the idea, and the people ran with it."

"Do you really think it could work?"

He shrugged. "The Council can't keep ignoring the people forever. The only way we're going to see a change is if we take a stand."

"You certainly did that today."

"For a moment there, I thought my chances of getting shot were greater than my chances of getting heard. In any case, I'm pretty sure my career in law enforcement is over."

"You could always go back to the rations warehouse."

Josh wrinkled his nose.

I laughed. "Was it really that bad?"

"That depends," Josh said. "If you like mind-anesthetizing boredom combined with back-breaking lifting, it was the perfect job."

"I didn't see Mom out here. Is she at home?"

Josh nodded. "She's in charge of the rations we've been saving up over the past few days."

"Let's go home. I'd like to talk to her about—everything."

"I don't think that's a good idea," Josh said. "If the officers catch you by yourself, they'll put you in jail for sure. We might not be able to get food and water to you in jail. I think you need to stay here." He motioned toward the airlock. "You know, safety in numbers and all that."

"But they hate me. Did you see the looks some of them gave me when I handed them their food? They think this is all my fault, that I betrayed them to the Council."

"How did the Council get their names?"

"Well, I didn't tell them, that's for sure." My gaze dropped to the ground. "But I did trust the wrong person. Officer Parizek gave me this sob story about wanting to be reunited with his family, and I believed him."

"Listen, everyone in there knows who's really to blame, and it's not you. Just lay low for a while and give them some time. They'll come around."

"I hope you're right."

# 40

I walked slowly back into the airlock. I wanted to do something. I wanted to help. I didn't want to just sit there and be safe.

Many of the people in the airlock had already fallen asleep, exhausted by the acclimatization process. I stepped carefully over and around people until I found an empty spot on the floor.

I thought of all the ways I might be able to help. I could sneak back to my car and drive somewhere to find more food. I could get ahold of one of the officers' guns and do some hunting. I could work in the fields—I'd done that at the cabin.

Josh was right. If I tried any of those things, it would undoubtedly just lead to my arrest. But I still felt restless and unproductive.

I lay back on the floor, closed my eyes, and took a deep breath, trying to quell the impatience swelling in my chest. *Lord, why can't I help?*

I took another deep breath. As I breathed out, I felt it, deep in my chest. *You can.*

"You're right," I whispered. I remembered what my job was.

I prayed with a level of fervor that I had never felt before. I prayed for the safety of the people in the biosphere, in the airlock, and in the village. I prayed for the officers, caught in the middle trying to do their jobs. I asked that God would give the council members wisdom and understanding, and especially that God would soften Chairman Lambrecht's heart. I prayed for my family, particularly for Josh's baby. And through every prayer, I asked that God's will be done, not mine.

My mind drifted to the last time I saw Scott, before he left Lincoln in search of his parents. I had finally mustered the courage to ask if I could pray with him, and he'd said yes. I'd never felt closer to him than I did when we were praying together. And then he was gone, leaving a feeling of emptiness that nothing else could fill. I longed to have Scott there in the airlock with me, joining me in prayer.

My stomach rumbled, reminding me to turn back to God. I started to pray again.

The next day around noon, a group of villagers came to continue the airlock sit-in. The newest evacuees, now well-rested and breathing without difficulty, were eager to get out and move around in the fresh air. I wanted to do the same, but I knew what Josh would say—"You have to stay; it's not safe for you out there."

So, I greeted my new roommates, spent some time talking with those I hadn't seen in a while, and accepted another tiny packet of food and water. After everyone claimed a piece of floor, the commotion in the airlock calmed, and I resumed my prayer crusade.

The hours dragged on. Each time I felt impatient or bored or hungry or thirsty, I tried to refocus on God, offering my discomfort as part of my prayer.

At midnight, the newest evacuees returned to the airlock, and the villagers went back out to work.

At first, the people returning to the airlock excitedly shared stories of their adventures—their successful hunts, their run-ins with officers trying to keep them from getting to the fields where the winter vegetables were growing.

But after a few days, no one had the energy to tell tales. Most people spent their time in the airlock sleeping. When we were asleep, we could forget about the hollow feeling in our stomachs.

The sit-in had been going on for five days when Josh escorted the midnight shift into the airlock with a "Ho-ho-ho. Merry Christmas!"

All around the room, expressions of hunger and discomfort softened into smiles.

Jesus had come into the world on the first Christmas as a baby who had to sleep in a feed trough because he didn't even have a bed. Throughout his life, he stood up for what was true and right, no matter what it cost him.

*Jesus, thank you for coming here to show us how it's done. Give us your strength to persevere in our pursuit of truth and justice. And—happy birthday.*

When Josh got to me with the day's packet of food, I

gave him a hug.

"Merry Christmas," I said.

"You, too." Josh smiled, but his eyes still looked sad.

"I'm sorry I couldn't get you back inside so you could spend Christmas with Lauren."

Josh looked at the door to the biosphere. "I know Lauren and I will have a lot of Christmases together in the future." He turned back to me with a look of determination. "But this is where I need to be right now."

"It's going to be worth it," I said. "I know it will."

"I hope so." Josh continued around the room, passing out the rest of the food and a little Christmas cheer.

I believed that my job through all of this was to pray, but it became harder and harder to do. It felt like God wasn't listening. The officers were doing everything they could to get in the way. The Council wouldn't even talk to us. We stuck with our commitment to a peaceful protest against the Council's unfair policies, but it seemed like nothing was changing.

*Lord, I trust that you know what's best for us, and your timing is perfect. But when you're so quiet, sometimes it's hard for me to believe that you can hear me.*

A reminder from Paul's first letter to the Thessalonians crept into my consciousness: "Pray without ceasing."

*That's what I'm trying to do.*

Then I recalled the rest of the verse: "Rejoice always. Pray without ceasing. In all circumstances give thanks, for this is the will of God for you in Christ Jesus."

I had been doing a lot of asking and quite a bit of complaining, but I couldn't remember the last time I'd rejoiced. I held my empty abdomen, which had long since ceased rumbling, and looked around at the concrete room that had become my home. Did Paul really mean I should give thanks in all circumstance, even these?

Of course, I knew the answer to that question.

*Lord, thank you for . . .*

It was so much easier to think of things I wished would change, than to think of things I was grateful for.

*Thank you for keeping my family safe and healthy. Thank you for the food and water I get every day. Thank you for the courage and commitment of all the people participating in the sit-in.*

I really did have a lot to be thankful for.

*Thank you for the officers' restraint, which kept them from resorting to violence to break up the protest. Thank you for saving a few of the animals from dying in the Change, so we could have something to eat. Thank you for the man that Josh is becoming, willing to stand up for what he believes in, even when the cost is high.*

*Thank you, Jesus, for reminding me that I am blessed.*

Rejoicing still didn't come easy, but I forced a smile and made it a point to thank God every day.

# 41

Almost two weeks into the protest, I heard voices outside the airlock.

I tapped the people who were asleep near me. "Sounds like your shift is up."

People began gathering their belongings and picking up. But no one came in.

Several people clustered at the door, pulling the heavy blankets back to see what was happening on the outside. Word drifted through the crowd, "The officers are out there."

Questions were whispered around the room: "What are they doing? Won't the officers let the other people in?"

I moved toward the entrance, but I couldn't get close enough to see or hear anything. I climbed up on the loading dock, which was on the opposite wall. From there, I could see a little over the heads of the people gathered around the door.

Outside of the airlock, the officers were standing on the right. The people who were coming to take their shift for the airlock sit-in were standing on the left. Josh was in the center, face-to-face with one of the officers. What was he doing? He wasn't confronting the officer, was he?

The officer's right hand moved toward his belt.

"No!" I yelled.

Several people ran up the steps onto the loading dock to

see what was happening.

The officer extended his hand toward Josh. The sun glinted off the metallic parts of the object in his hand.

"Stop!" I screamed.

I pushed through the crowd on the loading dock and ran down the steps. I had to stop that officer before he hurt Josh. I zigzagged across the room, trying to avoid stepping on the people who were sitting or lying on the floor. I just knew I wasn't going to make it in time. I tried to find a way through the tightly-packed cluster at the door, but I couldn't make any progress.

"We have to stop them," I shouted.

Several people in the crowd at the door glanced back at me and then returned their attention to the scene in front of them. I pushed between people to try to get to the door.

I felt a hand on my shoulder. I turned to look. It was one of Josh's friends.

"Christy, it's okay," he said. "The officer just handed Josh a radio."

"A radio?" The way the sun reflected off of it, I thought for sure the officer was brandishing some kind of weapon.

Josh's friend nodded. "The Council finally decided they were ready to talk."

He helped me move to the front of the cluster. The officer had joined his colleagues, and Josh was standing alone, holding the officer's radio.

The sound coming from the radio was laced with static, but it was loud enough we could still understand ". . . *cannot meet your demands. If we let one hundred and seventy-three people back in, the atmosphere will not hold up.*"

Josh held the radio to his mouth. "All of the people who move back in are willing to work on the outside. They will be out of the biosphere eight hours a day. That will significantly decrease demand on the atmospheric conversion system."

"*It might not be enough. If all of those people move back in, they will put the lives of everyone in the biosphere at risk. Is that what you want?*"

Josh caught my eye through the airlock door. I pantomimed swabbing the inside of my cheek.

Josh's brow wrinkled and his lips twisted to one side.

I pointed back toward the biosphere and pretended to swab my cheek and put the swab in a test tube.

Josh's eyes widened, and his mouth formed an "o."

He quickly raised the radio. "What if we found more people in the biosphere who, once acclimatized, could work on the outside?"

Josh held the radio out. There was a long pause. Josh bit his lower lip.

After several seconds of static, the voice re-emerged. "*If you can identify one hundred and fifty more people who can work on the outside, then we will allow your hundred seventy-three back in.*"

Cheers erupted, both inside the airlock and out. A few of the officers even smiled.

When the commotion had died down, Josh picked up the radio again. "In order to identify those people who can work outside, Christy will need to be admitted to the biosphere to take more genetic samples. We will only relinquish control of the airlock, so Christy can return, if you provide us with a signed copy of the agreement we just made, and if you allow one hundred people to move back into the biosphere today."

The radio was silent for several minutes. No one spoke. We barely breathed.

"*We will allow ninety-eight people back in today.*"

Josh scanned the crowd and nodded. "We agree to those terms."

There were more cheers and tears and high-fives.

"*You have two hours to return control of the airlock to us, or this agreement is void.*" Few people heard this last communication over the celebration, but it spurred Josh into immediate action. He said a few words to the villagers who had gathered to take their shift in the airlock. The group rapidly dispersed.

He strode toward the airlock. Those of us gathered at the entrance stepped back to make room for him to enter. He crossed the room and stepped up onto the loading dock. No action was needed to get the people's attention. Every eye was already on him.

"As most of you heard, the Council is going to allow ninety-eight people to move back into the biosphere today, as long as they agree to work on the outside." Josh smiled at me. "Soon, even more people will be allowed back in.

"We are so grateful for the sacrifice you made to allow families to be reunited. Your generosity will not be forgotten.

The ninety-eight people who will return today will be selected by random drawing. If you changed your mind and wish to return to the biosphere, you are welcome to enter the drawing. Write your name down and bring it to me.

"Things will be a little crowded in the village for a while. We'll all need to share the available houses until we can get more built.

"If you can stick around and help disassemble the structures holding the airlock door open, we would appreciate it. Thank you again."

The people in the airlock left, and villagers began streaming in. They stopped at the loading dock to write their names on pieces of food containers, bags, or whatever they could find. Each person then selected a spot in the airlock to sit and wait for the results of the drawing.

When the stream of people coming in stopped, I turned back toward the loading dock and caught Josh's eye.

"Where's Mom?" I mouthed.

Josh shrugged his shoulders and returned his attention to the people dropping off their entries.

Josh clapped his hands to quiet the room. "Has everyone turned in their name?" He scanned the room. "If your name is called, you will have one hour to gather your belongings and return to the airlock. If you are late, you may lose your chance."

He lifted the plastic bag containing all of the names, shook it, and reached inside. "Jennifer Zinkula," he read.

A woman shrieked excitedly and raced to the door.

I watched the faces of the people around me as the

names were read. I saw a progressive loss of hope in each person's eyes, punctuated occasionally by joy when a familiar name was heard. When the last name had been read, there were way too many people whose dreams of being reunited with their families were not going to come true, yet.

I circulated among those remaining in the airlock, offering encouraging words. I already had seventy-five names that I hadn't yet given to the Council. It shouldn't take too long to get seventy-five more positive tests.

By the time all of those who had been chosen to return to the biosphere were back in the airlock, the newest villagers had finished disassembling the structures protecting the airlock door.

Josh approached the officers. "We're ready to go. You can tell the airlock operator to begin the transition."

One officer nodded and pulled out his radio.

Josh motioned for me to return to the airlock and followed me inside. The people nearby looked confused to see us again. Our names hadn't been called. In fact, we hadn't even put our names in the drawing.

Josh held up his hand. "I'm only here to review the contract and make sure the Council holds up their end of the bargain." He gestured toward me. "Christy needs to collect more DNA samples so more of our friends can come back home. Both of us will return to the outside as soon as these tasks are completed."

Josh's explanation seemed to satisfy the people. They returned their attention to the conversations that had occupied them before our arrival.

The garage door opener ground to life. I felt a surge of fear. What if they just closed the doors and left us here as punishment for our crimes? I turned toward the garage door. If I ran and rolled, I could probably make it out before the door finished closing. But I couldn't make my legs move. I watched the garage door descend, inch by inch. The door hit the floor with a thud. My fear blossomed into panic.

I swallowed hard and carefully backed away from the door. I couldn't lose it now, in this enclosed space with so many people. I looked to Josh for some reassurance.

His gaze was focused on the door to the biosphere.

I stepped closer to him. "Do you really think they're going to keep their promises?"

Josh nodded. "It wouldn't gain them anything to make the promises if they weren't going to keep them."

"Why do you think they changed their minds?"

Josh shrugged. "I'd like to think it was because of their common decency and respect for their fellow man, but those things have never factored into the Council's decisions before."

I glanced back at the garage door. "It just makes me nervous that they were suddenly willing to compromise. Like maybe they know something we don't know."

Josh put his arm around my shoulders. "Let's just celebrate this little victory. We can deal with the Council's ulterior motives later."

# 42

The light over the walk-in door turned from red to green. Excited murmurs erupted around the room. Josh walked up the steps onto the loading dock. He put his hand on the doorknob. I saw his shoulders rise and fall as he took a deep breath. He opened the door halfway, keeping one leg behind the door.

Someone on the other side handed Josh a packet of papers. He glanced through the packet, exchanged a few words with the other person, and then closed the door and turned toward the sea of expectant faces in the airlock.

"At first glance, the contract looks good. I'm going to read it aloud, so together we can make sure that it meets our expectations."

There were a few nods, but most of the people did not look pleased. Some checked their watches. Others adjusted their bags farther up on their shoulders. Most of the people in the room did not appear to care about the particulars. They just wanted to get back into the Bubble as soon as possible.

Undeterred, Josh proceeded to read every word of the contract. Looking past the legal mumbo-jumbo, the contract sounded good. Ninety-eight people would be allowed back into the biosphere. They would each be required to work an eight-hour shift on the outside five days a week. When 150 more people who could work on the outside were identified, then seventy-five more people would be allowed to move back into the biosphere.

There were paragraphs about the consequences of breaches of contract, the duration of the contract, and the circumstances that would void the contract. I started shifting my weight from one foot to the other. *Enough, already. These people just want to see their families. And I just want some food.*

Josh finally reached the end of the contract. People crowded closer to the loading dock.

"Are there any objections to this contract?" Josh scanned the room. "All in favor of approving the contract without revision, please raise your hand."

Hands shot up all around the room.

Josh smiled. "Excellent."

He stepped into the biosphere and closed the door behind him. The people who were closest rushed up the steps onto the loading dock.

Moments later, Councilman Jacobs opened the door and stepped inside. "You may now enter the biosphere. Please move in an orderly fashion, giving me your full name before you leave." He looked around the room. "Welcome home."

The councilman stepped to the side and began writing down the name of each person re-entering the Bubble. There were a few quiet struggles on the floor among people trying to get to the steps. But once on the loading dock, everyone followed Councilman Jacobs' instructions, maintaining calm and order.

I hung back, remembering the first time I walked—or rather, sprinted—through that door to meet my family. As each person stepped into the Bubble, my smile grew a little bigger. I knew the joyful reunion that awaited them on the other side of that door.

I followed the last person up the steps. Though she hadn't tried to push her way to the front of the line, I could see in her wide grin and glistening eyes how excited she was.

Councilman Jacobs and I were the only people left in the airlock.

"Hello, Councilman," I said. "Don't worry; I'm not moving back in. I'm just stopping by to collect some more DNA samples."

He looked up from his pad of paper. His face was serious. "I'm afraid the Council has other plans for you at present."

He took hold of my elbow and gently but firmly steered me through the door.

Josh was standing a few feet to the left with his hands behind his back and an officer at each elbow. He smiled at me, but his eyes looked vacant.

Councilman Jacobs turned me over to two officers standing to the right of the door and strode away. The officers secured my hands behind my back and pushed me after the councilman, down the street toward the administration building. I heard several sets of footsteps behind us. Josh and his officers must be following us.

*Lord, I thought you had this thing under control. What's*

*going on now?*

Had I learned nothing, spending day after day in the airlock?

*Thank you, Lord, for reuniting these families today, and for opening up the opportunity to bring even more people together. I praise you, Lord, because you are loving and merciful, and you know how to give us good gifts. Please, Lord, Josh has worked so hard to help other families. And he didn't even put his name in for the opportunity to return to the Bubble. If there is any way, please give him the chance to be with his wife again, so they can start their life together. In everything, Lord, I desire your will above all else.*

I wish I could say I felt great peace and I knew that everything was going to work out. But I didn't. I was afraid that God's will wasn't the same as mine. I was afraid that my family wouldn't get back together, and Josh wouldn't get to see his baby's birth, and the people outside the biosphere would have to stay there because I wouldn't be able to collect any more DNA samples. I wanted to trust in God's will. But if any of those outcomes were part of God's plan, I certainly wouldn't call his plan good.

*Thy will be done, Lord. Thy will be done.*

Maybe if I said it enough, I would really start to want God's will instead of my own.

We stopped in the anteroom outside the council chamber. Josh was staring ahead but still looked like he saw nothing.

I tried to think of something encouraging to say. "Josh,

you were amazing out there. Lauren would be so proud of you."

He turned to me when I said her name. "All I wanted to do was to come home to my wife. I reunited ninety-eight other families, but I couldn't manage to figure out a way to get mine back together."

The clerk opened the door to the council chamber. The officers pushed us inside, forcing us into the chairs at the center of the room.

Chairman Lambrecht struck his gavel on the desk. "Here begins the sentencing trials for Ms. Christy Phillips and Mr. Joshua Phillips."

What about a trial to determine our guilt or innocence?

"Ms. Phillips, we bring the following charges against you." The chairman picked up a document and read, "Disobeying a direct order of the Council by not providing the list of names requested and interrupting a council meeting in session without authorization."

He put the paper down, removed his glasses, and motioned around the room with them. "We have all witnessed these infractions firsthand; therefore we have no need to call further witnesses. How do you respond, Ms. Phillips?"

I'd known they wouldn't just let my uninvited outburst during the council meeting go unpunished. Sitting in the airlock, I had thought up what seemed to me like a brilliant defense. Now I couldn't remember any of it.

"Mr. Chairman, sir," I said, haltingly, "I didn't have a list I could have given you, and I had to interrupt the council meeting because you were in the process of violating the good faith of the people. If you didn't stop immediately, I was afraid you would never be able to regain the people's trust."

"The list in your head could easily have been transferred onto paper, as Officer Parizek demonstrated for us. It is our job to keep the people safe, not to make them like us. Urgent safety concerns could be justifiable reasons to interrupt a council meeting. Concerns about trust and good faith are not."

The chairman pounded the gavel against the sounding block. "Mr. Phillips."

Josh raised his eyes and looked around as if noticing for the first time what was going on around him.

"The following charges have been brought against you: insurrection, leading an illegal political uprising, and trespassing. The officers on the outside have kept us fully informed of the actions of all people during the sit-in, and in particular, of your leadership during the uprising. How do you respond?"

"Ladies and gentlemen of the Council." Josh looked at each member of the Council. His eyes were clear, and his voice was strong. "The people who volunteered to leave the biosphere so that others could return put their trust in the Council. Instead of honoring their sacrifice, you violated their trust and forced them out of the biosphere, with no plans to allow anyone back in and without even following the recommended acclimatization process. I could not, in good conscience, continue to defend and enforce the unjust rules and decisions being made by the Council.

"Freedom of speech has always been a highly valued right in the United States of America. We've been speaking out for a long time about how we want our government to treat its citizens. But apparently, we weren't talking loudly enough, because it seemed like no one ever heard us. The people decided they wanted to make a statement you couldn't ignore. And I was happy to help them do that."

Chairman Lambrecht pressed the tips of his fingers together. "And what means did you use to communicate with people on the inside?"

Josh's eyebrows drew together, and his head tilted to the side. "Sir?"

"Did you confiscate a radio?" The chairman leaned forward. "Hijack the communications systems in the USCSBS watch towers?"

Josh shook his head. "The only communication I've had with the inside was this morning when I spoke with you, sir, using one of the officers' radios."

"Then how did you coordinate the protests on the inside with those in the airlock?"

"What . . . I . . . don't." Josh's eyes darted back and forth.

He took a deep breath and looked at the chairman again. "I was unaware of any protests on the inside, sir."

"You're telling me you had nothing to do with the people of the biosphere walking out of their jobs and clogging the streets day and night?"

"No, Mr. Chairman."

Chairman Lambrecht pounded his gavel. "The Council

will begin deliberations now. You are dismissed."

The officers pulled us to our feet and pushed us into the anteroom. Josh and I sat next to each other in the center of the room. Two of the officers guarded the doors. The other two hovered over us.

"Protests on the inside," Josh whispered, "did you know anything about that?"

In the tiny room, I knew the officers could hear every word, but it still seemed appropriate to stick to a whisper. "The people who wanted to move out had mentioned some protests when I was taking their DNA samples, but it didn't sound like they amounted to much—nothing like what the chairman just described."

"That must be what finally convinced them to listen."

"Could be." I nodded. "It's one thing to shut down the airlock, but shutting down all the businesses in the Bubble, that's another story."

Imagining the streets of the Bubble crowded with protestors, I couldn't hide my smile, even though the officers were watching.

I leaned closer to Josh. "When we walked in there, I thought you were about ready to give up. Then you went and delivered that brilliant speech. What happened?"

"You were right, I do want Lauren to be proud of me," Josh said. "But even more than that, I want my child to grow up in a better world. And if I'm not willing to stand up for the truth, I can't make this world any better."

"Did I ever tell you I think you're going to be a great

father?"

Josh smiled at me and then looked away. "As long as the Council doesn't lock me up for the rest of my life."

I wanted to give my brother a hug. Instead, I leaned toward Josh again and spoke softly. "Jesus, we leave this in your hands. Only you have the power to soften hearts. Lord, we pray that you would guide the Council to a just and merciful decision. But whatever happens here, we pray it will bring glory to you. Holy Spirit, calm our fears, and give us the strength to face—"

The door to the council chamber opened. The officers escorted us to our seats.

"The Council has reached the following decisions." Chairman Lambrecht sounded bored or maybe tired. "Ms. Christy Phillips, you are sentenced to three months in jail, with work release during the day to serve the needs of the village community. You will be given a one-month stay of your sentence, during which time you will identify one hundred and fifty more residents of the biosphere who can acclimatize to work on the outside. Your sentence is subject to revision, depending on whether you meet this objective."

I tried to imagine spending three months in the jail cell. Could I make it three months sleeping on a dirt floor, unable to see Dad or my friends in Lincoln and at the cabin? Three months seemed like such a long time. But I could hear my mother's voice saying, "It'll go fast. Three months will be gone before you know it."

They were giving me a free pass for a month. I could

drive away, pretend I was going to test some DNA samples, and never come back. They wouldn't send someone after me—at least, I didn't think they would. I could be a free woman.

But if I made that choice, families would remain divided by the biosphere wall—families that I had the power to reunite. If the population of the Bubble continued to grow, there would be no one to collect and test DNA to find out who could work or live on the outside. The biosphere systems could fail, killing Dad, Lauren, and my friends in the Bubble. And I could never come back to the Bubble; could never see my family again. Those were sacrifices I was not willing to make.

"Mr. Joshua Phillips," Chairman Lambrecht said, "as you know, your right to free speech does not also give you the right to ignore the laws and the authority of the government. You will be permanently stripped of your duties as an officer."

I knew Josh expected this, but he still winced when he heard it. He had felt like he was doing something worthwhile, working as an officer. And he was good at it. It might take some time for him to find another niche into which he fit that well.

"And you will be sentenced to three months in jail with work release." The chairman struck his gavel. "You are dismissed."

The officers pulled us to our feet and pushed us out of the council chamber, through the anteroom, and into the hallway. I picked up speed, coming up beside Josh. He sniffed and blinked rapidly. I could tell he was trying hard not to break down in front of his colleagues.

"I'm so sorry, Josh," I said, softly.

He took a deep breath. "At least I'll be out before the baby's born."

"I know you loved being an officer."

He nodded. "Looks like we'll all be working the fields this winter."

The officers pushed us through the doors of the administration building and down the sidewalk to the street.

"Christy." Josh's voice was strained. "You've got to get those names for the Council."

The officers holding my arms turned me to the left, away from Josh and toward my parents' house.

"I'll do the best I can," I said over my shoulder, raising my voice to be sure Josh could hear me.

"I need to be with my wife and my baby," Josh said.

*Lord, please find a way to bring Josh back into the Bubble. Lauren and Josh need each other. I know I can't make it happen—I've tried. But if there's anything I can do to help, just show me the way.*

# 43

When we reached my parents' house, one officer cut the cord holding my wrists while the other knocked on the door. There was no answer. I used my key to unlock the door and poked my head inside.

"Dad?" I didn't hear or see anyone. "Looks like no one's home."

I turned back to the officers. "Does that mean you guys have to follow me around?"

They exchanged a glance.

"I'll stay," the gray-haired officer said.

The other officer nodded and walked away.

"We're not allowed to leave you without supervision," the officer explained.

I started to sigh but stopped myself. It could be helpful having a member of law enforcement with me.

I held out my right hand. "Christy Phillips."

The officer chuckled, deepening the wrinkles at the corners of his eyes. "Believe me, I know." He shook my hand. "Officer Cartwright."

His eyes reminded me of my grandpa's—a soft grayish-blue that lit up when he laughed. I felt like I could trust him, and I needed his help. But trusting other people had gotten me in trouble before.

"Look, I'm sorry you got stuck with me, but I could really use your help. I've got to collect a lot of DNA samples in a hurry. I haven't had much luck trying to collect from workplaces. If you could have a chat with the supervisors, letting them know the DNA collection was mandated by the Council, I think we could make some headway."

Officer Cartwright crossed his arms. If I wanted his help, I needed to give him a good reason.

"Listen," I said, "this will help to reunite families and increase the workforce on the outside working the fields to make sure everyone has enough to eat."

His expression was unchanged.

"And, the sooner I get my samples, the sooner I will leave. Then you won't have to babysit me anymore."

"Well, let's get started, then." Officer Cartwright turned and headed down the street.

"Hold on. I've got to get the supplies first."

I went inside, filled a backpack with swabs and tubes, and tucked the notebook in the back. There were less than a hundred testing kits left at my parents'—not near enough to yield seventy-five more positive tests. That meant I was going to have to make at least two trips to Lincoln and back to meet the Council's expectations.

I grabbed a handful of crackers and headed out the door. I didn't want to waste any time, but I didn't think I could walk another block without something in my stomach.

Now that he knew what he had to do to shorten his sentence of one-on-one supervision, Officer Cartwright was a man on a mission. I almost had to jog to keep up with him on the way to the industrial district.

He strode into the first building on the left. He knocked on the door and stepped into the office just to the right of the entrance.

Holding up his badge, he said, "Council is requiring DNA samples from all citizens of the biosphere. We'll get the office staff first. Then we'll circulate through the factory floor. Should cause minimal disruption in production."

The woman behind the desk looked confused, but she nodded. Apparently, Officer Cartwright's badge was enough to keep her from asking questions.

I handed the clipboard and a pen to Officer Cartwright. I tried to imitate his authoritative tone. "I need to swab the inside of your cheek, ma'am. It'll be quick and painless. Open up."

I took the sample, the officer wrote down her information, and we moved on to the next office.

When we hit the factory floor, we faced a little resistance from the foreman, but Officer Cartwright quashed it with a few words and a flash of his badge.

We repeated the process on the second and third floors without a hitch. By the time we left the building, every test tube in my backpack was full.

It was amazing how smoothly things went when I let God take control, and didn't try to do it all myself. I had to smile at God's sense of humor. I figured having an officer tagging along everywhere I went would slow me down. But

God used that officer to help me achieve my goal even more quickly.

Officer Cartwright escorted me back home. Dad had supper cooking by the time we arrived. My stomach began rumbling as soon as he opened the door. The first bite of food almost came right back up. My stomach didn't quite know what to do with a hearty, hot meal anymore. Giving Dad the play-by-play of the past several days forced me to eat slowly, so I didn't make myself sick.

# 44

I was in the airlock, ready to go, when the sun set that evening. I sped through the crowded highways to Lincoln, stopped at the lab to drop off the samples and pick up more testing supplies, and drove to Max's house. I was disappointed to find no one home. I scrawled a quick note to Max and Ashley and lay down on the couch for a nap.

It seemed like I had just lain down when I was awakened by whispers in the next room. A glance at my watch informed me that the brief nap I'd planned had turned into a four-hour siesta. I stood, stretched, and walked to the kitchen. Ashley and Max were sitting at the table.

"Hi, guys," I said.

Ashley jumped up, knocking her chair over, and ran to me. "Where have you been?" She wrapped me in a hug. "I thought you'd be right back on your delivery route, coming through every three or four days. What happened?"

I launched into the story of Officer Parizek's betrayal, the sit-in, and the sentencing. Tears welled up. "I'll be gone for three months—maybe longer if I can't come up with a list of a hundred fifty names. I'm going to miss you guys so much."

"You could stay," Max said.

"I thought about it," I said. "I doubt they'd send anyone after me. But if I don't go back and bring a list of survivors with me, Mom and Josh will never get to go back in the Bubble. Three months in jail is a small price to pay if it will allow my family to be together again."

"Maybe if you turn in an even longer list of survivors," Ashley said, "they'll shorten your sentence."

"It's worth a try," I said, "though I wouldn't hold my breath."

"How can we help?" Max asked.

"You two have done so much already," I said.

"We want to help," Ashley said. "What can we do?"

"I left more samples at the lab," I said. "If you have time to start some of the tests, that would be great. I have to run back to the Bubble to get more samples. Hopefully, I'll be back within a week, and I can help with the rest."

I was reluctant to ask my friends for more help. But I knew my chances of meeting the Council's one-month deadline were slim if I tried to do everything myself.

"Consider it done," Ashley said.

"Thank you both, so much," I said. "I have to get going. I want to get the rest of those samples collected as soon as possible. I'll be back soon."

# 45

It was two in the morning by the time I reached the checkpoint. After inspecting me and my vehicle, the officer insisted that I wait in my car at the checkpoint until the first-shift officers arrived. I wanted to visit Mom, but I knew I couldn't risk any sort of a confrontation with law enforcement. So I quietly complied, reclining my seat and trying to catch another nap.

At six thirty, two officers arrived to escort me on foot to the airlock. One of them spoke into the rock at the entrance. When he finished, I stepped toward the rock wall. It didn't move. I looked back at the officers. They were leaning against the pile of rocks, chatting. I looked back at the wall. Nothing.

It was a full ten minutes before the rock wall slid to the side and the garage door opened. I stepped toward the door again. I jumped back as people poured out of the airlock. They were dressed in work clothes, and most of them seemed happy to be leaving. There was no sign that they had just endured a grueling acclimatization process. The airlock was nearly empty before I realized what was going on. These were the people who had been allowed to return to the Bubble, going outside for their workday.

That meant the Council had kept its word. It hadn't just waited until Josh and I were out of the way and then kicked everyone out again. My excitement grew. Maybe Mom and Josh would be able to move back into the Bubble. Maybe God would reunite our family.

The officers motioned for me to enter the airlock. They remained outside. After the atmosphere in the airlock had been converted, the walk-in door opened.

I was surprised to see Officer Cartwright on the other side. "You drew the short straw again, huh?"

He smiled. "No, I volunteered. I thought we made a pretty good team."

The industrial district was adjacent to the airlock. We got to work right away. Between Officer Cartwright's commanding tone and our efficiency in collecting the samples, we encountered little resistance.

By four in the afternoon, most of the businesses were shutting down. Officer Cartwright knew of a few that operated multiple shifts. We returned to those buildings to collect samples from the second-shift workers.

It was six when I finally said, "Let's call it a night. We can pick up here tomorrow."

I was exhausted but thrilled with the progress we'd made.

I began walking toward my parents' house. "Thanks for your help today. I really couldn't have done it without you. You were brilliant."

I stopped and glanced back. Officer Cartwright wasn't following me. Did he actually believe that I could get back home without his watchful eye?

He motioned for me to come back. I took a few steps toward him, confused.

"The Council decided that you can only be in the biosphere while you're collecting samples. If we're done for today, then you have to go back outside." He pointed over his shoulder with his thumb, toward the airlock.

"Oh, okay." This was actually good. I would get to spend some time with Mom and maybe even stop at the jail to say hi to Josh.

We walked toward the airlock.

"Do you have any names for the Council yet?" Officer Cartwright asked.

The question surprised me. I was only gone a day. How could I have gotten DNA test results back already? But, of course, I had the seventy-five names from earlier tests that I hadn't yet turned over. Perhaps it would be a good show of faith if I gave them to the Council now.

"Yes," I said, "I have a few."

He held out his hand. "I can deliver them to the Council tomorrow if you'd like me to."

"Sure, that would be great." I pulled the list of names out of my backpack and handed it to the officer.

We approached the airlock operator's booth.

"Christy is going to spend the night on the outside," Officer Cartwright said. "She'll need to be admitted again in the morning."

The airlock operator nodded and began punching buttons on her console. The officer and I walked to the airlock entrance.

"I had fun today," he said. "Sometimes in law enforcement, you can have entire days when you feel like you accomplish nothing. It was nice to actually get something done today."

I opened the door. "Shall we do it again tomorrow?"

He smiled. "You got it."

# 46

I was surprised that there wasn't an officer waiting for me on the outside. Maybe Officer Cartwright forgot to call. Or maybe he trusted me enough that he didn't think a call was necessary.

I decided to take advantage of the moment of freedom. After hiding the boxes of DNA samples just outside of the airlock, I went in search of the jail. I knew that I needed to go to the right and that it was some distance from the biosphere wall. But I had never gone there under my own power, so I didn't have a good feel for how far away it was or what landmarks I should be looking for.

I had been crisscrossing the area in which I thought it had to be for forty-five minutes before I finally spotted the stumps of the trees that had been removed to make room for the jail. I walked carefully to the edge of the clearing, watching for any signs of officers on guard. I stood behind a tree for several seconds. Hearing and seeing no indications of other people in the area, I slowly approached the cell.

I continued to scan the area around me. My head was turned all the way to the right, toward the wall of the Bubble, when my foot caught on a stump. I let out a squeal as I pitched forward. I stumbled, trying to get my feet under me. This effort was unsuccessful. I landed hard on my side, rolling once before I was stopped by another stump.

If anyone was in the area, they now knew I was, too. And I was sprawled on the ground in the middle of the clearing, right out in the open. I lay still, listening. The only movement I heard seemed to be coming from the jail cell. At least I hoped it was coming from the jail cell.

After several seconds of silence, I eased myself up onto my hands and knees and crept to the door.

"Josh, are you in there?" I hoped the sound would travel through the narrow crack between the door and the frame.

There was no reply.

"It's me, Christy."

"Christy?" The thick wall between us made it sound like Josh was at the opposite end of a football field. "What are you doing here?"

I couldn't tell if he was upset or just surprised.

"I've been working on collecting DNA samples inside the Bubble." I raised my voice a little, to make sure he could hear. "They don't want me using up their air at night, so they sent me out to spend the night with Mom. But before I went to the house, I wanted to make sure you were okay."

" 'Okay' might be stretching it."

There was a long pause.

"I have everything I need," Josh said. "They even gave me the materials to build a fireplace in here. And I get to spend eight hours a day working outside. But—"

I put my hand on the doorframe.

"Three months," Josh said. "I can't see or even talk to Lauren for three months. She needs me now more than ever, and I can't be there for her."

I wanted to put my arm around his shoulders. "Lauren understands. And she has her family to help her, and Dad."

"But that's supposed to be my job. It's not fair."

"You're right. It isn't. Listen, this officer on the inside is helping me collect more samples. Officer Cartwright. I don't know if you know him, but he's great. I think we're going to be able to get a lot more samples than I'd planned. Maybe we'll get enough positives that the Council will let everyone back in who wants to. Once your three months is up, you might be able to walk straight from this cell back into Lauren's arms."

Josh's voice quieted, so I had to strain to hear. "What if she's not willing to wait that long?"

"She chose to marry you. She loves you. She's not going to give up on you just because you're apart for a few months."

"I hope you're right."

"I've seen the look in her eyes when she talks about you. I know I'm right."

I heard a twig snap somewhere in the woods.

"I better go before someone finds me here," I said. "Hang in there."

"I'll try."

I slid around to the back side of the cell, staying close to the building. I made a quick sweep of my surroundings and then darted into the woods. I circled wide around the jail and away from the Bubble, hoping to avoid crossing paths with anyone headed toward either place.

I reached the road just this side of the checkpoint. I

walked up to the checkpoint booth. The officer inside was intently watching the road leading in and sipping on a mug of coffee. I knocked on the window of the booth. The officer jumped, spilling coffee down his shirt. He drew his gun and threw the door open.

I raised my arms. "Sorry. I didn't mean to startle you."

"What do you want?"

"I was just going to ask if I could pull my car up a little closer, to make it easier to load the DNA samples."

"Wait here." The officer stepped back into the booth and closed the door, keeping his gun trained on me.

After a brief exchange with the radio on his shoulder, he opened the door again. "The car stays here."

I resisted the urge to demand an explanation. I couldn't risk getting in trouble again. Not while I was still seventy-five names short.

"Okay. Thank you, officer."

It took three trips from the airlock to get all of the samples we'd collected into the Civic. The long walks intensified my exhaustion, but I was still thrilled to see my trunk fill up with DNA samples.

When the last boxes were finally safely stowed and the car doors locked, I made my way to our family's house in the village. I had hardly knocked when I found myself smothered in a hug from Mom.

"It's good to see you, too," I said when we finally let go.

It was. While I was stuck in the airlock during the sit-in, Mom was at home, divvying up the food people had collected and trying to make it last. It had been weeks since we'd seen each other.

Mom pulled me over to the bunk along the right wall. "I thought you'd be inside, collecting samples."

"I was," I said. "In fact, I just loaded a bunch of them into my car. But they don't want me using up their air, so they're kicking me out at night. I'll go back tomorrow to collect more, but it looks like I'll be spending my nights here until I have all the samples I need."

"That's wonderful."

"How have things been going since the sit-in ended?"

"As soon as they finished moving people back into the biosphere, they brought out a big shipment of rations, thank goodness. I think there were a lot of people who wouldn't have made it much longer."

"I wonder how long the Council would have held out if there hadn't been officers out here starving along with everyone else."

Mom shook her head. "Who knows?"

"During our trial, the chairman said there were protests on the inside, too. A bunch of people walked off their jobs and blocked the streets. I have a feeling that helped sway the Council, too."

"When Josh didn't come back home after the drawing, I assumed he had been selected to go back in. I was so excited that he and Lauren were going to be together again. I had no idea they only brought you and Josh in to arrest you."

"Why didn't you come and put your name in for the

drawing?"

Mom sighed. "There are so many people out here who have left their children or ill relatives back in the biosphere. I couldn't put my name in if it meant I might get selected before them. Your dad and I have been apart before. We can wait our turn."

I hugged Mom. Her generosity was inspiring.

After having a bite to eat, I went to bed. I needed to get up early to make it to the airlock before seven.

# 47

By the end of the third day, Officer Cartwright and I had collected almost five hundred DNA samples, far exceeding my goal of three hundred. Confident that I had enough to produce a list of seventy-five positives for the Council, I returned to Lincoln. I spent every waking minute in the lab, running tests and recording results. Ashley and Max helped when they could, usually stopping by in the evening after the market closed.

The list of positive results was growing steadily, but my window of time was closing rapidly. I began staying at the lab day and night, catching naps when I could and working whenever I was awake enough to do so.

Finally, a week before the deadline, I began the test on the last sample. Now I just needed to hang around and watch the results come in. By the next day, the list of positive test results had reached the magic number of seventy-five.

*Lord, should I go back now?*

I remembered Mom talking about the people who had left behind young children and family members who might not have long to live. I couldn't leave yet. Not if there was a chance that I might be able to help more people get back to their families in the Bubble.

The day before my deadline, the list was up to 115, and

there were only thirty tests that were not yet complete. It was time to return to the Bubble.

I had gotten in the habit of alternating between my two favorite routes from Lincoln to the biosphere. But I knew that if my actions became predictable, it would increase the likelihood of someone figuring out where I was going, or at least getting curious enough to follow me.

I opted for a more southerly route this time. The route involved a lot of back roads, including long stretches of road with few obstacles, where I could really open it up. But it also required frequent checks of the map, and a close eye on the odometer, so I didn't miss turns onto unmarked country roads.

After the first few turns, my memory of the route started to come back, and I didn't have to refer to the map as often. I found myself enjoying the change of scenery and appreciating the clearer roadways.

I saw a flash of brown out of the corner of my eye.

*Was that a deer?*The populations of smaller animals, like insects and rodents, had started to recover. But it was rare to see anything even as big as a dog or a cat. I hadn't seen any deer or cows since the Change. The resource acquisition teams from the cabin had traveled all the way to North Dakota before they found horses to use in their farming operation.

I scanned the roadside. Unless it was moving, a brown animal would be hard to see against the brown grass, wilted bushes, and dry fallen leaves.

I heard a deafening crash. A sharp, hot smell seared my nose. My head whipped forward, and the world went black.

# 48

*I have to wake up. I'm going to run out of time.*

I tried to pull myself out of the realm of sleep, but the heavy comforter seemed to press me down into the softest bed I had ever felt.

*I can't stay here. I have to get back.*

But why? I couldn't remember.

I lifted my left leg to roll onto my right side. Pain exploded in my left thigh and screamed all the way down to my foot. I cried out, tears instantly overflowing.

"Easy now."

The voice was gentle but unfamiliar.

I took a few deep breaths, willing the pain to calm down. I blinked several times and tried to focus. I looked to the left. Even a little movement made my head throb.

The man sitting beside the bed smiled at me. His smile was nearly hidden by his scruffy, gray facial hair, but the sparkle in his eyes and the wrinkles bordering them gave it away.

"You had quite the fender-bender out there." He spoke with a soft southern drawl. "Good thing your airbags were working, or you might not have made it."

The memory of the sound of metal impacting metal reverberated. I must have run into one of the stalled or abandoned vehicles.

"Name's Carl." He extended a weathered hand.

I reached up. Every movement I made seemed to awaken another area of soreness. "I'm Christy. Thanks for the help."

Carl clasped my hand in a firm but gentle handshake.

"My leg?" I gingerly touched my left side.

"Can't tell if it's broken or just a deep bruise. We'll give it a couple days to heal, and then see if you can stand on it."

I pushed myself up to sitting, wincing at the rekindled pain in my leg. "I can't stay here. There's somewhere I have to be."

He put his hand on my shoulder. "Right now, your job is to get better. Whoever's waiting for you, they can wait a couple more days."

"No, I have to go now." I tried to ease my legs over the side of the bed. "I have to get there before morning, or I'll miss my deadline."

My left foot slid off the edge of the bed. I squeezed my eyes shut against the pain and continued to scoot forward.

"Well, as long as you're sitting up," Carl said, "you might as well have something to eat."

I nodded. The pain had filled my stomach with knots, leaving no room for food. But I figured if Carl was out of the room, I could test my injured leg a little more.

"I'll be right back." He left the room, glancing over his shoulder before he turned down the hall.

I got my right foot on the floor and slowly stood up.

Even with all of the pressure on my right leg, the pain in my left still made me feel like I was going to pass out. I sat down, took a few deep breaths, and stood again. It wasn't quite as bad the second time.

I touched my left toe to the floor. It felt a little better when the leg was supported, rather than hanging in the air. I put my foot flat on the floor. Not too bad. I shifted a little weight onto my left leg. The pain flared. I grabbed onto the dresser. The sharp edge of the pain began to dull. At least the leg didn't give out.

I heard footsteps in the hallway. I reached back for the bed and gently eased myself down.

Carl entered with a glass of water and a bowl. The smell of the soup made my stomach rumble. Perhaps I was hungry, after all.

"A little meatless chili." He handed me the bowl and put the water on the dresser.

"Smells delicious," I said. "Thank you so much."

I raised a steaming spoonful, blew on it, and put it in my mouth. The perfect amount of spice united the flavor of the beans and tomatoes into a delectable combination. While most people were throwing together whatever they could find and calling it a meal, this man had somehow found just what he needed to make the perfect batch of chili.

"This is amazing," I said between bites. "Are you a chef?"

Carl laughed. "No, but I have been cooking for a lot of years."

He sat in the chair on the other side of the dresser.

"Aren't you going to have some?" I asked.

"Already ate."

I took a few more bites. The ache in my stomach eased, and my head was clearer.

"How did you find me?" I asked.

"Things are usually pretty quiet around here. That crash could have woke the dead." He frowned and looked out the window. When he turned back to me, his eyes had lost a little of their sparkle. "I came running as soon as I heard it. When I saw your car, I thought there's no way anybody survived that wreck. But there you were, alive and breathing. You could even walk a little when I helped you to the house. You were out of your head, though. Kept talking about going to jail and bubbles.

I smiled. *Not bubbles,* the *Bubble.*

"Could I see the car?" I asked.

Carl motioned toward the window across from the bed. I put my bowl down and used the dresser to pull myself to standing. I hardly recognized the mangled pile of purple metal resting in the ditch. The hood looked like it had been folded into an accordion. The windshield and all of the side windows had shattered. The driver's side door hung down at an angle.

I inhaled sharply, recognizing the truth of Carl's words. *Thank you, Lord, for saving my life.*

I looked at my watch. Four o'clock. I hadn't made it very far before my accident, and the route I was taking was not the quickest one. I probably had ten or eleven hours of driving ahead of me. I needed to get going by six—seven at the latest—

to make it to the Bubble before it started to get light.

I swiveled on my right foot to get closer to the window. I looked up and down the street. There were a few stalled and abandoned cars. I hadn't had much luck looking on the roads for cars to drive. The abandoned cars were generally locked, and the stalled cars were usually out of gas, the drivers having been overcome by the atmospheric change while they were still trying to outrun it.

I scanned the horizon. There was no sign of a town nearby. The nearest car lot could be dozens or even hundreds of miles away.

I turned to Carl. "Are there any cars here I could borrow?"

"There's a few cars and a tractor in the barn. Don't know which ones run, but you're welcome to take whatever you can find. I still think you should stay here until you heal up a little, though."

"I know, and I wish I could. But I really have to meet this deadline."

I gripped the dresser, slid my left foot forward, and tried to take a step with my right foot. The pain almost forced my lunch back up. I swallowed hard and took another tiny step with excruciating pain. I wasn't going to make it out of the room, much less all the way to the barn.

"Hold on," Carl said. "I just thought of something that might help."

Moments later I heard footsteps and doors slamming above me.

Carl returned with a set of wooden crutches. "Don't know if these are the right size, but they're better than nothing."

He taped towels over the top of each crutch and washcloths around the handgrips, where the pads were missing.

"Here you go." He handed the crutches to me. "Just like new."

I stood and tucked a crutch under each arm. I had to lean down a little to reach the handgrips. I slid my left foot forward, leaned down on the crutches, and took a step with the right. The pain was still there, but it wasn't overpowering.

I smiled at Carl. "Perfect."

I slowly made my way to the door of the bedroom. Carl nodded his approval.

"Do you have the keys to the barn?" I asked.

Carl laughed. "You don't need keys to get into the barn. You just open the door."

"What about the car keys?"

"They're in the cars. Nobody gonna travel this far out in the middle of nowhere to steal a car that may or may not run."

I grinned. He had a good point.

The grass and gravel were a little harder to navigate on crutches, but I managed to make it to the barn.

Everything inside was covered with dust. The three cars looked like they hadn't been moved in years. A green tractor towered over the cars. Though its shine was dulled by the layer of dirt, I could tell that it was newer and had been maintained better than all of the cars.

I tried each of the cars, repeating the painful process of sliding in and out of the driver's seat three times. I couldn't get any of them to turn over. I looked at the tractor. It was more likely to start than anything else in that building, but going at a tractor's speed, I would never make it to the Bubble in time.

I searched around the barn and found several gas cans and a couple lengths of hose. If I couldn't use the cars, at least I could use their gas. Siphoning from all three cars, I nearly filled two five-gallon gas cans. That wasn't enough to get me all the way to my destination, but it should at least get me close enough to civilization that I could find more.

I held one can in each hand and looped my thumb over the handgrip of the crutch. When I swung the crutches forward, the sloshing liquid threatened to send me sprawling.

The barn door opened, and Carl stepped in. "Need a hand?"

"That would be great," I said. "I couldn't get any of these cars to start, so I want to get these gas cans up to the road and see if I can find something there I can drive."

"I can help with that." Carl took the gas cans from me and headed toward the road.

I hobbled behind him on the crutches. The sun had already set and there was barely enough light for me to find my way. My back was starting to ache and my hands were tingly. But right now, those were the least of my worries. The only cars on the road with keys were the occupied ones. That meant I would have to remove the car's inhabitants before I could drive away.

Carl waited for me at the edge of the road. The car I had run into was behind him, perched precariously with one rear tire hanging off the opposite side of the road. It was in almost as bad a shape as mine—definitely not a viable option.

I limped down the road, forcing myself to look in the windows I was usually so careful to avoid.

*Jesus, give me strength.*

Lunch threatened again to re-emerge.

I spotted a silver Taurus that looked like it had only one occupant. I turned back and waved to Carl. "Let's try this one."

I grabbed the handle of the driver's side door. I took a deep breath, squeezed my eyes shut, and opened the door. The sharp odor, amplified by the confined space inside the car, stung my nose and made my eyes water. I covered my mouth and nose with the sleeve of my coat and tried to stifle a cough.

I hit the unlock button on the door, still trying to avoid looking directly into the car. I limped to the trunk, opening the back door on the way by. I rummaged through the box in the trunk, finding what I was looking for at the very bottom—a blanket. I continued around the other side of the Taurus, opening both doors to let in some fresh air.

I stood at the opening on the front passenger's side and leaned the crutches against the doorframe. I forced my eyes across the front seat to the spot where the driver's seat belt was fastened. I reached in. Flies swarmed around me. I squeezed my eyes shut. When the buzzing subsided, I stretched forward and pressed the button to release the belt, careful to avoid touching the elbow resting just above the button.

I backed out of the car and stood, taking a deep breath of fresh air.

I got hold of the crutches and the blanket and continued around the front of the Taurus to the driver's side door. I glanced quickly inside the car. I turned to Carl, who was standing a few feet away, watching.

"I hate to ask," I said, "but I don't think I can do this alone. Will you help me?"

Carl nodded, his face serious. "Just let me know what you want me to do."

I unfolded the blanket and threw it over the body. The driver's left arm stuck out from under the blanket, pinned in place by the retracting seatbelt. I pulled the seatbelt out and slid it free from his arm.

I motioned for Carl to come closer. "I want to try to roll him out of the car, keeping the blanket under him, so we can use it to move him. See if you can get his legs."

I wrapped the blanket around his right shoulder and put my hand on his back, keeping the blanket between my hand and the body. "Let's roll on the count of three. One, two, three."

I pulled forward. I felt tissues give way under my hand, but the body didn't move.

I stepped back and turned away, trying to quell the nausea swelling in my gut.

I looked at Carl. "Any ideas?"

"I can get the blanket wrapped around his legs. We can

use it to slide his legs out of the car. Then maybe we can tilt him forward onto the blanket."

I was sort of hoping Carl would come up with an idea that didn't require my help. "It's worth a try."

Carl wrapped the lower part of the blanket around the man's legs. I lifted the end of the blanket, raising his feet over the edge of the doorframe. Carl lifted the blanket at the knees, using the legs to turn the body so it was facing out the door.

The man's upper body began to slide toward the passenger's seat. Carl let go of the legs and reached behind the man to keep him from falling over. I tucked the blanket farther around the man's left shoulder until Carl could reach it and pull it around the man's back.

"We can't get the blanket around his hips," Carl said. "I'll push his hips from the other side while you pull his upper body out."

Carl half sat on the passenger's seat with one boot against the man's lower back. Carl was amazingly limber for his age. He pushed with his foot, inching the man to the edge of the seat. I kept hold of the blanket around his shoulders, to make sure he didn't fall over backward.

"All right, he's at the edge," Carl said. "Start pulling him forward. Keep that blanket wrapped around him, so he doesn't roll out.

I dropped the crutches and leaned against the back edge of the doorframe, keeping my weight on my right foot. I grasped the blanket around the man's shoulders with both hands and pulled him toward the opening. He barely moved.

Carl gave another push from behind. The body slid off the seat and toppled forward. I went down on my knees, sending a fresh hot poker of pain through my left thigh. But I kept the blanket around the body.

Carl came around and took hold of the blanket at the man's head. "I'll do all the pulling, but I need you to hold onto the foot of the blanket, so we can make sure everything stays inside."

I picked up the crutches and used them to hoist myself back onto my feet. I wrapped the end of the blanket around the handgrip of one of the crutches and held it tightly.

We made our way awkwardly through the ditch, me hobbling forward on crutches, and Carl pulling with everything he had to move the body an inch or two.

When we finally got the body into the bean field on the other side of the ditch, I stopped and leaned down on my crutches, trying to catch my breath. "I would love to give this guy a proper burial, but I've got to get going. Carl, I can never thank you enough for all you've done for me. I promise I'll stop and visit next time I'm coming through."

"It was nice to meet you," he said. "You take care of that leg as soon as you get where you're going, and I'll look forward to seeing you soon."

The hard part was over—the body had been removed. I limped to the wreckage of the Civic and retrieved my backpack and maps. I marked Carl's house on the map. It might be months down the road, but I would stop and see him again, as soon as I could.

I climbed out of the ditch and filled my new ride with the gas I had collected. Everything was ready. I just had to get inside and drive away. Get in the car that buzzed with flies and smelled of decomposition. Sit on the seat that, minutes before, had been occupied by a corpse. Even after all we had gone through to get it ready, I didn't know if I could do it.

I swallowed and took a deep breath. I walked to the front seat, but I just couldn't sit down. I went to the trunk and found some paper towels. I used them to brush off the front seat and wipe down any surfaces the man's body might have touched—the seatbelt, the steering wheel, the shifting lever, and the inside of the door. I knew a dry paper towel wouldn't make much of a difference, but it still made me feel better.

I closed all of the other doors and stood beside the driver's seat. I held my breath, sat down, and swung my legs in. I pulled the crutches inside and quickly slammed the door behind them. I started the car, opened all the windows, and turned the fan on full blast. I couldn't bring myself to put on the seatbelt. I was just going to have to drive carefully, and not get into any more accidents.

I couldn't pretend that I felt comfortable, but at least now I had a chance of reaching my destination in time.

I turned on the dome light and checked my watch. It was already six thirty in the evening, and I still had to find someplace to stop for gas. I leaned over to see my reflection in the rearview mirror. My nose and cheeks were red, and there was a bandage on my forehead. With the severity of the pain in my leg, I hadn't even noticed my other injuries. I touched each area gingerly. They were tender, but the pain wasn't too bad.

I turned the Taurus around and headed west. I went as fast as I dared, keeping my eyes fixed on the road. I hadn't investigated the car lots along the southerly route I was taking. Because I was driving mostly through rural areas, I decided to try a small town instead—one of these friendly little places where everyone leaves their cars unlocked.

I found what looked like a quiet residential street in a town of about five hundred. With no streetlights, it was easy to sneak down the street, checking car doors. I was disappointed to find several locked doors, but I still only had to check about a dozen cars before I found three that were unlocked. Access to the inside of the cars allowed me to open their gas cap covers and siphon enough gas to fill my tank. I was hoping to find a car with keys in the ignition, so I could trade in my tainted Taurus, but no one on the street I chose was that trusting.

I didn't have to make any more stops before I reached the Bubble. But still, sunrise was approaching way too fast.

It was a quarter to six when the sky in my rearview mirror began to lighten, and I was still a half hour away from the checkpoint. If I continued on, I would again be violating the rules, arriving during daylight hours. If I stopped and waited until the next night, I would miss my deadline, and the Council could use that as an excuse to renege on their part of the agreement. I was not willing to let that happen.

I stopped one more time to look and listen for anyone who might be following me. Then I cut the lights and sped toward the Bubble.

# 49

The officer at the checkpoint ran to the center of the road as soon as he saw me approaching. He held his hand out, signaling me to stop. He kept his other hand on his gun, while he spoke into the radio clipped to his shoulder.

Seconds later, two other officers were running down the road toward me, guns drawn. I raised my hands in the air. Even though I knew they were overreacting to my minor infraction, the sight of their guns still made my heart pound. If they decided to just take care of me, right there, they could make up any story they wanted to justify their actions. And I would be dead, so I couldn't defend myself.

The two approaching officers stepped up to the front windows of the Taurus, one on either side. Once they got within a couple feet of the open windows, the officer on the passenger's side started to cough.

"What in the world?" the officer closest to me mumbled.

"Yeah, sorry," I said. "I got in a wreck, so I had to borrow a car from a dead guy. If you hang out here a while, though, you'll actually get used to it."

The officer ignored my comment. "Get out of the car for your inspection."

"Sure thing," I said. "It's just going to take me a minute. I got a little banged up in that car accident."

I eased myself out of the Taurus and leaned on the hood while the officers patted me down and went over every inch of the vehicle. They confiscated several items from the box in the trunk. I hadn't paid attention to what was in there, so I doubted I would miss whatever they took.

"Come with us," one of the officers said.

"I'm going to need my crutches." I pointed to the front passenger's seat, where the crutches were propped.

"Then get them," he said, rolling his eyes.

I limped back to the door and pulled out the crutches. "Now, I have to talk to the Council today, in order to meet my deadline. Were you able to get me on the schedule for today?"

"Oh, you're on their list, all right," the checkpoint officer said. "I'm sure they won't waste any time getting you in there for sentencing on your latest infraction."

Two of the officers escorted me to my mother's house, verbalizing great impatience at my slow pace. We arrived just as Mom was leaving for work. While I was disappointed that I couldn't spend time with her, I was grateful for the chance to catch a nap. I had only been up for fourteen hours, but they had been exhausting hours. The long car trip had stiffened up my left leg. It felt good to stretch it out on the bed.

I dozed off a little but tried not to fall sound asleep. I didn't want to miss the officer when he came to escort me to the council chamber. I was looking forward to the meeting. I knew they would be pleased with the list I'd brought. And I was excited about the prospect of reuniting more families. But I also knew that meeting meant the beginning of months of imprisonment, sleeping on the hard ground, eating cold food, and being separated from my friends. And after arriving late that morning, I could only imagine how eager the Council would be to lengthen my sentence. I was glad the officer didn't come to get me right away in the morning; grateful for a few more minutes of freedom.

As the afternoon wore on, though, I began to get nervous. If the Council didn't see me that day, they would accuse me of missing my deadline. They could use that as an excuse to make my prison sentence even longer or to go back on their word and take my list without letting anyone move back into the Bubble.

I stepped out of the house and looked around. I needed to stay close by. If I wasn't at the house when the officer came to pick me up, I would miss my deadline for sure. But if there wasn't an officer on the way, I had to find one soon.

I circled the house in widening arcs, looking in all directions trying to spot a navy blue uniform. When I finally saw what I was looking for, I hobbled down the street as fast as my crutches could carry me, yelling, "Officer, Officer."

I glanced back. I couldn't see the house from here. Hopefully, I wouldn't be out of sight of it for too long.

"Officer." I paused to catch my breath. "I need to find out when they put me on the Council's schedule."

"Someone will come and get you when it's time," the officer said. "You don't need to worry about it."

"But today is my deadline. I need to make sure I'm on the schedule for today. Otherwise, I'll get in trouble for missing the deadline."

"Just sit tight. As long as you stay where you're supposed to be, we'll make sure you get to the council chamber on time."

"Yes, sir." I stuffed my frustration. Why wouldn't he just give me a straight answer? "Thank you, officer."

I hurried back to the house. There was no one around. What if I had missed the officer who came to get me? What if he had come when I was just out of sight of the house?

I paced back and forth in front of the house, my crutches and shuffling steps creating a unique rhythm. Had I blown it again? Messed up my chance to help my family and the other people in the village because of my impatience?

I leaned against the side of the house. I took a few deep breaths. Why was it so hard for me to trust?

*Lord, I know you've got everything under control. I leave it all in your hands. I know, whatever happens, you will use it for good. Jesus, I trust you. It's your will I want, not mine.*

I went in the house and began fixing supper. Mom would be home soon, and I was sure she would be hungry. The soup had just started to boil when I heard a knock at the door. I moved the pot off to the side, away from the direct heat but where the bricks would help it to stay warm.

I opened the door.

"Time for your appearance before the Council," the officer outside said.

I smiled and turned to lock the door. God knew what he was doing. He'd just wanted to make sure I believed he was the one in charge.

# 50

The officer escorted me to the airlock, where he left me alone. When the door to the biosphere opened, I was surprised to see Officer Cartwright. We started down the street toward the administration building.

"Welcome back," he said. "How'd we do?"

"Great." I said. "One hundred fifteen more names. That should make the Council happy."

"That's wonderful."

"I couldn't have done it without you."

"Glad I could help."

"It's too bad we won't be able to work together again for a while."

"I suppose you'll be getting back to your delivery route."

I shook my head. "Not for a while. I've got a three-month prison sentence to serve yet."

"After all you've done to help them?"

I shrugged. "The chairman's always been suspicious of my motivations, like I'm trying to take advantage of him or something. I suppose it's because I'm an outsider. I came here uninvited, and I think they would have executed me right then if they hadn't figured out that they needed my help."

"So, what's this prison sentence for?"

"Well, I wouldn't give the Council the names of the

people who had tested positive, because the Council wouldn't agree to the people's terms. And then I burst into a Council meeting uninvited and started yelling at them."

Officer Cartwright chuckled. "And they didn't appreciate that?"

He held the door of the administration building for me.

"Not hardly," I said.

"Christy Phillips is here for her appearance before the Council at four," he said to the woman at the reception desk.

"I'll let them know you're here," she said. "Go on back to the anteroom, and they'll come and get you when they're ready."

"So, what's with the crutches?" Officer Cartwright asked. "You looking for sympathy votes?"

"No," I said, "I got in a car accident. I might have broken my leg. I haven't had a chance to get it checked out yet."

"If it's broken, you shouldn't be walking on it, even with crutches," he said. "You need an x-ray before you make things even worse."

"Yeah. I don't think there's an infirmary in the jail. I might have to wait a few months for that x-ray."

The council clerk opened the door from the anteroom to the council chamber. I took a deep breath and limped in. I handed the list of names to the clerk and sat in the chair at the center of the room. Officer Cartwright stood just inside the door.

Chairman Lambrecht took the list from the clerk. "How many names?"

"One hundred fifteen, sir," I said.

The chairman looked over the top of his glasses at me. "Well done."

"Thank you, Mr. Chairman."

Chairman Lambrecht cleared his throat. "It has come to our attention that you are still having trouble abiding by the stipulations in your contract. Do you care to explain your arrival this morning during daylight hours?"

"Yes, sir. I was delayed by an accident that disabled me and incapacitated my car. I resumed my journey as soon as I could. I did not wish to postpone my return until tonight, as that would have caused me to miss my deadline for turning in the list of names. Mr. Chairman, the sun was not yet visible on the horizon when I arrived at the checkpoint, and I took every precaution during the drive to make sure I was not being followed."

"In recognition of your service to the USCSBS over the past month, no additional time will be added to your three-month sentence for this latest infraction. During the jail sentence, your work release will be spent in the biosphere collecting more DNA samples. I want every person of working age tested."

"Yes, Mr. Chairman." I swallowed, trying to bolster my courage. "May I make a request, sir?"

The chairman pulled his glasses off. "What is it?"

"Officer Cartwright's assistance has been invaluable. I would like to request that he be assigned to me during my work release in the biosphere."

The chairman and I turned toward Officer Cartwright. He nodded.

"That can be arranged," Chairman Lambrecht said. He raised his gavel.

"And," I said, before the gavel fell, "I would like to request that Joshua Phillips be released from jail on good behavior and allowed to return to the biosphere so he can take care of his wife, who is expecting a child."

The chairman leaned forward.

I held my breath.

"Perhaps, Ms. Phillips," Chairman Lambrecht said, "your brother should have thought about his wife and child before he decided to lead a political uprising."

Josh was thinking about his wife and child when he made that decision—he did it for them.

The chairman banged his gavel. "You are dismissed."

A mix of emotions swirled in my gut as I walked to the door. I was glad my sentence hadn't been increased and grateful that Officer Cartwright had agreed to continue helping me. But I would have given all of that up if I could have helped Josh get back to his wife sooner. I dreaded facing Josh when I got to the jail.

When we reached the door to the airlock, Officer Cartwright said, "I'm sorry about this, but I have to follow protocol. Give me your wrists."

I shot him a confused look.

He nodded and held out his hand.

I sighed and laid my right wrist across his hand. He

secured the end of a cord around my wrist.

So this was how it was going to be. My month of freedom was over. And now even Officer Cartwright didn't trust me. I held up my left arm. He secured the other end of the cord around my left wrist, leaving enough slack that I could barely reach both crutches.

"Just have to make sure you don't give the officers on the other side any trouble." He opened the door to the airlock. "See you in the morning?"

I turned my back to him and stepped inside.

"Christy?"

I wiped away a tear before I turned to face Officer Cartwright.

"First thing tomorrow," he said, "we're going to get you to a doctor to check out that leg, okay?"

I nodded.

"We're a team, right?" he asked.

I held up my bound wrists. Right now it felt like we were on opposing teams.

"I'm sorry. I really am. Sometimes we just have to play the game." Officer Cartwright closed the walk-in door.

The garage door to the outside opened, revealing two officers waiting for me. They hurried me through the woods, barely preventing me from pitching face-first into a tree when my crutches caught on the underbrush. One officer unlocked the door to the jail, and the other shoved me inside. I stumbled, catching myself on the wall of the cell.

The first officer shone a flashlight around the inside of

the cell. "Remember, you try to escape, and you will never see the inside of the biosphere again."

The door slammed and the padlock clanged shut.

I burst into tears. "I'm sorry, Josh. I tried to get them to let you go, so you could be with Lauren, but they wouldn't listen."

"It's alright." Josh knelt and worked to untie the cord binding my wrists. "I've already made it one month. A couple more won't kill me."

He looked up at me. "Did you get the names?"

I nodded. "Forty more than what they asked for. The Council was so pleased, they're going to have me use my work release time to collect more DNA samples. It shouldn't be long before we have enough people working on the outside that everyone who wants to can move back in."

"That's great news." Josh smiled.

# 51

I paced back and forth in front of Lauren's parents' house, where she and Josh were living until they could get a place of their own. Every time we heard a cry of pain from inside, Dad sprang out of the lawn chair, shifted his weight side to side a few times, and sat back down.

Mom stepped outside for some fresh air. She looked tired, but she was smiling. "Things are moving along nicely. It shouldn't be long now."

Less than half an hour later, we heard a new sound from inside the house—a baby's cry. I giggled at the adorably cute sound that expressed such tremendous displeasure. Dad and I waited eagerly at the door. The baby's cries softened and then stopped. The door opened. Josh stepped out, holding a swaddled bundle.

"It's a boy," he said with a huge grin. "Theodore Bashkim Phillips."

It seemed like a long name for such a tiny person. But when I saw his pudgy pink face and the dark curl resting on his forehead, I knew it was perfect for him.

When it was my turn to hold little Theodore, I thought my heart would burst with joy. "Hello, little guy. It's your favorite aunt, Christy."

His eyes were closed. Every now and then he turned his

head to the side and puckered his lips. I bent down and kissed his head. It was warm and soft, like nothing I'd touched before. Even the wrinkles on his forehead felt smooth.

My joy was joined by an intense longing. I wanted a baby of my own. Someone I could love and take care of. Someone so innocent and beautiful, yet fragile. The hole that Scott had left in my heart when he drove away seemed to grow, my longing for Scott joined by a longing for the first child we would have had together. Scott could still be out there somewhere. I couldn't imagine starting a family with anyone else. But what if I never found him? What if he wasn't still alive? Was I holding onto a dream that could never come true?

I gave Theodore a gentle squeeze. "You are going to be my little Teddy bear. I promise I won't let anything happen to you."

Theodore's grandmothers had finished cleaning up, and it was Grandma Cosgrove's turn to hold him. I walked to the bed, where Lauren lay looking exhausted and thrilled.

"Congratulations." I gave her a gentle hug. "You have a beautiful baby boy. You are so brave."

She chuckled. "Not hardly. I've been scared out of my mind ever since I found out I was pregnant. Dealing with morning sickness and hormones and not being able to bend down to tie my shoes was so hard without Josh's help. I hope we'll never have to be apart again."

The Council had allowed everyone who wished, to come back into the Bubble two weeks before, when the atmospheric conversion system upgrades were completed. Josh and Lauren were finally together again, after spending the first five months of their married life apart.

"Thank you all for your help and support." Josh's voice carried above the chatter in the room. "Lauren is exhausted and needs some rest. You are welcome to come back and visit tomorrow."

Secretly, I thought Josh only asked us to leave so he could hold Theodore. Still, it was good to see him taking charge and looking after his wife and son.

I squeezed Lauren's hand. "You guys are going to be great parents."

The excitement and worry and waiting left me emotionally exhausted. Holding little Teddy in my arms reminded me how badly I wanted to start my own family. Maybe it was time to let go of Scott and move on. That might be the only way I could see my dream of having a family come true.

I excused myself and went to the firing range, hoping to clear my head and sort some things out.

I was still getting used to my new gun. I had finally earned enough to purchase it three weeks before. After a couple of wild shots, I found my groove, hitting one bull's-eye after another. I had been shooting about five minutes when someone began firing from the stand next to mine. I was surprised to see a slender ankle beneath the partition, sporting a delicate rose tattoo. The firing range was usually a boy's club. Rarely did I see other women there.

When I left my stand, I had no further clarity about my

future. But I knew my job right then was to be the best aunt, sister, daughter, and friend I could be. For now, that had to be enough.

I was cleaning my gun in the reception area when the woman in the stand beside mine came out.

"How was your practice?" I asked, motioning toward the empty chair at my table.

"I'm just getting started." She sat across from me. "I'm not very consistent yet."

"Keep at it. You'll be surprised how fast you improve."

"I hope so."

I put gun oil on a pad and started oiling the barrel. "I noticed the rose on your ankle. I used to have a friend who had a tattoo just like yours."

The woman stopped cleaning and looked at me. "Who?"

"Excuse me?"

"What was her name? Your friend with the rose tattoo."

"Kayla. She was my roommate in college."

The woman sitting across from me looked like she'd seen a ghost.

"Are you okay?" I asked.

"You're Christy? Kayla's roommate? Kayla is my little sister. Is she . . . Did she . . ."

"I'm sorry." I shook my head. "I stayed with her during the Change. She was at peace and comfortable at the end."

Kayla's sister stared at her lap for a long time, silent tears dropping onto her folded hands. Finally, she looked up. "Thank you," she whispered.

I nodded. "She was so excited when she found out you and your brother had been selected in the lottery to live in the biosphere. I think it helped make her last moments easier, knowing you and your families were safe."

She sniffled and resumed cleaning her gun.

"If you would like—" I hesitated. The offer I was about to make would not be easy to fulfill "—I could go to our dorm room and bring back some of her things."

"Would you do that for me?"

The thought of going back into that room gave me goose bumps, but I smiled and nodded.

"There's a locket Mom gave her and her favorite stuffed bunny. If it's not too much trouble. It would mean a lot to me."

"No trouble at all."

She wrote down her name and address and a list of things for me to look for in the dorm room. She hugged and thanked me.

I walked slowly to my parents' house, glad I had met Kayla's sister but dreading the task that lay ahead. When I arrived, Mom was still talking excitedly about Theodore's birth and what a perfect baby he was and how great Lauren had done.

"We need to take them some food," Mom said. "Lauren is in no shape to cook, and I'm sure she's starving after all that work."

"Tomorrow, Mom," I said. "Josh said we could come back tomorrow."

In the morning, I had to convince Mom it was not okay to stop and visit her new grandson before work. She reluctantly left the Bubble with the rest of the first-shift field workers. I stopped at the school to collect DNA samples from the students who would be graduating later that month.

I met Mom at the airlock after her shift, and we walked to Dad's office. When he finished the report he was drafting, we all went to Lauren's house. Josh opened the door for us, looking a bit disheveled but still with a big grin on his face.

Mom smiled. "Not much sleep last night?"

Josh sat next to Lauren on the couch and put his arm around her. "Lauren has been dealing with sleepless nights for weeks. Now I finally have a chance to shoulder some of the burden for her."

Lauren finished nursing Theodore, and Josh changed his diaper. We bundled him up and took him for a walk, hoping to give Lauren and Josh time to get a little rest.

I got to hold him first. In the cool evening air, Theodore's eyes were bright. I knew he couldn't see much yet, but he looked around as if eager to take it all in. I felt a twinge of sadness when I realized he might spend his whole life in the Bubble, never having a chance to feel the unobstructed warmth of the sun, to clearly see a rainbow, or to explore a forest.

By the time I handed him to Mom, Theodore's eyelids were beginning to droop. The warmth of Mom's embrace and the rhythmic movement of her walking soon lulled him to sleep.

When we returned after our hour-long walk, Lauren and Josh were also sound asleep. Dad held the sleeping baby, and we sat on the patio talking softly about Josh's beautiful new family.

Josh came to the door, and we motioned for him to join us. Theodore was still content, and we didn't want to wake Lauren if we didn't have to.

I reached behind my chair. "I got Teddy a little gift." I handed Josh the baseball bat left behind by the guys who tried to break into my car, and a ball and glove I had found at the Lincoln market. "It might be a few years before he can use it."

Josh put on the glove, threw the ball in the air, and caught it. "It's perfect. Thanks, Christy."

"My little brother is a daddy." I shook my head. "I still can hardly believe it."

"Me neither," Josh said. "This little guy is dependent on us for everything. It's kind of scary. But at the same time, I know there is nothing I wouldn't do for him. I never knew I could love someone I just met so much."

A year earlier, I couldn't have imagined Josh talking like that. He had grown up a lot in a few months.

Theodore started to cry. Josh scooped him up to comfort him and make sure his needs were met. I excused myself to pack for my trip back to Lincoln. Mom and Dad stayed so they could play with Theodore and chat with Lauren when she awoke.

Walking away, I felt a tug on my heart, pulling me back

to little Teddy. I would be in Lincoln for at least a week while we tested the latest batch of DNA samples. I couldn't imagine going more than a week without seeing or holding my new nephew. I experienced a little taste of the love and connection Josh had with his baby. The ache I felt leaving Theodore made me want a baby of my own even more.

# 52

I had a lot to accomplish on my trip to Lincoln, and I wanted to get back to the Bubble as soon as possible to spend more time with my nephew. *I'm an aunt.* Sometimes it still didn't seem quite real.

I stopped at Max's house first. He wasn't home. I figured he was probably at the market, but I didn't want to take the time to look for him. I left him a note and went to the lab to begin testing the DNA samples.

Max joined me a few hours later, starting in right away on the untested samples. I told him all about the birth of the cutest baby ever. He didn't try to contradict me, but I could tell from the look on his face that he was skeptical, certainly believing his own kids to be the cutest.

I was grateful the awkwardness between us was gone. To me, Max was a comfortable mix of good friend and father figure. I occasionally caught him looking at me with an expression that said he still wanted to be more than friends. But he never spoke of or acted on his feelings. Maybe, when I was a little older and the memory of Scott wasn't so fresh, I would be able to reciprocate his feelings. For now, though, we were happy as friends.

It took us three days to get all of the samples started. Max offered to monitor and record the results as they came in, and I went to the farmhouse to see Ashley.

Ashley was working in the garden when I arrived. She had traded for some seed adapted to the atmosphere, and she was growing food to trade at the market. It was hard work, and she wouldn't see results for months. But nothing traded better in the Lincoln market than fresh food. She was certain all of the work would be worth it.

Ashley greeted me with a dirt-covered hug. "How is Aunt Christy?"

I giggled. "Almost as proud as Lauren and Josh but not nearly so tired."

"Was it a boy or a girl?"

"A healthy baby boy. Theodore Bashkim." I knelt and started pulling weeds. It amazed me how quickly the weeds had adapted to the new atmosphere.

"Is that a family name?" Ashley hoed another row.

"No. They picked it for its meaning. Theodore means 'gift of God,' and Bashkim means 'united.' "

"That's really cool."

"Anything new around here?"

"I had a run-in with bandits on my way to Lincoln a couple days ago."

I stopped working and looked up. "Are you okay?"

"Sure. I just kept driving. Once they figured out I wasn't afraid to run them over, they scattered pretty quickly."

I chuckled, imagining Ashley running down the guys who thought she would be an easy target.

"I met someone new at the firing range this week," I

said.

"Yeah? Anyone I know?"

"Kayla's older sister. I recognized her tattoo." I turned to another area of the garden. "I offered to go back to our dorm room to get some of Kayla's things."

Ashley stopped and looked at me. "You did?"

I nodded. "It seemed like the right thing to do."

"When are you going to go?"

"Tomorrow morning. I want to get it over with as soon as possible."

"I'm going with you."

"You would do that for me?"

"You shouldn't have to go there alone."

"Thanks."

We wrapped up work in the garden in time to grab a bite to eat and get cleaned up before leaving at dusk to drive to the cabin.

Dr. Franklin opened the door when we arrived. "Good to see you. Come on in."

I smiled, still remembering the less-than-friendly greetings Dr. Franklin had offered for months after we first left the cabin.

"We're just finishing supper. Would you like to join us for dessert?" Dr. Franklin motioned toward the common room.

"Sure," Ashley said.

I followed her inside, and we found a couple of empty

seats next to Ryan. I was disappointed that Angela wasn't sitting with him. I'd missed their wedding while participating in the sit-in. Since the wedding, Angela seemed to be glowing every time I saw her. Just being around her was enough to boost my spirits.

"Where's Angela?" I asked.

Ashley put a freshly-baked brownie on the table in front of me. Hers already had a bite out of it before she sat down.

"She's not feeling well today," Ryan said. "She's downstairs resting."

Panic bubbled up inside me. "What's wrong? Is she all right?"

Ryan smiled. "She's fine, just a little sick to her stomach."

"Wait, is she . . . Are you . . ." Ashley looked at Ryan, her eyes and mouth open wide.

Ryan nodded. Ashley jumped up and attacked him with a hug.

"We're going to have a baby." Ryan laughed.

"Congratulations! That's awesome." I added my hug to Ashley's.

"The baby is due in November," Ryan said. "We were going to wait to tell people, but it's pretty hard to keep a secret around here."

"Tell Angela congratulations for us. I'm so excited for you both." Ashley squeezed Ryan again.

The news stirred up my desire to get back to the Bubble and hold little Teddy. And it amplified my longing for a baby of my own. When I imagined holding and feeding and caring for my baby, it sparked a passion inside me I had never felt before. I just knew I was meant to be a mother.

After we finished our dessert, we distributed the mail I had collected in the Bubble. I was still on probation after my incarceration, so I was running a very limited mail service, fearful that if I got caught I would end up back in the slammer.

Dr. Franklin bustled around the common room, clearing the tables. It must have been his day for kitchen duty. He seemed to be happy. I imagined it hadn't been easy for him to give up the power he had previously exercised. But his health scare had given him a new perspective on things and an appreciation for life in whatever role he found himself.

Sue gathered the representatives for an informal board meeting in the library. Ashley and I brought in the delivery from the biosphere, including propane and several walkie-talkies with extra batteries. The Board conferred briefly about the Council's request for more seed. When they had agreed on the amount of seed they were willing to give, Ashley and I went to the shed to get it.

Ryan met us at the car with the list of additional items the Board wanted from the biosphere. He handed the list to Ashley and pulled me to the side.

"You've been looking at the genetics of survival, right?" he asked.

I nodded.

"Is survival a dominant or recessive trait?" he asked.

"We've only identified the gene. We haven't looked at how it's passed on. I don't think we have enough data to figure that out."

"Then how do we know if our baby will be able to breathe?" Ryan's voice was strained.

"The chances are really good since you guys were both able to adapt," I said, "like at least seventy-five percent."

"That means there could be a twenty-five percent chance that Angela has to watch our baby suffocate right after giving birth. I can't let that happen."

I knew too well the helpless feeling of knowing a baby's life is at risk and being powerless to help.

"I know," I said. "I wish there was something more I could do."

I gave Ryan a hug, and Ashley and I got in the car to drive to the farmhouse.

I stayed in bed long after I awoke the next morning, dreading the trip back to my old dorm room. When I heard Ashley moving around downstairs, I reluctantly pulled myself out of bed. Much as I wanted to postpone the trip, I knew we needed to get started as soon as possible so Ashley could get back to her planting.

The smell of freshly-baked biscuits greeted me at the top of the stairs. I hurried to join Ashley for breakfast.

"Courtesy of Max," Ashley said, holding out the cookie sheet full of biscuits.

I grabbed two and sat at the kitchen table to savor their

flaky goodness.

Max had been helping Ashley by taking some of her things to the Lincoln market to trade for food, to keep her pantry stocked while she worked to get her produce business going. Since the Change, Ashley had become quite a proficient cook, producing wonders over an open fire. I always ate well when visiting her.

I closed my eyes and allowed the last morsel of biscuit to melt on my tongue. I sighed with satisfaction and resignation. "I'm going upstairs to get dressed. Meet you in fifteen minutes at the car?"

Ashley nodded. "It's going to be okay, Christy."

"I know. It's just hard."

An hour later, we were driving through Lincoln, approaching the "Gerald Ford College" sign. Bittersweet memories of my freshman year at college flashed through my mind—the fun and excitement, the new friends, the stress of preparing for exams, the late nights spent studying. Through all the memories, good and bad, there was a sense of freedom and security. With the Change, that feeling of safety had been replaced by constant fear. I had to be alert all the time, never letting my guard down. I longed for a return to those carefree college days.

Ashley parked the car outside my dorm. Memories of the last time I was there—the fear of the anticipated change and the angst, desperation, and finally, peace, that accompanied Kayla's last hours—pressed down on me, making it hard to breathe. *Jesus, I need you. Give me courage and strength. I can't do this without you.*

Ashley turned off the car. "Do you want me to come in with you?"

I nodded.

I got out of the car and walked to the door, trying not to imagine what I might find inside. The dorm had been broken into, so the door swung open easily. The buzz of flies swarming around the doorway reminded me of a noisy window air conditioner. I stepped inside. Bugs crawling on the floor scattered. The air smelled of old dirt like someone had tried to clean with an antique vacuum. I expected a more noxious smell.

I looked down the first-floor hallway. The contents of the rooms had been strewn about the hall by whoever had broken into the building. I spotted a long, thin tail disappearing into one of the rooms. I shuddered. I was not prepared to battle rodents for Kayla's possessions.

We entered the stairwell closest to the door and headed up. I could almost imagine I was on the way to my room to get ready for tomorrow's chemistry test.

I paused when we reached the landing at my floor. I was scared of what I would see and how I would react. But at the same time, I felt like I needed to be there. The things I retrieved from our room would be treasured by Kayla's family and would help them to say goodbye, to have closure. I was the only person who could do that for them.

Ashley linked her arm in mine. I smiled at her and pushed the stairwell door open. We walked through together. I coughed. The pungent, dusty smell was stronger in the hallway. A few belongings were scattered around the third-floor hall, but it wasn't as much of a mess as the first floor. I kept my eyes fixed on the window at the end of the hall, avoiding the temptation to look in the open doors as we walked by.

The door to my room was closed. I hoped that meant the looters had skipped it. My room key was still on my key chain. I unlocked the door and pushed it open. I looked up to survey the room and saw something taped to the door. "Christy" was scrawled on the outside of the folded piece of paper. I immediately recognized the handwriting. I tore the paper off the door and opened it, barely able to make out the words through my tears.

"It's Scott." I shoved the paper at Ashley.

Ashley read it aloud, "*Dear Christy, I came back as soon as I could. I don't know where to find you, but I'll keep looking. I love you. I will love you forever. Hugs and Kisses. Scott.*

*"P.S. I'm staying at 210 Walnut Street in Pleasant Dale."*

Ashley and I hugged, laughing through our tears.

"He's alive. I can't believe it. He came back for me. I need to see him." I couldn't think. I hardly understood what Ashley had read. But my heart pounded with a joy I hadn't felt in a long time.

I pulled away from Ashley, suddenly cognizant of where

we were and who was on the other side of the door. "But I have to do this first."

I pushed the door open and glanced at the blanket on the couch covering what was left of Kayla's body. The sight reminded me how certain I was, when she passed away, that Kayla was no longer there with her body. She was someplace much better. It had been the hardest night of my life, sitting with her, seeing her struggle, trying to find the right things to say. But it had also been a privilege to share her last minutes in this world and to bring even a little comfort as she prepared to let go. I closed my eyes, imagining how excited we would be to see each other when I joined her in heaven. The picture brought a little smile to my lips.

We went through Kayla's closet, dresser, and desk, picking out those things her sister had requested and anything else that was special to Kayla or might remind her family of her. Ashley and I recalled many great memories from our year together at Ford College. I grabbed a few things out of my closet before we left.

Back in the car, I pulled out my maps. It didn't take long to locate the town of Pleasant Dale, a few miles outside of Lincoln, but I didn't have a detailed map of the town. There wasn't any GPS we could turn to for directions. I navigated for Ashley, directing her west out of Lincoln on Highway 6 to avoid the obstructions on the interstate.

I was thrilled to know that Scott had survived the Change, but I had no idea how long ago he had left that note. What if he had left Pleasant Dale to try to reconnect with his extended family? What if he had given up on me and found someone else? What if he had survived the Change only to fall victim to an act of violence?

It only took forty minutes to reach Pleasant Dale. Still, by the time we arrived, my tears of joy had quieted to sniffles of fear. We made several turns in the small town before we located Walnut Street.

Despite my trepidation, I jumped out of the car before Ashley came to a complete stop at 210 Walnut. Whether good news or bad news awaited me, I needed to know the truth.

I ran onto the porch and rapped loudly on the door.

Nothing happened.

I pushed the doorbell several times and knocked again.

I heard nothing from inside the house.

I looked around for another note or any indication that someone lived there. I saw nothing out of the ordinary. This house looked like every other house on the block—dark windows with curtains pulled, a smattering of overgrown weeds in an otherwise brown front yard, a few budding trees amidst bare branches and peeling bark. Any hope I still had was rapidly draining away. This house was probably empty, just like most of the other houses on the block undoubtedly were.

I was turning to walk back to the car when I saw the curtains in the window next to the door move slightly. I froze, unsure whether I could trust my eyes but clinging to my last drop of hope.

The door flew open. I caught a glimpse of Scott's wide

smile and the dancing light in his eyes before he pulled me close and lifted me up. I wrapped my arms around him and pressed my cheek against his rough stubble. I didn't ever want to let go. He set my feet back down on the porch. I still felt like I was floating.

*He's here. We're here. Together.* This moment had happened so many times in my dreams. The smell of cedar and spice in his cologne and the feel of his strong arms assured me that my dreams had become reality.

"Thanks for coming back for me," I whispered, the joy rising within making it difficult to choke out the words.

"Thank you for waiting for me." Scott's lips brushed my ear, lingered on my cheek, and sought out mine, first with gentle tenderness, then with an intense passion that made my heart dance.

I knew I was right where I was supposed to be, and I never wanted to leave.